HELP FOR THE HAUNTED

ALSO BY JOHN SEARLES

Boy Still Missing
Strange But True

HELP
FOR
THE
HAUNTED

JOHN SEARLES

wm
WILLIAM MORROW
An Imprint of HarperCollins*Publishers*

FIRST EDITION

Designed by Jamie Lynn Kerner

Library of Congress Cataloging-in-Publication Data has been applied for.

ISBN 978-0-06-077963-4

13 14 15 16 17 ov/rrd 10 9 8 7 6 5 4 3 2 1

For Maia, Cristian, and Shannon,
with love

WHAT MAKES YOU AFRAID?

Whenever the phone rang late at night, I lay in my narrow bed and listened.

My mother picked up on the first ring so as not to wake my sister, if she was home, or me. In hushed tones, she soothed the caller before handing the phone to my father. His voice was stiffer, more formal, as he made plans to meet somewhere or offered directions to our faded and drooping Tudor on a dead-end lane in the tiny town of Dundalk, Maryland. There were times when the person on the other end of the line had called from a pay phone as nearby as Baltimore. A priest, I guessed, had scratched our number on a scrap of paper and handed it over. Or maybe it had been found by simply searching the tissuey pages of the phonebook, since we were listed, same as any ordinary family, even if ordinary was the last thing we were.

Not long after my father put down the receiver, I heard them dressing. My parents were like characters on an old TV show whose outfits stayed the same every episode. My mother—tall, thin, abnormally pale—wore some version of a curveless gray dress with pearly buttons down the front whenever she was dealing with the public. Her dark hair, threaded with white, was always pinned up. Tiny crucifixes glimmered in her ears, around her neck too. My father wore suits in somber shades of brown, a cross nestled in his chest hairs beneath his yellow button-down, black hair combed away from his face so that the first thing you noticed was his smudged, wire-rimmed glasses.

Once dressed, they brushed past my door and down the stairs to wait in the kitchen with its peeling blue wallpaper, sipping tea at the table, until headlights from a car turning into our dirt driveway splashed against my bedroom ceiling. Next I heard murmurs, impossible to decipher from my room above, though I had my ideas about what was being said. Finally, I listened to the *clomp clomp clomp* of footsteps as my parents led their visitor or visitors into the basement and everyone grew quiet below.

That's how things went until a snowy night in February of 1989.

When the phone rang after midnight that evening, I opened my eyes and listened, same as always. Never once, not one single time, did I claim to experience the sort of "feelings" my mother had, and yet something sawed at my insides, giving me the sense that this call was different from those that had come before.

"It's her," my mother told my father instead of passing him the phone.

"Thank God. Is she okay?"

"She is. But she says she's not coming back."

Three days. That's how long Rose—my older sister, who shared my mother's name but none of her gentle temperament—had been gone. This time, all the shrieking and plate breaking and door slamming had been about her hair, I guessed, or lack thereof, since she had hacked it off again. Or maybe a boy, since I knew from snatches of overheard conversations that my parents did not approve of whomever Rose had been spending time with since her return from Saint Julia's.

As I lay in my bed, listening to my mother act as a translator between my sister and my father, I stared at the textbooks on my desk. Eighth grade had become easy, just like sixth and seventh before it, and I couldn't wait for the challenge of Dundalk High School next fall. The shelf above was lined with hand-carved mahogany ponies. In the glow of the nightlight, their long, wild faces, complete with flared nostrils and bared teeth, appeared alive.

"If we want to talk," I heard my mother tell my father across the hall, "she says we can meet her at the church in town."

"The church in town?" The more agitated he became, the deeper and louder his voice. "Did the girl happen to notice the blizzard outside?"

Moments later, my mother stepped into my room, leaned over my bed, and gently shook my shoulder. "Wake up, sweetheart. We're going to meet your sister, and we don't want to leave you here alone." I opened my eyes slowly and, even though I knew full well, asked in a groggy voice what was going on. I liked playing the part of the daughter my parents wanted. "You can keep your pajamas on," my mother said in her whispery voice. "But it's cold out, so slip your coat over them. And you'll need your boots. A hat and mittens too."

Snow fell all around as we walked outside, hands linked paper-doll style, to our little blue Datsun. My father kept a tight grip on the steering wheel as we backed past the NO TRESPASSING! VIOLATORS WILL BE PROSECUTED! signs nailed to the crooked birch trees in our yard. As we drove the snowy roads my mother hummed a lullaby I recognized from a trip to Florida years before. The tune climbed higher until we turned into the church parking lot. Our headlights illuminated the simple white structure, the stack of cement stairs, the red wooden doors, the barren flower boxes that would burst with tulips and daffodils come spring, and the steeple with a small gold cross at the top.

"Are you sure she meant *this* church?" my father said.

The stained-glass windows gave off no light from inside, but that wasn't the only reason he was asking. Since the building was not big enough to fit the entire congregation, masses were held across town in the gym at Saint Bartholomew's Catholic Elementary School. Every Sunday, basketball hoops and volleyball nets were wheeled into a storage room while an altar was wheeled out. Felt artwork depicting the Stations of the Cross was draped on the walls, folding chairs and kneelers were arranged over the court markings on the wooden floor. So the *actual* church was a place we rarely visited, since it was reserved for weddings and funerals and the Tuesday night prayer group my parents used to attend but didn't anymore.

"Someone was going to drop her here," my mother said. "Or that's what she told me anyway."

My father turned on his high beams, squinting. "I guess I'll go in alone first."

"I'm not sure that's the smartest idea. The way you two carry on . . ."

"That's exactly the reason I *should* go in alone. This nonsense has to stop. Once and for all."

If she had her "feelings" about the predicament, my mother did not speak up any further. Rather, she let my father unbuckle his seat belt. She let him step out of the car. We watched as he followed a lone trail of footprints through the lot and up the stairs to the red doors. Though he left the engine running, heat pumping, he turned off the wipers and soon snow blanketed the windows.

My mother reached over and flicked a switch so the blades swished back and forth a single time. The effect was that of adjusting an antenna on an old TV: suddenly, the static gave way to a clear picture. She suggested I stretch out in back and sleep, since there was no sense in all of us staying awake. For the second time that night, I gave her the daughter she wanted, lying across the stiff vinyl seat with its camel hump. Inside my coat pocket, the book about my parents poked at my ribs, nudging me to pay attention to it. My mother and father were angry about so much of what the book's author, a reporter named Sam Heekin, had written, so I was not supposed to read it. But the things my sister said before leaving home had gotten to me at last, and I'd snatched a copy from the curio hutch in our living room days before. So far, I'd only been brave enough to trace their names in the embossed subtitle on the red cover: *The Unusual Work of Sylvester and Rose Mason.*

"I don't know what's keeping them," my mother said, more to herself than me. The faintest trace of an accent, left over from her childhood in Tennessee, bubbled up whenever she felt nervous.

Maybe it was that lilting sound, or maybe it was that book; either way something made me ask, "Do you ever feel afraid?"

My mother glanced my way a second before facing forward again and flicking the wiper switch. Her eyes, glittery and green, watched for my father. It had been twenty minutes, maybe more, since he left the car. She had turned down the heat and things were getting cold fast. "Of course, Sylvie. We all do sometimes. What makes you afraid?"

I didn't want to say it was the sight of their names on that book. I also didn't want to say that a prickly feeling of dread filled me up at that very moment as I wondered what was keeping my sister and father. Instead, I paraded out smaller, sillier fears, because I thought that's what she wanted to hear. "Not passing my tests with perfect grades. Not being the smartest in my class anymore. The gym teacher changing her mind about giving me a permanent pass to the library and forcing me to play flag football or Danish rounders instead."

My mother let out a gentle burble of laughter. "Well, those things *do* sound terrifying, Sylvie, though I don't think you have to worry. Still, the next time you feel afraid, I want you to pray. That's what I do in scary situations. That's what you should do too."

A plow rumbled down the street, its flashing yellow lights reflected on the snow covering the rear window. It made me think of when Rose and I were younger, the way we used to drape blankets over the wingback chairs in our living room and hide beneath with flashlights. "You know what?" my mother said when the roar and scrape of the truck faded in the distance. "I am getting a little worried now. I better go inside too."

"It hasn't been that long," I told her. It had, of course, but I didn't like the idea of her leaving. Too late, though, since she was already unbuckling her seat belt. She was already opening the door. A gust of frigid air blew into the car, causing me to shiver in my pajamas and coat.

"I'll be right back, Sylvie. Just close your eyes and try to rest some more."

After she stepped outside, I reached over the seats and adjusted the switch so the wipers would stay on and I could keep an eye out for her. All alone, listening to the patter of wet snow, I braved the book at last. The darkness made it difficult to read, and though I could have turned on the interior light, instead I made my way to the photo section wedged like an intermission in the middle of the text. One picture in particular, a blurred image of a farmhouse kitchen, caused my breath to catch: the chairs and table were toppled, the window over the sink shattered, the toaster, teapot, percolator scattered on the floor, the walls smeared with what looked to be blood.

It was enough to make me shut the book and let it slip to the floor. For a long while, I did nothing but stare at the church, thinking how my father's and sister's faces contorted at the height of their arguments until they resembled those horses on my shelf. Five, ten, fifteen minutes passed; still none of them emerged. At last, I grew tired and allowed myself to lie back once more. The cocooned feeling of the car led me to think again of those tents Rose and I used to make over the chairs. Some nights Rose convinced our mother to let us sleep in them, though the blankets always collapsed. I used to drift off imagining endless stars twinkling in the vast sky overhead; I woke with nothing covering us, and only the blank white ceiling above.

Those were my last thoughts as my eyes fell shut in the backseat.

All my life until that night, I'd never heard such a horrible and unforgettable sound. When I did, I woke with a start, sitting up in the backseat. The car had grown cold, all the windows except the front covered with a thick layer of snow. Staring out at that church, it appeared as peaceful and sleepy as one inside a snow globe, and I wondered if I had dreamed the noise, if the images from that book had slipped into my sleep. But, no. I heard it again, the second time more ferocious than the first, so loud it seemed to vibrate against my chest, causing my heart to beat faster, my hands to shake.

I don't know why, but the first thing I did was reach forward and turn off the car. The wiper blades halted in their path across the window. Except for the wind and the scuttling branches, the air was quiet when I pushed open the door and stepped outside. I hadn't thought to turn off the headlights and they lit the footprints before me, the first set almost completely dusted over with snow. How long had I been asleep? I wondered as I left the Datsun behind.

The next time you feel afraid, I want you to pray . . .

I tried. I really did try. In my nervousness, however, too many prayers clashed in my mind and tangled on my tongue so what came out was a mangled version of them all: "Our Father who art in heaven, the Lord is with thee, I believe in his only Son, who was born of the Virgin Mary, was crucified and buried. He rose from the dead, ascended into heaven, from thence he shall judge the living and the dead. As it was in the beginning, is now, and ever shall be. Amen. Amen. Am—"

At the bottom of the cement steps, I fell silent. For a long moment, I stood listening for some sound of them inside the church. But none came.

THINGS IN THE BASEMENT

How would you describe yourself now?
Arnold Boshoff asked a lot of questions each time we met in his windowless office decorated with Just Say No posters, but he returned to that one again and again. Boshoff gave a taffy stretch to the word *nooow* while resting his hands on his mountainous belly and steepling his fingers. Always, I looked up at his puffy pink face and watery blue eyes and fed him the obvious. I was an Advanced Honors student at the top of my class. My long, black hair was too stringy to stay in a ponytail. My skin was pale. Eyes, hazel. Sometimes, I informed him, I thought my head was too big for my body, my fingers and feet too small. I doled out those sorts of details before moving on to more minor things, like the flea-sized freckles on the inside of my right wrist. God kisses, my father used to call them. Hold them to the wind and they might blow away. By the time I started talking about how I used to make a triangle with those freckles by drawing on my skin with a marker, Boshoff unsteepled his hands and moved onto a new topic.

"I have something for you, Sylvie," he said, after we finished that routine one chilly October afternoon. He opened his desk drawer and pulled out a present, wrapped in polka-dot paper.

"What is it?" I asked as he placed the gift in my hands.

"You have to open it to find out, Sylvie. That's the way it works with presents."

Boshoff smiled and clacked his cough drop around his mouth. Judging from his rumpled sweaters and stain-splotched khakis, he wasn't the neatest person. Somehow, though, he managed to do a careful job wrapping that present. I peeled back the paper just as carefully, to find a diary with a miniature lock and key.

It had been some time since anyone thought to give me a gift, and I wasn't sure what to say. Finally, I managed, "Thank you."

"You're welcome."

Except for the flippity-flip of my hand turning the diary's empty pages, things were quiet. Boshoff was the teen drug and alcohol counselor for all of Baltimore County, Maryland, and rolled through towns like Dundalk on a weekly basis. Unlike his regulars, I had never puffed on a joint or tasted a drop of alcohol. Even so, I was excused from study hall once a week on the principal's suggestion that an hour with him might be helpful, seeing as there was no budget to fund a professional who had experience dealing with my "situation." The first time I went to his office in September, I asked Boshoff if me visiting him was like a person going to a vet to treat a burst appendix. He laughed and clacked his cough drop before using a serious voice to tell me, "I suppose most veterinarians could perform an appendectomy on a human if the situation called for it, Sylvie."

That ruined the joke.

"I've come to realize in these meetings of ours," he began now, so many weeks later, "that there are things you might not want to share with me or anyone else. But you might find it helpful to write them down in that journal, where they'll be safe."

I fingered the flimsy lock. With its violet cover and pink margins, the diary looked meant for some other girl, one who would fill the pages in loopy cursive with tales of kissing boys, slumber parties, cheerleading practice. Instead, my father's voice rolled through my head: *People don't need to know what goes on inside our house, so you and Rose shouldn't say anything to anyone—no matter who it is.*

"What are you thinking?" Boshoff asked, another favorite question of his.

"I'm thinking I don't know what I'd possibly write about in a journal," I told him, even though I knew what he intended. But I'd spent so much time in other windowless rooms, recounting the details of that night at the church for a white-haired detective and a haggard-looking assistant district attorney, that I felt no desire to do it again.

"Well, you could at least start by writing about your day, Sylvie."

I walk the hallways of Dundalk High School and people clear a path. No one makes eye contact or talks to me unless it is to taunt me about my parents and the thing that happened to them—the thing that almost happened to me too. . .

"You could write about what's going on at home with your sister now that things have, well, changed for you both."

Rose refuses to bother with grocery shopping except when Cora is scheduled to come by with her clipboard. Most nights, we eat Popsicles for dinner. Potato chips for breakfast. Mayonnaise smeared on bread in the middle of the night. . .

"Or you could just open the book and see what memories come."

To give the illusion that I was at least considering his suggestions, I turned to the first page and gazed at it, picturing the loopy cursive of that girl: *A boy kissed me in his car on Friday night for so long the windows steamed up. . . . My best friend slept over on Saturday and we watched* The Breakfast Club *on video. . . . I spent Sunday practicing cartwheels for cheerleading tryouts. . . .*

Somewhere in the middle of her happy life, I heard Boshoff. "Sylvie, the final bell rang. Did you not hear it? You know, on account of your ear?"

My ear. I looked up from the blank page, my expression blank too. "I heard it. I was just, I don't know, thinking about what I'd write."

"Well, good. I'm glad it's got you thinking. I hope you'll give it a try."

Although I had no intention of doing so, I told him I would before sliding the diary into my father's tote. It used to be that he carried his notes in that bag when he and my mother went on their trips, but I'd been using it to haul my books around since so many break-ins had led me to abandon my locker. High school may not have been the challenge I hoped for, but it certainly was louder. Slamming lockers. Shrill bells. The roar that filled the halls at the end of the day. Any other student stepping out of Boshoff's office into the stampede risked getting shoved against the wall. Not me. As usual, the crowd parted to make room.

Normally, after last bell, I walked against the foot traffic to the rear exit and out onto the winding path through the woods, past the distant hum of the highway and along the fence behind Watt's Poultry Farm toward home.

Today, though, my sister was picking me up to go shopping for school clothes at a place everyone in Maryland seemed to have been except us: the Mondawmin shopping mall. She never would have arranged the excursion if Cora hadn't shown up on a rainy Monday weeks before. When I stepped into the house that afternoon, I'd been thinking only of peeling off my wet clothes and taking a hot shower. Instead, I found a light-skinned black woman waiting on the sofa in the living room, gazing up at the wooden cross on our wall. In her pressed skirt and blouse, she looked too together to be someone who had come in search of help from my parents. And yet, I decided that's what she was.

"They're . . ." I said, my heart kicking into a speedy ticktock, ". . . they're not here."

"Oh, hello," she said, glossy lips parting into a smile when she saw me. "Who's not here?"

"My mother and father. You must not have heard, but—"

"I know that. I came to see you, Sylvie."

"Who are you?"

"Cora. Cora Daley. From Maryland Child Protective Services." Her smile froze as she took me in. "No need to look so worried. I just want to check in on you. That's all."

Had our previous caseworker, a man whose primary focus had been studying for his real-estate agent exam rather than me, mentioned that another person would come in his place? I remembered talk of interest rates, square footage, appraisals, though I'd lost track of the rest. "What happened to Norman? And how did you get in?"

"Norman is no longer working with you. I am. And your sister let me inside. I was waiting in the driveway when she got home. Poor thing was wet just like you. She went upstairs to change. I didn't have an umbrella, but I used this clipboard to cover my head. So long as my hair stays dry, I'm a happy camper. My mom's the same way. Don't mess with our hair and don't make us break a nail. Then we're happy."

As she rambled, I studied her hair, yanked into a bun, and her long nails, perfectly manicured. Her clothes looked so creaseless and new that I would not have been surprised to see a price tag poking out from a sleeve. I noticed down by her ankle what looked to be a small dolphin tattoo—or was it a shark? Despite her efforts, Cora Daley looked too young for the job, not much older than my sister, in fact.

"Do you want to change into dry clothes, then we can chat, Sylvie?"

Yes, I wanted to change. No, I did not want to chat. "I'm okay if you just want to get started."

"Well, all right then." Cora glanced at the damp papers on her clipboard. Her hands shook ever so slightly, and I wondered if being inside our house made her nervous. "Let's see. There are plenty of questions my supervisors tell me I'm *supposed* to ask. But the most obvious one that comes to mind is not on here." She looked up, flashing her warm brown eyes. "I'm wondering if that's what you wore to school today?"

Standing before her, dripping in my capris and T-shirt and flip-flops, what answer could I give but yes?

"If you don't mind me saying, Sylvie, those don't seem like the most appropriate clothes. Especially on a day like today."

"I guess we don't pay attention to weather reports around here lately."

"Well, I am going to have a talk with your sister about that. As well as the missed doctor's appointments for your ear that I see noted here on these pages."

Good luck, I wanted to say.

As I waited in front of school, weeks after that rainy Monday, dressed in nearly the same outfit and shivering in the cool October air, I looked over at a smoking area tucked beneath an overhang. Ratty couches and recliners were scattered so haphazardly it might have been mistaken for a rummage sale if not for the derelict students flopped on the furniture, squeezing in a last smoke. I'd seen most of them coming and going from Boshoff's office too, their clothes a kind of uniform: hoodies, thermals, ripped jeans, pentagrams and 666's doodled on their knuckles.

"Hey, Wednesday, you see something you like?"

This question came from Brian Waldrup, a freshman who lived in the golf course development, when he caught me staring. Brian was not the only person at school to call me by that name: Wednesday Addams. I reached into my father's tote and pulled out the diary, if only to look like I was doing something. As I stared at that empty first page again, I wondered what memories would come if I allowed myself to break my father's rule.

"You know what?" Brian said. He had folded up his recliner and was making his way closer. When he reached me, I felt his breath, skunky with tobacco, against my good ear. He paused, and I thought of so many things I wished he'd say: *I see you leaving Boshoff's office too. Are you okay?* Or, *I remember the homemade paper hearts you handed out on Valentine's Day in first grade. You gave me two because I'd broken my arm and you felt bad.* Or even, *I know what happened to your parents—we all do—and I hope at the trial this spring the jury puts that psycho, Albert Lynch, behind bars.* Instead, he asked, "What did your parents keep in the basement?"

"Nothing."

"Don't lie, Wednesday. Gomez and Morticia wouldn't approve."

"I'm not lying. There's nothing down there."

Impossible as it seemed, Brian came closer still, his tight body pressing into mine as he whispered, "You're lying. Just like they did. And you know what else? Your mom got what she deserved. Your father too. Right now, the two of them are burning in hell."

That might sound like the worst thing a person could say, but I tried not to feel bothered. It was a lesson I used to get every Sunday, when my family still went to Mass in the gym at Saint Bartholomew's Catholic School, where we arrived early and sat in the front pew at the edge of the three-point line. As we followed along with Father Coffey in the epistle—my sister and me in Sunday dresses that I loved but she hated—whispers came from the pews behind us. Even if I didn't hear what was being said, I understood that it had to do with us, the Mason family, and our presence in that makeshift church.

I smiled at Brian Waldrup. After all, despite those symbols and devil numbers drawn in pen on his knuckles, he was just a kid my age whose mother picked him up from school in her Volvo every afternoon. I had seen them rolling out of the parking lot on their way to that pretty yellow house on the golf course, where I imagined her sliding a roast or chicken into the oven most nights, flipping pancakes or scrambling eggs most mornings. Thinking of the differences between Brian's life and my own made it less difficult to smile because I was reminded how harmless he was. And when I finished smiling, I tucked the diary back into my father's tote and headed toward Rose's enormous red truck rolling up the drive at last, AC/DC screeching from her speakers.

"Boo!" Brian yelled as he watched me walk away.

When Rose came to a stop, I opened the truck door and climbed inside. Since she'd hacked off her hair again a second time last winter, it had grown back long and wild, black as mine still, but with a reddish hue that hadn't been there before. Rose liked to keep the windows down and let the strands whip around her, so that when she came to a stop she had to pull the mess away from her face.

"Hey," she said from behind her tangled hair.

"Boo!" Brian called from the curb, waving his hands and jumping up and down.

"What's his problem?" my sister asked as her pale, broad face made an appearance, dark eyes blinking.

"He's trying to scare me."

She made a *pfft* sound, then leaned over and gave him the finger. My sister flipped people off like nobody else: thrusting her arm, popping that middle digit fast and flashy as a switchblade. "Butt-holes like him are the second reason I hated this school."

"What was the first?"

"Food sucked. Teachers blew. And I *hated* homework."

That's three, I thought but didn't say since she had moved on to yelling at Brian.

"Step in front of my truck so I can squash your balls!"

"Boo!"

"Is that the only word in your vocabulary, you moron?"

In a quiet voice, I said, "Just go. It's easier to ignore him, Rose."

She turned back to me. "Sylvie, if we don't stand up to him and all the rest, they'll never leave us alone. *Never.*"

"Maybe so. But right now, I'd rather go to the mall."

Rose blew out a breath and gave it some thought before letting it go. "Guess it's Dinky-Dick's lucky day. Otherwise, I'd get out and pummel him." She popped her middle finger one last time before slamming on the gas.

"Boo!" Brian shouted as our giant tires squealed. "Boo! Boo! Boo!"

He kept at it, like a ghost haunting an abandoned house on a hill. If you believe in ghosts. I did and I didn't. But mostly, I did.

Nine months. That's how long my mother and father had been dead.

And yet, despite what I told Brian, those things my parents kept in the basement—things so many people in Dundalk wondered about whenever they laid eyes on my sister and me—they were down there still.

THE *Shhhh . . .*

An hour—that's how long we spent roaming the echoing corridors of the mall, riding the escalators in a daze brought on by the bright lights and smells of chocolate chip cookies and cinnamon. There was so much to take in that Rose didn't even walk ahead of me the way she usually did. She was the more attractive sister, with a taller, more athletic body and what people call a handsome face on a girl. I caught men giving her a once-over as we passed, but Rose ignored them. As we wandered, I had a happy feeling for the first time in a long while, because our lives felt almost normal.

At JCPenney, the catalogs we had known for so many years, since our mother once shopped only from those pages, sprang to life before our eyes. In the Junior Miss department, I stopped to feel a knee-length black dress with a cinched waist and narrow collar. I liked the dress but worried it looked like one Wednesday Addams might wear, which would only encourage the Brian Waldrups of the world.

As it turned out, my opinion on that outfit was unimportant. Rose led me to a clearance rack in the back and told me to have fun choosing. The clothes there consisted of a hodgepodge of flared cords and snap-up shirts I had no interest in wearing. The moment my sister wandered away, I wandered too. No sooner had I found another rack when she appeared again and asked what I thought I was doing, then ordered me to wait in the dressing room while she picked my clothes. Considering the bickering we'd done about her driving on the way there (too fast, too much attention to the radio, too much wind through the windows, too much lane changing, not enough signaling), I didn't want to stir up more trouble. I went to a booth and stripped down to my underwear and bra, which fit too tightly after months of not buying anything new.

I was good at waiting. Last winter I had done a lot of it, lying in my hospital bed and listening to the footfalls of nurses in the hall, the tinny laugh tracks of sitcoms drifting from other patients' rooms, pages crackling over loudspeakers. And hearing, without having to listen for it, the unending sound that filled my ear. "It's like the noise inside a seashell," I told the doctors, "or when someone is telling you to shush."

Shhhh . . .

Not Rose. Not Uncle Howie. Not Father Coffey. Not anyone I knew. Other than a nurse or doctor or hospital social worker, the first person I saw standing by my bed when I opened my eyes was Detective Dennis Rummel. The man had bright blue eyes and snowy hair, the sort of blocky jaw you might see on an old statue. Odd, perhaps, that a detective would slip his large hand into my small one and hold it for so long. Odd that he would take the time to fill my cup with water from the plastic pitcher and ice from the noisy machine down the hall. Odd, too, that he would adjust my pillows and blankets to make certain I felt something close to comfortable. But he did all those things.

"The more you can tell me about what happened, Sylvie," the detective said in his steady voice that made me think of a statue too, the way one might sound if it parted its lips to speak, "the better chance we have of finding whoever is responsible. That way your mom and dad can rest in peace. And that's what you want for them, isn't it?"

I nodded, even as I thought of my father saying, *People don't need to know what goes on inside our house . . .*

"Why don't we start with what led you to the church in the first place?" Rummel asked, sitting on the edge of the bed, slipping his hand into mine once more.

The question left me suddenly thirsty. I wanted more water from the pitcher. I wanted more ice from the machine down the hall. I wanted my sister, but Rummel had not yet mentioned Rose. So instead of bringing up any of those wants, I told him that the phone rang after midnight, that my mother came into my room and woke me to go to the church.

"Did she seem upset to you?"

I shook my head.

"And did she tell you who called or who they were going to meet?"

Shhhh . . .

As Rummel fixed his blue eyes on me, that noise grew louder. I swallowed, my throat feeling even more dry than before, the answer nesting on my tongue.

"I know this is hard, Sylvie. No one should have to go through something so unspeakable, particularly at such a young age. So I appreciate you being brave. I also appreciate you giving me the answers as best you can remember. Understand?"

I nodded.

"Good. We'll have the phone records pulled. But in the meantime, it's important that you tell me, did either of your parents say who called?"

You and Rose shouldn't say anything to anyone. . .

"No," I said, my voice trembling over such a short word.

"Not a mention?"

No matter who it is . . .

"They never told me about the things they did. And on the drive to the church, we were quiet on account of how late it was and because of the slippery roads."

The detective looked away, and I had the sense that he was unsatisfied with that answer. His gaze moved from the drab curtains to the flickering TV. "Okay, then," Rummel said, turning back to me. "Tell me why your parents took you along but left your sister at home."

"At home?"

"Yes."

I was quiet, listening to that sound in my ear. I pressed my fingers to the bandage, squeezed my eyes shut.

"Are you all right? I can call the nurse. She's right outside in the hall."

"It's okay." I opened my eyes, looked at my feet by the end of the bed. "Didn't Rose tell you why she was at home?"

"Sylvie, she's at the station right now being asked the same questions.

After we discovered you and your parents at Saint Bartholomew's, an officer was dispatched to your house where we found your sister. Now it's crucial that we piece your separate accounts together in order to help. So tell me, why did your parents leave Rose behind?"

"They didn't say," I told him..

"Was it unusual for the three of you to go somewhere without her?"

Two pairs of cords flew over the top of the dressing room just then, followed by flannel shirts. "Hurry up and try the stuff on," Rose said. "I have to pee like a pony."

If there is such a thing as putting away a memory until later, that is what I did. I gathered the clothes from the floor, unable to keep from muttering the word, "Racehorse."

"Huh?" my sister said from the other side of the door.

"'I have to pee like a racehorse.' That's the saying. There's no pony involved."

A silence came over my sister that told me she was doing some big thinking. All that brainpower led to her saying, "Are you telling me ponies don't pee too?"

I had slipped on brown cords and a flannel, half listening as I studied myself in the mirror. Funny that we were discussing horses, because I looked like a stable girl. "Ponies pee," I said, tugging off the cords. "But that's not the—"

"Ha! Got you, nerd brain. Now let's move it, because I really do have to go."

"There must be a bathroom around here, Rose."

"Public toilets give me the skeeves. I'll go at home if I don't wet myself first."

My mood had shifted by then, same as it did whenever I thought about Rummel's questions. And even though I wanted to get dressed and walk out of the store, I needed new clothes so I kept trying them on. Each outfit looked worse than the next, until finally I dressed in the capris and tank I wore to the mall and stepped out of the booth.

"Where are you going?" my sister asked.

"To pick out my own stuff."

"You can't."

"Why not?"

Rose didn't offer up an answer right away so I turned in the direction of the Junior Miss department, figuring the dress on that mannequin deserved a second look.

"Because I need to watch our budget, that's why," she blurted.

I knew we didn't have much money, not even when our parents were alive. People didn't pay well for the services they provided. They wrote letters begging for help and only occasionally enclosed a check to cover gas or airline tickets. Or they showed up on our doorstep with a glazed look in their eyes, offering promises to undo the debt later if only my parents could make all that had gone wrong in their lives right again—there, too, money rarely materialized. Instead, we relied on income from my parents' lectures to support us. Once Sam Heekin's book was published, however, that income dried up. Still, I'd seen my sister blow plenty on things we couldn't afford, namely her truck, purchased with insurance money and the sale of our parents' Datsun after the police released it from impound. When I turned around and reminded her of that, she broke into an all-out fit, her voice pitching higher and higher until she yelled, "Whether you like it or not, Sylvie, I'm your legal guardian now!"

With that, she walked out of the store.

Whenever that phrase passed her lips it caused some part of me to fold in on itself. I remembered, of course, the lawyers, my parents' nonexistent will, the endless paperwork and court appointments, Norman's visits and now Cora's. I remembered, too, the afternoon Uncle Howie had been located somewhere near his apartment in Tampa, days after that night at the church. The way he came around, announcing his intention to take care of us, and the way that ended when Rose and the attorneys raised the issues of his DUIs, a drug arrest, and his lack of any consistent history of involvement in our lives. And yet, the knowledge of how our situation came to be did nothing to keep that feeling away. I stared down at the flat red carpet in JCPenney's while customers who had been watching our feud slowly returned to their shopping.

"Honey," a passing clerk said, "are you okay?"

I looked up at the *Can I help you?* pin stuck to her enormous bosom but did not make eye contact. Instead, I just nodded before heading out to the parking lot. I couldn't find the truck at first, and I wandered the rows of vehicles, certain Rose had left without me. When I finally did spot it, there was no sign of her inside. The heat of the passenger door warmed my back as I waited. For a place teeming with cars, it seemed strange that so few people were around. In the distance, a woman strapped a wailing baby in a car seat. Farther away, a man in a green uniform arranged bags in his trunk. Other than that, it was just me out there until I heard keys rattle nearby. I turned to see Rose coming my way, sipping a mammoth soda and devouring an oversized bun out of a carton.

"Where were you?" I asked.

"You wasted so much time, I had no choice but to use the scummy restroom. And then I got hungry."

She unlocked my door, went around to hers. As we climbed inside, Rose said she would leave it to me to explain the way I dress to Cora if the woman stopped babbling long enough to ask again. My sister started the truck, the monstrous engine vibrating the floor beneath my feet. "Besides, I barely notice what you wear when you walk out of the house anyway. More important: there's nothing I like less than hovering over a toilet seat in some filthy restroom. So don't make me do it again."

On the drive back to our faded Tudor hidden among the thinning cedars and birch groves at the end of Butter Lane, neither of us spoke. Rose kept the windows down and failed to signal when she changed lanes, but the radio remained off. As the last of the sunlight vanished, I stared at the dead leaves on the lawns we passed. One family had carved their jack-o'-lantern too soon and, with three days to go until Halloween, already the face was caving in on itself.

As we turned into our sloping driveway, past the faded NO TRESPASSING! signs, I couldn't help but glance at the basement window. A light used to remain on down there at all times. Considering the reasons my parents kept it on, I should not have longed for the sight of that yellowy glow seeping beneath the rhododendrons, but I couldn't help myself. Not that it mattered. The bulb burned out sometime after their deaths, and neither of us had gone down to replace it.

"Isn't it funny?" I said. "All those times Mom and Dad went away and you fought for us not to have a nanny so we could be alone. Now, here we are. Just the two of us."

Rose cut the engine. As we listened to the faint *tip-tap* beneath the hood, she untangled her hair, and I waited for that vibrating sensation to leave my feet.

"Like that time with Dot," I began.

"Why do you have to talk about that stuff?"

"I just—"

"I don't want to think about the past anymore, Sylvie. Mom and Dad chose their lives and beliefs and career. And look what happened. I know I should never have made that call. Believe me, I wouldn't have if I'd had any idea what would come of it. But Albert Lynch would have found a way to get to them anyway. Or if not him, some other freak. So I don't think it's good for either of us to go on about what used to be anymore. Once we get through the trial come spring, we have to leave it behind."

As she spoke, I stayed quiet, watching her undo the snarls in her hair.

"Someday, Sylvie, when you finish school and we move away from this house and live our separate lives, we're going to forget the one we lived here. I know it seems hard to believe, but one day it'll be just a bunch of lost memories from a long time ago."

Shhhh . . .

It had nothing to do with that sound; I heard her just fine. Yet I couldn't see how we would ever be able to leave any of it behind. But what more was there to say? I reached for my father's tote full of books, including the diary Boshoff had given me earlier that day. I opened the door and lowered my feet to the ground. That's when I felt something soft beneath my flip-flops. Part of me knew what it was right away. Still, the sensation made me gasp.

"What now?" Rose asked.

My silence did nothing to keep her from coming around to the other side of the truck. By then I'd stepped off the thing and placed the tote on the ground. We stood in our shadowy driveway, staring down at its splayed body and wide white moon of a face. Those blank black eyes and that peculiar shade of red hair. This one was smaller than usual: the size of a possum, but flattened, as though it had been run over.

With the tip of her boot, my sister flipped it facedown into the dirt. "Fuckers!" she yelled into the darkness surrounding our house. "You fuckers!" With each new outburst, she raked her hands over her hair until the staticky strays levitated around her head. I thought again of how she'd first razored it to the scalp more than a year before, mainly because some guy she liked had shaved his and wanted her to do the same. *If Franky told you to jump off a bridge, would you? If Franky told you to rob a bank, would you? If Franky told you never to speak to your family again, would you?* Those were the questions my parents asked, to which my sister responded, *Yes!*

"Fuckers!" she yelled one last time before letting out a breath and kneeling in the dirt. Slowly, her hands reached out for the thing.

"Don't!" I said.

"Don't what?"

"Touch it."

Rose looked up at me. She may have had our mother's name, but it was our father's face I saw on her: his wide chin, his pronounced nose, his eyes, dark and squinty behind his smudged wire-rims. Though our father never spoke to me the way Rose did when she said, "It's not going to do anything, you idiot."

"I know. But please. Just don't."

My sister sighed. She stood and walked to the rusted shed at the edge of our property. I heard her rattling around before she returned with a shovel. It took maneuvering, but she slid the foam-stuffed body onto the end and carefully walked to the well we hadn't used since the town of Dundalk installed city water. I followed and pushed the plywood covering off the top. Rose raised the shovel over the gaping black mouth and, with a flick of her wrists, dropped the doll inside.

"It never ends," my sister said, hurling the shovel into the darkness where her old rabbit cage once stood. "It never fucking ends."

"They'll get bored," I told her and pulled the plywood back over the hole, careful not to give myself a sliver. "They have to get bored."

Inside, our house was silent except for the hum of the fridge and the ticking of the antique clock that hung not far from the cross on the wall. I went to the kitchen with its peeling blue walls and ate my dinner: a cherry Popsicle, the best kind. All the while I slurped and felt my lips go numb, I stared at my mother's thick book of wallpaper swatches on the table and thought about another conversation with Detective Rummel, the morning after the first, at the hospital.

Rummel had slid a photo across the narrow table over my bed. "Do you know this man, Sylvie?"

"Yes."

"How?"

"He once was a friend of my— Well, not a friend. I guess he was what you'd call a client of my parents. His daughter, Abigail, was anyway. She was the one who needed them. Her father just brought her to us."

"Brought her to you?"

"Yes. Albert Lynch wanted my parents' help dealing with his daughter's, well, problems."

Rummel tapped his thick finger on the photo. "Okay, then. We are going to want to know all about that. But right now, I need an answer in order to help you. Is this the man you saw inside the church the night of your parents' deaths?"

I thought of the cold air inside that small building after I pulled the door open, so cold it hurt to breathe. I thought of how dark it had been after the door clicked shut behind me, the only lights from the car outside, the beams muted through the stained-glass windows. More carefully, I stared down at the picture. Bald head. John Lennon glasses. Wispy mustache that looked like something a teenager, maybe Brian Waldrup, might grow.

"Yes," I told Rummel. "That's who I saw."

When I finished eating, I tossed the Popsicle stick in the trash and headed upstairs. My sister had gone ahead of me, and a thin strip of light glowed beneath her door. No sound came from inside. As I got ready for sleep, I emptied my books from the tote and placed them on my desk until I pulled out the violet diary. Earlier that day, I had felt certain I would not bother, yet there I was searching for a pen. There I was turning to the first of so many empty pages as I sat on my bed. For a while, I did nothing but stare at the pink margins and lines, doing my best to conjure frivolous details from the life of that imagined girl. But she had gone silent, drowned out by the very different particulars of the life I was leading. At last, I clicked the pen and wrote the name *DOT* at the very top. But before I put down anything about the way the woman's visit to our house led, in its own peculiar way, to greater troubles for my family, I found myself writing out Boshoff's question: *How would you describe yourself nooow?* This was my answer:

> *I am the only girl in school who dresses like it is June, even though it is October. Last year's fall and winter sweaters and pants and skirts are hanging in my closet and folded in my drawers, exactly where my mother left them. But I cannot go near those things. Not because I am beginning to outgrow those clothes, but because putting them on would mean rearranging the things she left for me. Not that it matters since Rose really is my legal guardian now and, like she said at the mall, she barely notices what I wear, even if it's a flimsy tank top, capris, and flip-flops, and even if the temperature is dropping by the day, and even though she should—*
>
> *My sister really should notice.*

DOT

My parents always packed the same supplies. My father: an electromagnetic frequency meter, a motion sensor, thermometers, audio and video recorders, a high-resolution camera, ample rolls of film. My mother: a simple set of rosary beads, a well-worn King James Bible, pages dog-eared and highlighted in a rainbow of colors, and a solitary flashlight. As they prepared for their trip, Rose and I lingered by the front door in anticipation of the latest nanny's arrival. How many times had I been disappointed? Yet there I stood, hoping for Mary Poppins to glide over the cedar trees. Instead, the nannies were all so bland they blurred in my mind— except for Dot, who arrived at our house when I was eleven and Rose fifteen, and who came to be the last nanny we ever had.

I remember watching from the front steps as she shoved open the creaky door of her mud-splattered Yugo and climbed out. Dot had skinny arms and legs, but a bulging midsection, hugged tight by the elastic waistband of her yellow uniform. Instead of a suitcase, she pulled a plastic laundry basket from the backseat.

"This one's going to be an easy target," Rose said as we watched the woman lumber up the walkway. "I almost feel bad for her."

Run! I wanted to yell. *Get out before it's too late!*

When she met us at the front steps, Rose skipped over any formal greeting and asked, "What's with the bears?"

"Bears?" Dot had a foamy mouth with permanent spittle in the corners of her chapped lips. Tiny bubbles washed over her crowded teeth. She glanced behind her then looked down at her matching shirt and pants, where pastel bears decorated the fabric. "Oh, *these* bears. It's my uniform. I'm an LPN at the children's hospital in Baltimore. I'm hoping it'll turn into a full-time job. But right now, I'm just a substitute."

The geyser Dot produced pronouncing the word *substitute* kept me distracted until Rose said, "Well, this ain't the children's hospital. So climb back in your four-wheeled fuse-box and keep right on trucking."

"Seven-twelve, Rose!" my mother called, coming up behind us. She had developed a shorthand for the scripture she most often quoted to Rose—Matthew 7:12: "Do unto others as you would like done unto you." Or, as my sister liked to translate, cut the crap and be nice.

"I just came from the hospital where I work sometimes," Dot informed my mother after they introduced themselves. "Sorry I didn't change, but I worried I'd be late."

"Are you sure you want this lady bringing hospital germs into our house?" Rose asked my mother. "She could be carting along an army of bacteria for diseases like—" My sister looked at me. "Sylvie, name some weird diseases that might be contagious."

Normally, I would not have gone along with Rose's behavior, but my desire to show off my smarts trumped all else. "Elephantiasis. Progeria. Hypertrichosis," I rattled off. "Diptheria. Shigellosis. Leptospirosis."

My mother gave us a look and said more plainly, "Quit. Being. Rude."

"Rubella," I let slip.

"Sylvie!"

"Sorry."

She took a breath, then turned back to Dot, who stepped into the house, carrying her laundry basket. Inside, I saw her wrinkled clothing, deodorant, a worn toothbrush, and a bloated copy of *The Thorn Birds*. "You can change in the bathroom down the hall," my mother told her, "then I'll show you around and go over the rules."

Dot set her basket on one of the wingback chairs. "Actually, if you don't mind, I have to wash a few things. So I'll keep these clothes on until my nightie is clean."

"Nightie?" my mother repeated.

Dot smiled, her mouth foaming a little too. "Oh, don't get the wrong idea, Mrs. Mason. It's not one of those lacy Frederick's of Hollywood getups I used to break out for my husband. It's just a flannel nightgown any old lady would wear to bed. Thing is, my cat hopped up on the bed this morning and peed on it. I guess when she saw me filling her auto-feeder she realized I was skipping out for a few days. Got her revenge ahead of time. Anyway, I figured I'd wash it here."

"I see," my mother said, glancing at her slim watch and probably wondering if she had enough time to call the service and inquire about another nanny.

My father came clomping up the basement stairs then, carting the suitcase full of equipment and his tote filled with notepads where he recorded observations for lectures. In the hours before their trips, he grew serious and preoccupied—this time was no different. "The flight leaves in a few hours," he told my mother. "We better get going."

Not long after, the two of them were waving and honking from the Datsun as they pulled out of the driveway. No sooner had they disappeared down Butter Lane than Dot asked, "So what's on the docket, girls? Are you hungry?"

Rose didn't answer, but I shook my head.

"Good. Because I had some Burger King on the way over so I'm stuffed. You can help me get started on my laundry. Oh, and I assume there's a bathtub in the house."

"In my parents' room," I told her, "and one in the bathroom Rose and I share."

"Great. I need to soak these weary bones. This house has an awful chill to it. You'd never guess it's May."

"It's the spirits," Rose told her.

"Pardon?" Dot wiped the corners of her mouth with her thumb and index finger.

"The spirits," Rose repeated. "You know what my parents do for a living, right?"

"Well, I— The woman at the service warned me it was unusual. But I get all kinds. Money's money. I told her I didn't want to know the details. I'm a holy woman—"

"A holy woman who wears sheer nighties?" Rose said.

Seven-twelve, I thought. *Seven-twelve.*

"I never said *sheer.* I said *lacy.* And that was a long time ago, for my husband, Roy, on special occasions. Before he passed. I don't parade around like some flooz—"

"When our parents go on these trips," Rose interrupted, "they are asked to confirm the presence of unwanted spirits. Sometimes they are asked to drive them out too. Usually from places, but once in a while, from people. I'm talking about children, pregnant women, the elderly, even animals and inanimate objects too."

This information bothered Dot—that much was obvious by her pinched expression—but she shrugged. "Well, I want to get my laundry done then settle into the tub and finish my book. I'm just getting to the juicy part. Sylvie, could you pick up my laundry basket like a good girl? Old Dot's back hurts."

"The spirits need somewhere to go after they've been driven out of the host," Rose told her as I lifted the basket. "More often than not they end up— Well, I'll give you one guess where they end up."

Dot pushed her owl glasses to the top of her nose and grabbed her copy of *The Thorn Birds*—a priest dominated the cover, far more handsome than Father Vitale from Saint Bartholomew with his drooping skin and sagging shoulders. *"Here?"* she said in a quiet voice.

"Here," Rose told her, lowering her voice too. "In this house. Tell her, Sylvie. Tell her about the terrible things we've seen."

There were times when Rose's terrorizing of the nannies was, I confess, fun to watch. But this felt too easy somehow. "Let me show you the washer and dryer, Dot."

Dot ignored my suggestion, asking, "What do you see?"

"Sylvie won't tell you because we are not supposed to talk about it— *forbidden* by my father to talk about it, actually."

"So why are you talking about it then, Rose?" I asked.

My sister manufactured a creepy, distant voice. "Because Dorothy seems like a nice lady, and since she'll be staying here for the next five nights, I feel I should warn her." Rose looked at Dot. "Ours is not an easy house to sleep in. Some nights they've even—" She stopped, as though snapping out of a trance, returning her voice to normal. "Well, never mind. Don't worry. Mostly they mind their own business. *Mostly.*"

Dot stared at her a moment, pinched-faced still, before pushing back her shoulders and squeezing the handsome paperback priest tighter. "I don't buy into that nonsense. Tell you what. Sylvie, I'm gonna let you put the laundry in since you're familiar with the machines. Meanwhile, if anyone needs me, I'll be in the tub."

For a while at least, Rose left her alone. I took care of the laundry. Slipped into my pajamas. Spent time completing a paper I'd been writing for the first ever Maryland Student Essay Contest—a two-hundred-dollar cash prize would be awarded to a student in each grade from fifth through twelfth and the deadline was the next morning. My topic was inspired by a documentary my mother and I had watched about the aftereffects of Martin Luther King Jr.'s assassination. When I mentioned it to Ms. Mahevka, my pasty, yawning English teacher, she told me it was "overreaching" considering my age. I kept at it for weeks anyway, my electric typewriter conking out before I did, since the last of my ink cartridges ran dry that night. The letters of my final sentence were so faint I backspaced and typed over them again and again.

"Boo!"

I glanced up to see Rose lurking in my doorway. "Stop it."

"What are you doing?" she asked.

"Just homework."

"What kind of homework?"

The kind you never do, I thought. "A paper. I'm finishing the last line."

"Read it to me."

"The entire paper?"

"No. The last line."

"Why?"

"I don't know. Guess I'm curious what goes on inside that egghead of yours."

Why I did not simply refuse her request, I don't know. Maybe the pride I felt clouded my judgment. I cleared my throat and, rather than read, recited: "Only by entering into the most crystalline of consciousnesses and by raising our voices vociferously enough to be heard by those in power

will the citizens of this great but troubled country of ours send such big-
otry and phobia tumbling toward obsolescence."

Rose stared at me, blinking. "Now that you're done speaking in
tongues, what are your plans tonight?"

I tugged the sheet from the machine and placed it beneath the others
on my desk. My parents had given me that typewriter, a brand-new Smith
Corona Spell Right, for Christmas, and even though other students were
getting pricey word processors, I treated it like a favorite pet, wiping down
the keys and fitting the dustcover over the top after unplugging the cord.
Rose kept her eyes on me, smirking. So many things she'd been given
ended up neglected, like those mahogany horses, gifts to each of us from
Uncle Howie on one of his rare visits. I'd given mine fairy-tale names that
suited their looks: Esmeralda, Sabrina, Aurora, Megra, Jasmin—and arranged them on my shelf according to color and height. Rose's had long
been banished to a dark corner of her room.

When I was finished shutting down the typewriter, I pulled back the
covers on my bed, climbed in, and turned off the light. "Good night, Rose."

"Come on, Sylvie. It's early! Why turn in when Dot the Twat is soaking
her lazy bones in the next room? The woman's *just begging* for us to mess
with her."

"Seven-twelve."

"Enough with the seven-twelves already. It's like some pathetic police
code. Ten-four good buddy."

"Good buddy is more of a trucker saying than cops."

"Whatever. The point is, I'm not a *baby*. So therefore, I don't need a
*baby*sitter. Especially some fart-face who comes around here claiming she's
going to take care of us when all she's doing is taking care of her own fat
ass. You mean to tell me a substitute nurse at a children's hospital is smarter
than me? I don't think so. And even if she is, there's no way she's smarter
than *you*, Sylvie. Listen to that sentence you wrote. That is *not* the sentence
of a person who requires a babysitter. That's why I've taken the liberty of
locking Dot in the bathroom."

My eyes, which had fallen shut, snapped open. "What?"

"I locked Dot in the bathroom."

I reached over and switched on the lamp. Got out of bed. Slipped on my slippers. Walked across the hall to my parents' room. On account of our father's back trouble, they had slept separately for as long as I could recall. Their room resembled one in a roadside motel: two full-size beds, a nightstand between, even a bible tucked in the drawer. On this particular night, a bright yellow rope stretched from my mother's heavy wooden bedpost to the bathroom door. Behind that door, Dot hummed away, making bubbling sounds in the water, oblivious to her predicament.

"Pretty cool, huh?" Rose whispered.

"I don't think it's pret—"

Rose yanked me into the hall. "Don't blow this with your big mouth. Whether you like it or not, you're going to help me, Sylvie."

"No, I won't."

But Rose ducked into my room, returning with the pages of my freshly typed essay in her hands. "'The Aftereffects of Martin Luther King Jr.'s Assassination on American Society,' by Sylvie Mason," she read. "Bet you'd hate to see all your hard work go tumbling toward obsolescence too."

I reached for the paper, but she pulled back.

"Careful." Rose gave a little tear to the title page, the sound causing me to wince. "Oops. Are you sure you don't want to help me?"

I looked away, into my parents' room. Their beds perfectly made, their bedspreads the swirling colors of a leaf pile. That rope, stretching between my mother's bedpost and the bathroom door. From the other side, the sounds of Dot splashing about, making those hapless bubbling noises. I turned to Rose. "What do I have to do?"

The question was as good as a yes—we both knew it. My sister did an about-face and headed downstairs without answering. I followed until we were standing in the kitchen at the door to the basement. Our parents had only recently moved their workspace from the living room to below, so the place didn't hold the same fear that would come later. Even so, I avoided it. But Rose pulled open the door and descended the wooden steps. Again, I followed, breathing in the musty air and gazing around at the cinder-block walls. In one corner, the beginnings of a partition separated a small area by the sliding glass door. My father had long ago begun constructing those walls, only to give up on the project. Through the sloppy cage of two-by-fours and snarled wires, I watched as my sister navigated among the heap of bicycles, a forgotten dental chair, and on deeper into the shadows.

While she did who knew what over there, I studied my father's new desk and file cabinet, a compact TV and VCR on top. A hulking bookshelf had been positioned in front of the cavity in the wall that led to the crawl space, the shelves filled with boxes they'd yet to unpack, a basket of cassettes and a tape player, a few stray videotapes. My mother never cared for sitting at a desk, so she kept a wooden rocker there. The cushions tied to the seat and spindled back were worn thin, her knitting basket situated nearby so she could occupy her hands whenever they discussed their work.

Darkness cannot put out the light.
It can only make God brighter.

The words were engraved on a paperweight atop a pile of snapshots. I lifted it and flipped through the photos. A dingy hall in an old hospital. A hillside cemetery, names and dates worn from the stones. Only one photo had I seen before: a run-down theater with an empty marquee. In each, a stray sliver of light or odd shadow turned up. I tucked the photos beneath the paperweight and opened a drawer, where I found a bundle of tarnished dental instruments bound by rubber bands. Probes and explorers, bone files and orthodontic pliers—I knew all their names, because I'd once asked my father.

"Damn it!" Rose shouted from beyond the skeletal partition. "I stepped in a glue trap."

That should slow you down, I thought, listening to her foot scrape the floor. "What are you doing over there anyway?"

"Just hold your horses, Sylvie." She kept scraping. "You'll see soon enough."

I wandered to the bookshelf. Something made me pick up a video, push it in the VCR. A grainy nothingness filled the screen, then my mother appeared. On that fuzzy TV, it felt the way it must glimpsing an image in a crystal ball. She stood outside a brick house in a beige raincoat I'd not seen before, the belt tight around her slender waist. My father's voice could be heard saying, "Okay. We're rolling. Go ahead."

My mother gave a nervous smile. "Go ahead, what?"

"Go ahead and explain where we are and what we're doing here."

"I feel . . . *silly.*"

"Just give it a try, Rose."

She let out a breath. "All right then. My name is Rose Mason. I'm here with my husband, who is holding the camera. Isn't that right, husband-holding-the-camera?" My father nodded so that the frame moved up and down. "We are at the home of—" My mother stopped, looked at the ground. "Oh, I don't like this, Sylvester. Can't we just record the details in a notebook or on a cassette like we used to do?"

"Here," my father said. "You hold the camera. I'll give it a—"

From the far side of the basement, there came a loud snap before the lights went out, the TV along with it. In an instant, the basement was enveloped in black. Apparently, it was the same throughout the house, because two floors above Dot called from the tub: "Girls? Hello? Girls?"

"Not funny," I told Rose.

"Girls? Anybody hear me? Yoo-hoo! Girls?"

Rose clicked on a flashlight and shined it at her face, transforming her features into something ghoulish. She handed me a flashlight too. "First of all, who the hell says, 'yoo-hoo'? Second, it is so funny and you know it."

"Sylvie? Rose? Hello?"

"Dick Van Dot is calling," my sister said. "We better go see what she wants."

By the time we stepped into my parents' room again, I could hear her splashing around in the dark, like some oversized, floppy fish washed ashore. The sound made me want to put an end to whatever more Rose had in mind, but, ashamed as I was to admit it, the thought of my essay and how much I wanted to win led me to keep my mouth shut. I sat on my mother's bed, where Dot had discarded her uniform with the tiny bears. Since the rest of her clothes were folded in the laundry basket downstairs courtesy of me, I knew she had nothing in the bathroom except a towel.

Rose went to the door. Scratched at the wood.

"What the devil?" Dot said.

Scratch. Scratch. Rose kept at it, which brought on another onslaught of, "Girls? Hello? Girls?" At last, she gave up on that too. The woman sighed, followed by a splash, loud enough that I knew she was standing up in the tub. I listened to her feet pad across the linoleum. Her hand found the knob, and I watched the rope tighten. The door did not budge. Dot banged on it, crying out more frantically. "Girls! Can anybody hear me?"

Rose walked to my mother's bed and sat on top of Dot's uniform. Leaning close, she whispered in my ear, "Do *The Scream*."

I should have figured that's what she wanted. I shook my head.

"*Do it,*" she insisted.

The Scream was a talent—if that's the word for it—I had stumbled upon a few nannies before when Rose lured us into a game of indoor hide-and-seek. We were actually having fun until my sister decided to hide where neither of us could find her. After an hour of searching, we gave up and got ready for bed. When I climbed into mine and turned off the light, Rose reached out from where she had jammed herself between the wall and the mattress and grabbed my neck, which caused me to release the most blood-curdling scream. From that night on, Rose begged me to do *The Scream* in all kinds of places: store parking lots, outside of church, the library. Since it felt good to have her appreciate me for a change, there were times when I gave her what she wanted. But that night with Dot locked in the bathroom, I kept shaking my head.

Still, Rose went right on whispering: "*Do it. Do it. Do it.*"

"If I do it, can I get my essay back and go to bed?"

"Girls? I don't know what the bejesus you're up to, but I don't like it one bit."

Rose ignored her, mulling the deal. Finally, she whispered, "Okay. Give her one good one, and I'll take over from there."

I knew exactly the kind of performance my sister expected, so I stood and went to the bathroom door. "Dot," I said in my quietest voice. "It's Sylvie. Can you hear me?"

"Yes. I mean, no. Not really. Can you speak louder?"

"Are you okay?"

"If you call freezing and dripping in the dark okay, then yeah, I guess I'm just dandy. Now what is going on? And talk louder for cripes' sake. I can't hear you."

"Press your ear to the door," Rose told her, joining me at my side.

Dot shifted around in the bathroom. "Okay. What is it?"

"I warned you about the spirits," my sister said in a hushed voice. "Now do you believe me?"

"Not really. More likely your parents didn't bother to pay the electric bill."

Rose poked me with her flashlight. I took the deepest of breaths and out it came: a scream—*The Scream*—so sudden and shrill it would put the best horror movie actress to shame. In the silence that followed, I clutched my throat, since it always hurt afterward.

When she was done fumbling, Dot called out, "Sylvie, dear? Are you okay?"

From the tremble in her voice, I could tell she felt genuinely afraid now. I opened my mouth to let her know I was fine, but the thought of my essay being handed back to me as confetti made me close it again. Rose forked over the pages, and I stepped away from the door. Before leaving the room, I glanced back to see my sister making herself comfy on our mother's bed. She pulled out the bible from the nightstand, flipped the thin pages and in a slow, methodical voice began reading a random passage from Revelations: "And there was war in heaven: Michael and his angels fought against the dragon . . . And the great dragon was cast out, that old serpent, called Satan, which deceiveth the whole world: he was cast out into the earth, and his angels were cast out with him . . ."

"Let me out of here!" Dot screamed. *"Please!* Let me out! Help!"

I should have helped her.

I should have shredded that essay myself and untied the rope.

Instead, as Dot kept pleading, as she kept pounding her fists against the door and Rose kept right on reading, I crossed the hall to my room. I climbed into bed, pulled a pillow over my head, and squeezed my eyes shut.

For centuries humans have believed in God, Buddha, Yahweh, and so many forms of a higher power. And yet, not one can be seen. Why do the same people who believe in those deities doubt the existence of darker spirits? I ask all of you, how can a person believe in the light but not the dark? *How,* when all evidence points to the basic facts of dualities? There is the light of the sun and the dark of the moon. There is the heat of summer and the cold of winter. Even a simple magnet demonstrates positive and negative energy. So when people ask for proof, I know they want stories about things my wife and I have encountered, and I can tell plenty. But first, I point out that they already have all the proof they need. Any of us here has only to observe the opposing energies of the world we live in, and it's proven time and again: If there is good, there is bad. If you believe in one, you must accept the existence of the other."

I opened my eyes. The house was dark, silent. My nightlight and digital clock were still dead, which meant the electricity had yet to be turned on. My pillow had fallen to the floor. I retrieved it and rolled over, staring at the wall. Those words I'd heard before coming fully awake, they had been spoken by my father. In my drowsy haze, I imagined them taking shape, drifting across the hall into my room, surrounding me in my narrow bed and filling my head. But then I remembered: my father was not home.

"There are times when people of confused faith misinterpret a psychological or medical disorder and carry out barbaric methods to rescue the sufferer. There are many such stories, but this evening I'd like to talk about a girl named Lydia Flores from a village in Mexico. When Lydia was fifteen, her mother—a widower—noticed a change in her daughter. Where she had once been affable, outgoing, she became sullen, withdrawn. Simply leaving the house became an act she resisted. According to reports, the girl's appetite vanished; her weight loss was drastic. Nights, she spent awake in her room, thrashing in bed. Days, she slept with such stillness it disturbed her mother. As things worsened, her behavior became violent toward others and herself. She spoke of voices and the horrible things they told her to do. Now any of us might contact a psychiatrist. But Lydia's mother lived all her life in that village, where people held antiquated beliefs about what was to be done in such a situation. Unfortunately for Lydia, her mother sought out a village priest with the same beliefs. This priest devised a plan for her treatment."

When I opened my eyes again, morning sun shone through my window. My nightlight was still out, clock too. I lay there, surrounded by my father's words, wondering how they had come to me. Before I could think too long, though, I remembered: *Dot.* I got out of bed and crossed the hall. My parents' door was shut and locked. I slipped back into my room a moment. My mother and I had a tradition: whenever they were about to leave on their trips, she helped me pick out the clothes I'd wear to school while they were gone. I found the soft blue spring dress and simple white flats she had chosen for that day and put them on without bothering to shower.

Downstairs, the antique clock ticked in the living room. I was running twenty minutes late, long enough that the bus was likely blowing past the end of the lane at that very moment. Inside the kitchen, I found Rose hunting down a fork, the toasty smell of something heating in the gas oven filling the room. "Where is she?" I asked.

"Who?"

"Rose, you know who I mean."

"Oh. *Her.* Where do you think?"

"After what you put her through, I'm hoping she's in mom's or dad's bed catching up on sleep."

Rose pulled open the oven door, reached inside. Out came two waffles, which she tossed on a paper towel before blowing on her fingers. "Don't you mean what *we* put her through? After all, you were the first one to scare the crap out of her." As she spoke, I watched her slather butter on those waffles and dump on so much syrup that it drooled through the paper towel onto the counter.

"You're making a mess," I told her. "Just put them on a plate."

"Won't fit under the door if they're on a plate."

"What door?"

"The bathroom door."

"She's *still* in there?"

"Go to school, Sylvie. I'm taking the day off myself. Too much to do here."

"Rose, you have to let her out. It's been almost twelve hours."

"Eleven, actually. And of course I'm going to let her out. I even told her I would last night, but that's when Miss Mary Snatch said she planned to call the police as soon as she was free. So no can do just yet. The woman's not getting out until we broker a deal. I guess you could say we've got a hostage situation going on up there."

For a long moment, I stood watching as she flattened each waffle with a fork so they'd slide more easily beneath the door. Finally, Rose looked up at me. "Sylvie, you don't want to be a part of this. I promise she'll be out by the time you get home. Now go on. Don't you have to turn in your paper so you can prove how smart you are?"

My paper. She was right that I needed to turn it in soon. But it wasn't going to happen, I told her, since I already missed the bus and had no way of getting to school.

"Just walk."

"*Walk?*"

"It's not that far. Not if you take that path behind the foundation across the street. Just follow it past Watt's Farm, and it'll lead you to the high school and middle school just beyond. I've taken it plenty of times when I bailed from school. Thirty minutes tops." With that, she grabbed the paper towel with those flat waffles on top and walked by me in a whiff of maple syrup. The smell made me hungry, and I thought of that Mexican girl I'd imagined—or maybe dreamed of—my father speaking about, the way her appetite had vanished, the way she had turned violent before the village priest devised a plan for her treatment. As Rose headed up the stairs, I called to her, "Wait."

Rose stopped, looked back.

"If I walk to school, do you promise to let her out soon?"

With her hands still holding that paper towel, she made what was meant to be an X but looked more like a lopsided U over her chest. "Cross my heart. Now go."

After she disappeared upstairs, I went to the rickety curio hutch and pulled a map of Dundalk from the drawer. Rose's path was not marked, of course, but I traced my finger through the woods and saw that what she said looked possible. I gathered my books and walked across the street, past the foundation, where a house had been started but never built. Behind it, I found the opening in the trees, a kind of wide-open mouth that swallowed me into those woods. Rose's shortcut turned out to be not much of a shortcut at all, since so much of those woods was thicker than I thought, but eventually, I emerged by the athletic fields, the middle and high school waiting for me.

For weeks, so much of what fueled me was the thought of placing my essay into Ms. Mahevka's hands, but she was out sick so a substitute collected my paper. After that, I had to sit through an entire day of classes, unable to think about anything but Dot upstairs in my parents' bathroom. Had she eaten those pathetic waffles? Had she promised not to call the police? Would she keep her word once she was free? By the time I stepped off the bus, those questions consumed my mind.

In the driveway, Dot's Yugo was parked where she left it. On the second floor, I saw that my parents' bathroom window, which led out onto a slanted section of the roof, was wide open, the shade unraveled and flapping in the breeze. Nearby, shingles were missing, and I spotted them among the rhododendrons below.

" . . . There is the heat of summer and the cold of winter. Even a simple magnet demonstrates positive and negative energy. . . ."

Even before stepping inside, I heard the faint sound of my father speaking again. This time, I realized how it was that he had come to me during the night. I walked through the door, listening to his words. When I flipped a light switch, no lights came on. I went to the kitchen, but no Rose. By the time I returned to the living room and reached the staircase, pausing to stare up at the darkened hallway above, my father had begun talking once more about that girl, Lydia Flores.

"The priest put the child in isolation. She was allowed no visitors except her mother. Her food and water were rationed. The priest spent hours each day, placing feathers between her toes in belief that it would enable the evil spirits to take flight. . . ."

At the top of the stairs, I turned and walked down the hall to my parents' door.

" . . . After a month of feathers and shouted prayers and the girl's cries for help, Lydia began to speak of her desire to die in order to atone for her sins. That's when doubt stirred in her mother, and she wondered if this priest was helping her daughter after all. She went to the city and spoke to people there. That is how she learned of my wife and me. And when she was told that our approach to these situations was more gentle, more humane, unlike the clichés we see in movies and books, she made contact with us . . ."

When I reached their door, I expected it to be locked. But it opened right up. The first thing I saw was Rose passed out on our mother's bed, mouth open in a lopsided *O*, bible facedown on her chest. On the nightstand: the tape recorder from that basket in the basement. The wheels turned inside, and I looked at my father's cramped writing on the cassette: *Sylvester Mason, Light & Dark Lecture at The Believers Circle. 11/9/1985.*

"... When we arrived in that village, it was immediately apparent to my wife and me that this was not a girl in need of our help, but one who desperately needed a doctor to address her medical issues, a psychiatrist to treat her emotional problems. You are probably all wondering how were we able to tell the difference. Let me explain—"

STOP.

When I hit that button, the air inside our house fell silent. On the other side of the bathroom door, things remained eerily quiet. I waited for my sister to wake, but when she didn't, I went to the door. "Dot? Are you okay in there?" She did not answer, and my sister remained dead to the world. I went to work, attempting to undo the rope around the knob. When it wouldn't give, I moved to the bedpost, where the knot came loose more easily.

When the rope fell to the floor, my sister's eyes opened. Groggy voiced, she asked, "What are you doing?"

"What do you think, Rose? She's been in there for hours."

I expected her to argue. Instead, my sister rubbed her eyes and got out of bed, then found her flashlight and strolled out of the room. I grabbed the other flashlight off the dresser and pointed it toward my parents' pink-tiled bathroom. Inside, I found a slumped and shivering figure, huddled in the corner on the floor. Except for a towel wrapped around her waist and another around her shoulders, she was naked.

"Dot?"

Slowly, she lifted her head. One hand shielded her eyes from the glare of the flashlight. I moved it away. Asked if she was all right. Not a word in response. Quickly, I went to the bed, grabbed her uniform with the bears, and returned to hold it out to her. Dot stood, legs shaking, towel slipping from her body so that her skinny legs and sagging breasts and drooping pouch of a stomach, even the thatch of gray hair at her crotch, were exposed. I saw that her legs and arms were scraped and realized she must have tried, unsuccessfully, to crawl out the window onto the slanted section of our roof.

Before I could look away, Dot reached out and snatched the uniform. She began to clumsily dress, gripping the towel rack for support. In the end, her shirt wound up inside out and backward, the tag in front, the V of her neckline dipping down the wrong side. It didn't seem to matter: Dot picked her bloated paperback off the floor and walked past me, bumping my shoulder so that I stumbled back. She felt her way down the hall in the dark as I regained my balance and trailed behind, doing my best to light our path. When we arrived in the living room, she grabbed her laundry basket off one of the wingback chairs right where I'd left it.

"I washed and folded your clothes just like you wanted," I told her.

She did not respond, though the house seemed to, because all at once the lights came on and Rose clomped up the stairs. She paused when she saw Dot at the front door.

"Dot," I called when she pulled it open. "You don't have to go."

Those words caused her to pay attention at last. She whirled around, eyes wide behind crooked glasses, more spittle on her lips than ever before. "Oh, yes, I do," she told us, pointing a trembling finger between Rose and me. "I don't care if I ever work for this service again! You girls are horrible! *Horrible!* You say your parents travel the country searching for demons. Well, I can save them the trip. Because they've got two of the most wicked little girls right here in their own home!"

With that, she stormed out into the bright daylight, leaving the door open behind her. I walked to the steps and watched her climb into her mudsplattered Yugo. As the engine turned over and she rolled backward up the driveway, Rose joined me at my side. We watched as Dot narrowly missed one of the birches before reaching the road. And when she shifted again, grinding the gears in a terrible grating noise, before sputtering away down Butter Lane, my sister actually put her arm around me.

"What if she calls the police?" I asked.

"She won't."

"How do you know?"

"I just do," Rose told me. "And anyway, the good news is, it looks like it's just you and me until Mom and Dad get home at the end of the week."

Once and for all, my sister had made her point. After that visit from Dot, never again would we have another nanny. But Rose *did* and *didn't* get what she wanted, because from that day on, whenever our parents went on their trips, they took us, their two daughters, their two very own wicked little girls, right along with them.

THE CAR WITH ONE HEADLIGHT

Those first few weeks after our parents died, I heard noises in the basement. A kind of rattling, things breaking and smashing. This was back before that bare bulb went dark. Back when its yellowy glow still oozed from the filmy casement window by the dirt, illuminating the lowest branches of the rhododendrons. I felt certain of what the noises were: down below, the things my parents had left behind were lamenting their untimely deaths—no different from what Rose and I were doing up above.

Those were the nights and days we spent shipwrecked in the living room. Together, though not really. I lay on the worn Oriental carpet, staring at the ceiling like there was something up there, a world of constellations that might spell out an explanation instead of just a vast white space with dust in the corners. Rose took up residence on one of the wingback chairs, dragging a second so close it formed a cradle. Her legs hung over the sides, covered by a blanket our mother had knitted years before.

"I don't understand," I said again and again. "Why would you make a deal like that with Albert Lynch?"

When Rose answered, her voice held none of its usual bark. Instead, she sounded as dazed and faraway as me. "I made it . . ." she began then stopped, before starting again, " . . . I made it because I had no idea what it would lead to, Sylvie. He told me he just wanted to talk to them. He told me he wanted to set things straight about what happened with Abigail that summer she came to live here. He told me—"

I waited for her to finish. When she didn't, we both fell silent. Time had a funny way of moving in those early days and weeks after they were gone. An hour might have passed, or maybe just a few minutes. It all felt the same. Finally, some part of my consciousness rose up to prod her. "He told you what?"

"I don't know. He just made it sound simple. Like if I got them to meet him, he'd be happy and would leave them alone. Even though I was in a fight with them, I thought it might be a good thing. You know, for them to be finally rid of the guy. So I went to the pay phone outside that bar, dropped a dime in, and made the call."

"And Albert gave you the money before he left?"

She did not respond, but I remembered the way my mother once tried to teach me how to understand a person's silence. And though I had never been good at it before, for the first time, I thought I understood Rose.

"How much?" I asked.

My sister stayed quiet for a long time. At last she said, "I'm tired, Sylvie. So tired you have no idea. And I've been forced to answer questions over and over for that detective and all those lawyers. It's gotten so I can't think straight. What does any of it matter? Nothing I say will bring them back or undo my part in it all. But you know who you saw inside that church. And the police found his fingerprints and footprints all over the place. So let crazy old Lynch keep telling Rummel and the rest of them that I made the call. It's our word against his. And all along we've both said the same thing: that I was here at home, nowhere near that pay phone. Now, please can we take a break from talking about it?"

I gave her the break she wanted.

If our parents were alive, our slothlike behavior never would have been allowed, and they would not have tolerated the endlessly blaring television. *The Price Is Right. Tic-Tac-Dough. General Hospital. Phil Donahue. Cheers. Family Ties.* So many shows came and went with applause and tears and dramatic music and canned laughter, while Rose and I remained immobile and numb, barely sleeping before waking and repeating the cycle. Neither of us said much else until I started asking if she heard the sounds coming from the basement.

"Huh?" she responded each time, lifting her head in the fog of that room.

Inevitably, there it would be again: something shifting beneath us, something shattering. "I said, 'Did you hear that?'"

"Hear what?"

"That noise, Rose. *Those noises.* Down in the basement."

My sister dug out the remote, lowered the volume. I wanted her to mute it altogether so we could listen properly, but she never did. After lifting and tilting her head, she said, "Nope. I don't hear anything. You should have that ear checked, squirt."

She was right. I should have had my ear checked. Foolishly, I still believed it was her responsibility to make that happen—at least that was the understanding when the hospital released me into her care. The gaggle of nurses and administrators at the discharge counter made a fuss over me: the girl with bandages on the left side of her head, a tube snaking into her ear, all because she walked inside a church on a snowy night to see what was keeping her parents. They plied Rose with forms to be signed. They plied her with papers listing doctors I needed to visit. They told her about appointments already made in my name. After we left the hospital, however, the dates came and went.

Clatter. Clang. Crash. Another night brought no movement or sound from us, but a cacophony from below. I began pressing my ear—the good one—to the floor, picturing Penny, that toddler-sized doll with the moon face and vacant black eyes, rattling the walls of her cage. If I pressed my ear to the floor long enough, I could swear some moments I heard what sounded like something breathing. Sucking in air, blowing it back out. Lifting my head, I spoke to Rose in a quivering voice, near tears, "You're crazy if you don't hear those things. They're pissed off. They're sad. They want them back. I can tell."

Rose turned down the volume once more. With less enthusiasm each time, she did the lift-and-tilt motion with her head. "I'm sorry, Sylvie, but I really don't hear anything. And why would I? There's nothing down there except some rag doll and a bunch of dusty crap. *You're* the crazy one if you believe the stuff Mom and Dad claimed to be true."

"I'm not crazy."

"Well, neither am I. And if you're so convinced, go see for yourself."

We both knew I was too afraid to go down there alone.

As the days wore on, Rose's scoffing chipped away at me. I began to wonder if it was just a matter of me hearing things. After all, a doctor should have been the one to remove the tube from my ear. Instead, I woke one night to find it resting beside me on the carpet like a small worm. Apparently, I'd yanked it out in my sleep. Perhaps I'd done more damage than I realized, I started to think. After nearly a month, when we no longer spent so much time in the living room, the rattling and shaking and all the rest grew silent, sudden as a needle lifted from a record. Part of me believed my hearing was improving, that someday the *shhhh* would fade as well. But another part couldn't help believe that down below those things my parents left behind had made their peace. If that was the case, they'd done it much faster than my sister and me up above.

For those reasons, for so many reasons, ours was not a house people should have visited on Halloween. Trick-or-treaters would have made better use of their time roaming the golf course, where oversized colonials were piled one on top of the other, instead of venturing down our street with its half-dozen cement foundations. Despite mosquitoes, puddles, and weeds rising from the cracks, Rose and I used to play in the one across the street when we were little. In pastel chalk, we outlined imaginary bedrooms for our imaginary children. We drew furniture on the floor, pictures on the walls, careful to stay away from the rusted steel rods on the far end that Rose speculated had once been the start of a fireplace. Our time down there was the closest anyone came to living in those structures, since they were abandoned years ago when the builder went bankrupt. The sole property he unloaded before trouble hit was the one my parents purchased.

Still, trick-or-treaters walked right past the NO TRESPASSING! signs and made their way down our driveway. Some behaved so casually I could tell they had come only for candy. But there were others who came on a dare, who giggled nervously as they approached, who fell into uncomfortable silence the moment they stepped onto our porch. It used to be that what they wanted was a glimpse of my mother or father—to leave with a story to tell. How disappointed they must have been those years when the most they encountered was a basket of candy on the doorstep along with a note in my mother's careful cursive telling them: *Please help yourselves, but be mindful of other trick-or-treaters and don't let greed get the better of you.* . . . And the years when we were at home, they were met with still more disappointment when the door was answered promptly and my tall, pale mother smiled as she dropped Butterfingers into their pillowcases.

But who knew how the details were altered in the retelling?

No one answered for a long time and we heard chanting in the basement. . .

When that woman opened up, she had dried blood caked around her cuticles. . .

That moon-faced doll with the red hair was rocking in a chair all on its own. . .

You cannot control the things people say. That much I had learned.

Despite Rose blasting Lynyrd Skynyrd on her stereo upstairs, and despite the never-ending *shhhh,* I heard the initial group of trick-or-treaters drawing near that first Halloween after our parents were gone. More than other years, I had good reason to worry about who might show up at our door. But I tried not to think about that. When I opened up, three girls stood on the stoop. Short skirts rustling in the wind. Torn fishnet stockings. Glittery tops. Ample lip-gloss and eye shadow. At the mouth of our driveway, smoke plumed from the muffler of a station wagon, headlights illuminating the old well and the dirt patch where Rose's rabbit cage once stood. Those girls couldn't have been much younger than me, so my voice should not have sounded motherly when I asked, "And what are you young ladies supposed to be?"

They burst into laughter, shrieking out their answer in unison so that it mashed into a single word, *"Hookerscantchatell?"*

I felt relieved that they had come for candy and nothing more. As I dropped peanut-butter cups and mini candy bars into their sparkly purses, I noticed something shiny down by their heels. Before I could get a closer look, one of the girls began cooing, "Ooh, ooh, ooh! I'll do anything for an Almond Joy! I mean *anything!*"

I gave her extra. After all, it wasn't every day a junior high student showed up on our step pretending to be a candy-addicted prostitute. After I watched them totter back to the station wagon, I bent and picked up a bowl covered in foil.

Once, sometimes twice a week, Rose and I returned home to find foil-wrapped offerings on our doorstep. Casseroles. Lasagnas. Chocolate cakes. Never once did they come accompanied with a note, so we had no idea who left them. As a result, no matter how hungry or tempted, we felt too suspicious to eat them. Instead, Rose shoved all the food on the counter to take out to the trash later.

I carried the bowl into the house and lifted the foil to find a Jell-O mold with walnuts and tangerine slices beneath the surface, like insects embalmed in amber. As usual, no note. I considered sticking my finger in and tasting it anyway.

"What are you doing?"

I turned to see my sister coming down the stairs. Black cape. Pointy hat. Face slathered with green makeup. I'd been so preoccupied with those make-believe hookers and the bowl that I'd failed to notice her music go dead above me.

"Nothing."

"Doesn't look like nothing." Rose reached the bottom of the stairs, took the bowl from my hands, peeked beneath the foil. "What the hell is it?"

Beef bourguignon, I wanted to say. "Jell-O."

"Did you see anyone leave it?"

I shook my head, which made me think of Louise Hock, the haggard-looking assistant district attorney who attended our meetings with Rummel at the police station. Lately, Louise had begun telling me I needed to get in the habit of speaking my answers, since there would be no nodding allowed when I was questioned in the courtroom come spring. "I didn't see anyone," I told Rose.

"Well, I hope you weren't about to eat it."

"Seems like a lot of effort just to do us in. By now, whoever it is must realize it's not exactly working, seeing as we're still alive."

"Maybe it's a slow poison. Or maybe the freak is waiting until we get used to stuffing our faces with these innocent 'donations' before sprinkling in Drano. All those goodies down the hatch then—*wham!*—the unsuspecting Jell-O mold does us in."

I stared at her, blinking.

"What?" she said.

"Or maybe someone out there feels bad about our situation and is being nice."

My sister gave the bowl a wiggle, then sniffed the slick red surface before holding it out to me. "Okay, then. If you're so brave and determined. Help yourself, Sylvie."

I hesitated, waiting for her to retract the bowl. When she didn't, I reached two fingers in and scooped out a blob. The walnut inside made me think of those embalmed bugs once more. I opened wide, my breath causing the Jell-O to wiggle on my fingertips, and then, at the last second, said, "I can't do it," and tossed it back.

Rose set the bowl aside. "Thought so." She fussed with the knot on the collar of her cape while telling me about a warehouse party she was going to two hours away in Philly. Normally there was something impenetrable about my sister's face, but in contrast to all that green, her eyes looked red and tired, her teeth smaller, more yellow. The effect was not scary so much as gloomy.

"You know, Sylvie, it wouldn't hurt you to act fourteen instead of forty for a change. Throw a sheet over your head. Go out with your friends."

"I don't have friends," I told her.

"Yes, you do. That girl with the weird name and the other one with the weird face."

"Gretchen moved when her dad got a job in Cleveland."

"And Elizabeth?"

"She moved too." That part wasn't true, but I didn't feel like explaining the way Elizabeth stopped sitting with me at lunch after I came back to school last winter. "Forget about them," I told my sister, and then I thought of what I'd overheard in the school library, the reason I felt nervous about who might show up tonight. "Besides, one of us needs to watch the place in case anyone decides to make trouble."

"Oh, don't you worry, Sylvie. I've got us covered on that front."

A fist pounded on the door, startling me. When I opened up, it took a moment to place the driver, since her face was caked with witch makeup too. The extra features didn't help: matted wig, fake eyebrows, rubber hands with noodly fingers. Instead of a "trick or treat," she launched into an explanation of how she'd been listening to Rose and me until she remembered the doorbell was broken. "You really should put a sign up, letting people know the thing doesn't ring. Lucky I figured it out, because someone el—"

"All right, all right," Rose said, cutting her off. "Come in already, Cora."

I stared at Cora's noodly fingers, thinking of that rainy afternoon when I first found her waiting for me in the living room, the way Rose had returned downstairs a few minutes later only to peek over her shoulder at the clipboard and ask us both the questions listed there: *How many hours of sleep do you get a night? Do you ever feel anxious during the day? If so, how often and why?* "I didn't recognize you without your clipboard," I told Cora now, as I remembered the reluctant answers she'd given my sister that day: *Four or five at best . . . Yes . . . Quite a bit . . . I'm supporting my sister and me with this new job. . . . And I guess you could say I don't have enough fun in my life. . . .*

She tilted her green witch face and said, "Really? Well, it would have been odd for me to bring it. I mean, witches don't carry clipboards."

"That was a joke, Cor," Rose told her. "It might come as a shock, but we do make jokes in this house. Even Great-Grandma Sylvie ekes one out now and then."

Cora pressed her fake fingers to her mouth and let out an *"Ohhhhhh!"* Then she smiled. "How are you doing, Sylvie?"

"Fine."

"How's school?"

"Good."

"No problems?"

"No problems."

"While I was waiting at the door, I heard you saying something about your friends. Is something wrong?"

"One moved away. That's all. I have plenty of others."

"Well, don't forget if you ever need anything, how do you reach me?"

"RIBSPIN," I told her, repeating the acronym she'd worked out for her number.

"Good. And do you have paperwork from your doctor visits like we discussed?"

"All right already," Rose said. "You're off duty, so let's skip the official business. We are supposed to be having fun, remember? And where the hell is your date?"

So this was not an unexpected visit after all, I thought, as Cora informed us that "the Hulk" was waiting in the car. I went to the window and looked out to see an enormous rottweiler leaping from the front seat to the rear and back again, its tail a drumstick beating the seats.

"The Hulk belongs to Dan," Cora explained. "Dan lives upstairs from my mother. He let me borrow her for the night."

"Her? The Hulk's a girl?"

"Yeah," Rose told me, thrill rising in her voice. "We're going to tie her to a tree. She'll scare the crap out of anybody who comes around to mess with the place." My sister turned away and started rummaging through the closet.

The news should have made me feel safer. But that dog would also keep away ordinary trick-or-treaters, like my happy hookers, spoiling what little fun I looked forward to. I didn't bother saying any of that, though. "So are you going to the party with my sister?" I asked Cora.

She gave a tight-lipped smile. "Guess that's probably breaking some sort of code. But it's just one party. You don't mind, Sylvie, do you?"

I shook my head then remembered Louise's warning about speaking up. "No."

"Here we go." Rose unearthed two brooms, buried so far behind the coats it made me realize how seldom we swept. One had a wooden handle and cinched straw at the base, the other, a lime-green plastic handle and stubby plastic bristles. Rose handed Cora the bad broom before opening our front door and stepping into the dark. On the top step she paused, adjusting her hat so it didn't blow off in the wind. Then she stuck her broom between her legs and leaped off the stairs. She went so high that for a second it seemed she might actually keep on soaring before she landed on the mossy lawn.

"Not bad," Cora said, taking her place on the step.

"Well, I did date a former track star. It's how I learned everything I know."

"Come on!" my sister called to Cora. "Your turn!"

As the wind whipped the dead birch leaves into a whirl, Cora hesitated. I could tell she felt nervous about jumping, even if it was just three measly steps. But then she surprised me by letting out a cowgirl's "Yeeehaaaw!" and leaping off the step. She didn't soar nearly as high as my sister, and she made a crash landing, stumbling as leaves spun around her feet. But she managed to regain her balance and danced around the lawn, cackling.

Once they released the Hulk and hitched her to a tree, Rose and Cora climbed into the car. The engine started, and I noticed that one of the headlights was out. Isn't that a game for some people? I wondered. When you see a car with one missing, you punch the person you're with. Or maybe you kiss them, I was never sure of the rules. Either way, I realized they'd forgotten to leave water for the dog. I went to the kitchen and filled a bowl. Before taking it outside, I opened the freezer and dug out a bone behind my father's glass tumbler that I saw every time I reached for a Popsicle. My mother had frozen that bone to make stock for her beef barley soup.

When I put both the bowl and the bone by her paws, the Hulk didn't growl or bark. She didn't drink or bother with the bone either. She just sniffed my toes and slobbered on my flip-flops before rolling on her back in an invitation to scratch her belly.

"You're real fierce, aren't you, girl?" I said, kneeling and rubbing her velvety fur.

It was early enough that we had hours ahead. I stared off into the woods, thinking of Albert Lynch in a holding cell not twenty miles away, because of the answer I'd given Rummel that day in the hospital. And then I thought of what I heard those boys talking about while I'd been tucked in a study carrel at the school library days before.

"What would it take?"

"You've seen the dude's picture."

"It's not like I've jerked off to it. I didn't memorize what the hell he looks like."

"I guess we need a skullcap to look bald. We definitely need his weird 'stache. I could grow one. But you might need help, pansy. Use burned cork. Plus there's those glasses. Little round things that make him look like a bug. Then all we need is a weapon."

"A weapon?"

"Not a real one, moron. But you know, like a rubber hatchet."

"Dude, a hatchet isn't what he used to do it."

"Okay, so now you're the expert. How the hell did he do it?"

"He blew their—"

Shhhh . . .

That day in the library, I pressed my hand over my good ear and shut out their voices. Now, just as I'd done then, I pushed the thought away. I quit petting the dog and stood to go inside, which was when I glimpsed the brake lights down the street. Cora and my sister had come to a halt by one of those cement foundations. As the car idled, the moon shone down, making it possible to see their pointy-hatted silhouettes. Funny how I'd been thinking about that game with the missing headlight and what you were supposed to do when you see one, because this is what I witnessed: two witches who had just completed their first successful broom flights of the night and were stopping a moment.

They were stopping to kiss.

Thunder, Lightning, Rain

Ocala, Florida—of all places, *that* turned out to be the first we visited with our parents. They were scheduled to give a lecture at the city's conference center. The event was going to draw their biggest crowd to date—more than three hundred tickets sold, my father informed us, reading from a fax that came as we were stuffing our suitcases. Even though the auditorium only held two hundred, the coordinators were setting up a spillover room where people could watch on a monitor. My father was thrilled, though my mother never cared one way or another about those sorts of details. She was too busy making sure Rose and I packed our toothbrushes and plenty of underwear.

Kansas. California. Texas. Pretty much any location they'd traveled to interested me more. Still, I was grateful for the chance to see something outside of Maryland for a change. Mostly, I couldn't wait to splash around the hotel pool, even if that meant having to sit next to Rose on the fifteen-hour drive south. Ever since that night with Dot, my sister had developed an obsession that made her even less fun to be with. She'd been carting that bible around from the moment she pulled it from my parents' nightstand. Flipping pages. Underlining passages. Scouring the text in search of ludicrous scripture that she recited to my parents as evidence that the book was "nothing more than an outdated fable." So while other families we passed on I-95 might have been playing I Spy or Twenty Questions, the Masons kept busy listening to Rose.

"'And God made two great lights; the greater light to rule the day, and the lesser light to rule the night,'" she read from Genesis before pointing out, "First of all, the moon is *not* a light; it only reflects light from the sun. And why, if God made the moon to 'rule the night,' does it spend half its time moving through the daytime sky?"

Sometimes my parents ignored her—the best tactic as far as I was concerned, since it led to her quietly staring out the window, a faraway look on her face. Other times, my mother or father offered an explanation, which almost always led to an argument. Every once in a while, they'd try some version of: "It's nice to see you taking an interest and using your intellect, Rose. Perhaps all your questions will lead to a newfound faith."

"I *seriously* doubt that," she'd tell them. And soon, she'd be back at it. "Oh, here's a winner: Genesis 1:29: 'And God said, Behold, I have given you every herb bearing seed, which is upon the face of all the earth, and every tree, in which has the fruit of a tree yielding seed; to you it shall be for meat.'"

From the front seat, our mother asked, "What's so wrong with that?"

"Well, let's see. Since a huge majority of plants and trees are poisonous, God's advice is a tad reckless, don't you think? I mean, would you tell Sylvie to wander out into the woods and eat whatever plants she found?"

"Of course not."

"Well, lucky for Sylvie, otherwise she'd be dead. I guess you're smarter than God who is apparently a moron."

"Enough!" my father said, growing angry whenever she took things too far.

After that, my mother killed a few miles humming what sounded like a lullaby, one I'd never heard before. The tune climbed higher and higher until I think even she grew tired of it, and then she said, "Why don't you read us some of your paper, Sylvie?"

I kept quiet, anticipating a groan from Rose. But my sister just pressed a cheek to the window, and her lack of protest led me to take out my paper along with the envelope announcing that I had won first prize for fifth grade, along with two hundred dollars.

"The Washington, D.C., riots that took place in early April of 1968, following the assassination of civil rights movement leader Martin Luther King Jr., affected at least 110 U.S. cities," I read after clearing my throat. "Chicago and Baltimore were among the most impacted. The availability of jobs in the federal government attracted many to Washington in the 1960s, and middle-class African American neighborhoods prospered."

"That's a very good point you raise," my father told me.

"It is, Sylvie," my mother said. "Good job."

Rose let out a *humph.*

"What?" I asked her.

"Nothing."

Okay then, I thought, and I started reading again, "Despite the end of mandated segregation, the neighborhoods of Shaw, the H Street Northeast corridor, and—"

"It's just funny that the people in the front seats agree with you," Rose said, "since the Bible is racist and they are such big believers in everything the book says."

"The Bible is not racist," my mother told her.

My sister cracked hers open and began flipping pages. "Exhibit A: 'If a man beats his male or female slave with a rod and the slave dies as a direct result, he must be punished, but he is not to be punished if the slave gets up after a day or two, since the slave is his property.' If that's not enough, here's another gem: 'Your male and female slaves are to come from the nations around you; from them you may buy slaves. You may also buy some of the temporary residents living among you and members of their clans born in your country, and they will become your property.' Should I find more?"

"Some of the things in the book are from a long time ago. Back when the world was a different place."

"So what you're saying is the book is outdated."

"In certain areas," my mother conceded.

"So you and Dad get to pick and choose what is and isn't worth believing in?"

"Enough!" my father said again.

After that we went back to being quiet. I waited to see if anyone wanted me to read more of my essay. No one did, so I pressed my cheek to the glass too.

Despite so many difficult moments on that trip south, there were times when my sister put away the Bible and nobody argued. We stopped at South of the Border, where my father bought us sparklers and people didn't stare at our family as much as they did in Dundalk. At the motel where we spent a night to break up the drive, we ate Kentucky Fried Chicken in our beds while watching black-and-white movies on the small TV. When we crossed the state line into Florida, we pulled into the Welcome Center, where my father asked a woman to snap our picture in front of palm trees. Even though the wind gusted and the sky grew dark too early, we wore the sunglasses my mother picked up at a pharmacy especially for the trip. In the remaining hours of the drive, however, the wind continued to gust and the sky grew darker still. One by one, we pulled off those glasses and tucked them away.

At 3:25 in the afternoon, my father turned the Datsun into the hotel parking lot. No one would have guessed the time since things were dark as dusk. After we checked into our room on the second floor, I didn't bother unpacking my bathing suit. Instead, I lingered by the window, staring out at the raindrops splashing against the surface of the pool. Somewhere back in Georgia, my father had confiscated Rose's bible, but she wasted no time finding another in the nightstand and stretching out on one of the beds to comb through the pages. My mother clicked on the clock radio and spun the dial until she found a meteorologist who made the same prediction as the others we had listened to in the car: heavy wind, heavy rain for the next two days.

"Here we go," Rose said, not caring about the weather. "A gem from Leviticus, which is quickly becoming my favorite source of all things ridiculous. 'The Lord said to Moses and Aaron, Speak to the Israelites and say to them: When any man has a bodily discharge, the discharge is unclean. Whether it continues flowing from his body or is blocked, it will make him unclean. This is how his discharge will bring about uncleanness' . . ."

"Tell you what, tadpole," my father said, ignoring her and putting a hand on my shoulder. "I've been looking forward to a swim too. Let's do it."

"What about the rain?"

"We're going to get wet anyway. What's the difference?"

Across the room, Rose kept at it. "'Any bed the man with a discharge lies on will be unclean, and anything he sits on will be unclean. Anyone who touches his bed must wash his clothes and bathe with water, and he will be unclean till evening . . .'"

How desperate must my father have been for a break from her if he was willing to go swimming with me in the middle of a storm? But what did his reasons matter? I ran and got my bathing suit. When my mother realized what we were planning, she put up a fuss. Once my father promised to yank us from the water at the slightest threat of lightning, she gave in and even watched from the window, waving as we circled the pool before holding hands and jumping into the deep end.

With the wind blowing through the palm trees and rain splattering against our heads, I had the feeling we'd been tossed overboard from a ship during a storm. I flipped onto my back and kicked my way around the pool, squinting against the rain. In the shallow end, my father found a water jet and pressed his back to it. I watched him gaze up at the sky. More to himself than to me, he said, "I hope the weather doesn't scare away the crowds."

"It won't," I told him, though what did I know?

He looked across the rippling water at me. Without glasses, and with rain dripping down his face, he looked younger, less serious. It made me think of years before when he and my mother would take us swimming at a pond in Colbert Township near Dundalk. Back then, they used to swim with us too, though we never went there anymore. "Listen, tadpole," he said. "Your mom and I agreed that you and your sister are going to wait in what they call the greenroom during our talk this evening."

I said nothing, kicking my feet and picturing a room with green walls and a green carpet, maybe a green ceiling too.

"They'll have lots of food for you both."

Green M&M's. Green Jelly Beans. Green grapes and kiwis and limes.

"You can read or play a game," he said.

"Or listen to weird bible passages."

He smiled, water dripping from his chin and from the cross nestled in his wet chest hair. "Or listen to weird bible passages. Anyway, we figured you'd prefer that to sitting in the audience."

I dipped beneath the water, swam closer before emerging. "Sounds good to me."

"Sylvie, you know how your mother gets her feelings sometimes?"

I did know. Everyone in our family knew. "Yes. Why?"

"Well, she keeps saying that she has an unsettled feeling about tonight. My guess is that she's worried about Rose."

"What about her?"

"That she'll, let's just say, *act up*. And I know it's unfair to put this on you, seeing as you're the youngest, but I'd like it if you could do your mother and me a favor. Will you promise to keep your sister in line?"

"Promise," I said right away, because I didn't want to disappoint him. But then I thought of that night with Dot and how helpless I'd been to stop Rose. I thought, too, of how little control my parents seemed to have when it came to her.

My father must have sensed what I was thinking, because he wriggled his back against the water jet and sighed. "It's probably more than you need to worry about. But your mother and I are aware that your sister has developed some, well, behavioral issues. We are trying to figure out the best way to handle it. In the meantime, whatever you can do to keep her under control is appreciated. You're a good girl, Sylvie. And prominent lectures, like the one tonight, are very important. Unlike those silly talks I get suckered into doing every Halloween, these can make all the difference. They build our careers and notoriety."

I bobbed in the water, thinking about his desk in the basement, that paperweight with the inscription about God lighting the dark, his old dental chair in the far corner reminding me of how much I wished he still had a job like that. "Do you want to be famous?" I asked, the words tumbling from my mouth before I even realized what I was asking.

The question surprised my father as much as me. "*Famous?*" He shimmied against that nozzle, rain sopping his hair, dropping from his lashes. "Well, now that you mention it, I suppose it would be nice to show them."

"Show who?"

"My parents."

My mother and father rarely said much about the families they had come from, so I knew little about them, other than that their parents were deceased. The only extended family I knew of was my father's brother, Uncle Howie. "But they're gone, Dad."

"Your parents are never gone from you, Sylvie. You'll see that someday, hopefully, a very long time from now. But I don't just mean my parents. I suppose it would be nice to prove something to your uncle. Not to mention so many of the people who used to laugh when I told them about the things I saw. Really, though, what I want most is security for our family. To put you and Rose through college. But you don't need to worry about all that."

Thunder rumbled in the sky just then, startling us both. Seconds later, a flash of lightning.

"That's our cue," my father said, climbing out of the pool. "Come on, tadpole. Let's head for dry land."

I swam to him, feeling the urge to reach my arms up so he could lift me from the water like a much younger girl. On account of his back, I scurried up the ladder instead. As we made a mad dash for the room, our feet sounding a quick *slap-slap-slap* against the walkway, I thought of my mother's feelings about the night that lay ahead. To look at her waiting in the doorway of that second-floor room, no one would have ever guessed her concern. She smiled as we ran closer, then wrapped us in the scratchy hotel towels. While helping us to dry off, she kissed my forehead, my father's too, before shutting the door to keep out the driving rain and rumbling thunder and crooked branches of lightning that crackled in the daytime sky.

OUT THERE, IN THE DARK

It used to be that every Halloween my father was invited to give a lecture at Fright Fest in Austin, Texas. Those talks paid the best, though he liked them the least. "The audience lacks serious interest in the subject matter," he'd complain while packing his brown suits, yellow shirts, and pills for his back, which acted up in the cramped airplane seats. When we were little, Rose and I reminded him to bring us something from the trip, and every year he arrived home claiming to have forgotten. He'd hold up his empty suitcase, shaking it to prove there was nothing inside, and only once we believed that he really had forgotten would he laugh and reach into a compartment, pulling out cowgirl statuettes, plastic cactuses, or some other surprise.

Still, the next year we reminded him all over again while he packed and leveled the same complaints to my mother: "Those crowds want nothing more than the cheap chills they get watching that phony Dragomir Albescu, with all those ridiculous rings on his fingers, as he carries on about the ghosts and goblins he encounters on his trips home to Romania. No one is interested in hearing from an *actual* deacon in the Catholic Church with *actual* knowledge and *years* of experience with the paranormal."

My mother used her most soothing voice as she pulled clothes from his suitcase, folding them more neatly than he had, before putting them inside again. "If that was true, dear, the organizers wouldn't keep asking you back."

"Yeah, well, maybe one of these years they'll realize their mistake. The experience is downright degrading. I'd make a request to appear with someone else, but I'm afraid I'll end up in what they call the 'odditorium' speaking with Elvira, Mistress of the Dark. Now *that* would truly be the bottom of the barrel."

"Elvira who?" my mother asked.

"Never mind. You don't want to know."

"Well, are you sure you wouldn't like me to come too? We're a team, after all."

My father took a shirt from my mother and set it aside. He held her hands, looked into her eyes. "It's bad enough I have to share the stage with a man as legit as a sidewalk fortune-teller. I won't allow you, who is every bit authentic as he is phony, to play second fiddle to a fraud."

After that, my father said he didn't want to discuss it anymore. They finished filling his suitcase as he joked that he better not forget to pack wax fangs and a tube of fake blood. Once he had left for the airport, my mother's mood lightened. She loved trick or treating with us, and even if there had been other houses on Butter Lane, I still think she would have made the twenty-minute drive into Baltimore every year and led us along the narrow streets of Reservoir Hill, where she and my father had a tiny apartment when they first married. The old women who remembered her carried on at the sight of Rose and me dressed as vampires or princesses or aliens. One ancient, heavyset woman with a name that sounded like it should be flip-flopped, Almaline Gertrude, insisted on inviting us in each year. Her kitchen smelled of spicy stews that I imagined came from the deli downstairs, since there was never anything but crumpled dollar bills and envelopes on her stove. While Mrs. Gertrude sat at the table with my mother, sipping microwaved tea from dainty cups that clanked against the saucers, she told us to help ourselves to her candy basket.

My sister may not have been good at school, but she was a master at the art of moping. That's exactly what she started doing as the years went on and she grew into her teens. One Halloween night, we made the pilgrimage to the old neighborhood and found ourselves once again in Mrs. Gertrude's kitchen, where the air was thicker than usual with the smell of spices, though there was still nothing but money and mail on her stove. I was dressed as a scarecrow, stuffed with real hay my father picked up from Watt's Farm before leaving for his trip. Never mind that the straw poked and scratched my skin, never mind that I smelled like the livestock section at a state fair, I was thrilled to be wearing a genuine costume.

My sister, however, refused to wear any costume at all. "Not including her mope," my mother joked when Mrs. Gertrude asked about it. Everyone but Rose laughed. And the more she moped, the more the old woman made an effort to cheer her up. "I don't understand," Mrs. Gertrude said when all her attempts, from cookies and milk to free rein of the TV, failed. "No costume. No appetite for sweets. Something has changed about you, Rose. Why the long face?"

My sister looked up from where she was sitting at the table with the rest of us. I thought she was about to participate in the evening at last. Then she said, "Because I'd rather be at a party with friends my own age instead of being forced to spend the night in a stinky, disgusting apartment with a dumb old fatty bat like you."

My mother's mouth dropped open. Her hand shot up and slapped Rose so hard across the face my sister slipped off the chair and crumpled on the floor.

"Rose!" Mrs. Gertrude shrieked, but she was not talking to my sister.

My mother jerked her hand back and brought it to her mouth, horrified by what she'd done. Neither of our parents had ever taken a hand to us, never mind with such force. The next thing I knew, my mother was ripping us out of the apartment, spewing trembled apologies to Mrs. Gertrude, Rose, me, and most of all, God.

Now, on the first Halloween without my mother or father, I looked away from the sight of Rose and Cora kissing and walked into our house, twisting the locks behind me. In some ways, my sister's behavior was no different from all the other surprises she delivered over the years, from that night with Almaline to the morning last year when she came downstairs with a shaved head, still nicked and bloody from the razor. But hadn't she done those things to antagonize my parents? What could be her reason now?

With the Hulk standing guard, I figured I'd seen the last trick-or-treaters. I helped myself to dinner—a handful of Mr. Goodbars—clicked off the lamps, and made my way upstairs. My sister didn't make a habit of telling me where she was going and when she'd be back, so I felt a sense of freedom as I pushed open her door. Squashed soda cans, scratched off scratch-off tickets, her old globe—those things and more littered the floor. A humidifier puffed away, mold gathered at its mouth. The tub of witch makeup sat on her dresser, the epicenter of a green fingerprint storm that moved from the window to the walls to the tissues scattered everywhere but the wastebasket.

It had been eleven weeks exactly since we heard from my uncle. After the courts rejected his request to be made my guardian, he promised to return to Florida, "tidy up his affairs," then move closer and be part of our lives anyway. Instead, all spring we had received late-night calls with rambling explanations about leases, debts, and so many other reasons why things were taking longer than he hoped. When the calls stopped, letters arrived, claiming he had devised a plan to help us all if only we'd be patient. After that: no word at all. Good riddance, my sister said, though I'd taken it upon myself to finally write him without telling her, if only to make sure our sole living relative was okay. It would have been much easier if I could've checked our mailbox for a return letter, but when a car came by and kids batted it off the post, Rose set up a P.O. box in town. Carrying mail home from that box put her in an even worse mood than usual, so it didn't help to ask if anything was for me.

"Not unless you count these love letters from the electric and gas companies," she told me last time. "What could you be waiting for anyway? An invitation from Harvard? Don't get ahead of yourself, squirt."

I moved slowly around the room, unearthing a laminated prayer card from Saint Julia's that I was surprised she had not thrown away, and a newspaper where she'd circled an ad: *PARTY PLANNER WANTED: MUST BE DETAIL-ORIENTED & ORGANIZED.* Even though Rose talked about going back for her GED, so far she had done nothing about it, instead taking random office jobs only to get fired because she lacked the exact skills listed in that ad. I gave her old globe a spin and thought of the way she used to do the same, planting her finger on random locations and bringing it to a stop, announcing Armenia or Lithuania or Guam.

I was about to check out her closet when the Hulk's chain rattled on the lawn.

I went to the window. Outside, the dog's bone must have thawed, because she gnawed frantically on it, causing her chain to make that clanging sound. Except for Rose's truck, the driveway remained empty. Relieved, I stepped through the minefield on her floor and opened the closet. Since so few of Rose's belongings were ever put away, the space was mostly vacant. Nothing from Howie, but I located a plastic bag labeled *Baltimore County Police Department*. Flashlight, road map, repair bills, oil change receipts— its contents included everything the police had removed from the Datsun before returning the car to us. I stared at my father's signature on a receipt, imagining his hand moving a pen across the bottom. Finally, I pulled out the only remaining item: *Help for the Haunted: The Unusual Work of Sylvester and Rose Mason* by Samuel Heekin.

Despite all the months that had passed, holding that book in my hands made me every bit as nervous as it had that night in the backseat. Some part of me worried about Rose coming home still, so I clicked on the flashlight and turned off the ceiling lamp, then sat down on the floor and flipped pages. My mother used to complain about Heekin's convoluted way of stringing together sentences. Judging from passages that leaped out, I understood why:

> *If you are a believer who has come to this narrative, there is nothing that I, the author, can do to prepare you, the reader, for what you are about to discover . . .*

> *. . . The Masons could very well open a museum of curiosities in the basement of their home, for that is where the remnants of their excursions in the realm of the paranormal live. I use the word "live" because, to this visitor at least, many of the things I encountered on my tour beneath their house did feel exactly that: alive. One of the very first artifacts I took note of upon entering the basement was a hatchet, which seemed to carry a life force all its own. This weapon was used in a tragic family slaying at what was once the Locke Farm in Whitefield, New Hampshire. But that, as they say, is only the beginning . . .*

. . . Perhaps the most infamous case that the Masons have spoken about in lectures and media outlets is that of Penny, the child-sized Raggedy Ann doll hand-sewn by a mother from the Midwest with instructions from a mail-order kit. A gesture of hope, it was a gift to her only child, a girl who lay terminally ill until she died with the doll at her side . . .

"He writes like he talks," I could still hear my mother saying as I sat in Rose's dark bedroom, her humidifier puffing away like a sick old lady reading over my shoulder.

"You mean a lot of hogwash?" my father said in response.

"I mean too many words. Someone should take a vacuum cleaner to his sentences. No wonder the man's a reporter for the *Dundalk Eagle* and not a big-city newspaper. We never should have let him into our lives."

"You're right about that last part," my father told her. "But his writing style is the least of our problems."

I skimmed the mess until I came to the photo section with the image I'd lingered on in the backseat of the Datsun. That night, it had been too dark to make out the caption, but I saw it now: THE VANDALIZED KITCHEN IN ARLENE TRESCOTT'S APARTMENT, DOWNTOWN BALTIMORE. 1982. *Not a farmhouse after all,* I thought, turning to the table of contents. The book was divided into three sections. The first detailed each of my parents' childhoods and their early years together. The second consisted entirely of case studies, including only the briefest mention of Abigail Lynch. The final section was titled simply: "Should You *Really* Believe the Masons?"

Their childhoods—those were the chapters I turned to first, since what details I knew of their lives before me were fuzzy. I knew my father grew up in Philadelphia, and that my grandparents owned a movie theater with a candy store in the front. But I didn't know that at age nine, he reported his first paranormal experience when he saw "a globule of energy among the seats" while sweeping that theater. When he told his mother and father, they laughed and suggested that his "globule" was probably a couple who stayed after the movie to kiss. Over dinners, my grandparents and their friend, Lloyd, who helped run the theater, coaxed my father into telling the story. When he described the lightless mass that shifted and reshaped in the shadows among the seats, the room exploded with laughter, filling my father with shame. For that reason, he quit mentioning the globules, even as they began to appear with increasing frequency.

Maybe it was all the cavity-inducing sweets from the candy shop that gave him the idea to become a dentist. Maybe it was all the teasing and those persistent sightings that made him want to study away from home. Whatever his reasons, despite the fact that there were perfectly good dental schools in Philly, my father applied to the University of Maryland. Moving into an apartment in one of the old Pascault row houses for students, he reported a newfound sense of freedom, having left his family behind. But he soon discovered that not everything had been left behind.

The ghosts—as he began calling them, plain and simple—had followed.

At this point in the chapter, Heekin broke from his own tangled writing and allowed my father to describe the moment, referencing a quote from a lecture he gave to the New England Society for Paranormal Research. Reading my father's words reminded me that when he spoke of the things he encountered, I felt no tug-of-war between believing and not believing. I simply believed.

> *Not far from my bed in the dim light of that apartment stood a figure no more than four feet tall. Before that night, the things I'd seen had been shapeless, shifting masses. Their lack of a fixed form is what led me to refer to them as globules from an early age. But this figure was different: its body looked like that of a dressmaker's dummy. No arms, but also no sliver of light between its legs, so it seemed to be wearing a dress. Although there were no eyes, no nose, no mouth to gauge her emotions, I sensed that she was studying me with great curiosity and need before she vanished . . . Just as some people forever attract stray animals, others tend to draw out the humming, peripatetic energies in this world. After that experience, I realized I was in the latter category . . .*

My mother reported no such paranormal experiences growing up in a tiny mountain town of Tennessee. Heekin said that her father had died in an accident on the farm, one she witnessed at the age of eleven, and the mere mention of it forever held the power to bring her to tears. He persuaded my mother into offering a description of the man: gentle, soft-spoken, scrupulous, devout. He took their small family of three to church each Sunday and to breakfast afterward. He built birdhouses in his wood-shed and allowed my mother to paint them whatever colors she wanted before nailing them up in the trees. With binoculars, they watched from the second-floor windows as families of birds came and went with the sea-sons. Those birdhouses, those binoculars, were the loveliest pieces of her childhood, my mother told Heekin during their interview, but they also exacerbated the heartbreak she felt after her father was gone.

Here, too, he allowed my mother to speak for herself. As I read her words, I couldn't help feeling that in some way she was there with me in the dark:

> I remember waking in the mornings to hear those birds singing out-side my window—a sound that once brought me happiness but no longer. I tried closing my windows. I tried putting a pillow over my head. But still that chirping found me. Finally, there came a day when I couldn't stand it any longer. Desperate to make their singing stop, I waited until my mother went into town then pulled the ladder from my father's woodshed and climbed into the branches of those trees in our yard. My intention was to knock the birdhouses to the ground one by one, but typical of my father, he secured them to survive even the strongest storm, never mind an eleven-year-old girl. That's when I had an idea. I climbed down and went to the kitchen, where I located a bag of steel wool, which my mother used to keep mice from getting into our house. I made my way back up into the trees and stuffed the entryways my father had drilled, then snapped off the perches so there was no hope of birds getting inside. Sure enough, their singing stopped, or at least I didn't hear it so close to my bedroom window after that. Those birds moved on and took my father's spirit with them, I believed, be-cause that's when Jack Peele entered the picture . . .

Jack Peele. A man my mother never once mentioned to me, but whom my "practical, plain-speaking" grandmother had apparently married without her daughter present. One night, she simply set a third place at the dinner table and introduced him by saying, "Rose, I'd like you to meet your new daddy. Now let's eat." My mother expected this new daddy of hers to have the sinister qualities of a wicked stepparent in a fairy tale. But Jack pulled coins from his floppy ears. He recited the alphabet backward. He built towering card houses and let my mother blow them down. Instead of going to church, Jack lingered in his pj's and watched cartoons, busting a gut each time the Road Runner escaped a free-falling anvil. One Sunday, they skipped cartoons and went out in the yard, where he kept spinning my mother by the arms and letting her loose into a leaf pile. When he grew dizzy, Jack lay on the grass, my mother beside him. Staring up into the branches of the trees, he asked, "What do you suppose is going on with those birdhouses?"

Reluctantly, my mother told him about her father securing them up there, about the binoculars and the notebook and the songs that filled her with melancholy after he was gone. And then she told him about the steel wool and the snapped-off perches. Jack's face grew serious. "What time of year did you do that, darling?"

"Spring," she answered.

Jack stood and climbed one of the trees. He didn't need a ladder; he was tall and lanky and moved chimplike through the branches. Slowly, his fingers tugged out the steel wool from one of the birdhouses before he peered inside, shaking his head and letting out a dive-bomb of a whistle.

"What?" my mother asked from down on the ground. *"What? What? What?"*

"Nothing," Jack told her.

But that night, after he and my grandmother spent a long while whispering in the kitchen, they sat my mother down. In their most somber voices, they asked what had caused her to kill the baby birds inside those houses by making it so their mothers could not feed them. Horrified at the realization of what she'd done, my mother had trouble finding words. "It's like I told Jack," she stammered, tears leaking down her cheeks. "I did it . . . I did it because Daddy went away, so I wanted the birds to go away too."

A fist pounded on the door downstairs.

My head jerked up, and I dropped the flashlight. My mother, or at least the feeling of having her right there with me, vanished at once. I looked for a clock to figure out how long I'd been lost in those pages, but saw none. Outside, the Hulk's chain rattled, though she did not bark.

The pounding stopped then started again. I reached for the flashlight, which had rolled beneath the bed. When I pulled it out, I found a letter written to Rose—the return address on a random street in Baltimore. The fist pounded on the door again, so I slipped the letter in my pocket to read later, then tossed the book and all the rest in the plastic bag from the police station, returned it to the closet, and hurried downstairs. A laugh—deep, male—came from the other side of the door, followed by another, which made me certain those boys I'd been waiting for had arrived.

Astonishing the thoughts that can fill a person's mind in a single instant. For one solitary second after I put my hand on the knob and pulled, it was them standing before me. Not those phony Albert Lynches. Instead, I saw her in an ash-gray column dress with pearly buttons. I saw him in a rumpled brown suit and smudged wire-rimmed glasses. All my reading about their childhoods had summoned their spirits, the same way my father drew out those leftover energies late nights in the theater and in the dark of his university apartment.

That's what I first believed anyway.

But those thoughts gathered in my mind only for a moment. In the next, I noticed my mother's necklace, gold instead of silver, tight around her neck. The loose bun she wore to church not held up by bobby pins, but staples. My father's blazer may have been brown, but his pants were black and torn beneath one knee. His shirt, white rather than the mustard yellow he favored, was splattered with a substance meant to look like blood but too bright to be the real thing. The lenses of his glasses were popped out; without the usual smudges, I had a clear view of the cold, unfamiliar eyes beneath.

No longer was it enough to call me names in the halls.

No longer was it enough to knock down our mailbox.

No longer was it enough to toss rag dolls on our lawn.

Where would it end? I wondered. What would it take for them to leave us alone? Scream, slam the door, crumble to the floor—any of those reactions seemed possible until all that I'd read about my parents' childhoods returned to me. I thought of the way people mistreated them each time they offered a glimpse into their inner worlds. What good did it do my father to let his family know of the things he saw? What good did it do my mother to confess her ties to those ruined birdhouses? And then I thought of the kindness they always showed people, and I resolved to do the same. Those boys may as well have dressed as bums or superheroes, I offered the candy basket no differently.

"Go ahead," I said as they stared at me, expecting something more.

After some hesitation, the boy dressed as my mother reached out his large, knuckley hand and foraged through the basket, coming away with a couple of Charleston Chews. The boy dressed as my father did the same, grabbing Milk Duds and Sweet Tarts. My gaze shifted over their shoulders to the end of the driveway, where reflectors moved round and round, glimmering like the eyes of a demon out there in the dark. More boys on bikes, I realized. All the while, the Hulk licked and chewed her bone, not bothering to offer up so much as a growl.

"Can we see the doll?" my father, or the one dressed like him, asked.

"No," I told him.

"Where is she?" This question came from the one dressed like my mother.

I thought of Penny in the basement, slumped inside her cage, the sign written in my father's handwriting attached to the door: DO NOT OPEN UNDER ANY CIRCUMSTANCES! Abandoned down there all these months, the spiders had likely made a home out of her, crawling across her moon face, stringing webs between her floppy arms. "She's at the bottom of the well," I told those boys, a lie hatched out of old wishes.

"The well?" this version of my father repeated.

"We put it down there with all the others you and everybody else throw on our lawn. Go get it and the rest of them if you want."

With that, I slammed the door. Standing there in the dark, flashlight in hand, I listened to their feet thump down the steps. I went to the window and watched as they shoved off the plywood, same as I'd done a few nights before. I knew from experience they'd never see a thing in the absolute blackness below. Soon, the boys realized it too, because they gave up and headed to the street, where their friends still pedaled in figure eights. The boy in the dress tugged off his wig and dropped it among the cedars before picking up a bike by the curb. The boy in the blazer climbed on the back before they pedaled away into the night.

Once they were gone, my hands, my body, all of me began to shake. In an effort to make the trembling stop, I roamed the living room, dining room, kitchen, moving aimlessly through the shadows. I pictured my parents the last time I saw them. Snow gathering on the shoulders of my father's wool coat as he stepped from the car. Wind gusting my mother's hair when she got out too. Then I remembered stepping inside that church, where the air was so still, so absolutely frigid, it stung my lungs with every breath. Something smoky mixed with the faint trace of incense. It took time for my eyes to adjust, but once they did, I made out three silhouettes near the altar.

"Hello," I called out, the word pluming in the air like a question: *Hello?*

To distract myself, I located the diary Boshoff had given me. I forced myself to think of some other memory, to put it down in order to keep so many others at bay. That night in Ocala came to mind, and I started writing and did not stop or bother to even look up until the Hulk barked outside.

Once again, I went to the door. Daylight had yet to come, but the electric blue tinge in the air told me it was imminent. I had been writing for hours. Now, I spied the dog out there, lunging on her chain in the direction of the house.

"It's okay, girl," I said, stepping outside, moving across the lawn. Afraid to get too close, I stopped at the edge of her reach, missing the way my mother had of calming, not just people, but animals too. Above us, streams of toilet paper rippled. While I'd been lost in that journal, someone had come by and tossed those rolls into our trees, soaped the windows of Rose's truck too—pranks that seemed quaint by now. As the dog kept at it, I found the courage to make my way around to her bone, slick and shimmering with saliva. No matter how much I waved it in her face, the thing held no interest for her anymore. All she wanted was to bark and growl and lunge on her chain.

What more could I do but leave her to exhaust herself? I dropped that bone, wiped my fingers on my T-shirt, and turned toward the house. That's when my hand went to my chest. That's when my breath caught in my throat. Earlier, when those boys came and went, I believed I'd faced down the most frightening event of the night, but not once I understood the cause of the dog's alarm. Down among the tangled branches of the rhodo-dendrons, I saw it: the yellowy glow from the basement window. After all those months of darkness, whatever it was down there had turned on the light once more.

GHOSTS

Maybe it was coincidence. But the books my mother gave me to read at an early age—*Jane Eyre*, *Great Expectations*, *Pippi Longstocking*, and so many others—were almost all about children who had been orphaned. Sometimes I wondered if those "feelings" she used to get allowed her to sense our family's fate, and if so, maybe those stories were her way of preparing me. That night at the Ocala Conference Center, I had no idea about any of that of course. I simply kept busy with *Jane Eyre*—or *tried* to, anyway. I never would have admitted it, but, despite my smarts, the book was too advanced considering I was only entering the sixth grade. It didn't help that Rose had left her bible back at the hotel, so she served up plenty of distractions.

She paced the small greenroom. (Not green, but peach, by the way.)

She picked grapes off the fruit platter.

She bounced them off the ceiling and caught them in her mouth.

The ones that missed, she mashed into the carpet with her sneaker. I didn't say a word, figuring it would be easier to clean up after she finished entertaining herself. I'd taken to underlining passages in the book that stood out to me, the way my mother did in her bible, and was about to put a pen to the page when I glanced up and noticed that Rose had slipped out of the room. *Let her go*, I told myself, but that promise to my father in the pool nagged at me, and so I put aside *Jane Eyre* and wandered the hall in search of Rose. It didn't take long before I found her standing in a large room filled with row upon row of chairs, all of them facing an enormous TV, all of them empty. The spillover room, I realized, but the weather had kept so many people away there was nobody to spill.

On the screen, I saw my father. If the rainwater had made him appear boyish and less serious earlier that day, the stage lights did the opposite. Shadows fell across his face, carving his features into a jumble of sharp angles and deep wrinkles. His glasses caught the light in such a way that his eyes seemed to flash as he spoke, stiff voiced, to the crowd. "Well before this century, those in the medical community had begun to discard the idea of possession as an explanation for abnormal human behavior. Instead, experts resolved that specific conditions were symptomatic of schizophrenia and other psychosis. These afflictions were dealt with by putting the sufferer away in an institution, or with crude and harmful methods of electroshock therapy, and more recently, experimenting with medication . . ."

"Rose," I said.

"*Shhhh*. I'm listening."

" . . . Of course, it would be foolish to deny the importance of the myriad of advances in the treatment of mental disorders. But in the hurry to embrace the science of psychiatry, the medical field might have been a bit too eager to relinquish belief in evil forces, demonic oppression, and to accredit natural causes to all mental diseases of unknown etiology . . ."

"Rose, we're not supposed to be here. Let's go."

My sister whipped around. "'The mouth of a righteous man brings forth wisdom, but a perverse tongue will be cut out.'"

"What?"

"It's a bible proverb, stupid. In other words, keep it up and I'll cut out your tongue. Now *shhhh*. I'm trying to listen."

" . . . While the majority of psychiatrists are satisfied to diagnose mental illness in terms of abnormal brain function, chemical imbalances, and personality disorders, there are those who admit that a tiny percentage of cases defy medical science. These cases do not allow for an easy explanation because they exhibit symptoms traditionally associated with demonic influence. . . ."

"Rose," I said, even though it meant risking my tongue. "Let's go."

This time, she turned from the TV. "You know what? You're right. Let's go."

With that, she stepped out the door and headed down the hall. Where she should have hung a left into the peachy greenroom, however, Rose kept going. Through a set of doors. Up a flight of stairs. I followed until she slipped through one last door into the back of the auditorium where my parents were speaking. For a long while, I waited outside, wondering what she was up to and what, if anything, I could do about it. The entire time my father's voice drifted into the hallway. He described how so often people came to them as a last resort, after all attempts at treatment had failed, and I thought of the people who showed up unannounced on our front steps, a look of desperation in their eyes. Then I heard my father say, "No doubt you came here expecting a ghost story. You'll get plenty, I promise. But first, I'd like to start with a love story. I guess you could say it's a Christmas story *and* a love story, because it takes place in December and it's how I met my beautiful wife."

I didn't know how my parents met, and my curiosity led me to tug open the door the tiniest bit. I spotted Rose crouched in the rear of the auditorium. When I slipped inside and joined her, crouching and pressing my back to the wall as well, she did not acknowledge my presence. My father continued, and as we listened, I looked around at the empty seats. The crowd of three hundred he'd been anticipating had dwindled to no more than seventy. I wondered if that's why he seemed so distracted and uncomfortable up there. Talking in that stiff voice. Fidgeting with a stack of index cards, fanning and flipping them this way and that. Beside him, my mother stood, calm as could be, hands joined together, listening intently, as though she'd never heard the story before.

Which details am I recalling from that night and which have I filled in from things my parents told me when I asked questions later? And which, if I'm truthful, did I color in myself, lending their meeting a fairy-tale quality in my mind? Rather than attempt to separate those versions, I'll tell the story I carry with me.

When my father finished his coursework at the dental school in Baltimore, he spent a year working at the university clinic, clocking in the hours required to graduate. Although his career as a dentist had yet to officially begin, he had grown bored. The field lacked a sense of mystery, he said, and silly as it sounded, he despised the one-sided conversations with the people in his chair. ("How much can you learn when you're the only one talking?" I heard him once say.) So while his days were spent drilling and filling cavities, he found a more satisfying activity to occupy his evenings: he began studying the paranormal to make sense of the unexplained things he had seen since childhood.

As for my mother's life, the events of her childhood led her to spend an inordinate amount of time in prayer. On her way home from school each afternoon, she stopped at her small brick church, slipped into a back pew, and spoke to the Lord. On Sundays, she arrived early and distributed prayer books to worshippers entering the service. Afterward, she taught in the Bible school, where the pastor overheard her singing to herself and found her voice so melodic he convinced her to join the choir. When she was nearing the end of high school, that same pastor helped her get accepted into a small Christian college in Georgia on a voice scholarship.

One Christmas, the choir was scheduled to give a concert for inner-city children in Harlem. In the predawn hours of December 24, 1967, my mother boarded a bus with her fellow students and headed north. It began to snow on the East Coast that morning and kept up all through the afternoon. "Lift Jesus Higher," "The Lord Is My Shepherd, I Shall Not Want," "Amazing Grace"—with those songs and so many others, the girls sang away the miles until the choir director—out of genuine concern or, more likely, boredom—suggested it would be wise to save their voices. Except for the rumble of snowplows and rattle of salt trucks rolling past on the highway, the bus grew quiet. Soon, the girls had fallen asleep. My mother slept too, though she woke before the others with what she first experienced as a headache. Those "feelings" she sometimes got about the world didn't normally come to her in the form of physical pain, but the sensation was so intense she couldn't help but wonder if it was a sign.

By the time they reached D.C., snow spit frantically from the sky, blotting out the world outside my mother's window as pain crept to the side of her face and bloomed in her jaw. Despite the agony, my mother (being my mother) kept quiet. Nothing anyone could do until they reached New York City, she told herself. Besides, if she did say something, those girls might lay hands on her. Not only did my mother dislike being the center of attention, she did not believe they had the kind of faith to make that sort of healing possible.

Late in the afternoon on that same day, my father finished work and got ready to leave the clinic. In truth, he had seen his last patient hours before, though for once he felt no urgency to leave, since he faced the prospect of his first holiday alone. His final patient, a blowsy, red-haired woman doused with lilac perfume, whose oddly fanglike teeth he'd been capping and crowning for months, brought a Christmas gift to thank him for all his work. The gesture touched my father more deeply than he might have guessed, because it would be the only gift he'd be receiving that holiday. He peeled away the reindeer wrapping paper to find a leather-bound copy of Charles Dickens's *A Christmas Carol*.

> *"There are some upon this earth of yours," returned the Spirit, "who lay claim to know us, and who do their deeds of passion, pride, ill-will, hatred, envy, bigotry, and selfishness in our name, who are as strange to us and all our kith and kin, as if they had never lived. Remember that, and charge their doings on themselves, not us."*

The fang-toothed woman hugged him too long, leaving him smelling of lilacs. After she walked out, my father allowed himself to lounge in a dental chair. Page after page he turned until the Ghost of Christmas Future appeared and he glanced out the window to see the sky had grown dark. He decided to finish the story at home.

On the slippery drive back to his apartment, my father's thoughts turned to the ghosts of *his* past. Not the ones that appeared to him as apparitions, but rather his family. His mother had passed from lung cancer a few years before. (Hadn't he always warned her about all those cigarettes?) Since she'd been gone, his father and brother had done away with even the skimpy holiday traditions she once maintained and instead spent hour upon hour drinking from their freezer-chilled glass tumblers—getting good and sloshed in front of the TV. The year before, my father, who always shared one glass with them, had felt so gloomy during the visit that he vowed never to return. Even though he kept that promise, there he was on Christmas Eve, allowing those same old ghosts to haunt him anyway.

Your parents are never gone from you. . .

Perhaps those words flickered in his mind as he carefully navigated the slick roads that night. He'd already gone to an early mass—to his way of thinking, Christmas Eve mass was a candle-lit tourist trap, not meant for serious believers like himself—and now there was only dinner to think about. But he wasn't much of a cook and all the decent restaurants he passed were closed. That must have been what led him to pull into a Howard Johnson's off the highway.

Once he stepped inside, his eyes caught sight of a row of pay phones. Would he regret the call? Probably. But he walked to a phone anyway, fished out a fistful of change from his pockets, punched in the 215 area code and number he knew by heart. The phone rang and rang and he was about to give up when a craggy voice came on the line. "Hi, Dad," my father said. "It's me, Sylvester. I just called to wish you a Merry Christmas."

After a silence, "Same to you, son. Same to you."

"Some storm, huh?"

"Guess so. But it'll melt. Always does. Nothing to get upset about."

"I'm not getting up—" My father stopped, took a breath. "So I imagine you and Howie are spending the night together?"

"Nope. Howie's gone off. Here with Lloyd having a drink."

"Howie's gone off where?"

"Joined the navy. You know that."

"Well, *how* would I know that, Dad? I never hear from either of you."

"Phone rings both ways, son. Phone rings both ways."

Perhaps that was the moment my father first shifted his gaze toward the window and saw the idling bus in the parking lot. Emergency flashers blazed, turning the snow red then white then red again. Perhaps that was when a matronly, gray-haired woman stepped inside and approached the row of pay phones, opening the phone book and flipping pages. "I'll try to call more often in the New Year," my father said, putting his back to the woman since he didn't like people knowing his business. "But, well, there never seems to be anything to say."

Silence. More silence.

"Dad? Are you there?"

The tinkling sound of glass and ice. The sound of a sitcom laugh track. Finally, his father's voice: "Your mother was the talker. Not me."

What his father said was true, though his mother's conversations were limited to gossip: which neighbor was having trouble paying rent, whose husband was screwing another woman. Things that held little interest for my father. "Well," my father said, "Merry Christmas." Those bus lights blinked outside and he thought of the artificial tree his mother used to assemble. The angel on top wore a white dress splotched with yellow from all her time spent in the attic. Year after year, her blank face stared down at the four of them before she was stowed away once more. At last, my father pushed the thought of that angel and that tree and his mother and even his father who was still on the line from his mind. It had been a mistake to call, he decided. It always was.

"Same, same," his father said, then fumbled with the phone in a clunky good-bye.

Whatever appetite my father felt had vanished. He made up his mind to head home on an empty stomach. But as he walked out to the parking lot, he came upon a young woman with long, raven-black hair and impossibly narrow shoulders sitting on a suitcase outside the bus. She held the thick end of an icicle against her face. Her skin was so translucent, her features so delicate, he thought she might very well be an apparition.

> *"Ghost of the Future," he exclaimed, "I fear you more than any spectre I have seen. But as I hope to know your purpose is to do me good, and as I hope to live to be another man from what I was, I am prepared to bear your company, and do it with a thankful heart. Will you not speak to me?"*

The woman glanced up at him, and my father heard himself asking, "Did someone sock you?"

"Sock me?" Her voice was like the rest of her: soft, fragile.

"You know, *hit you*? I'm wondering on account of the icicle."

"Oh. No. I have a terrible toothache. I'm on a choir trip, and the director is inside looking through the phone book, trying to find help. I thought I could bear the pain until we got to where we are going, but now that the bus is having problems, I just don't know."

My father stepped closer, reached out a hand, and lifted the icicle away from her face. "If it's a toothache, the pain you are feeling is in your nerves. So you can put all the ice in the world on your face, and it is not going to make you feel better."

"It's not?"

"No. But I can help you."

Did that broken-down bus and the rest of the choirgirls make it to Harlem? How did my mother convince that matronly choir director to allow her to go off with a man she met in the parking lot? Or was the pain so severe that she made one of the few rash decisions of her life and simply picked up her suitcase and got in his car without telling anyone? I don't know those answers. However it came to be, less than an hour after he lifted that icicle from her face, my father was back at the clinic with my mother. X-rays revealed her need for a root canal. He was far from a specialist, and he couldn't perform one on his own that night, but he gave her a pulpotomy, removing the dead tissue to alleviate the pain and pressure until she could be properly treated.

That night in Ocala, after my father shared a modified, less personal version of those events with the crowd, my mother spoke up for the first time. In her lilting voice, she said into the microphone, "Since my mouth was stuffed full of instruments, Sylvester got to do all the talking. What better way to make a man fall in love with you?"

Not the funniest joke ever told, but something about her mild-mannered delivery ignited a burst of laughter from the crowd. All at once, the feeling in the air of that auditorium shifted. People had been won over, I sensed. They were on my parents' side now. Even my father relaxed, placing his index cards on the podium and putting a period on their how-we-met story by saying he and my mother spent that Christmas together and every one since. One of the things that drew them to each other, he explained, was their belief that the world consisted of more than just what we see and understand. And when he first confessed to her the strange things he'd witnessed starting as a child in his parents' movie theater, she did not laugh like so many before. Instead, she asked questions. She tried to make sense of it all.

"In this way, together over time, my wife and I began to investigate 'the otherness' of this world we live in," my father told the crowd. He pressed a button on the podium and the screen behind him filled with an image of an institutional hallway with a light in the corner that looked amorphous until you stared long enough and an elongated face emerged, its mouth open in a ghoulish howl.

"Ladies and gentleman, meet Caleb Lundrum. Caleb was one of the first, and certainly one of the most powerful, spirits my wife and I encountered when we began working together in the years after we were married."

People leaned forward in their chairs. My father began to explain how he and my mother became involved in the case when a man in the audience, about twenty rows from the stage, stood. From where I crouched in the back, I made out a bit of his profile, though mostly what I saw was from behind. His hair was dark and unkempt. His shoulders, round and beefy. His jeans, sagging. "Excuse me," he said in a slurred voice.

Earlier, when we turned into the parking lot of the conference center, my father commented to my mother that at least the weather had kept their detractors away. At the time, I didn't know what he meant. Rose, of all people, informed me later that at certain of their events, religious groups waited outside, shouting at the people who walked through the doors, calling them devil worshippers and sinners. My mother always felt genuinely confused by their venom, since she considered herself to be a woman of faith and did her best to live by the Bible. When this man first disrupted their talk, I thought maybe he was someone who had it out for my parents.

"You mentioned seeing ghosts in the movie theater when you were young," he said, his tongue sloshing around his s's. "But in the dark of a theater, there are all kinds of shadows and strange lights, especially if the projector's still, you know, running. Isn't it more likely that you saw something that *looked* like a ghost in the dark?"

People craned their heads around to see who had cut off my father just when he was getting to the good stuff. Rose and I watched too. My father removed his glasses, rubbed them on his yellow button-down, then returned them to his face. "At the moment, we are discussing Caleb Lundrum, whose image is here on the screen, so I'd—"

"Well, your friend Caleb looks to me like he might just be a problem with a camera flash. Or maybe you need to get your lens cleaned."

Lookshhhh to me . . . Jussshht be a problem . . . Lensshhhh cleaned . . .

He acted so drunk it seemed put on. Still, his comment drew a laugh from the crowd nearly as big as the one my mother's joke stirred earlier. My father kept calm and explained that the photo was taken with a special camera and that the image was most certainly not the result of a faulty flash or an unclean lens. As he spoke, Rose jabbed me in the side. "You know who that is, don't you?"

I stared at the man, seeing only his unkempt hair, those droopy jeans. "No."

"If ghosts are real," the man said, cutting off my father again, "I mean, if they're spirits who've been left in this world after their bodies have passed on, wouldn't it be a huge epidemic? I mean, billions of lives have come and gone from this planet. So wouldn't that mean there would be billions of ghosts wandering around taking up space?"

"Spirits don't occupy physical space in the way that you and I do."

"Oh, yeah? And how do you know? Do ghosts all go on a diet?"

The audience let out their loudest laugh yet. Now that the man's tone had tipped over into aggressive, I waited to see if my father would match it. "Ladies and gentlemen," my father said, "before we go any further, I may as well use this opportunity to introduce you all to my brother, Howard."

The small crowd might not have actually gasped, but the news brought about yet another shift in the air of that auditorium. People twisted their necks around to see. As much as I wanted to get a better look too, I crouched lower for fear of being discovered. The last time I'd seen my uncle had been a few summers before when he rolled into the driveway on his motorcycle, making an unannounced visit and staying nearly a week. Nights, he spent watching *M*A*S*H* and *Odd Couple* reruns in the living room. Days, he passed out on the sofa. The clock that ticked not far from the cross on our wall made him jittery, and he insisted my parents stop it. "Feel like I'm living inside a time bomb," I remembered him saying, though we were all so used to the sound it had no effect on us.

The visit came to an end one evening at the dinner table. My uncle, his mouth full of food, said, "This pork piccata, or whatever you call it, is dry. That's what happens when the cook tries getting too fancy. Me, I like things simpler."

"Well, if you like things simpler," my father told him, not looking up from his plate, "get on your motorcycle and go find the sort of fleabag flophouse you're used to."

"Come on, buddy," my uncle said. *"Relax."*

"I'm not your 'buddy.' And don't—*do not,* whatever you do—tell me to relax." Still, my father kept from looking up. He cut a carrot, put it in his mouth. I thought he was done talking, but after chewing and swallowing, he continued, his gaze never leaving his plate, "Maybe I tolerated the way you and our parents treated me years ago. But I won't tolerate it here in my own home. My wife worked hard to prepare this meal for my family to enjoy. So shut up and enjoy it too. Or, like I said, leave."

My uncle waited a moment before balling up his napkin and tossing it on the table. He stood and walked to the living room, where he gathered his clothes quick as a burglar. The front door opened and closed. Outside, his motorcycle roared, the sound rising then fading as he sped away.

Only after Howie had left did my father stop eating. He, too, stood, then walked to the living room and locked the door before starting the clock. The house filled with that familiar ticking sound once more as he returned. Our cutlery clanked against our plates while we finished the meal without another mention of Howie or any conversation at all.

Despite how many years it had been, I felt foolish for not realizing it was my uncle that night at the conference center. I whispered to Rose, "What's he doing here?"

"What does it look like? Busting Dad's stones."

"The difficult thing about the business my wife and I are in is that many people don't believe us. We accept that fact. Sometimes, however, those skeptics are family. That's the case with my brother," my father told the crowd before directly addressing my uncle. "But, Howie, these people paid to be here tonight. They came with open minds and a desire to hear what we have to say. So I'd appreciate it if you would take a seat and listen too. If not, I'd appreciate it if you would please exit the auditorium."

In the silence that followed, my uncle swayed slightly, as though blown back and forth by a breeze. When he did not sit but did not leave, either, a man in a security uniform approached him, taking him by the arm. My uncle jerked it away, nearly falling, before shoving past. Rather than walk down the steps to the main doors, he headed to the back of the auditorium, the guard trailing him. When he reached the wall behind the final row of seats, my uncle came to a halt. Up close, I saw that he looked different from the way I remembered. He had a belly and a beard now. His once close-cropped hair had grown bushy. His eyes were mapped with tiny red veins. Rose whispered hello, though I felt overcome by an unexpected shyness and managed only a slight smile. Howie reached out and patted our heads before winking and hustling away down the back aisle. When he arrived at the exit, the guard snatched his arm again, keeping a tight grip as he escorted my uncle out of the auditorium.

After the door clanged shut, my father began the slow process of winning back the audience. "Forgive the interruption. Where were we? Oh, yes, Caleb Lundrum . . ."

Rose hissed in my ear, "Let's go find Uncle Howie." She kept her back low and headed toward the door. I lingered, staring at that image on the screen. A trick of light or a howling demon? I couldn't be sure. Finally, I gave up thinking about it and headed toward the door too.

Outside, the rain had paused, though wind still gusted. The air felt hot and moist against my cheeks as I caught up with my sister in the half-empty parking lot, where the lamplights reflected in the deep puddles all around. "He's gone," Rose said. "It's your fault."

"*My* fault?"

"Yeah, you were so slow we missed him."

What good did it ever do me to argue? I kept my mouth shut and followed her back toward the building. That's when we noticed the man with scratches on his face, on his arms and hands too. He glanced at us before turning to a row of bushes, wet leaves shimmering in the lamplight too. The man made a kitten call into the branches. "It's okay. Come on out."

My sister must have found him as peculiar as I did, because both our paces slowed to watch. He kept calling, getting on his knees and reaching carefully into the dark of those bushes. When his hand was met by a sudden rustle and high-pitched snarl, he snapped it back. With his fingers in front of his face, we could see fresh blood glistening just like those puddles in the pavement. Rose and I might have stood there longer, waiting to see if he coaxed out what he wanted, but a horn honked behind us. We turned and saw my uncle at the wheel of a battered pickup, one side so buckled it didn't look like the vehicle should be allowed on the road. Over the chugging engine, Howie called out, "By any chance, are you lovely ladies looking for me?"

Rose jogged to the truck, rainwater splashing beneath her sneakers. By the time I caught up with her, she was leaning into the passenger window and they had launched into a conversation.

"The ghostbusters won't be done for a while," Howie said to both of us. "What do you say we go have some fun?"

I stepped up, poked my head inside the window. The air inside smelled of beer and smoke. The dashboard lights glowed orange and made the scruff of my uncle's beard glow too. An unlit cigarette dangled from his lips, bouncing when he spoke. "Hey there, kiddo. You've grown some, haven't you?"

My unexpected shyness returned. In the meekest of voices, I told him hello.

"Damn if you don't look like a carbon copy of your mother. I swear it's like she had you all on her own. I don't see my brother in you. Not one tiny bit."

Rose nudged me away in order to pull open the door and climb inside.

"You want to come with your sister and me?" my uncle asked.

"Where?"

"*Where?* We're going for a ride. Spin the wheels around this shit-box town for a bit. Who knows? Maybe we'll hit an arcade if we're lucky to find one. I'm guessing you like Ms. Pac-Man and Ping-Pong."

"You guessed wrong," my sister told him. "The girl doesn't like any of the normal things kids her age like."

Part of me wanted to climb into that truck simply to prove her wrong. I might have if Howie didn't look right at me, cigarette bouncing, and say, "Come on, Rose. What are you waiting for?"

"I'm Sylvie. She's Rose," I corrected him.

The lighter popped out of the dashboard. Howie reached for it and lit his cigarette so it glowed like the rest of him. "I know that. It's just, like I was saying, you look so much like your mother, a guy can get mixed up is all. Anyway, *Sylvie*, get in the truck."

His voice had changed, so it sounded more like an order than an invitation. Now I was the one who stood caught between two choices, while the wind blew and the palms made a frantic swooshing above and that man with the scratches called into the bushes, "It's all right. Come on. It's safe. I promise."

"Just forget her," Rose said.

My uncle leaned across the seat, his hairy, tattooed arm brushing Rose's stomach as he pushed open the door. "Get in the truck," he said again.

And then came another voice, "Sylvie!"

I whirled around to see the revolving door of the conference center still spinning even after it spit my mother from the building. She moved in my direction, one hand clutching her silver cross necklace. When she saw Rose sitting in my uncle's truck, her face took on a stricken expression. Over the sound of the wind and the chugging engine and that man calling into the bushes, my mother raised her voice louder than I'd ever heard, "Get out of that truck! Get out of that truck now, Rose!"

"You better step on it, Uncle," my sister said.

When my mother reached us, she must have realized that my sister had every intention of ignoring her. She looked at Howie and said, "Tell her to get out."

He laughed. "You want *me* to tell her?"

"Yes."

"Don't you think that's a little messed up? I haven't seen the girl in years and she's going to listen to *me*. Sounds like you have trouble controlling your own kid."

My mother gave up reasoning with him. One last time, she tried with my sister. "Rose, I'm asking you to get out of that truck."

Rose's only response was to pull the door shut. My mother tugged back, but Rose hammered down the lock and cranked up the window. I watched her say something to my uncle, but it was as though there were two worlds now: one inside the truck, which we could not hear, and another outside, where that man by the bushes was still calling into the bushes.

My uncle pulled away from the curb. As their taillights disappeared out of the lot, my mother clutched her cross and asked if I knew where they were going.

"For a ride. And maybe to an arcade if they find one."

Her eyes shut a moment, and I knew she was praying. When she opened them again, I asked how she knew that Rose and I were outside. I thought maybe she'd tell me she had one of her feelings, but instead she said that the security guard had checked the greenroom and reported back that it was empty. My mother had excused herself from the talk and left my father on the stage while she came to find us. "I can't believe she's gone off with him."

I wanted to tell her how sorry I was for not living up to the promise I made to my father, but someone else spoke first.

"Excuse me," the voice said.

My mother and I turned to see the man with the scratches. We had been so preoccupied, staring out at the parking lot, that neither of us noticed him approach. Beneath the visor of his baseball cap, I saw a long nose with flared nostrils and skinny lips. He must have wiped his hand on his face, because blood smeared across one cheek.

"I'm sorry to bother you, but—"

"This is not a good time," my mother told him, letting go of her cross and straightening her posture. It was never her way to be rude, but this moment called for an exception. "As I'm sure you just witnessed, we are having some family difficulties."

"I'm sorry." The man stepped closer, and I could see that beneath the smudges of blood, his skin looked smooth and creaseless. "I really am sorry. But, please. I drove all the way here, hours and hours, to hear you and your husband speak."

"Well, my husband is still inside speaking. If you hurry, you can hear him."

"I know that. I was in the auditorium earlier. But I had to leave, because, well . . ."

As his voice trailed off, my mother seemed to take him in for the first time. I watched her face soften in such a way that she appeared more like her usual, serene self. "What is it?"

"It's . . . well . . . I need your help."

He pointed to the bushes, and my mother walked toward them. I had the sense that she did not want me to follow, so I lingered behind. The man did too. From the curb, we watched as my mother gathered the hem of her dress and crouched to the ground. Rather than call into the darkness the way he had been doing, she began humming, the same song she hummed on the drive down to Florida to shut out Rose's bad behavior. At last, when her humming stopped, my mother held her hand into the shadows. I cringed, expecting the rustle and high-pitched snarl.

Except for the wind shaking the palm trees, things were quiet. I looked closer and saw, not far from my mother's hand, a pair of eyes. Wet and shiny, they made me think of an animal blinking there in the dark. And then, slowly, she appeared. Not an animal. A girl. She was older than me, I could tell, though not by much. Thirteen, I guessed. Maybe fourteen. Her blond hair was matted. Her expression, empty and dazed. She placed her hand in my mother's. Together, they stood. On the girl's forehead, my mother made the sign of the cross over and over again, so many times it was not possible to count. When that was done at last, she placed her palms on the girl's cheeks. Eyes closed, my mother's lips moved in prayer. "In the name of the Father," she said finally, "the Son, the Holy Ghost."

The girl's hand in hers now, she led her to where we stood by the curb in the spot my uncle's truck had been only a few moments earlier. As rain began to fall once more, misting my cheeks and dampening my hair, I studied the girl more carefully. No shoes. One sock. Ratty shorts and T-shirt. Her cherub cheeks and arms scratched, same as the man's. Her bright blue eyes stayed trained on my mother and no one else. She opened her mouth, actually moved it up and down in a vague, marionette sort of way, but no sound came.

Still, my mother seemed to understand. "It's okay," she said, turning to the man. "Come take her."

With my mother's blessing, he stepped toward the girl and held out his hand. When she took it, he spoke in an astonished voice to my mother, "It's true what people say. You have a gift."

She gave a small nod, but that was her only response. After so many years, my mother still did not like to be made the center of attention. And more than likely, her mind was on her oldest daughter, out there on the dark roads with her drunken brother-in-law at the wheel.

Before they turned to go, the man reached out his scratched hand and shook my mother's. "Thank you, and God bless. My apologies for intruding on your difficulties."

"It's okay," she told him. "You needed help. And certain kinds of help are hard to come by in this world."

"Well, I'm grateful to you for understanding," he said. "By the way, my name is Albert Lynch and this is my daughter, Abigail."

LITTLE THINGS

WITNESS SURFACES WHO MAY CLEAR SUSPECT IN KILLING OF FAMOUS MARY-LAND COUPLE.

The headline could not be missed on the newspaper folded neatly in the wastebasket by Boshoff's desk. When I walked into his office the morning after Halloween, I glanced down to see those words and Albert Lynch's unlined face—his bald head, long nose, and wispy mustache—staring up at me.

I'd been avoiding stories about my parents' case in the papers ever since Cora gave me what I thought was her only worthwhile advice: "The things people write will mess with your head. Better off letting the detectives and lawyers keep you abreast of what you need to know." So I did my best to focus on Boshoff, who unwrapped a cough drop and placed it on his pink farm-animal tongue before telling me, "I read a poem last night that put me in mind of you, Sylvie."

"A poem?"

"Yes. I've been anxious to tell you about it all day." As I took a seat, he went on to say that when he had trouble sleeping, he read poetry. Cookbooks were his favorite reading material, but he had worked through all the titles on his shelf, and they were too costly to buy more. "Some people would claim that's not much of a change, since recipes are little poems in their own way. Wouldn't you agree?"

I nodded, remembering the recipe my sister recited before I left for school. Considering all that happened the night before, it was no surprise I never slept. Not long after the sun came up, a car turned into the driveway. Peeking through my window, I glimpsed Cora tugging the Hulk into her backseat while Rose burst through the front door and began vomiting downstairs.

"I know what you're thinking," Rose said, wiping her mouth and straightening up after I followed the retching sound to the kitchen. The green makeup was washed from her face, though clumps still clung to her hair. "You're thinking: don't puke in the sink. But who says the toilet's the only place a person can puke? Now that I think about it, the sink's way more sanitary."

Actually, I'd been thinking about the boys who had come to the door and the light in the basement. I opened my mouth to tell her about them, but Rose broke in before I could speak.

"I'm going to make a pizza. Want some?"

"*You're* cooking?"

She reached for a 7-Eleven bag on the table. "Here's my recipe: open box, remove frozen crap, nuke in microwave. I'm no Julia What's-Her-Tits, but I'll manage."

"The poem has nothing to do with your situation," Boshoff was saying, luring me back to the here and now of his office. "But it contains a few lines that might offer you a helpful approach. It's called 'Little Things' by Sharon Olds. I would have written it down, except I was in bed with my book-light on, so I didn't have a pen. Plus, I didn't want to wake my wife. She needs her rest these days."

The tight-fitting band on his finger should have led me to consider the existence of a Mrs. Boshoff, but I never had. When I tried to picture her what came was a woman with white hair and rosy cheeks, a kind of Mrs. Claus, tucked under the covers beside him. "Why does she need her rest?" I asked.

Boshoff quit clacking his cough drop. "I'm afraid my wife's not well."

I knew how it felt when people pushed on a sensitive topic, so I told him I was sorry, but I didn't ask more. He nodded his thanks and we let that be enough. I watched him slip on his glasses and lean over his desk, doing his best to recall the poem. As his pencil scratched across the pad, I felt Albert Lynch's eyes upon me. Since there had only been one witness at the church—*me*—I wondered who could have come forward to clear his name.

"Here we go, Sylvie. I can't remember the entire poem. Just the part that made me think of you." Boshoff swiveled his chair in my direction and read aloud. When he was done, he pulled off his glasses and asked if the passage put me in mind of anything in particular. I had no clue, so I shook my head before remembering to speak my answer. Glasses back on, he tried again. This time, I listened carefully as he read: " 'I learned to love the little things about him, because of all the big things I could not love, no one could, it would be wrong to.'

"As I told you, Sylvie, the poem itself is about an unrelated topic. However, those lines might offer a way for you to think about your sister."

I learned to love the little things about Rose, because of all the big things I could not love, no one could, it would be wrong to.

Never once had I mentioned the larger blame I placed on my sister for making that call and luring them to the church or my role in not telling the police about it, but perhaps Boshoff had sensed something in my silence, the way my mother once taught me to do.

"Do you think you could try that, Sylvie? Since you have to live with her for the next few years at least, it might help you to focus on the positive."

"I'll try," I said, unable to muster even a hint of enthusiasm in my voice.

"Well, why don't we start by making a list of little things about her that are lovable? We can begin it together. Do you have the journal I gave you?"

That small violet book came with me everywhere in my father's tote, since leaving it home meant Rose might discover all I'd been writing there about the things from our past I did not want to forget, like that night with Dot, that trip to Ocala and what came after. On account of what I'd written, I didn't like the idea of taking it out, so I told Boshoff I didn't have it. He riffled through the desk and found a pad instead. In his sloppy script, he wrote "Little Things" at the top, numbers one through three down the side, before handing it to me.

"You once mentioned Rose has a nice voice when she sings with the radio. That seems like a small enough thing to love, right?"

Reluctantly, I wrote: *My sister has a decent singing voice.*

When I was done, I stared at the impossibly vast spaces beside those next two numbers. "I'm sorry," I said, my gaze shifting to Albert Lynch in that photo once more. "I'm not feeling well. Do you mind if we stop?"

This time, Boshoff's gaze followed mine to the wastebasket. His lips parted and he brought a finger to his mouth, like he was pushing a button there and turning something off. "Sylvie, you're aware I share this office with a handful of rotating staff. I got here a short while before you today. Had I noticed the paper there, I would have removed—"

"I think I need to go to the nurse. But can I take that newspaper with me?"

"Of course. If that's what you want. But wouldn't you like to talk about it?"

After weeks of him gently circling the topic, I felt bad that this was the way it had come about. Even so, I shook my head, forgetting about Louise Hock's insistence that I practice speaking my answers. I reached into the basket, feeling as if I were reaching down and down into our well to fetch one of those rag dolls by its fingerless hands. I grabbed the edge of the newspaper, a coupon section and the sports pages falling away, leaving me with the pages I wanted. I carried them with me as I left poor, startled Boshoff and his list of "Little Things" behind.

The direction of the nurse's office—that's the way I headed, even though I had no intention of ending up there. Instead, I took a detour down the industrial arts hall, where the smells were unfamiliar: sawdust and solder. At a water fountain, I splashed my face, because it was true that I didn't feel so well, before unfolding the newspaper.

Dundalk—The killer shot Rose Mason, 45, leaving her to die by the altar in a small chapel in a quiet Maryland town twenty miles from the state capital. Sylvester Mason, 50, her husband, was killed a few feet away with a gunshot to the back of the head.

The younger of the couple's two children, a 13-year-old girl, had been sleeping in her parents' car outside the chapel when she woke to the sound of gunfire. "When I heard the second shot, I opened the car door and walked into the church," she told police, though no further details of her account have been released to the press. Officers reported that they did not find the girl, who was crouched beneath a pew, until hours after the investigation had begun. "Her head was bleeding and she was drifting in and out of consciousness," said Detective Dennis Rummel of the Baltimore County Police Force. "We got her out of there as soon as we could."

In the weeks following the investigation, a lone suspect emerged: Albert Lynch, 41, a drifter, originally from Holly Grove, Arkansas. Since 1986 Mr. Lynch had been seek—

"Excuse me, young lady."
I looked up to see a teacher I didn't recognize. "Yes?"
"Do you have a pass to be out here loitering during class time?"
"I'm on my way to the nurse's office."
"Well, this is a roundabout way of getting there."
I folded the paper, left the hall with its unfamiliar smells, and once more walked in the direction of the nurse's office. But when I came upon an exit, I slipped through it. Rarely did I miss class, never mind skip out in the middle of the day, but I wanted to go someplace where I could read the article without interruption. Considering how often I took it, the path I first followed when Dot had been locked in our parents' bathroom should have been well tread by then. But like some fairy-tale forest, it remained forever overgrown and unwelcoming. A maze of stone walls led me to the barbed-wire fence behind Watt's Farm close to Butter Lane. Most of the year, the field there held no sign of life, but come fall it teemed with white-feathered turkeys. The way they arrived, all at once and fully grown, left me suspicious about how many were actually raised on premises, but nevertheless, mornings when I was early for school, I stopped at the fence and watched those birds strutting about on their scaly, bent-backward legs. The high-pitched warble that rose from their throats made them seem like nervous old women.

That afternoon, I stopped at my usual spot, put down my father's tote, and rested a hand on the fence while I finished the article.

Since 1986 Mr. Lynch had been seeking counsel from the Masons—a couple who built a national reputation, admired in some circles, mocked in others, as demonologists. Those close to the case say Mr. Lynch was disgruntled with the Masons' treatment of his daughter. Lynch admits to meeting the couple at the chapel on the evening of the murders, but claims to have left the church before violence erupted. To date, he has lacked a substantiated alibi, insisting that he was at the Texaco on Route 2 at the time of the killings. The station's security monitors were not in service so no video exists to support his claim. Further weakening Mr. Lynch's case, he asserted through his attorney, Michael Cavage, that after fueling his car, he paid with cash. The clerk on duty has no recollection of seeing Mr. Lynch that evening.

For months, the suspect insisted that an elderly man had seen him in the restroom. With the court case approaching in April, police had all but stopped searching for another suspect, as the witness failed to surface. Yesterday, however, Cavage announced that the person had been located and would corroborate Mr. Lynch's alibi in court. Mr. Patrick Dunn, 71, of Kennebunkport, ME, claims to have seen Mr. Lynch in the men's room that evening while his wife waited outside in the car. The sudden emergence of Mr. Dunn leaves police and investigators without any apparent suspects.

In a final twist to an already bizarre account of the evening, Mr. Lynch has maintained that he paid the deceased couple's eldest daughter, Rose Mason Jr., now 19, a small sum to make a call from a pay phone outside the Mustang Bar in Baltimore, inviting her parents to the church that evening. The allegation has been denied by Ms. Mason who states that she was home at the time of the call, a claim supported by her sister.

Assistant District Attorney Louise Hock told the press a statement would be forthcoming.

"Hello!" a voice called from across the field. "Hey, you! Hello!"

I looked up to see a very tall someone trudging through the field of turkeys in my direction. He wore a tan barn jacket, gray sweats, and enormous boots, laces loose and slithering at his ankles. The sea of turkeys parted, flapping and gobbling in his wake. When he arrived at the fence, he said, "I've seen you here before."

"Sorry." I figured I must be in trouble for trespassing or loitering. I pressed the newspaper to my stomach, where the only thing I'd eaten all day—a single slice of Rose's microwave pizza—roiled.

"Don't be. I just wanted to warn you not to put your fingers on the fence. Turkeys are as mean as they are dumb. They'll bite." He tugged off a glove and held up his left hand, wiggling his thumb and index finger. His ring, middle, and pinky fingers were all missing.

I yanked my hand off the fence. "Is that how—"

"No. But the visual usually makes people listen. You're Sylvie, right?"

I nodded, thinking of those boys who showed up at the door the night before. This guy was older than them, the age my father must have been when he left Philadelphia and moved to that row-house apartment in Baltimore, where ghosts appeared to him in the evenings. "Sorry about your parents," he told me.

I kept quiet, waiting for the part where he turned the comment into something hurtful, but it didn't happen. "How do you know my name?"

"I used to date your sister."

"*Rose?*" Most of the dates Rose brought home looked like the derelicts in the smoking area at school and acted just as aloof. This guy seemed too athletic, too polite, to have been one of them. I studied his brown eyes, floppy brown hair, and bulky shoulders. His sweats clung to his crotch in a way that gave a pretty exact picture of the anatomy beneath—a sight that would have caused my mother to make the sign of the cross and mutter about the perversities of youth today. Then I remembered the fights she and my father had with Rose about one boy in particular. "You're not Franky, are you?"

"No, I'm Dereck." He reached his hand over the fence to shake mine. Between Cora's fake, noodly fingers and his missing ones, I wasn't sure which felt more odd. Behind him, the birds gobbled and flapped, moving closer. "Keep it down, ladies!" he yelled, letting go and waving his hands to shoo them away.

When he turned back, I asked if he ever felt bad about what was going to happen to them in a few weeks. Dereck smiled. At each side of his mouth, he had a pointed tooth, more yellow than the rest, lending him a wolfish look. "*Nahh*. Spend as much time with these morons as I do and you're glad to see them go. Besides, it's just a job I'm doing for extra cash this month. I work at my father's garage in town the rest of the time. But anyway, I wanted to ask about your sister. She was always so much fun. Is she still?"

"Some might think so."

"Yeah, well, you're her sister, so you probably don't. Tell her hello from me, okay?"

Despite—or maybe because of—the memory of Rose and Cora kissing, I found myself saying, "Maybe you should give her a call and tell her yourself. I'm sure she'd like that."

Dereck smiled again, flashing those wolfish teeth. "Maybe I will. Glad I ran into you, Sylvie. Remember, what's the rule?"

"Rule?"

He held up his hand, twiddling what wasn't missing. "Fingers off the fence."

"Fingers off the fence," I repeated.

With that, I picked up my father's tote and started down the last of the path until it opened up to the lot across from our house. As I passed, I glanced at the foundation, which looked like a drained swimming pool. A tree had fallen inside, knotted roots balanced on the ledge, twisted branches soaking in a puddle at the bottom not far from the rusted steel rods that rose up in one corner. I thought of how much time Rose and I once spent down there, drawing the details of our imaginary home. Nothing used to make me so gloomy as when the rain came and washed it all away. Back then, my sister cheered me up by pointing out how fun it would be for us to draw everything all over again.

I left those memories of what seemed like two other girls behind and made my way across the street. That's when I noticed another of those foil-covered dishes on our step. Not far from our house, a wood-paneled station wagon idled down the lane, a woman in a frumpy beige dress walking toward it.

"Wait!" I called, figuring she must be the one leaving all that food.

She turned my way, giving me a glimpse of her grim, head-on-a-totem-pole face, before quickening her pace, pulling open the door, and slamming it shut on the hem of her dress. As the station wagon sped away, I squinted at the license plate, making out the colors but not a single number.

After she rounded the corner and was gone, what was left for me to do but turn back to the house? Even in daylight, that bare bulb could be seen burning behind the dusty glass of the cellar window. Given how hung over Rose had been that morning, I expected to find her passed out in bed, but her truck was gone. With that light on, no part of me liked the idea of being home alone, but I hurried toward the door, scooping up the dish before stepping inside.

Stuffed shells—that's what we'd been tempted with this time. I deposited them on the kitchen counter for my sister to inspect then returned to the living room, where I pressed my good ear to the carpet same as I'd done months before. After hearing none of the rattling or breaking I once did, I sat on the sofa and turned on the TV. When the afternoon news came on at last, I listened as a perky anchorwoman repeated the same information about the elderly man who had come forward in the case. As she spoke, pictures flashed on the screen of Albert Lynch, then my parents, then, finally, a photo that news programs and papers loved to trot out: the shot of my mother standing on our front lawn, cradling Penny as if the doll was her living, breathing child.

After it was over, I lay back on the sofa and allowed myself to think of that night in the church. I remembered the way my eyes adjusted to the dark until I made out three silhouettes near the altar. When I called, none moved. Waiting there in the cold shadows, a detail drifted back to me from the few times I'd been inside that church. Painted statues surrounded the altar: a robed man with forlorn eyes and a beard, rosary beads dangling from his fingers; a nun with an oddly shaped habit, clutching a bible. But there had only been two statues. The thought led me to look more closely, which was when I saw that the third figure was moving after all.

"Hello," I called out again. And again, it sounded like a question: *Hello?*

And then there was the tumble of heavy footsteps moving out of the darkness in my direction, the sound of something exploding by my ear, then nothing until I woke in the hospital. How many times had I been over those details and so many others with Rummel and Louise? At some point during every meeting, Louise impressed upon me how crucial it was that my account never waver, saying, "We have Lynch's footprints and finger-prints inside that church. We have the details of his threats toward your parents. But what the jury needs to hear, Sylvie, is that you saw him with your own eyes when you stepped inside. That's what's going to seal the deal and put him away. That's what's going to make it so your mother and father rest in peace. And isn't that what you want?"

"Yes," I told her whenever she asked that question.

Yes, I thought as my eyes fell shut on the sofa.

When I opened them, the sunlight through the front window was gone. The TV had moved on to the evening news. As Peter Jennings droned on, I looked at the ticking clock: almost seven. What had caused me to wake, I realized, was the sound of someone at the door. Those boys again, I wor-ried. But before I could get up and twist the locks, it swung open and Rose stepped inside. She wore a top I'd never seen before, nicer than her usual, with a little bow at the collar as though she was making a gift of herself. In the flickering blue light, I saw that she held something in her hands. Mail, I guessed, since she set it on the stairs to carry up later. After that, she turned to the cross on the wall and brought her hands together in a gesture that looked like she might be about to pray.

"*Whooaa!*" She noticed me at the last second and spun around. "What the hell are you doing just sitting here in the dark?"

"I fell asleep in front of the TV. I was tired after school."

"Well, you scared the crap out of me. And try working a job when you're tired. It's not easy."

I let the mention of a job go for the moment. Her praying, too. "Dereck says hello."

"Dereck who?"

"I don't know his last name. He works at Watt's Farm and at a garage in town." I held up my thumb and index finger, twiddling the way he did. "Missing digits. Werewolf teeth."

"The one with brown hair?"

"Do you know a *blond* Dereck with missing fingers and werewolf teeth?"

"You know what, Sylvie? Every once in a while you're actually funny. But not this time. No one calls that doofus by his real name, so that's why I wondered."

"What do they call him?"

"Seven."

"Seven?"

"That's how many fingers he has left." Rose hunted down the remote and collapsed into a wingback chair. As she flipped channels, I watched her kick off her shoes and rub her feet. It took a while for me to work up the courage, but I managed to ask, "Have you been down in the basement?"

"Nope. Why?"

"The light's been on. Ever since last night."

"Probably something screwy with the wiring. Don't start thinking your weird thoughts. By the way, that detective called. So did Louise. There's been a development. They want us at the station in the morning. So you'll have to miss a few classes."

I waited to see if Rose would say anything more about the development, but she did not. Rather than tell her what I'd read in the paper and seen on the local news, I just took to watching bits and pieces of TV before asking: "What state has license plates with a blue background and gold letters and numbers?"

"You don't know, Sylvie? We see them all the time. They're from one state over. *Delaware*. Why?"

"No reason. Did you mention something before about a job?"

From the way she rubbed her feet, I thought she'd tell me she found one waitressing. Instead, she said, "Try not to be too impressed. But you're looking at a bona fide tele-researcher for Dial U.S.A. in Baltimore. Today was my first day. I completed three phone surveys."

"*Surveys?* About what?"

"Fast food. Deodorant. Cigarettes. They say opinions are like assholes and everyone's got one. But I say opinions are like teeth—everyone's got *hundreds,* and they love nothing more than to use them to chatter away."

"Thirty-two," I told her.

"Thirty-two what?"

"Humans have thirty-two teeth. Not counting the deciduous ones we lose and put under our pillow for the Tooth Fairy when we're kids. So according to your theory, every adult has thirty-two opinions. Not hundreds."

My sister stared at me, massaging her foot still. "How the hell do you know that kind of crap anyway?"

"Our father was once a dentist. Didn't you ever talk to him about it?"

She let go of her foot, slouched in her chair, not answering.

"So do you like your job?" I asked, changing the subject.

"It's work, Sylvie. Nobody likes work. But I've already sucked up to my supervisor real good. Fran even forked over a Dial U.S.A. calling card, so I can take surveys home and do them from here. A privilege only people with seniority usually get. Anyway, I was thinking, if you help me, I'll give you a cut. Fifty cents for every completed survey. What do you say?"

It used to be I had money hidden in my room from that first essay contest and the others I'd gone on to win. But that changed the summer Abigail came to live with us. As much as I liked the idea of replenishing my supply, I knew better than to accept Rose's initial offer. We haggled, stopping whenever she found something good on TV. As I waited for a commercial, I found myself thinking of what Boshoff told me about his sick wife and the way he liked to read cookbooks when he couldn't sleep. Maybe, I thought, if I made enough cash, I'd pick him up a new one.

"A dollar a survey," I told Rose when a commercial appeared at last. "Final offer."

"Deal."

I had plenty of questions: How would Fran know we weren't making up answers? What was the latest we could call people? But Rose told me she would explain everything in the morning. She didn't want to talk about Dial U.S.A. anymore. I knew better than to bother her, so I stretched out on the sofa again, figuring I'd stay up a while. My sister flipped channels until settling on a PBS documentary that I knew didn't interest her. But leaving that channel on was what we did when we wanted our house to feel the way it used to when our parents were alive, since that was all they watched.

This particular show was about famous speeches. As Winston Churchill addressed a crowd, I started thinking that I might do better than Rose when it came to making those survey calls. My voice was less pushy, like our mother's, which might put those people at ease. When I looked over, Rose had nodded off. Her eyes had a way of staying open the smallest bit when she slept. I kept staring at the milky slits until something caused her to stir.

"Why are you gawking at me?"

"I wasn't gawking."

"You were so. Just like when I came in before. Now cut it out."

I should have planned the next part, but the question came out almost of its own accord. "What do you think I should love about you?"

Rose opened her eyes more fully and sat up. I may as well have snapped on the lights, clapped my hands next to her ears. "*What?*"

"What do you think I should love about you?" I repeated, feeling more nervous the second time.

"What the hell kind of thing is that to ask, Sylvie?"

The Churchill speech should have inspired me to offer some eloquent response, but I felt stumped. Rose pressed the remote and the room went dark. Silent too, except for the ticking clock. I figured she'd given up waiting for an answer, because she told me she was too tired to go up to bed and that she'd just rest on the couch for a while. I picked up my things and walked to the stairs, glancing down at the mail and wondering if a letter from Howie might be in the stack. The moment I put my foot on the bottom step, I heard Rose's voice behind me. She sounded softer, a little like our mother for a change, when she said, "I'm your sister. Isn't that reason enough for you to love me?"

I wasn't sure what to say, so I told her she was right. Then I kept going up to my room, where I took out that small violet book and sat on my bed. Inside, I made a new list of "Little Things," a list that looked like this:

#1. *My sister knows Dereck, and Dereck seems nice.*

2. *My sister is giving me the chance to make money so I can buy Boshoff a present.*

#3. *My sister is my sister. She thinks that's reason enough for me to love her. And I guess I do too.*

THE LIGHT

When we left the Lynches in the parking lot of the convention center, I figured it was the last we would see of them. Or, more likely, I didn't think about it at all. I was too busy following my mother back to the greenroom and replaying the things I'd witnessed over and over in my mind: the way she knelt before those bushes, the way she hummed that pattering song, the way she grew silent before reaching her hand into the shadows.

Inside the building once more, my mother asked me to sit quietly with *Jane Eyre* while she returned to the auditorium to finish the last of the evening's talk with my father. There must not have been much left of their presentation, or perhaps my uncle's disruption and my mother's disappearance from the stage had caused people to lose interest. Whatever the reason, a short while later I looked up to see them standing in the doorway. The same security guard who chased Howie out escorted us through a maze of hallways and through the rear exit to where our Datsun was parked. As we climbed inside, he stood watch, making sure none of my parents' detractors appeared unexpectedly to confront us.

After my father started the engine, I apologized for failing to keep my promise. His dark eyes glanced at me in the rearview mirror. He told me that he was sure I'd done my best, so I should not feel bad. But he wanted to know how Rose went from sitting in the greenroom to joyriding around town with his brother. As we rolled along the Ocala roads, strewn with palm leaves and debris from the storm, I filled them in on everything that happened. Since I'd already disappointed them once that evening, I left out the detail about sneaking into the auditorium with my sister and instead said we'd wandered outside to check on the storm when we saw him there in his truck.

"Uncle Howie looks different," I finished.

We were passing a commercial strip, and I watched my parents turn their heads in search of that old pickup with the squashed side.

"Don't you think he looked different?" I asked, not letting it go.

"That's Howie," my father said. "A human slot machine. You never know what you're going to get when you pull the lever."

"Why do—" I started in on another question then thought better of it.

"Why do what?"

"I was going to ask why do you and Uncle Howie hate each other?"

My mother kept quiet, staring out the window still, though we were passing nothing but woods by then.

"Hate is a strong word, Sylvie. He's my brother and my blood. I suppose some part of me loves the man, despite our differences. I let him know we were coming to Florida, because I thought we could have a nice visit for a change. But clearly, we're better off keeping a distance between us. The stunt he pulled tonight proves once again how little respect he has for me and my work and my wife and my chil—"

"Sylvester," my mother said. "You don't need to go into all that with Sylvie."

So rarely did she challenge him that my father fell quiet. Never once had I heard them argue, but things were tense enough inside our car that it made me wonder if it might happen. After a pause, though, he told her she was right, that there was little point in rehashing it all. "The last thing I'll say on the topic, Sylvie, is that someday, when Rose gets her head straight, I hope the two of you can be close. Even though it's not the case with your uncle and me, it can be a very special thing to have someone who's a part of you in this world. Someone who knows how you think and feel."

"There," my mother said, tapping the glass. "Look there."

My father slowed the Datsun and we stared out the passenger side at a sign that announced simply: ARCADE. Our flash of hope faded the moment we pulled into the lot and spotted another sign on the door: CLOSED. Through the windows, it was possible to make out dozens of hulking video games, though none gave off any light. Teenagers hung out on the sidewalk anyway. A lanky boy on a skateboard, hair so long he might have been mistaken for a girl, tried jumping the curb only to wipe out. A group of girls sat close by, smoking as they watched him dust off and attempt the stunt again.

"Good evening," my father greeted them, rolling down the window.

The boy kicked the back of his skateboard and it leaped into his hands. He eyed our car as though ready to make a run for it. A girl with ropy bracelets around her thin wrists looked less skittish. My father's "good evening" had sent her into a fit of giggles. "Why, good evening to you, sir," she said, imitating the deep formality of his voice. "And how do you do this fine evening?"

If my father noticed that she was mocking him, he never let on. "I'm wondering if you've seen a truck."

"Well, I've seen plenty of trucks this evening, sir. Eighteen-wheelers. Dump trucks. Pickup trucks . . ."

"Tell her that this one is two-tone. Brown and cream," my mother said from the passenger seat as the girl rambled in that put-on voice. "It has a big dent on one side."

My father repeated the information, offering a description of Howie and Rose too.

"You a cop or something?" she asked in her real voice this time, which sounded squeakier than I would have guessed.

"No. I'm not a cop."

"So what are you? Besides *creepy*, I mean."

Her friends laughed, but my parents did not acknowledge them. I hoped my father wouldn't answer by explaining his occupation, so what he said relieved me. "I'm just a worried parent. That's all."

Who can predict the way people will react to a basic truth? I would not have guessed that my father's words would cause that girl to quit teasing, but they did. She smiled and told him, "Sorry to say, there's not been anybody like that here tonight."

"Maybe you can try Fun and Games over in Silver Springs," another of the girls with the same ropy bracelets suggested. "That place is open for another hour. Right, Duane?"

The skateboarder nodded and mumbled directions. My father thanked them and we were on our way. But a short while later we arrived in Silver Springs to find no sign of the truck there, either. Since the place was open, my father got out of the car. I had never been inside an arcade before, and if I asked to come in with him, I knew he'd tell me to stay behind. So I didn't ask. I just opened my door and got out too. My father looked at me, surprised, but didn't resist. After we stepped into the flashing lights, he weaved among the clusters of teenagers to a booth in the back where he spoke to the manager. I used the opportunity to take in those machines, blinking and buzzing away. A group of girls huddled around a game until it released a series of disappointing beeps and they stomped off. In the wake of their departure, I approached and stared at the round, yellow face on the screen, the pink bow, the dots in the maze. I put my hand on the control but had no money to make it work.

I'm guessing you like Ms. Pac-Man and Ping-Pong . . .

The girl doesn't like any of the normal things kids her age like . . .

"Ready, Sylvie?" my father said from behind me.

"Can I play?"

"Play? Now?"

"Just a quick one. It's only twenty-five cents."

My father sighed. "Sylvie, you are far too bright to waste your time with this nonsense. Besides, we need to get back to looking for your sister."

"But I don't want to," I said before I could stop myself.

My father grew quiet, same as when my mother challenged him in the car. In that video screen, I could see his blurry reflection—tilted head, raised eyebrows—a look usually reserved for Rose. "You don't want to look for your sister?"

"It's like you said about Uncle Howie. Maybe it's better we keep our distance. Let her do what she wants, since she's the one who chose to go with him."

"This is nothing like the situation with your uncle. He's a grown man. Your sister is a kid. Now I'm not sure what's gotten into you, but I won't have you acting out too. You're our good daughter. The one we rely on and trust to do what we need. Right now what we need is to get back to finding Rose. So let go of that game and follow me."

I took a breath. If Rose's behavior had proved one thing, it was that it was easier to give my father the daughter he wanted. That daughter pulled her hand away. That daughter followed him outside.

The Mustang. The Teeter-Totter. The Frog Pond. Those were just a few of the bars where we stopped so my father could inquire if anyone had seen them. But no one had. At each place, I waited in the car with my mother, listening to the rain pound on the roof. At last, after one in the morning, she suggested we call it quits.

"You want to stop?" my father said.

"It's not that I want to, Sylvester. But I don't know what more we can do at the moment. It's apparent we aren't going to find her out here tonight."

"Maybe they headed back to Howie's apartment in Tampa? It's only a hundred miles away. They could be there by now."

"It's a possibility. But even so, I don't think we should drive there without knowing for sure. Better we go back to the hotel and call first. At the very least, we can leave a message telling her to let us know where she is so we can come get her."

Reluctantly, my father turned the car around while my mother continued staring out that window. "I suppose you're right," he said once we were headed in the opposite direction. "We don't have much choice, do we?"

Back at the hotel, the three of us climbed the stairs to the second floor, a weary silence all around. The moment my father snapped on the light in our room, we saw Rose curled beneath the covers in one of the beds. She lifted her head from the pillow. "Hey."

"*Hey?*" my father said.

"Where were you?" my mother asked.

"Uncle Howie took me to—"

"You know what?" my father shouted. "Never mind. How did you get in here?"

"The lady at the front desk gave me a key." Rose yawned, messed with her hair. "She's one of those too-tan Florida freaks. I took one look at her wallet face and—"

"Let's go!" my father shouted, charging toward the bed. He ripped back the covers and yanked Rose by the arm, lifting her up and off from the mattress. "Let's go! Let's go!"

"*Ow!* Go where?"

"Don't ask! Just do what I say for a change! *Now!*"

My sister still had on her T-shirt and jeans from earlier, though her sneakers were off. While my father kept squeezing her arm, she made an effort to get her balance and slip her feet into them. All the while, Rose looked to my mother and me. The defiant expression she wore when slamming the truck door earlier gave way to something frightened. Normally, I knew my mother would have made some effort to calm the situation, but after the way Rose had behaved at the convention center, she just turned away, walked to her suitcase, and pulled out her nightgown. My sister barely managed to get her feet into her sneakers before my father began jerking her toward the door. Rose stumbled as she stared back at me. My mouth opened to say something that might stop it, but what words would he listen to? In the end, I just stood there, mute as that girl who emerged from the bushes.

Once they were gone, the room filled with a heavy silence. My mother walked to the window, not to stare outside, but to adjust the curtains. There wasn't enough fabric to cover the glass, so she had to choose where the light would come in the next morning: down the middle or at the sides. I watched her sample both before choosing the middle. After that, she told me I might as well get ready for bed too.

When she stepped into the bathroom and shut the door, I listened to the faucet handles squeak, the water run. The hard, cinnamon-colored suitcase I shared with Rose lay open on the floor across the room. I had every intention of doing as my mother said, but stopped to look out the window. Through the gap in the curtains, I could see fat moths doing a sloppy flutter beneath a light, but no trace of my sister and father.

At last, my mother emerged from the bathroom. She wore a knee-length white nightgown, her feet bare so she must have forgotten her slippers back in Dundalk. Since she was never the type to walk around the house in sleeping clothes, I rarely saw her this way. Unpinned, her hair fell past her shoulders, revealing more silvery streaks than were apparent in her bun. That hair, that gown, that pale skin, made her look ghostly—a vision worthy of those slides on the screen at the convention center.

"It's been a long day, Sylvie, and an even longer evening. We need our sleep. Now come away from the window and get ready for bed."

I stared outside again at those moths around the light. "Where did Dad take her?"

"I'm sure he just wanted to talk with Rose about what she did."

"Why outside?"

"Well, since it was not going to be the quietest of conversations, it only makes sense to have it someplace where they won't wake the other guests in this hotel."

"But I don't see them out there. I don't hear them either."

"They're probably farther away. Down in the parking lot. Now try not to worry, Sylvie. I know it's hard. Your sister's behavior this evening upset me too. But difficult as it is to watch your father be so tough on her, it's what she needs. Something has gone wrong with Rose, and we're working hard to make it right."

I didn't want to turn my attention away from the world outside that window, but I forced myself. Pajamas. Hairbrush. Toothbrush. Once I pulled those things from the suitcase, I slipped into the bathroom. When I stepped out, I saw that my mother had unfolded the cot my father ordered. On account of his back, he needed his own bed. He and Rose could work out who slept where when they returned, my mother told me, and I could sleep with her.

Before pulling down the covers, she knelt and clasped her hands in prayer. When I was little, I used to kneel with her each night when she came into my room to tuck me in. No longer. And my prayers had become more of a mental wish list I ticked off with my head on the pillow. Still, I knew she expected me to join her, so I knelt on the opposite side of our hotel bed. Eyes closed, I prayed that my father and Rose would stop fighting. I prayed that whatever had gone wrong with Rose would go right, just the way my mother said. After that, I waited in silence until I heard her stand, and I stood too.

In bed with the lights off, we listened to the rise and fall of each other's breaths. Rather than her usual milky scent, I smelled the perfumed hotel soap on her skin. How much time passed? I was not sure, but when my mind wouldn't give itself over to sleep, I whispered, "Are you awake?"

"Yes, dear. I am."

"Can I ask you something?"

"You know the rule."

The rule. It had been a while since she or my father mentioned it, but this is what it was: Rose and I could ask any questions or share anything we were feeling. In return, our parents would listen and do their best to understand. Despite the rule, I felt nervous saying, "Back at the conference center . . ."

"Yes?"

"That man. That girl."

"You mean, Albert and Abigail Lynch?" The way my mother said their names, it was as though she had been speaking of them all her life.

"Yes."

"What about them?"

"How . . . how did you, you know, do what you did?"

My mother paused before responding. I shifted my head on the pillow so I was that much closer. At last, she said, "The most truthful answer I can give you or anyone else, Sylvie, is that I don't know. All I can say is that it's something I have done for a long time without understanding the whys and hows of it all."

"How long have you done it?"

"Well, it began when I was a girl not much older than you. I find there are moments when I am overcome by certain feelings about things. You know that much already. But sometimes, what I feel most of all is another person's need for peace. A soul can be so scared, so troubled, so lonely and sad in this world, Sylvie, and when that happens, what's needed most is a promise of calm, of comfort, of safety. That's what I did my best to give that girl tonight."

"But you didn't even speak to her."

"It's not about speaking. It's about sensing what's inside a person. Most people could do the same if they tried. I know you certainly could."

"*Me?*"

"Yes, you." She laughed. "There's no one else here but us, is there?"

"But how would I do it?"

"I'm sorry to say I don't have a set of instructions. But, well, try looking at me."

My mother moved her pale, pretty face still closer on her pillow. In the slash of light that came through the gap in the curtains, I could see her glittery green eyes blinking. For a long while, the two of us were silent, gazing at each other, breathing softly, until at last, in her whispery voice, she said, "Tell me now. What have I been feeling as we lie here?"

I did not plan my answer, but out it came. "That you love me."

My mother smiled. She leaned forward, kissed my forehead.

"Was I right?"

"Right that I love you? Of course."

"No. Was I right in guessing that's what you were thinking?"

"First of all, Sylvie, 'guessing' is not the word for what we are talking about."

"Well, you know what I mean."

"I don't need to answer that question for you. You know the truth already. What I will say is this: each of us is born into this life with a light inside of us. Some, like yours, burn brighter than others. You don't see that yet, but I do. What's most important is to never let that light go out, because when you do, it means you've lost yourself to the darkness. It means you've lost your hope. And hope is what makes this world a beautiful place. Do you understand what I am trying to say?"

"I think so," I said if only not to disappoint her.

"That's my good girl. It won't always be easy, but you have to believe. Okay?"

"Okay."

"Now, like I said, it's been a long day so let's try to get some rest."

There was more I wanted to know, but my mother said good night and rolled away. Too soon, her breath grew heavy and I lost her to sleep. I waited, staring toward the window, feeling more alone in that room than I should have with her so close. But without her voice, without her eyes looking into mine, an emptiness spread inside me, until at last, I heard a hand jiggle the doorknob.

With so little light in the room, it was as though two shadows entered. Without speaking, they moved to their suitcases and took turns using the bathroom. Rose went to the cot as my father settled into the bed, releasing an enormous sigh as he pulled the covers over him. With all of us safe inside, I should have felt calm. Instead, I lay there thinking about that conversation with my mother. Despite what she said, my answer really had been a guess. It didn't take a gift to see the love she felt for me—her good daughter, the one my parents relied on and trusted to do what they needed. I thought of that pleading expression on Rose's face earlier, the way I'd watched our father yank her from the room without uttering a word.

Something has gone wrong with Rose, and we're working hard to make it right . . .

Why, if my mother's gift gave peace to that Lynch girl, did it not work to bring the same sense of calm to Rose, her very own daughter? My mind tugged and pulled at that question until it grew weary enough that sleep came at last, though the answer I wanted never did.

SNOWBIRDS

Snowbirds—that's a term I learned today. Now I'm certain to hear it all the time in that way new words have of popping up after you discover their existence, making you wonder how you missed them before. (Someone should come up with a term to describe that phenomenon.) Anyway, snowbirds was how Detective Rummel described the old couple who stopped at the gas station where Albert Lynch claims to have been at the very moment I followed the footprints toward the church last winter. As I stepped inside to see those three figures near the altar, he claims to have been washing his hands in the men's room at the Texaco. He claims to have been making small talk with . . . a snowbird.

"Have you always kept a diary, Sylvie?" Rummel asked.

"No. This is just something I started doing lately."

"And do you mind if I ask what sorts of things you write about in there?"

"School stuff," I told him, closing the book while being careful not to let the letter I'd found beneath Rose's bed on Halloween night slip out. I stared around at the gray walls of the interview room. They had become achingly familiar since that article appeared in the paper two weeks before, and Rose and I had been summoned to the station almost daily. "Just things I need to remember. It helps me do better on tests."

"According to your sister you don't need much help," Louise Hock said from the corner where she stood. Even though it was nearly three in the afternoon, her curly hair looked damp. Beneath her blazer, her shoulder pads had shifted in a way that gave her a lopsided appearance. "She says you're very bright. Top of your class."

"I study a lot. That's all."

Detective Rummel gave me a small smile, an event that felt increasingly rare. As he spread papers on the table between us, I picked up my journal and slipped it in my father's tote. I never would have taken it out, but since they'd begun separating Rose and me on our visits, I needed something to distract my mind from the nervousness I felt whenever they spoke to her in the next room. "The complete affidavit was filed in court this morning," Louise began. She paced behind the table, never sitting the way Rummel did. "The documents provide more detailed information than what we supplied you with on your previous visits here. I'm sure you remember everything we've gone over so far. Right, Sylvie?"

Patrick Dunn—that's the snowbird's name. What makes him one is that he and his wife live up north (Maine) all summer and down south (Carolinas) all winter. Normally, Mr. Dunn insists on fleeing for warmer weather immediately after Christmas, but last year they lingered in the cold temperatures because his wife's sister broke her hip and needed them nearby. By the time she was better, and by the time they finally hit the road, it was February. Their Crown Victoria ("The Vic," as Rummel keeps calling it) was jam-packed with Mrs. Dunn's garment bags and shoeboxes, plus her three Pomeranians. Despite predictions of bad weather, Mr. Dunn refused to wait another day, since he had already waited long enough and he firmly believed that all weathermen exaggerate. On their drive south, they could have pulled off the highway anywhere for gas, but Mr. Dunn chose Baltimore. He chose the Texaco off the White Marsh exit. There in the men's room, he washed his hands at the sink beside an odd-looking bald man with a wispy mustache. They chatted about the obvious topic: the storm, which turned out to be even worse than the weathermen predicted, before going their separate ways.

"I remember," I told her. "But like you said, it's Mr. Dunn's word against mine. The cameras at the station weren't working. Nobody else, not even the attendant at the register, remembers seeing Lynch."

Neither responded. I stared down at those papers, a choppy sea of words between us.

"You also said that Dunn is an old man," I went on, "and that chances are good the jury will believe my testimony over his."

"You're right, Sylvie," Louise told me. "I did say those things."

"Then what's wrong?"

The detective took a breath, blew it out. "More information has come forward. And I'm afraid to say it's not good for our case."

Out in the hallway, my sister's voice rose and fell, mixing with the *shhhh* in my ear. I couldn't hear her words but knew she was talking to Dereck, who had started coming around a few days after I saw him in that field. "What information?" I asked, doing my best to shut her out.

"It seems Mr. Dunn is not the only one offering Lynch an alibi," Louise told me.

Rummel slid the papers closer, but the words blurred before my eyes. When he saw me staring at them with no reaction, he asked if he should read it. I nodded, expecting Louise to give me her line about speaking my answers, but she kept quiet.

"This is directly from Mr. Dunn's court interview, all of which is reflected in his affidavit, Sylvie. Here goes: 'After I finished washing my hands and exited the restroom, I walked outside to my car, where my wife was waiting. When I opened the door, one of her dogs scrambled free and made a beeline toward the road. I can barely catch those dogs when there's no snow on the ground, never mind when things are as slick as they were that night. Had I gone after that dog, I risked breaking my hip just like my wife's sister. Had I let him run free, I risked breaking my wife's heart, because she loves those animals even more than she loves me. Thankfully, I didn't have to make a choice.'" He quit reading and looked up at me. "Give you one guess who saved the pooch from becoming roadkill."

I knew—of course, I knew—but something kept me from saying it.

Louise went right on pacing. "You're a smart girl, Sylvie. We don't have to tell you the answer."

"There's more," Rummel said. "Even though the attendant at the register doesn't recall seeing Lynch, he does remember Mr. Dunn. So it's no longer your word against one man's. It's become your word against a small web of people. Three, actually. Four, if you count Lynch."

"But what about his fingerprints and footprints at the church? And the things you said about his motive and his confession that he was there that night?"

"All that's still true. But our defendant now has what's called a time stamp on his alibi. The Dunns may have paid with cash, like Lynch. But unlike him, who could never produce a receipt, the couple turned theirs over. It shows they purchased gas at 1:04 A.M. The same time neighbors near the church reported hearing gunshots."

In a quiet voice, I asked why the Dunns waited so long to come forward. That had all been explained on previous visits, but I brought it up again as a way to stall, if only for a moment longer, since I sensed what was coming next. In the same gentle way he spoke to me that first night at the hospital, Detective Rummel described once more how neither of the Dunns thought about that evening for a long time afterward. Why would they? But that changed when Mrs. Dunn opened the paper a few weeks before and saw a photo of a man who looked familiar. She kept staring at that photo, finally showing it to her husband who immediately recalled the odd-looking man from the restroom, the same man who went on to save his wife's dog in the snowstorm.

When Rummel was done telling that story again, the air around us fell quiet. I thought of Cora, who had escorted Rose and me to meetings at the station when she was first assigned as my caseworker. Legally, she was not allowed in the interview room, and though I could request a break to see her at any time, I never did. Some part of me wished to see her now, however, if only for the distraction of her mindless rambling and cheerful assurances. But after Halloween night, Cora stopped coming by. Instead, Norman had been reassigned as my caseworker. The most he offered by way of explanation was that the Child Protective Services Department sometimes changed its mind, and this was one of those times.

"So what does this mean?" I asked now.

"It means we keep going forward just the same until the trial," Louise told me. "But our case is going to be significantly more challenging. Like you said, though, we have the evidence at the church as well as a clear motive. And the Dunns are elderly and may prove unreliable as we dig deeper. The man working the register that night has an arrest record. Nothing major, marijuana possession years back. But that's something we can use to discredit him in the jury's eyes. Most important, we have your eyewitness account. And when a girl who lost her parents gets up on that stand, when she points her finger at Albert Lynch and tells the court exactly what she saw—"

"Or thought she saw."

For months, those words had been waiting, sealed inside, like those baby birds in the whitewashed houses of my mother's childhood. Now that I'd set them free, a strange, humming silence followed. In the midst of that silence, only Dereck's voice could be heard in the hall, his words unclear, though the warm, meandering way he spoke had a way of soothing me before Detective Rummel said, "Excuse me?"

More quietly this time, I said, "Or thought she saw."

"What do you mean, 'thought she saw'? We've gone over every detail of that night dozens of times, Sylvie. We took your affidavit. We filed it in court. We have a man sitting not twenty miles from here, *behind bars* for the last nine months, awaiting trial on account of what you told us."

Beneath my flimsy tank top, my heart beat hard and fast. The *shhhh* grew louder, muddling even my own shaky voice when I said, "I know what I told you. But it was late. It was dark in that church. I had just woken up. And I was afraid."

Rummel leaned forward, pressed his hands to the table, the same hands that held mine during those visits at the hospital, the same that filled my plastic cup with water and adjusted my pillows. They seemed like someone else's now. "So what exactly are you saying, Sylvie?"

"I'm saying that maybe I was wrong," I told him, tears welling. "Maybe I didn't see him."

Louise came closer, her shoulder pads shifting again as she leaned down and spoke up at last. "If that's the case, this about-face in your testimony is quite serious, seeing as you've never so much as hinted at any doubt before."

"But that's because you made it seem like it had to be him. I insisted, because I felt pressured to give the right answer, the one that you and everybody else wanted."

"Are you saying *we* pressured *you?*"

Hands shaking, I reached for my journal, opened it and read, "'All we need to make certain a jury puts him away for a long time and that your parents rest in peace is your testimony.'" I flipped to another page. "'Your account is the key ingredient to our case. It will bring all the evidence together for your parents' sake.'" Again, I turned. "'We have Mr. Lynch's prints inside the church. We have the details of his threats toward your mother and father. All evidence points to his guilt. But we need you to seal the deal and bring justice in your parents' honor. Isn't that what you want?'"

"Maybe we did tell you those things," Louise said. "But never—*not one single time*—did we encourage you to lie."

"I didn't lie!" I shouted, my voice cracking, tears spilling down my cheeks. "I told you what you wanted to hear! I told you what would help my parents! I gave you the right answer because I didn't want to be wrong!"

"All right," Rummel said, pushing back his chair, standing up too. "Let's everybody calm down. Let's everybody take a breather."

Louise went to the door, yanked it open, stepped out. As her heels clicked away down the hall, Rummel became his old self for a moment, walking to the water cooler, filling a cup for me. After I wiped my eyes and took a sip, he told me he was going to give me a few minutes. "Would you like your sister and her boyfriend to come inside?"

Her boyfriend. It was the first anyone had referred to Dereck that way, though given the amount of time he spent with Rose lately, I supposed it was true. That need to practice speaking my answers didn't seem to matter anymore, so I just shook my head. Rummel went out to the hallway, shutting the door. I heard him say something briefly to my sister before his footsteps receded in the same direction as Louise's.

Alone at the table, I thought of the lingering doubt I'd lived with ever since Detective Rummel first brought Lynch's photo to the hospital and asked if it was the man I saw. How much of his and Louise's talk about making things right for my parents—of being their good daughter one last time, which was what they were saying even if they didn't know it—had helped me to feel certain? And how much was tangled in the lie Rose and I had told . . . were *still* telling? The thought led me to look at the folders Rummel left on the table. As I listened for the return of his footsteps, I leaned forward and opened one. On top lay a photo of a gun that I recognized: a small black pistol with a blunt silver nose. I turned it over, kept searching. Most details I already knew, but I found a piece of information buried in those papers that I'd always wondered about. I read the line over and over again, until Rummel's thudding footsteps moved down the hall in my direction. Quickly, I began to close the folder, but not before I noticed words scratched randomly on the inside in blocky script:

> *Howard Mason. Brother of male victim. Lacks verifiable alibi in the days surrounding murders. Motive?*

"Where's Louise?" I asked as Rummel opened the door, seconds after I pushed that folder away.

He stopped a moment, taking in the sight of me at the table, those folders he'd left behind. "Ms. Hock decided she's done for the afternoon. We all are, actually."

I reached for my father's tote and began to stand, but the detective held up a hand and told me to hang on a second. I sat back down, studying him. Judging from his grim face and hunched shoulders, I got the feeling that he and Louise had a fight about me. He folded his arms in front of his chest and said, "Here's how this is going to work, Sylvie. Right now, it's Friday. Just after three. Not much is going to get done at this point. But come Monday, nine A.M., the gears start turning. So we'll give you till then. That's—"

"Sixty-six hours," I said, staring at the watch on his hairy wrist.

Rummel glanced at it too. "Is that what it works out to?" He fixed me with a look I didn't recognize. "You're a quick thinker, Sylvie. And that's right: you've got sixty-six hours to consider exactly what you did or did not see in the church last winter. First thing Monday you will report back here and you will let us know whether or not you'll be recanting your account of that evening. Understood?"

"Understood."

Rummel gathered his folders from the table as I sat watching.

"And if I do recant, what happens?"

"What happens, Sylvie, is that the game changes. Significantly. Lynch will likely be released. We'll be back to square one."

"And will you look at other suspects?"

"That's my job."

"Who?" I asked, thinking of the note scratched inside one of those folders.

"Well, if it comes to that, I'd count on you and your sister to help. We should have talked about other possibilities in greater detail early on, before zeroing in on just Lynch. That was my slipup. But if things change come Monday, I'll want to hear from both of you if there was anyone else who had reason to do your parents harm. Someone you might not have thought of before. Also, we should talk again about why they left Rose at home that night. I know you both said that was normal, but other people might not think so."

Mr. Knothead—that was the name of Rose's pet rabbit who once lived in the cage out by the well. She had begged for him one Christmas years before and given him that name on account of the bony lumps between his ears. Unlikely as it seemed, I thought of that twitchy-nosed creature then, the way I used to press my cheek to its soft white fur, feeling the frantic *tic-tic-tic* of his heart beneath. That's how my heart felt the moment Rummel brought up my parents leaving Rose at home—a detail that had been dissected early on in the case but had since been accepted as fact. Now it was back, and I'd have to repeat the same story again, being more careful than ever not to give away the truth.

I took a breath. Swallowed. My mouth felt impossibly dry, but there was no more water in the paper cup Rummel had given me. Even if there had been, I thought it best not to speak for fear he might pick up some signal—a wavering in my voice, like ripples on water—that would give birth to new suspicions. And so I said nothing more. I stood from the table. I picked up my father's tote. I tucked my journal away.

"Guess you write about more than school in that little book of yours. Those things you read to Ms. Hock and me before? Not exactly notes on a homework assignment." Before I could respond, he turned and stepped out into the hall.

I took a minute to compose myself, then followed. Rose was sitting on a bench, flipping through one of the random safety brochures we both took to reading while we waited. *The Heimlich Maneuver. Stop, Drop, and Roll. Pedestrian Precautions.* By now, we were prepared for just about anything. I wondered if the detective might want to see her alone again, but he simply informed her in a more formal tone than usual that we were both required to be back at the station Monday morning at nine. As they spoke, I glanced down the hall where Dereck hunched over a water fountain, his height making it appear like one meant for children.

After Rummel walked off, my sister turned to me and asked what happened inside that room. Again, I glanced at Dereck, guzzling away still. "Maybe we shouldn't talk about it here—"

"Old Seven drinks more than a farm animal," Rose told me, "so it'll be a while. And the guy wonders why he has to pee all the time."

"He's your boyfriend," I told her, testing the label.

"I wouldn't go that far, Sylvie. Now what happened?"

Quickly, quietly, I ticked off the details about the second snowbird, about the dog that broke loose, about Lynch saving it from running into the street. I was about to tell her more when she stood from the bench. I watched her walk to the bulletin board, tack the brochure back where she found it next to one I'd already read about the dangers of going near a live wire after a storm. "I already knew that stuff," she told me, turning around again. "They talked to me first, remember?"

The doubt I felt about who I'd seen inside the church was something I'd never confessed to anyone before—not even Rose. I was afraid of how she would react if she knew I'd let it slip out at last, but she needed to know, so I pushed on, "Mrs. Dunn gives him a stronger alibi, which means—"

"It means it's some senile old couple's word against yours, Sylvie. You watch. It'll turn out she's half blind and he's bat-shit crazy. Or that the time was set wrong on the crap register at the station. So whatever you do, don't start panicking."

"Panicking about what?" Dereck had made his way back from the fountain. He towered over us, wearing the same barn jacket and clingy sweats as when we met.

"Nothing for you to worry about, Seven," Rose said.

"You okay, Sylvie?" he asked. "You don't look so great."

"I'm fine," I told Dereck, which was hardly the case. I spotted a clock on the wall, and the calculation seemed to do itself in my mind: sixty-five hours and forty-two minutes until I had to report back here and give Rummel and Louise an answer.

"Okay, then," my sister said. "Let's try to forget all this for a little while and go get some money."

All week long, we'd been waiting for the day when we could go to the Dial U.S.A. office and pick up Rose's check. Since striking our deal, my evenings had been spent making calls to faraway cities listed on number sheets Fran provided. At the start, most people cut me off to ask, "How old are you, young lady?" The ones who didn't wanted to know if it was some kind of prank. So I practiced making my voice sound mature while memorizing the instruction sheet Fran included for Rose but she never bothered with: *1. Be direct and clear with questions. 2. If respondent wavers, state exactly what you want to know, thus keeping respondent on point. 3. Never say, "Thank you for your time," because time is money and Dial U.S.A. does not pay for opinions.* Ridiculous as those rules sounded, they helped me rack up more surveys than Rose predicted. It meant I could begin replenishing my savings *and* buy Boshoff a cookbook.

On our drive into Baltimore, we passed the church and I did my best not to look at it. My sister did the same, pushing in her AC/DC cassette and beating her hands on the wheel. Dereck spread his legs east and west as he sat between us, so one of his tree trunks pressed against me, the other against my sister. More than once, Rose stopped singing to say, "Would you close your legs already, Seven? You're like an old whore!" He did as she said, but soon they drifted, and I'd feel him there, which I might not have minded if I didn't feel so bothered about what happened back at the station.

Every parking space outside Dial U.S.A. was taken except one with a safety cone in the middle. Rose got out and tossed the cone in the back of the truck before pulling in and cutting the engine. Dereck and I watched her walk toward the building and spin through the revolving door, his leg pressed to mine still. Once she'd been sucked inside, I glanced at the clock on the dashboard, something I'd been trying hard not to do: sixty-five hours and three minutes. The rabbitlike *tic-tic-tic* of my heart persisted.

"Want to guess?" Dereck asked me. When I didn't answer, he added, "Our game, I mean. Do you want to guess?"

What I wanted was for him to stop talking. My mind was too preoccupied with the myriad of unthinkable ways things might unfold now. Newspaper headlines would shout from the pages that I had been wrong to accuse Albert Lynch, that because of me, he'd been waiting behind bars all these months without bail. Worse still, Rummel and his men were bound to uncover the lie I'd told about Rose being home that night. Even though I knew my sister was not capable of killing her very own mother and father, no matter how troubled their relationship had become, that's the way it would look to the world. And it would appear as though I'd been a part of it too.

"Are you okay?" Dereck asked, nudging me with one of his tree-trunk legs.

"Not really."

"Want to talk about it?"

"No. Actually, I think I need to go for a walk."

"A walk? Where?"

I put my hand on the door handle. "Just around the lot. Until Rose gets back."

Dereck placed his hand on my arm, gently tugged it away from the door. "Hold on. Whatever it is, let's try taking your mind off it. Besides, selfishly I don't want to sit here by myself."

I sighed, doing my best to give him the person he wanted. "A woodshop accident?" I said.

"Already guessed that."

"I did?"

"One of your first actually. Not counting the turkeys."

"A raccoon with rabies?"

"Guessed that too."

"A rabid possum?"

"I know you don't want hints, Sylvie. But let me save you some trouble. No humans were harmed by animals in the making of my missing fingers."

Like a lot of Dereck's jokes, that one didn't quite work, but I forced a smile. Normally, the expression came naturally whenever we played the strange game the two of us had concocted in the random moments Rose left us alone. "No animals. No wood-shop or chain-saw accidents. This is tougher than I thought."

"Lots of ways a person can lose three fingers, Sylvie. You have to think harder."

"Does my sister know how it happened?"

He used his good hand to reach up and biff a Scooby head he'd given Rose. Scooby hung from the rearview mirror whenever we rode with Dereck. The second he was gone, Rose tossed him on the floor. The abuse had left the dog with a scuffed nose. "Robably," Dereck said. "Retty ruch reveryone rin rour raduating rass rew."

Probably. Pretty much everyone in our graduating class knew.

In addition to learning to talk so people would answer surveys, I'd also developed the newfound skill of deciphering Scooby-speak. "How long did you two date back in school anyway?"

"Ra ronth," he told me, before switching to his real voice. "Maybe two. Not long. It was probably when I was sixteen and she was fifteen, I guess. How old are you, Sylvie?"

The question surprised me. "Fourteen. Fifteen soon. In April. How about you?"

"Nineteen. Last August."

We were quiet, staring at that revolving door, waiting for Rose to be spit out of the building again. I knew the mood would shift the moment she appeared. Maybe that's what gave me the courage to say, "Four years. That's not much."

The words hung in the air until I felt Dereck's leg move away from mine. "You're right. But what a difference they make."

I kept quiet.

"Trust me, Sylvie. Things are so different than I thought they'd be back then. I mean, where did everybody go?"

"Everybody?"

"The people Rose and I went to school with. After my graduation, they just . . . left."

"Didn't you ever think of leaving too? You know, heading off to college."

"That'll make sense for you in a few more years. Not me."

"Why not? Your grades weren't good enough?"

"Actually, my grades were never a problem. You might not believe this, but I was in the Honors Society."

"I believe you," I said in a voice that sounded like I didn't.

"I can tell." He laughed. "I'll show you my yearbook someday and prove it." His leg drifted against mine once more, and he said, "I have my reasons for not wanting to go to college. I'll tell you sometime."

"What about the army?"

"*Nahh*. Too chicken. And not sure they'd take me. Hard to fire a gun when you're missing so many fingers."

I stared out the window. The *shhhh* in my ear. The *tic-tic-tic* of my heart. The mention of a gun. It was all too much.

"Sorry," Dereck told me after a moment.

"It's okay."

"Have you been back there? The church, I mean? I saw the way you barely glanced at it when we drove by before."

I shook my head. The conversation had nudged my mind back to what I should have been focusing on. I remembered that note about Uncle Howie inside the folder and wondered if that's why we had stopped hearing from him.

Dereck fell silent next to me, and not long after my sister emerged from the building. When she climbed into the truck, Rose tossed the envelope with her check on the dashboard. On our way to the bank, Dereck asked her about the safety cone still in the back. It belonged to Sheila, Rose told us, a woman who also worked at Dial U.S.A. "Sheila claims to have dibs on the spot. She throws a hissy if anyone even looks at it. It's not a handicapped space but may as well be because it's so close to the front door. That's why she wants it to herself. She's as lazy as they come."

"So how did she get her hands on a safety cone?"

"Her husband works road crew. And the woman has the balls to leave it in the spot to keep everyone away, like it's reserved parking."

"Not anymore," Dereck said. "Now that you have it."

"Oh, trust me. She'll have a new one tomorrow. Sheila pops them out like a chicken laying eggs. One of these days I'll shove them all right back up her ass."

Dereck laughed. Since we were pulling up to the drive-through window at the bank, and I was about to get paid, I should have felt happy enough to laugh too. But I couldn't manage it. Soon, Rose was scooping an envelope with cash from the teller's drawer. She asked for a lollipop they normally gave to children and popped it in her mouth, not bothering to get any for Dereck and me. I watched her suck on the thing while counting the bills before setting the envelope on the dashboard. As we pulled away from the bank, loose coins chattered inside.

I cleared my throat and asked, "Rose, can I have my seventy-seven dollars now?" The question came out just as she pumped up a song; a scratchy-voiced singer wailed about shaking someone all night long. Once more, Rose beat her hands on the steering wheel and crooned away. As we picked up speed, wind rushed through the windows, whipping her hair. I watched Dereck bat it away as the envelope slid back and forth across the dashboard with every turn. At last, the shaking all night long wound down, and Dereck smiled, showcasing his wolfish teeth. He said quietly in my good ear, "Must be morning."

When the inside of the truck grew silent, I knew I didn't have much time before the next song started. I used my most mature, survey-taking voice to say, "Rose, can I please have my seventy-seven dollars now?"

"Sorry, squirt. But you aren't getting that money just yet."

"Why do we have to wait until we get home? I want—"

"I'm not talking about waiting until we get home. I'm talking about you contributing to the expenses for a change."

"But that's not the deal we made."

"Well, it is now."

"I'll give some toward expenses, Rose, but not all. I have plans for that money."

"What *plans?*"

I shouldn't have told her how my savings had been wiped out after that summer Abigail came to live with us. I shouldn't have told her about the cookbook for Boshoff. But I did, and it ignited a rant about the people she had to waste money on too. "One is named Mr. Maryland Light and Power. Another is named Mrs. Baltimore Oil and Heat. They're *bills,* Sylvie. *Bills* we need to pay. So if you think buying a book for some crap counselor takes priority over keeping the lights and heat on, or putting food on the tab—"

"What food?" I could not keep from saying. "You mean Popsicles?"

"Surprise! They cost money too, and I don't see you complaining when you're shoving them in your face!"

"Calm down," Dereck tried, but nobody was listening to him anymore.

His leg felt too heavy against mine all of a sudden, and I shoved it away. "I worked hard getting those surveys, and I deserve the money!"

"Sorry, Sylvie. But the answer is no."

If my sister were smarter, she would have snatched the envelope off the dashboard by then. But maybe she didn't suspect me of being capable of what came next. As we rounded another corner, I watched that envelope with its bills and chattering coins slide in her direction. Before it could slide away for good, I sucked in a breath and did something I hadn't since that night with Dot years before: *The Scream.*

The sound caused Dereck to flinch as I lunged across his lap and grabbed at the envelope. Rose let go of the wheel and grabbed at it too. Before either of us could get it, the money slipped from the dashboard, coins spraying on the way down. I tried to catch what I could, my hand brushing Dereck's crotch in the process, which led him to grab my arm. The truck swerved. Rose put her hands on the wheel again, jerking us back to the right side of the road.

"Jesus Christ!" she screamed. "You almost killed us."

I wriggled free from Dereck's grip then dropped to the floor. Down on the gritty mats, I spotted the envelope by Rose's sneakers. I reached out but she kicked it away. Again, the truck swerved, this time more suddenly and forcefully. Someone in another vehicle laid on the horn as Rose slammed one foot down on the envelope, the other on the brake, then cut the wheel. I looked up to see Dereck's square face as the sky swirled above and things got bumpy.

And then, all at once, everything went still.

As the sound of the horn faded, I stayed on the floor, staring at Dereck's giant, unlaced work boots next to my sister's small black sneakers. I watched as Rose reached down and grabbed the envelope, quickly shoving it in her jeans. Three quarters. Two dimes. Three pennies. Since I didn't know what else to do, I gathered up those coins, a pathetic ninety-eight cents that I slipped into my pocket. When I sat up, I saw that we had made our way into an empty lot with patches of tar and muddy grass between two industrial buildings. I glanced at the clock, trying not to think about how much time I wasted doing those surveys—how much time I was still wasting not getting the answers I really needed.

"You're not getting the money," Rose told me. "And I don't want to hear any more about it."

Good, I thought as my hand found the door handle, *because I have nothing left to say on the topic.* Before Dereck could stop me, I shoved open the door and jumped out, tumbling onto the damp earth. I'd left my tote bag inside but managed to snatch my journal on the way and keep it with me.

"Sylvie!" Dereck got out and lumbered in my direction. "Are you all right?"

I stood and began hunting for one of my flip-flops, which had come free.

He pointed toward a patch of tall, dead grass. "There."

I limped over, picked it up, slipped it on.

"Just let her be." Rose hadn't bothered to get out of the truck, but she hung her head out the window and called to Dereck. "The girl's brain has finally shit the bed. She'll come to her senses and find her way home soon enough."

"Better go," I told him. "Your girlfriend's waiting."

"You don't have to be so upset, Sylvie. I know it's seventy-seven dollars, and you worked hard for it. But in the grand scheme of things, it's not much. You're going to make that and more in your sleep someday."

My sister revved the engine. Watching her made me think of the detail I found in Rummel's folder. Not the scribble about Howie, but that other thing I'd always wondered but never knew. "How about fifty dollars?" I asked him. "Is that a lot?"

"Fifty? I thought you said you made—"

"I'm not talking about what I made. I'm talking about how much Albert Lynch paid—or *offered* to pay Rose to call my parents and get them to the church that night."

Dereck's gaze shifted to my feet. He began cracking the knuckles on his bad hand—thumb, index finger then stopped abruptly, as though remembering the rest were no longer there. "But what does that matter if it's not true? The man is lying. Rose was home with you. You both said so all along."

I stared at him, thinking how easy it would be to let that final secret free.

"Train leaves the station in ten seconds," my sister called out her window. "All aboard or you're shit out of luck."

Dereck lifted his head and looked at me. "Get back in the truck, Sylvie."

"No," I told him, feeling the *tic-tic-tic* of my heart.

It seemed he might take a couple of quick steps, pick me up, and force me to go with them. But I was wrong. "Well, if you aren't going to come, then at least take my jacket. It's cold out, and you're not dressed warm enough. You never are."

"Ten seconds," Rose said from behind Dereck. "Nine. Eight. Seven . . ."

"Quit your counting!" he yelled, the first I ever heard him speak up to her. He pulled off his battered barn jacket and held it out to me. When I didn't take it, he tossed the coat on a patch of tar between us. He removed his boots too, set them beside the coat. With that, he turned, walked toward the truck, and climbed inside. A moment later, Rose stepped on the gas, the tires spun in the mud, and the truck picked up speed and disappeared.

Their sudden absence left a vacuum of quiet behind. A cool breeze moved through the trees surrounding the field, bringing with it the memory of Rummel's voice:

You've got sixty-six hours to consider exactly what you did or did not see in the church that night last winter. After that, your time is up.

I stepped forward onto the patch of tar where Dereck had left his boots and jacket. It looked as if he had been sucked into the earth, pulled down to the underworld depicted in the pages of those books my father kept in the curio hutch. I slid out of my flip-flops, stepped into Dereck's boots, roomy and warm from his large feet. I lifted his jacket, put that on too. Slowly, clumsily, I began walking out of the field in the direction of those industrial buildings. I hadn't let on to Dereck, but I knew exactly what I was going to do once they were gone. It was something I'd decided while down on those truck mats, getting knocked around, same as that Scooby head. Inside my journal was the letter I found beneath Rose's bed. For more than two weeks now, I'd been carrying it with me, taking it out and reading the words:

> *Dear Rose, I'm probably the last person or spirit on God's green earth you want to hear from right now. Yet, here I am writing you anyway . . .*

Those coins from the floor of the truck, the only income I'd see from all my hard work, might not have been enough to replenish my savings or buy poor Boshoff that cookbook. But it was enough to make a call to the number on the top of that letter. If my parents were alive, they never would have wanted me to do it, but he was the only person who knew more about their lives, about our family, than me. And maybe, I thought, he might be able to tell me something about that night and all that had come before it.

I had little more than sixty-three hours left.

I was going to call Sam Heekin and ask for his help.

GIRLS

There should be a word to describe the specific kind of melancholy that creeps up during the final days of a trip. Whatever it would be called, that feeling began infecting each of us the very next morning in Ocala—a bit too soon, considering our time away from Dundalk was only just beginning. The plan had always been that we would spend a few days after my parents' lecture doing what most tourists do in the Sunshine State: going to Disney World. We stuck to the plan but, unfortunately, that end-of-vacation feeling stuck to us.

More than anything, what brought it on was the dramatic change in Rose.

Over breakfast at an IHOP off the interstate, my sister was quiet and polite. Not overly friendly. Not chatty. But she smiled and paid attention when each of us spoke. She answered questions when asked. She ordered chocolate chip pancakes. Used her knife and fork to cut them before chewing softly and cleaning her plate. On the way out of the restaurant to get back on the road to Orlando, she even thanked my parents for the meal.

Those were the results my parents had hoped for when my father dragged her out of that room. And yet, even though they seemed pleased, the change was so sudden, so drastic, I had the sense none of us really trusted it.

Since my mother and father were never ones for rides, they spent most of their time at Disney World waiting on benches while Rose and I stood in eternal lines. I knew most of the attractions didn't appeal to my sister, yet she climbed on board and buckled up, feigning excitement as we glided through Wendy and Peter's window out over the twinkling lights of London. She put on the same cheery face as we floated through countries where children sang "It's a Small World" in so many different languages. When it came time for Space Mountain, I suspected that hurtling through the dark might shake out the true Rose. But same as me, she gripped the safety bars and held in her screams. In the end, she offered just one glimpse of the person hidden beneath. While riding our "doom buggy" through the Haunted Mansion, a trick mirror reflected the image of a ghost in a top hat seated between us.

"What?" I asked when I saw Rose sneering in the reflection.

"Nothing."

"Not *nothing*. What?"

"I was thinking that they should have come on this ride."

"Mom and Dad?"

"Who else, stupid?"

"Why?"

"For starters, maybe they could have taken a picture of that ghost and put it on the screen at their next phony talk."

"You don't believe them?"

"Do you, Sylvie?"

"Yes. Well, at least I think I do."

"Think harder. Uncle Howie told me stuff that might convince you otherwise."

"What stuff?"

In the same way that ghost appeared in the mirror then vanished, the true Rose had appeared for a moment too, but then she gave a little shake to her head, as though flinching at the thought of something unpleasant, before vanishing as well. Around her wrist, she wore an elastic band I'd noticed for the first time that morning. All day long, I'd been watching her snap it until the skin beneath grew red and irritated. She yanked and released it then too, telling me to forget she said anything. "Let's just enjoy the ride. It's fun, huh?"

"Guess so," I told her.

When our buggy wheeled to a stop, we followed the path of railings outside, where the sun felt harsh compared to the dim lights of the ride. In the throbbing heat, our parents waited. The warm weather had led them to abandon their usual attire. Rather than a column dress, my mother wore jeans and a pale purple top I'd never seen before. Rather than a brown suit, my father wore a pocket tee and plaid shorts, putting his hairy legs on display. Even though they were dressed not much differently than other adults in the park, I caught people staring anyway.

I'd brought my underlined copy of *Jane Eyre* with a plan to mark more passages I liked while waiting in line. But the thought of that conversation Rose and Howie had about me not being like kids my age led me to instead give the book to my mother, who had begun rereading it herself. My father sat by her side, a glazed expression on his face as he dabbed his forehead with a hankie and watched people pass by. "How was the ride?" he asked when he saw us. "Anyone inside ask for help from your mother and me?"

I looked at Rose, wondering if that sneer might reappear. Instead, she gave my father her cheery new smile. "No, but they should have. It's pretty scary in there."

"Next stop, Frontierland," he told her. "Don't think we'll have much to worry about there. Except cowboys and Indians."

From Frontierland to Adventureland and every other land in the park, Rose did not break from her new persona again. And when the vacation ended at last, we drove north with her seated quietly beside me in the backseat. Instead of shouting obscure scriptures, she took her turn reading that now beat-up, dog-eared copy of *Jane Eyre*. All the while, I glanced over to see her snapping that elastic against her wrist, which had become even redder and more irritated.

Once we settled back in Dundalk, where the air had grown cooler and autumn loomed, Rose kept up her good behavior. She began junior year by joining the track team and doing homework each night without complaint. Some evenings, she even made Hamburger Helper or sloppy Joes so my mother could get a break from cooking. Rose also brought home her first boyfriend: a senior named Roger who had the straightest part I'd ever seen, a crisp white line that divided his scalp. Except to answer my father's questions about his academic interests and to compliment the food, Roger was mostly quiet during dinner, even quieter when we watched a documentary afterward and he held Rose's hand on the couch. After that night, Roger didn't come around again, though Rose didn't seem to care. As weeks passed, and still there was no trouble from her, I had the feeling our parents had begun to trust that my sister had settled down again.

I started to believe it too.

In late September, Rose's seventeenth birthday arrived. Since Rose had begun attending confirmation classes at Saint Bartholomew, my parents invited the new parish priest to dinner. Every birthday, my mother baked a Lady Baltimore cake, which, despite the name, she told us was not a Maryland tradition but a southern one. Father Coffey, however, took it upon himself to arrive with an ice cream cake. When he set it on the table, we all stared at the words *Happy Birthday, Rosie* in loopy cursive across the top. "Who the hell is Rosie?"—that's the question my sister normally would've muttered beneath her breath. Instead, after Father explained that the people at the shop slipped in the *i* all on their own, Rose laughed and said she kind of liked being Rosie for a night.

After dinner, I cleared the table and arranged candles on Rosie's cake while my mother's creation—with its white frosting, nuts, and candied fruit—had been banished to the refrigerator out of politeness. If my mother was bothered, she didn't let it show. She sang "Happy Birthday" just the same, her voice more pleasant than the rest of ours, before my sister squeezed her eyes shut then blew out the flames in a single breath. As Rose sank a knife into the cake, my mother asked what my sister had wished for.

"She can't tell you," I said, watching the bricks of vanilla and chocolate ooze apart.

"Why not?"

"Because then the wish won't come true."

"Who made that rule?" my father asked.

Smart as my parents were, some basics about the world escaped them, but it usually came down to a lack of knowledge about things like MTV and Swatches and Reeboks. "I don't know," I told him.

"Wishes are like certain prayers," Father Coffey said, seated between my mother and father and wearing a black turtleneck. "Some are best to carry privately in your heart."

Our family was used to Father Vitale, who had come to dinner many times. Vitale never brought his own cake, never showed up without his collar, and never challenged my father even on a point as small as that. But Vitale was retiring soon, which was why Coffey had been brought to Dundalk. My father considered his comment before saying, "I suppose that's one way to look at it. But to my way of thinking, prayers and wishes are nothing alike. The former is a sacred conversation with the Lord. The latter is a whimsical expression of worldly desire."

My father seemed to be waiting for Coffey to keep the debate alive, but the man stared down at the fast-melting cake on his plate and let the point die.

"Well, then," my father said. "Since what we are talking about here is a simple birthday wish, I think the rule seems a bit silly. Don't you, Rose?"

The rest of us had been calling my sister Rosie for a good hour by then, so my mother assumed the question had been meant for her. "Maybe so," she answered, poking at the dark crumbles with her fork. "Although there's nothing wrong with keeping something to yourself, Sylvester."

"And what about you, birthday girl?" he asked. "Do you think it's silly?"

"A little," Rose said.

"If you can't tell your family and your priest what you want most, who can you tell? Besides, depending on the wish, we might be able to help make it come true."

No one spoke for a moment after that, though the silence in the kitchen begged for the news of what Rose's wish had been. My sister must have felt it too, because after she took a bite of a baby blue flower on top of that cake, which left smudges on her lips, she said, "Do you all really want to know?"

"Only if you feel comfortable sharing," my mother said.

Rose eyed my father. "You promise you won't get mad?"

"Promise," he told her.

"Okay, then." It didn't take my mother's gift to sense from the way Rose inhaled that she felt nervous. "I wished . . . I wished that I could get my learner's permit."

The phone rang. My father excused himself, slid back his chair, and crossed the room to pick it up. As he talked to the person on the other end, my mother took a bite of cake at last, and asked in a quiet voice, "A learner's permit for what?"

Again, I thought of that disconnect between them and the world. Father Coffey and I both spoke up for my sister, saying, "For her driver's license."

My mother mouthed an *Ohhh,* though that was all. I knew she'd never offer an official answer until my father weighed in, but he was deep in conversation by then. "Of course I remember you," he said into the phone as he stretched the cord tighter into the living room. "I did get the letter. It was very flattering. But, well, I need to speak with my wife about the matter. We make all decisions together so she gets an equal vote. . . ." And after a pause: "We liked it very much. Thank you again. We will certainly consider your request." With that, my father hung up and returned to the table. I expected the topic to go back to my sister's wish, but my mother asked who had called.

"That reporter," he told her.

"Which reporter?"

"You know, the one from the *Dundalk Eagle.*"

She squinted, as though reading something in small print. "Samuel Heekin?"

"The one and only."

"I see," my mother said. "But we gave him the interview for that paper months ago. The story has already run. What could he possibly want?"

"Says he's interested in meeting again. He's got this idea about writing a book."

"About?"

"What else?" My father smiled. "*Us.* Who would have thought?"

"Oh, Sylvester. I don't like the idea. A book only invites more attention."

"I understand, my dear. But let's discuss it later. Now Rose, about your wish—"

"I'm sorry," my sister said, pushing the last of her melting blue flower around her plate. "Never mind. I shouldn't have said anything. It was a dumb idea."

"It's not dumb," my father told her.

Rose looked up. "It's not?"

"Not in the least. After all, you're seventeen now. I think it's a very smart idea."

"You do?"

He smiled and looked to my mother to see if she objected, though she gave no sign of it. "Yes, of course. We know how your mother hates to drive, so it will be handy having another person around here willing to get behind the wheel. Of course, there's just the Datsun, so it's not like you'd have your own car."

"That's all right," my sister told him. "I don't need my own car."

"I hear there's a driving school right over on Holabird Avenue," Father Coffey said.

"We don't need to waste money on a school. I can teach her, same as my father taught me. Except I promise not to yell the way he did if you forget to signal. Okay?"

"Okay!" Rose leaped up from the table and actually hugged him, a sight I had not seen in a long time. She even kissed his forehead, leaving the last of the baby blue smudges from her lips on his creased skin.

Happy as that moment made them both, some part of me still worried and waited for that once hostile Rose to resurface. I thought for certain the driving lessons would end in a screaming match. But I was wrong. Things went so smoothly that within a few months Rose had her license, with a DMV photo that showed her smiling big and wide. And she loved nothing more than being behind the wheel, so she found any excuse. When I stayed after school, she picked me up. Sunday mornings when the four of us needed to get to church in the gym, Rose was always ready and waiting at the wheel. She even began grocery shopping with my mother just so she could drive. Best of all, as far as my father was concerned, she willingly played chauffeur when we headed out on more of my parents' lecture trips and television bookings.

Hagley Museum and Library in Wilmington, Delaware . . .

Philips Convention Center in Pittsburgh, Pennsylvania . . .

Webster Center in Cambridge, Massachusetts . . .

None of those places or any others brought about the drama of Ocala. Rather, things went as originally intended: while my mother and father talked to crowds, which grew larger each time, or when they appeared on a dozen local and a few national TV shows, Rose and I waited in the green-room. No grapes thrown at the ceiling. No sneaking through doors to hear what they were saying. My sister simply passed the time spinning the car keys on her finger while reading those classics about orphans my mother pressed upon us, books Rose once refused. I spent the hours reading as well, though a different type of book held my attention now:

Encyclopedia of Visions, Possessions, Demons & Demonology by M. E. Roche.

Hard to believe, but soon nearly two years had passed since that visit from Dot, which meant the deadline for the Maryland State Student Essay Contest had rolled around again. This year I was working on a slightly less overblown paper than my first contest submission. Late one night, after hours spent working on my new entry about the Cold War, I went down-stairs for a drink. I had just turned on the faucet when a voice came from behind, "You a real girl? Or one of those things I keep seeing?"

I whipped around. A man was slumped in a chair at the table, his face riddled with so many creases and folds it looked stitched together. His eyes were bleary and red, his salt-and-pepper hair mussed from sleep, his beard scraggly. "You're . . ." I began as the water kept running behind me, " . . . you're not supposed to be up here."

The man did not respond. He just blinked his bloodshot eyes and tapped his fingers against the table in such a determined way he might have been typing. A few nights before, I'd heard the phone ring then lis-tened from my bed to the knock on the front door not long after, followed by the *clomp-clomp-clomp* of footsteps heading to the basement. So I knew we had someone with us in the house, but I'd never actually seen him. I'd never actually seen any of them before, I realized.

"There's a cot downstairs," I said. "And I saw my father take down a sandwich and a pitcher of juice earlier tonight. So you have everything you need down there. My parents don't allow—" I stopped, searching for the word to describe this man and the others my parents welcomed into our home. "They don't allow haunted people up here."

That strange finger tapping of his came to an abrupt stop. He stood from the chair, and I saw that he was much taller than I realized, so tall his head knocked the ceiling lamp that hung above the table, causing it to rock back and forth. In a voice as distant as his expression, he told me, "Your mother. She's been reading scripture to me. Things in that book never sounded so good as they do they coming from her mouth. And your father, well, he mostly asks questions about the things I've been seeing."

The shifting light created a helter-skelter feeling in the kitchen, making me all the more nervous. I reached behind and turned off the faucet before walking to the basement door and pulling it open. When the man moved by me toward the steps, the air smelled like sweat and old clothes and damp leaves. At the top of the stairs, he paused, and I couldn't help but ask, "What did you mean before? When you wanted to know if I was a real girl?"

"Since the night I got here, I've been seeing things. Down in that basement."

I looked past him at the bottom of the stairs, expecting to see whatever it was dart between the shadows. "What . . . things?"

He just shook his head and started down the steps without answering. I watched until he was gone from view, then shut the door. Before going back up to my room, I found myself walking to the curio hutch in the living room and staring at all those books behind the glass cabinet. I thought of what that man just said. Then I thought of my sister sneering at that phony ghost at Disney World, of her asking if I believed the things our parents claimed to be true. In search of some sort of proof, I dragged over a chair, climbed up, and reached for the key my father kept hidden on top. Possessive as he was about those books, it was odd how carelessly they were shelved: haphazardly piled, upside down, wrong side in. I pulled out what looked to be the oldest and thickest of all. Back in my room, I made a cover out of a paper bag, same as for my textbooks, writing simply *HIS-TORY* on the front.

Inside the worn pages, I *did* discover a history, different from any I'd read before, about people from long ago who suffered strange afflictions and reported otherworldly visions. Of all the stories I read, none stayed with me so much as those about the girls. The first I encountered was Marie des Vallées, born in 1590 into a poor family in Saint-Sauveur-Landelin, France. At the age of twelve, Marie's father died. Her mother remarried a butcher, "whose humour and manners resembled those of the animals he worked with" and who beat Marie with a stick until she fled. For years she lived on the streets until in 1609 a female "tuteur" took her in. After moving into the woman's house, Marie began to experience what the clergy labeled as symptoms of demonic possession. On countless occasions, she fell to the ground, "mouth agape, emitting otherworldly cries of agony and terror." If she walked by a church, never mind attempting to enter, her body collapsed and convulsed until she was carried away.

Another girl, more famous than the first Marie, was also born in France, though later, in 1844. Her name: Marie-Bernarde Soubirous, though she came to be known simply as Bernadette. A devout peasant girl, Bernadette began seeing apparitions at the age of fourteen. She described her first sighting as, "a gentle Light that brightened the dark recess, and there in the Light, a smile. A girl dressed in a white dress, tied with a blue ribbon, a white veil on her head, and a yellow rose on each foot." Despite early skepticism, the church declared Bernadette's sightings worthy of belief. The site in Lourdes where her body was buried became a shrine where millions search for miracles.

And then came a different kind of trip for our family. I first learned of it when Rose picked me up one Friday from school. On the dashboard, I noticed a map with a route highlighted in yellow. "Planning a vacation?" I asked.

"If I was, it would be to pretty much any place *but* the Buckeye State."

"Texas?"

Rose groaned. "Texas is the Lone Star State, Sylvie. Buckeye, that's Ohio. Anyway, Dad will tell you, but we're going there this weekend."

"For another talk?"

Rose shook her head. "You know those calls we've been getting at night lately? Apparently they've all been from the same person."

"Who?"

"Don't know. Didn't ask. My guess: the owner of a house where weird crap keeps happening. Or maybe a parent with a kid who's messed up, like so many of them."

It had been some time since I thought of that girl in the bushes out front of the convention center in Ocala—long enough that it took me a moment to pull the memory into focus. As I stared out the window of the Datsun, I saw not the houses we passed, but that father with blood on his face as he called into the shadows. I remembered the way he approached my mother for help, the way she knelt, humming that song while reaching a hand toward those shiny, blinking eyes. "Albert and Abigail Lynch," I said aloud as we made the turn onto Butter Lane.

"What?"

"That night in Ocala. Remember the man with the scratch marks? The one calling into the bushes?"

Rose smiled. "How could I forget a freak like that?"

"I thought maybe he was calling for a lost cat. But it was actually his daughter. A girl named Abigail. Mom helped them after you drove off with Uncle Howie."

The most Rose had to say was, "Mom helped them, huh?"

"Yes. I witnessed it."

"Well, good for you, Sylvie." When Rose spoke next, we were turning into the driveway, and a trace of her old self shimmered beneath her words. "We better go inside and pack. Dad wants to leave at some ungodly hour in the morning so we get there by noon. You've seen firsthand how helpful they are when people need them."

Five and a half hours—that's how long it took to reach the Ohio state line, another two to Columbus. Rose drove except for a break in Pennsylvania when my father insisted on taking the wheel so she could rest. Otherwise, he sat beside her in the passenger seat, making notes on a legal pad. My mother sat in the back with me, knitting or reading her bible while humming that tune I recognized by now but still did not know the words to. My book kept me busy, but the more I read, the more the stories began to seem like just that: *stories*. Ancient and far away. Not much different than if I'd been reading about a world inhabited by witches who tempted pretty girls with poison apples. I began to get the sinking feeling that I was getting further from proof instead of closer.

At a gas station stop in Wheeling Creek, Ohio, I ran inside to pee in the grimy restroom. When I came out, my mother and father stood by the car, stretching their legs while Rose waited behind the wheel. As I got closer, I caught scraps of their conversation.

My mother: " . . . scratches again."

My father: " . . . needs to be removed from the home."

But that was the most I heard. When we climbed into the car, however, my mind filled with thoughts of the Lynches.

The plan had been that my parents would pick up Kentucky Fried Chicken for Rose and me then leave us at the hotel until they returned. When we arrived, though, the gum-chomping woman at the counter informed us that the room would not be cleaned for a few hours. After some back and forth, my parents decided Rose and I would drop them in the Grandville neighborhood where they were headed. We had permission, along with a twenty my father pulled from my wallet, to see a movie at the Cineplex downtown.

Orchard Circle, like Butter Lane, turned out to be a pretty name for a place that wasn't. Neglected two-story homes surrounded a dilapidated park with a rusted chain-link fence. When Rose stopped the car, my father gathered his equipment from the trunk while my mother took out her bible. She told Rose and me to enjoy our time at the movies then gave us kisses before getting out.

As we drove away, I stared at that second-floor apartment—the Lynches' place, I felt more and more certain—where the curtains were all drawn. I watched my parents move up the outdoor stairs to the door at the top. After knocking, my father fussed with his tote while my mother waited beside him, hands clasped, that bible between, in a way that told me she was praying. I kept staring back to see if it would be Albert who answered the door, but we turned the corner before anyone opened up.

Despite my preoccupation with whoever was inside that apartment, I was excited to go to the movies so I did my best to put it out of my mind. It wasn't that we weren't allowed to go to the movies at home. My father grew up working in a theater, after all, so he loved them. But we went as a family, which meant my sister and I ended up sitting through films like *Agnes of God* or *Mask*—not exactly our top choices. That afternoon in Columbus, we looked at the splashy posters outside the theater for *Die Hard, Beetlejuice, Who Framed Roger Rabbit?*, and I could tell Rose was as excited as me. We compromised on our mutual second choice then spent what was left on popcorn, Kit-Kats, and sodas, something my parents never allowed.

As Rose and I sat in the dark, fingers sticky with butter and chocolate, watching Michael Keaton play a cartoonish ghost, that unsettled feeling slipped away and I forgot about what my parents were doing back on Orchard Circle. When the lights came up, the happy mood lingered as we walked to the lobby. We didn't get far before an old man, broom in hand, called to us. "You wouldn't happen to be Rose and Sylvie Mason, would you?'

"Who wants to know?" Rose said.

He pressed his lips together, confused by her answer. "Well, I do. Is that you?"

"Maybe. And what if it is us? Do we—"

"That's us," I said. "Why do you ask?"

"Oh, good. Your dad called the theater. He asked us to keep an eye out for you. Good thing it's the middle of the day, because I'd never have spotted you girls in the crowds at night. Anyway, he wanted us to let you know that he and your mom aren't ready to be picked up yet, so you can take in another movie if you like."

The news thrilled me, though my sister let out a groan. "What's wrong?" I asked.

"How does he expect us to do that? He only gave me twenty, and we blew the extra cash on the popcorn and crap."

As Rose and I debated our options, the old man went back to sweeping. Finally, we decided there was nothing to do but drive around town for another couple hours, though even Rose said she was sick of driving by then. We were walking toward the exit when that man called us back. "Follow me," he said, leading the way to a set of doors. "This movie's about to start. It's a personal favorite. Not many people watching, so the show's on the house. Just don't tell anyone."

When the title appeared on the screen, *The Last Emperor,* I expected Rose to complain. She stayed quiet, though, rubbing her sticky fingers on her jeans and leaning forward. Before long, both our minds drifted into the world of that film, far from my parents and whatever might be happening back on Orchard Circle. And this time, when the lights came up, neither of us said a word as we exited the theater and made our way toward the parking lot, where it was something of a shock to discover that it was nearly dark outside.

After Rose and I climbed in the Datsun and headed in the direction of that dreary neighborhood, I broke the silence. "Sorry, you must have hated that."

"Hated what?"

"The movie."

"Clearly, you know nothing about me. I *loved* it, Sylvie."

"You did?"

"Don't sound so shocked. I could have done without the sappy crap, but places like that—faraway places, I mean—they're where I want to go someday."

"China?"

"Yeah, China. But Australia, Africa, the Middle East, and who knows where else?"

I thought of the old globe in her room. Like Mr. Knothead, it had been a gift she begged for one Christmas. I remembered how she liked to give it a spin, planting her finger on random locations to see where it would stop: London. Sydney. Honolulu. "Why?" I asked.

"More like, *'why not?'* I just don't feel I belong anywhere I've been so far. Certainly not Butter Lane. I keep wishing Mom and Dad would get a call to go someplace really far away, so we could tag along. But what do we get? Stinky Columbus."

"It's not so bad. At least they've got a good movie theater."

Rose laughed a little as we pulled in front of the apartment where we'd left our parents. Streetlights cast a cozy glow on the houses and that park, making things appear less dismal. I stared up at the second floor, where the curtains were drawn and only the dimmest light shone from behind. "What now?" I asked.

"Don't know. Guess we knock."

"Knock?"

"What were you thinking? Smoke signals?" My sister opened her door and got out. That unsettled feeling I'd had on the drive earlier returned as I watched her walk to the stairs. If only to get another glimpse of that girl from the bushes and confirm what I'd come to believe about this trip, I forced myself to get out of the car too.

My sister didn't waste time before tapping on the door. I prepared myself to come face-to-face with Albert Lynch. Instead, my father opened up, his eyes wide and weary. "I'm glad you girls are here. Sorry it took longer than expected. But you got the message at the theater, right?"

"We did," Rose told him.

"Where's Mom?" I asked.

"She's just finishing up with something inside. We'll be down in a minute. Why don't you two go wait in the car? And, Rose, you may as well get in the back. We've got a long drive ahead of us, and I'll do it this time. It's only fair."

"But the hotel is just across town."

That's when I caught sight of something I hadn't when my father first opened the door: a faint but noticeable scratch along the back of his hand. The blood there glistened just as Lynch's had outside the convention center that night. "We're making a change of plans," he told Rose, "and heading back to Maryland tonight."

"*Tonight?*"

"Afraid so. We're taking—" He stopped.

"Taking what?" my sister asked.

"I need to explain, and I will. But for now, let's just say that in a way, well, we aren't going to be alone. And so I'd rather not stay in a hotel."

"Sylvester," my mother called.

"I need to go. Now you girls get in the car. We'll be down any minute."

After the door shut, my sister turned and pounded down the stairs, leaving me to trail behind. She let loose a string of complaints, sounding more like her old self than I'd heard in some time. "This is *ridiculous*. We drove all the way here only to turn around and drive back the very same day. And who the hell is coming with us anyway?"

Rose reached the Datsun, but kept walking, crossing the street into that park. I hesitated before following her until we came to a stop by those broken swings. She slipped a hand into her sock and pulled out a lighter and a cigarette. I watched as she brought the cigarette to her lips and lit up, inhaling deeply before exhaling into the night air. Against the backdrop of that dreary, moonlit park, she looked mature and sophisticated—someone who had already been to those faraway places on that globe.

"I didn't know you smoked."

"Yeah, well, like I told you in the car before, there's a lot you don't know about me. Just don't say anything to Mom and Dad."

"I won't. But I'm surprised you risk it, seeing as you never fight with them anymore."

"Oh, we still fight, Sylvie. But it's more of a cold war these days. You know, like that paper you're writing."

"What do you fight about?"

Rose took another drag, her gaze fixed on the apartment, where the streetlight illuminated the stairs leading to that door at the top. "Don't worry about it."

Inching that close to a topic only to back off put me in mind of another time she'd done the same. "Can I ask you something?"

"Can I stop you?"

"You could, actually. If you don't want me to, I won't."

"No. Might as well go ahead. Apparently, we've got hours to spare while they do God knows what, leaving their children out here in this creepy park in the dark."

"They told us to wait in the car, not the park."

"Keep defending them, Sylvie, and I won't answer your question. Now what is it you want to know?"

I pushed one of those dangling chains. "Remember that ride at Disney? The Haunted Mansion?"

Rose blew a cloud of smoke between us. "What about it?"

"When we passed those mirrors—the trick ones that made it look like a ghost was seated between us—you told me Howie said something about Dad and Mom. Something that would make it so I no longer believed them. What did he tell you?"

Rose was quiet for a minute, staring at the apartment door. Then she said, "I don't remember, Sylvie. Whatever it was, I'm sure it was a bunch of BS. Our uncle is a drunk and liar, just like Dad always says. So I'm doing my best to stay out of it. You'd be smart to do the same. Just write your papers and win your prizes. Let everyone tell you what a perfect angel you are. Must be nice living in the Sylvie Bubble."

"I don't live in a bubble," I protested. I hated when she held my good behavior and grades against me.

Rose let out a laugh. "You have no idea." She stubbed out her cigarette and pointed across the street. "Look."

I turned to see the door opening at the top of those stairs. My father stepped out onto the deck, carrying his bag of equipment. Next, my mother emerged. And that's when I saw her: the reason we were returning to Maryland that very night held tightly in my mother's arms. My father led the way, and my mother moved slowly down each step, careful not to trip and drop her.

"I don't understand," I said to Rose.

Beside me, my sister slid her lighter back into her sock. She pulled a stick of gum from nowhere and popped it in her mouth. "Me neither. But we better get over there."

The two of us walked so quickly across the street that we arrived at the car before them. Rose knew enough to pop the trunk for my father so he could put his equipment inside. He did just that, then took the keys from my sister and went to the passenger door, opening it for my mother. As she came closer, I heard her humming that familiar tune. Every bit as slowly, she lowered herself into the front seat before my father shut the door and went around to the driver's side. Rose and I climbed in the back. She moved my bulky *HISTORY* book out of the way, but it slipped from her hands and fell open on the seat. In the dim light, my sister glanced down at a page I'd folded over and bookmarked with a scrap of paper. On that paper, I'd scratched a simple list meant for nobody's eyes but my own:

Marie des Vallées, 14
Bernadette, 14
Rose Mason (Mom), 14

Rose glanced at that list then at the contents of the page, before closing the book and handing it to me. "You too, huh? I thought you were smarter than that, Sylvie."

"Smarter than what?" my father asked, starting the engine.

"Nothing," Rose and I answered at the same time.

He didn't push further. Rather, he leaned over and helped my mother buckle her seat belt, a difficult task considering the passenger she held so tightly in her arms. Once they were settled in, my mother positioned her-self in such a way that the strange face, one I'd seen before but never quite like this, was leaning over her shoulder, gazing directly at me. As my father pulled the Datsun away from the curb, I could not help but stare at her dark eyes, her mess of hair. All day long, I'd been wrong about the reasons for that wary, unsettled feeling.

I had to wait until we reached the highway east before my father began his explanation, sharing with us the sort of story that might have been torn from the pages of my oversized book. What made it more real, however, was that the biggest part of the story was traveling along with us in that car.

"Her name is Penny," my father began. "And for a lot of complicated reasons, the family who owned her cannot keep her anymore. Now she belongs to us . . ."

Now Penny, the rag doll from Columbus, Ohio, was coming to stay.

You and You and You

Dear Rose,

I'm probably the last person or spirit on God's green earth you want to hear from right now. Yet here I am writing you anyway. I have tried the phone but no one answers at your house these days. The reason I'm writing is because I feel such terrible guilt for the terrible trouble that has befallen your family. Please give me a chance to explain my part in it all. I know how headstrong you can be when you want to be, but please. If it sounds like I'm begging, it's because I am. My number is right at the top of this newspaper letterhead. All you have to do is pick up the phone and call it.

Yours,
Sam Heekin

The pay phone outside the first of those industrial buildings reeked of beer. I picked up the sticky receiver anyway, dropped in a coin from the floor of Rose's truck. Not far away, two men leaned against a Pinto with a smattering of Bush-Quayle bumper stickers, watching. Otherwise the place was deserted.

On the other end of the line, a receptionist answered, and I asked to be connected to Sam Heekin. His line rang and rang until she came on to ask if I wanted to leave a message. I gave her my name and the number on the phone, letting her know I'd wait for the next twenty minutes in case he returned. That plan sounded fine until I hung up and realized I had nothing to do but stand by the phone as those men stared.

"Don't know if you've noticed," the one with a belly popping out of his unzipped jacket told me, "but your clothes are kind of big."

"They're not mine," I said, staring down at Dereck's jacket and boots.

"Whose are they? The Jolly Green Giant's?"

"Easy, Trigger," the other guy told him. He had the same large belly, though he was zipped up tight in his coat. To me, he said, "You waiting for a ride or something?"

Or something, I thought. "No. But someone is going to call me at this number." I willed the phone to ring to prove it, but the air around us remained silent.

"We're splitting in a minute," the zipped-up one said. "It's going to be just you here. You sure you don't want a ride someplace? We could drop you."

I shook my head. Right on cue, Louise's reminder about speaking my answers stirred, though I no longer cared. Even though I'd read Heekin's letter dozens of times, I read it again, thinking of my mother's complaints about his convoluted sentences, of the way she and my father came to dislike him once his book was published. Why, I wondered, had he written to my sister? And did she bother to respond?

When I looked up, the men were climbing into their Pinto. The one who made the comment about my clothes got behind the wheel, giving me a quick salute before they sped off. I waited, feeling time slip away, bringing me closer to the moment I'd have to return to the station and give Rummel and Louise an answer.

After what seemed like an eternity, Heekin still had not called. It would be dark soon, so all I could do was begin trudging out to the road toward home. Cars and trucks zoomed past as I walked along the sparse grass bordering the road for a long while before rounding a corner and looking up to see it.

It's where Rose asked us to meet her. Someone was going to drop her here. . . .

In an effort to restore some life to the place, mums had been planted in the church's window boxes. Earlier when we drove by, there had been a dozen or so cars in the lot. Now, though, only a maroon Buick remained. *Keep walking,* I told myself. But the thought of Rummel telling me to figure out exactly what I'd seen lured me off the road. When I arrived at the steps, I felt another urge to turn away, but my hand reached for the handle. Same as that night, the door opened right up. I took a breath and stepped inside. The place felt drafty, but nowhere near the extreme cold it had been the previous winter. The last of the day's sun lit the space, and I saw that the statues by the altar had been removed and the white walls were covered with a new coat of paint, so fresh I could smell it.

"Hello," I called out, just the same as I had before. *Hello?*

No answer. I walked slowly toward the altar, the clomp of Dereck's boots echoing around me. When I reached the front, I stood in the exact spot where my mother and father had taken their last breaths. If I waited, I thought perhaps a more clear memory might surface from that night, but none came.

Walking in those boots had left my feet tired, so I slipped into the first pew. Head down, hands clasped, eyes closed, I said a prayer the way I was taught. When I was done, that tune my mother used to hum came to me, and I began softly humming it too.

That's when the church door opened. The sound caught me off guard, and some instinct led me to sink in the pew. I heard heavy shoes shuffle against the wooden floor, and I craned my neck around, peeking over the back of the bench.

Just like the first time he visited our house with that ice cream cake, Father Coffey wore stiff jeans and a black turtleneck. His posture was slouched. His splotchy skin was flaking. Since he was bound to notice me, I stood and said, "Hello."

Coffey gasped, nearly dropping the bag in his hand.

"Sorry," I said, my voice echoing. "Didn't mean to scare you."

"Well, you did," he snapped back. But after a second, he looked at me and his tone softened. "Sylvie?"

I nodded.

"You've . . . you've grown since I last saw you."

When exactly had that been? I wondered. "I guess so."

"And you are just about the last person I expected to see here."

"The doors were open," I said, trying not to sound defensive. "When I came in, no one was around, so I decided to sit for a while. Sorry again for startling you."

"It's okay." He looked around, let out a breath. "This place belongs to you as much as it does me."

We fell silent after that. In the midst of the quiet, I remembered when I'd last seen him: at my parents' burial, a raw morning last March, after the ground had thawed. Since it was not a public service, no one had been present except for Father Coffey, Rose, Howie, and me. It struck me as odd, suddenly, that a priest—even one who had a strained relationship with my parents—would not visit the orphaned children of his parish. "I saw cars in the lot earlier—" I began just as he said, "So I imagine you are in high school—"

We both stopped.

"You go," he told me.

"I saw cars in the lot. The flowers in the window boxes. I guess the place is, well, open for business again."

"We held a wedding rehearsal this afternoon for a ceremony that takes place tomorrow. It'll be the first since . . ." Coffey stopped, let out a sigh. "I'm sorry, Sylvie. You should know many prayers were said for your parents' souls, and this place was reconsecrated before opening the doors." He walked up the aisle, his heavy black shoes echoing against the floor too. That's when I noticed the statues in the back of the church. They hadn't been removed as I'd thought, only relocated. Their painted faces watched as Coffey slid into my pew without bothering to genuflect. Up close, I could see more of his skin peeling at the sides of his nose and chin. "I need to lock up and head over to the school. But do you mind if I sit with you a bit first?"

"I don't mind," I told him, taking a seat again too.

"I didn't eat before the rehearsal. After, I was famished. One of the parishioners gave me a ride over to—" He held up the bag so I could see the Herman's Bakery logo. "Against the rules to eat here. But I won't tell if you won't."

Coffey fished a piece of a marshmallow doughnut from the bag and popped it in his mouth before reaching in for a cruller. Behind us, the church door opened—or I thought it did. When I turned, no one was there.

It's only the *shhhh,* I told myself. After offering to break his cruller in half and share, an offer I declined, Coffey began wolfing it down. He asked about my coat and boots, which I explained belonged to my sister's boyfriend without telling him anything more.

"How is Rosie anyway?" he asked, smiling when he said that name.

"Same," I told him, trying not to think of the fight we'd just had. "Rosie's always exactly the same."

"I'd tell you to say hello from me, but I'm not sure she wants to hear that."

When I asked him why not, Father Coffey told me that a week after the funeral he'd come by our house. "It was a school day, so you weren't there. But your sister was. I brought food with me. Not that awful stuff Maura, the rectory housekeeper, makes. I stopped at Burger King."

"Well, Rose never gave any to me."

"That's because she told me she didn't want it."

I thought of all the food left on our steps by that woman with the grim, head-on-a-totem-pole face, the way my sister refused to take even a bite for fear it might be poisoned, the way she instilled the same fear in me. "Did Rose think you put something in it?"

Coffey swallowed the last of his cruller and began picking crumbs from the bag. "Put something in it?"

"Poison, I mean."

"*Poison?* No. Well, at least I hope she didn't suspect me capable of such a thing. Your sister said she didn't want anything from me or the church. Her specific words were that I had been nothing but trouble for your mother and father, and that it was better if I kept away. Believe me, Sylvie, I've thought many times of you girls out there living on that empty street. But Rose made it quite clear she was the one in charge of your lives now, and she didn't want me in it."

Once more, we fell quiet. I glanced back at those statues on either side of the closed door. I imagined the door opening, imagined seeing myself from this vantage point just as whoever killed my parents had that night.

"Has there ever been any word from the girl?" Coffey asked.

I turned back around. "Girl?"

"The one who came to live with you? The daughter of—"

"No," I told him, shaking my head. "We never heard from Abigail again."

"Someday, perhaps."

Considering the way she left, I doubted as much. Outside the stained-glass windows, the sky was growing darker. Inside, the air around us was darkening too. Sixty-two hours left, I guessed. Maybe less. Fran's instructions about being direct when asking the survey questions flickered in my mind. "Father," I said, "since we're talking about things back then, can I ask why my parents stopped coming to Saint Bartholomew's?"

Coffey wiped his fingers on the bag, crinkling the mouth of it and giving up on whatever crumbs were left inside. "Well, I guess I'd start by saying that when I came to this parish, I inherited your parents."

"Inherited?"

"They'd been here with Father Vitale before me. Vitale shared their beliefs about the power of demons and souls banished to hell for eternity. Personally, I take a less extreme approach to faith. Even so, your father struck me as a decent man. And your mother, well, there was something so tranquil about her. To be in her presence, it just made you feel . . ." He trailed off, before adding, "In fact, Sylvie, you have a good deal of her in you. I don't know if anyone has ever told you that."

"I look like her. People have said that."

"I'm not talking about looks. I mean whatever that thing was about her. You have it too."

As he spoke, my mind filled with the memory of that hotel room, my mother lying close to me, her whispery voice telling me: *It began when I was a girl not much older than you. . .*

"After Father Vitale left," Coffey said, pulling me away from that memory, "I made a decision that as long as the things your parents did weren't happening in my church, I would put it out of my mind and embrace them, same as I would any other parishioners."

"If you embraced them, why did they stop coming?"

Coffey looked away at the altar, running a few fingers beneath the collar of his turtleneck, before taking a breath and answering. "I want to make it clear that I came to like your parents, Sylvie. Genuinely. I understood their choice for privacy, given the nature of their work, but that also made them seem remote, *secretive* even. And as their notoriety grew, it became difficult for me not to think about who they were and what they did, especially when parishioners began to complain."

"Complain?"

"Yes. Frankly, Sylvie, people found your parents' presence in the church distracting. They didn't much like the idea of people doing what your parents did all week long, coming so close to Satan I guess is how you could put it, then attending Mass on Sundays. Never mind serving as a Eucharist minister as your father did."

"So you told them to stop coming?"

"No. Actually, I defended them, reminding those parishioners that gossip had no place in the church. It worked for a while. But once that photo of your mother and the doll appeared in the paper —not to mention the news of the hatchet and so many other things kept in your basement— and once Abigail came to live with you, well, after that, no amount of scripture put an end to their gossip and complaints. I don't know how else to say it, Sylvie, but people were afraid of them."

The light through the stained glass had shifted again. Father Coffey and I would be nothing more than shadows soon, but neither of us made a move to get up just yet. Seated so close to him, I could smell the sugary sweetness of those doughnuts on his warm breath. In a quiet voice, I said, "People misunderstood my mother and father. They took the things they did and twisted it around. All my parents wanted was to help people."

"Maybe so. But I'm not sure that's what ended up happening. I read the book by that reporter. It painted a very different picture of their motives. Your father's anyway. Have you read it, Sylvie?"

"Yes," I told him, though that wasn't entirely true. I still hadn't been able to brave the final section—"Should You *Really* Believe the Masons?"
"You were saying that people were afraid of my parents, but they didn't care what people thought. So that couldn't have been their reason to stop coming to church."

"Imagine, Sylvie, how awkward it was for your father to serve Communion when no one would go to his line except your family. And when I asked him to offer the wine instead, the handful of people who took that did not anymore. Finally, I had no choice but to tell your father his assistance was no longer needed."

I remembered those Sundays at church, how awkward they had become, and how grateful I felt when we suddenly quit going. "So that's why they stopped?"

"Yes, and at first, he grew angry and said he was going to complain about me to the bishop. He never did, though."

"Why not?"

Father Coffey glanced behind us at the silhouettes of those wooden statues, as though he worried someone might be listening. In a whisper, he said, "I think we should finish here, Sylvie. I need to get to the school. The nuns arranged to have the floors of the gym waxed, and the smell is so noxious they don't think people will make it through the service on Sunday without passing out. Someday, God willing, we'll raise enough money to build a church where students don't dribble balls all week long. Now do you need a ride somewhere? Or is that car outside for you?"

"I thought that car was yours?"

"The Buick belongs to me. But there's another one out there—a Jeep with the engine running and someone behind the wheel. Do you know who it is?"

"I might," I said, because I had a hunch.

Coffey stood and exited the pew, this time making a hasty sign of the cross. As we walked out of the church, I looked back at the altar, thinking of my parents entering that building, not knowing they would never leave, thinking of Rummel who asked if anyone in their circle had reason to do them harm. When Coffey pushed open the door, I saw the Jeep and gave a small wave. "Do you still keep a spare under the flower boxes?" I asked, as he jangled his keys, locking up. It was a detail I recalled from my father's deacon days.

"Not in a long while. I'm the only one who can open this place now."

I saw a quick flash of silver as he slipped his keys into the pocket of his jeans and headed for the Buick. I knew he didn't want me to follow, but I did anyway. On the backseat of his car, I could see stacks of boxes. Whatever was inside must have been heavy, since the car looked sunken in the rear.

"Just getting rid of some things from the rectory," he said when he saw me looking. He opened the door, got inside. I worried he'd drive off without answering my earlier question. But then he said, "The reason your father never went to the bishop had to do with that girl."

"Abigail?"

"Yes. She came to the rectory one night."

"When?"

"At the end of her time with your family. I opened the door and there she was, looking bedraggled and troubled. In some ways, she appeared just as she had when you first brought her to church. Only now there were two wounds on her palms, like stigmata."

I knew about those wounds. I remembered the shock and confusion I'd felt seeing blood pool on her skin without warning. "What did she want?"

"A place to spend the night. I welcomed her inside. Isn't that a priest's job, after all, to take in the needy? The girl spent much of the time begging me not to contact your parents or her father. Maura made her something to eat then made up the old couch in the basement. After we attended to her wounds, she went down to bed. While she slept, I lay awake, praying about the best thing to do. Times like that I missed Father Vitale. He always seemed to hear God's voice when I didn't, which is more often than I care to admit."

"What did you decide to do?"

"I made up my mind to track down her father. It only seemed right."

"And so Albert Lynch came and got her?"

"No. I never had the chance to contact him. In the morning, Maura took tea downstairs and found the couch empty. The girl had slipped out during the night."

"I don't understand. What does that have to do with my parents not coming to church anymore?"

"Abigail told me things, Sylvie."

"What things?"

"Things about what went on that summer she lived with you. Things I don't think your father wanted getting out. That's why he went quiet. That's why he walked away."

"Because you threatened him?"

"He was the one who threatened me, remember? I simply let him know what I'd been told."

"And what did Abigail tell you?"

Again, he ran his fingers back and forth beneath the rim of his turtleneck. This time, I noticed his nails were chewed, his cuticles raw. "We really do need to stop here. I've taken this conversation too far. You should get your answers from someone else. Now good-bye, Sylvie. Please come see me again, though not about this. I think it's better to let the past stay where it is."

"Who?" I asked as he pulled the door shut and started the engine. "Who should I get answers from?"

He rolled down his window. "I meant what I said before. You have a great deal of your mother in you. I can sense it. That's probably what got me talking so much."

"Who should I go to for answers?" I asked again, ignoring the comment.

"Your sister, of course. *Rosie*. I'm certain she can tell you things that I cannot. It's not my place. I'm sorry."

With that, he said good-bye one last time. I stepped back from the car, watched him drive out of the lot and away down the road, his trunk drooping with the weight of those boxes. When he was gone, I walked to the Jeep. The moment I opened the door, Dereck started talking, "I got here just as that guy was walking into the church."

"That guy," I told him, "is the parish priest."

"Oh. Well, I saw him head inside, then I started in too. But it sounded like you were having a pretty heavy conversation, so I waited out here until you were done."

So my ear wasn't playing tricks after all, I thought. I had heard the church door open and close. "But how did you know I was here?"

"I didn't. After I left your sister, I stopped at the farm to grab another pair of boots. I kept thinking about you, Sylvie, wondering what you'd done after we drove off. So I went to that field, only you were gone. When I was driving back and passed the church, I remembered asking if you'd been back here so I wondered if this is where you might have gone."

By then, it was completely dark. The air carried a chill. I glanced at the clock on Dereck's dashboard. Sixty-one hours and forty minutes remaining. Walking home would be a waste of time, and if the conversation with Coffey had done anything, it heightened my sense that I needed to stop wasting it. I climbed up onto the passenger seat and was about to buckle my seat belt when I felt something beneath me. A pair of gloves, I saw when I pulled them out. The interior lights glowed enough for me to make out flecks of something on the material. Before I could look closer, Dereck reached out his hand with the missing fingers and snatched those gloves from me, shoving them under his seat. I said nothing, leaving my seat belt unbuckled instead. As we pulled out of the lot, streetlamps cast shifting shadows over our faces. For some time, that Jeep rolled along, neither of us speaking. Finally, Dereck said, "It's turkey blood. I left my regular gloves in the pockets of the coat I gave you. So I grabbed a spare pair at the farm."

I reached in his coat that I was still wearing. Sure enough, his gloves were inside. "I thought you didn't slaughter the turkeys until Thanksgiving?"

"We're only six days away, Sylvie. We do some each day. Makes no sense, I know, to go through the effort to buy a fresh one, only to freeze it first. But people don't care, and we've got a lot of birds to slaughter."

I looked at Dereck's hands on the steering wheel, at his handsome face in the shifting light.

"You're trying to figure it out, aren't you?" he said.

"Yes."

"Then go for it. Make a guess."

I was quiet, thinking of all that I really was trying to figure out. At last, I gave him what he wanted. "A firecracker went off in your hand at a Fourth of July party."

"Now you're getting somewhere, Sylvie. It happened at a party. That's the closest you've come."

We reached Butter Lane, and Dereck made the turn. After passing the empty lots, he pulled into my driveway. Same as it had since Halloween night, the basement light glowed. The rest of the house was dark, Rose's truck gone. "Where's my sister?"

"Don't know. Not my problem anymore. We broke it off."

The news was the smallest of so many disappointments that day. And yet, it poked at something inside. Now I'd only see Dereck at the farm if he happened to be outside when I passed. After Thanksgiving came and went, he'd go back to just working at the garage, and I wouldn't see him at all.

"So," he said, flashing his wolfish teeth in the dark. "Do you finally want to know how I lost my fingers?"

I told him I did.

"First you have to admit that you couldn't figure it out on your own."

"I admit it."

"See, Sylvie. And you're still here just the same. It's not the end of the world if you don't always know all the answers."

It will be soon, I thought, glancing at the dashboard clock.

"Well, here goes. The fall after graduation, when everyone was home for Thanksgiving, one of my buddy's parents went out of town. So we got the idea to throw a party. Not just any old lame kegger; what we wanted was a rager people would remember. A reunion blowout. All the guys from every team I ever played on were invited along with their girlfriends. Plus, all my Honors Society buddies were there. For once, everyone got along. Word got out and tons of people crashed. Your sister was there, too, with her friend. Rose was lucky to walk away without getting hurt the way a lot of us did. She never mentioned any of this to you?"

I shook my head.

"Well, none of us saw it coming. The house was mobbed. People were spilling drinks, dropping food, breaking glasses. This guy's parents lived in a raised ranch with a deck off their kitchen on the second floor. The grill and an army of kegs were out on the deck, so that's where the fun was. Fifty-seven of us, by the police officer's count."

"Why were the police—"

"I'm getting to that. Someone plugged in a boom box. It was cheesy music. Madonna or Paula what's her face. But the girls started dancing, and they got the guys dancing too. Next thing I know, I feel something shift beneath me. At first I thought I was just dizzy from all the beer, but before I knew what was happening, we were tipping. That deck couldn't support the weight.

"Some people got burned by the grill. Others broke arms or legs."

Dereck held up his hand. "My fingers got wedged between two boards and ripped right off."

I lingered there, putting the pieces of Dereck's story together in my mind. Finally, I said, "I'm surprised I never heard about it. It's a small town. Seems like I would have."

"It was in the paper. Probably the biggest news story ever to hit Dundalk."

I was quiet, thinking of my parents, so many headlines about them.

"Sorry," Dereck said, realizing.

"It's okay." I tugged off his jacket and boots. "But I better go."

"Remember, I'm right through those woods if you need me. And even if you don't, you better come visit anyway. We'll think up some new game to play."

I forced a smile, told him I would. That's when Dereck leaned close, the stubble on his face brushing against me. The warm, earthy smell of him—wood chips and autumn leaves and worn clothes—was all around for an instant as he kissed my cheek. Four years between us—I couldn't help but think of what he'd said earlier about all the differences they created. Even so, some part of me wanted him to kiss me again. Instead, I opened the door and got out, my eyes automatically scanning the lawn for more rag dolls. Dereck flicked on his high beams and waited as I stepped in my bare feet up the walk. On the doorstep a foil-covered bowl shimmered in the headlights. I picked it up.

Inside, I flashed the porch light and Dereck beeped a few times before driving away. Alone in the house, I went to the kitchen, put the bowl on the table beside my mother's book of wallpaper swatches, and opened the freezer for a Popsicle. None left, so I made up my mind to go to bed. But on my way out, something made me stop. I stood at the door to the basement. Pressed my ear—the good one, of course—against the hollow wood.

When I heard nothing, I put my hand on the knob and pulled. The yellow glow lit the staircase from below. I took a step down, then another, then two more, before stopping in the middle and bending to look around the shadowy space. I saw my father's desk, messy with papers, which was not how he had left it, but the way Rummel and his investigators had when they came, again and again, to look through his things. There was my mother's old rocker, the shiny blue knitting needles she had used forever waiting on the cushion for her return. Just beyond, I saw the bookshelf covering the hole in the cinder blocks that led to the crawl space. On top, the cage with Penny inside. Her blank face stared back at me just as it had on the ride home from Ohio so long ago. I read the sign on the bars, remembering the day my father had written those words: DO NOT OPEN UNDER ANY CIRCUMSTANCES! At last, I looked away at the partition wall my father had finally finished. I thought of what Coffey had told me about people's gossip, the things they talked about happening here.

Courage—that's what I wished for, so I could keep walking down those stairs and turn off the light. But Penny and the hatchet on the wall and all the rest filled me with enough fear that I turned back. At the top of the stairs, I shut the flimsy door behind me. Rather than go to my room, something made me walk back to the kitchen. I lifted the foil on that bowl. Chocolate pudding. Again, I thought of Coffey and how he claimed my sister had refused the food he brought.

I dipped my fingers into the bowl. It had been a long time since I'd tasted anything remotely homemade, and once started, I could not stop. Without bothering to find a spoon, I kept dipping my fingers in, kept eating until the bowl was all but licked clean. At last, I buried the Tupperware container in the trash so my sister would not find it, then washed my hands before going upstairs.

For the next few hours, I waited for whatever poison to take hold. My stomach felt fine. My mind, however, drifted more than usual. I thought of Boshoff and his ailing wife and that cookbook I'd never be able to get him. And then I thought about a lady I had called in the 561 area code while doing those surveys. The crackle of her voice told me she was very old. She was so happy to talk to me I had the feeling nobody called her very often. All through the survey, she kept excusing herself then muffling the phone to cough, deep and rattling, like there was something swampy inside her. We were almost at the end when it got so bad I said we didn't have to finish. "Maybe you should have a glass of water," I told her, since I felt guilty taking up her time asking meaningless questions about shampoos and deodorants.

She laughed a little, then said, "You are sweet to suggest it, dear. But I can drink all the water I want, and I'm never going to cough a pearl out on my pillow."

I don't know why I thought about that, but afterward, I did one last thing I wasn't planning: I went to my closet and opened the door.

Inside, all my clothes from the previous winter fought for space. Sleeves and cuffs and hems tangled and twisted in such a way that it made me think of a pack of girls on a crowded bus. I reached in and pulled out a soft pink sweater with pearly white buttons. The sweater was warm, I remembered from the year before. Next, I pulled out a brown skirt. The wool was scratchy, I remembered as well, but it was warm too. The sweater and skirt matched enough that I set them on my chair the way my mother would have. I turned to the closet again and chose another outfit from the crowd. Then another. I imagined myself picking girls off that crowded bus. *You,* I said to them in my head, *and you and you and you* . . . I kept on picking until a week's worth of outfits was draped around my bedroom. Once that was taken care of, I was about to get back into bed when the phone rang.

Sometimes, those haunted people still called, seeking my parents' help. Rose usually just hung up on them, but I always took the time to explain that they were gone and apologized for not being able to do anything for them. I crossed the hall to my parents' room, figuring it would be another one of those calls. But when I answered, the person on the other end said, "Is Sylvie there, please?"

"This is Sylvie."

"It's Sam Heekin. I got your message but not in time to call you back at the number you left, so I thought I'd try you here."

"I see." His voice did not stumble or ramble the way my father once complained, and I found myself skipping ahead in the conversation, coming to the point sooner than was polite. "I found the letter you wrote my sister, and I was hoping to talk to you."

"Your sister? I never wrote any letters to your sister."

"You didn't?"

"No. But your mother. I used to write letters to her sometimes."

"My mother?"

"Perhaps we can meet in person, so I can explain. Would you like that?"

I looked around my parents' bedroom—at the pillows plumped beneath their bedspreads, at my father's striped tie draped over the back of a chair, at my mother's hairbrush and bobby pins on her dresser, and at the glowing green alarm clock, reminding me how little time I had left. I took a long, deep breath, before saying, "Yes. Yes, I would."

DOLL

In the beginning, there was no cage for Penny. She simply slumped in my mother's old rocker, which my father dredged up from the basement and situated in the corner of the living room. Same as the cross on the wall, the desk in the corner, the drapes over the window, Penny remained positively, perfectly, one hundred percent inanimate. Strange as I found the doll's sudden arrival into our lives, she had no effect on my behavior. Her mere presence, however, did something to my sister. In the way paint can peel from a house, revealing the true color beneath, the façade Rose had maintained since the night my father dragged her from that hotel room peeled away too.

The erosion began almost immediately on our car ride home from Ohio. Except for the occasional soft humming of that song I still did not know the words to, my mother spent the ride in silence. She cradled the doll in such a way that Penny's head propped over her shoulder, and so Rose and I found ourselves staring at those blank eyes hour after hour. We did our best to look away out the window at the 18-wheelers rumbling by in the dark, but while rolling through the hills of Pennsylvania, I noticed Rose's hand reach slowly forward. She grasped a strand of Penny's red yarn hair, tugged—hard, fast—and it came free. We went still, waiting to see if anyone noticed. My father was listening to a religious program on the radio, which put him in a trance. And my mother had been in her own kind of trance since coming down the stairs on Orchard Circle. When it was clear neither noticed, Rose set the yarn on the hump in the middle of the backseat and reached forward again.

"Stop it," I whispered, after watching her grasp and tug five strands free.

"It's not like I'm hurting her," Rose whispered back. "She's a doll, Sylvie."

"Yeah, but if they catch you, they'll—"

"I know what they'll do," Rose said, her old self shimmering beneath those words. "But you know what I decided just now? I don't care anymore."

"Care about what?" my father said from up front.

"Nothing," I answered.

We were quiet after that, listening to the voice of a radio preacher boom through the speakers, "Say to the people of Judah and those living in Jerusalem, 'This is what the Lord says: Look! I am preparing a disaster for you and devising a plan against you! So turn from your evil ways and reform!'"

"By the time I'm done, that thing will be bald," Rose whispered, leaning close to my ear. "Shove a lollipop in her creepy puss and we'll call her Kojak."

"Ko-*who*?"

"You know, Sylvie, you really should sneak downstairs with me and watch reruns some night. It might help you see the world the way everyone else does."

Sneaking downstairs to watch TV, scalping that doll—those things would only lead to trouble, and I told her so. But a few minutes later, her hand reached forward and then six strands rested on the seat. Soon there were a dozen. I worried she might keep her word and not stop until the doll was bald, but eventually Rose must have grown bored, because she fell asleep.

I slept too.

How much time passed before I opened my eyes to the sensation of the car stopping and the engine going silent? I was not certain. But I looked around and saw more 18-wheelers idling by a row of fuel pumps. WELCOME TO SENECA HILL TRUCK STOP read a sign above the glass doors of a shingled building not far from where we parked. My father got out and stood by the car. I expected him to make a show of kneading his hands on his back the way he did after sitting too long, but he simply let out a yawn. Rose and my mother had yet to stir. Same as before, Penny smiled in my direction, her blank black eyes holding my gaze until I looked down and noticed the yarn in my hand instead of on the seat.

"Very funny," I said to Rose, poking her awake.

She sat up, rubbed her eyes. "What?"

I opened my palm to her. "Putting these in my hand while I slept."

"Sylvie, I nodded off before you. And in case you didn't notice, I just woke up. So don't look at me."

"Next stop, Dundalk," my father said, ducking his head into the car. "*Pee* now or forever hold your *pees*."

Rose and I shoved on our sneakers while he walked to the passenger door and pulled it open. My mother finally opened her eyes and got out. She was about to start toward the building when my father suggested that it might be best if she carried Penny along with her. When Rose saw that in her sleepy haze our mother was actually going to do as he suggested, she shook her head and began walking ahead toward the truck stop. I hurried to keep up. Through the glass doors, past the counter where men shoveled eggs in their mouths—Rose and I kept going until we entered the oversized ladies' room. After ducking into the stalls around one wall, we emerged to find our mother standing in the middle of the restroom, cradling the doll. A uniformed waitress with smudged makeup and tired eyes bent over a sink, washing her hands.

"Do you need me to hold her, Mom?" I asked, even though I felt nervous about the idea. "That way you can use the bathroom."

My mother didn't respond. With her pale, papery skin, crosses in her ears, and black hair threaded with gray, she looked the same. Yet something about her felt altered.

"Mom?" Rose tried. "Why didn't Dad let you just leave that thing in the car?"

"Pardon, dear? Well, I guess he has his reasons. I mean, we both do."

"Are you okay?" I asked, before Rose could speak again.

"I think so."

"Do you want me to hold her?"

"Penny?" my mother said. "Oh, no. No, thank you. Now that I think about it, I don't want you girls touching her at all."

"Not a problem here," Rose said.

"Can I ask why not?" I said. "I mean, she's just a—"

"A doll. I know. Still, it's a feeling I have."

"But you're holding her," I pointed out.

My mother looked down at that doll cradled so tightly in her arms. I imagined a heart thumping inside Penny's small body. I imagined warm, milky breath escaping her thin lips. "You're right. I am. But that's just so I can get her home."

"There's always the trunk," Rose said. "Or the roof rack. It might even look decent as a hood ornament. A little bit big but what the hell?"

My mother's expression grew pinched, reminding me of that Halloween night when she slapped my sister for mouthing off to Almaline Gertrude. "Not funny, Rose. Strange as it may seem to you, your father and I know what we're doing. The way he sees it, a door was opened when we were upstairs at that apartment today. A door that's yet to be closed. So we need to be careful. Now how far are we from home? I've lost track."

"We're outside of Harrisburg," my sister told her. "A hundred miles from the Maryland border."

I'd been trying to forget the waitress at the sink, but it was impossible once she twisted the faucet and the running water stopped. A silence fell over the restroom. I looked at her more closely. The woman's skin appeared clayish, a valley of wrinkles beneath her eyes, slivery cracks around her lips. She tugged a paper towel from the dispenser and dried her hands over the trash can. Her gaze trailed my mother, who walked around the dividing wall to the stalls. A brief rustling followed before she emerged a moment later.

"Problem?" Rose asked.

"I can't lift my dress and hold Penny at the same time."

Even though I'd offered, a small surge of panic moved through me at the thought that she was about to put the doll in my arms. Thankfully, my mother went to a sink. After wiping down the edges, she propped Penny up and left her there before returning to the stall. That's when the waitress tossed her paper towel in the trash and spoke to us in a hushed voice at last. "She's that lady, isn't she?"

"What lady?" Rose asked.

"The one from TV. I saw the man out in the lot before. They were on Channel Eight and on that talk show I watch some afternoons. Not *Donahue*, but the local one. Anyway, I don't remember anybody ever mentioning they had kids. You're their kids, aren't you?"

Rose and I were accustomed to getting stared at around Dundalk, but nothing like this had ever happened before. Neither of us said anything.

"Don't act all *spooked* by me!" She let out a rattling laugh. "I'm sure you've seen scarier things in your day. What are your names? I want to tell my boyfriend I met you."

I looked at Rose, but even she seemed stumped. My mother, meanwhile, began coughing, deep and unrecognizable, in the stall.

"*Come on!* I'm Shawna. There, I told you mine. Now tell me yours."

"I'm Sabrina," my sister said, glancing my way and making her eyebrows jump. "And that's my sister . . . Esmeralda."

Who would have guessed Rose remembered the names I'd given those horses? I thought of them on the shelf above my desk back at home, a place that felt impossibly far away at the moment.

"Such pretty names for such pretty girls," the waitress was saying. "I wish I had a camera to get a picture with you and your folks. But who knew I'd be hobnobbing with practically celebrities in this dump? I bet you two could tell some stories, huh?"

Inside the stall, my mother's coughing grew so loud and guttural, she sounded on the verge of vomiting. "Mom," I called. "Are you okay?"

"*Mom*," that waitress repeated as though turning the word over and inspecting it. "Who knew a person like her could be a mother?"

"What do you mean, 'a person like her'?" Rose asked.

The waitress didn't answer. She walked to the sink, where Penny slumped against the wall, red-and-white-striped legs like oversized candy canes dangling from the ledge. "What's her story?" she asked, leaning in for a closer look.

"Been sleeping with her since I was born," Rose said, keeping her voice low so my mother wouldn't hear. "Can't go anywhere without her. That includes the bathroom."

Things were quiet on the other side of that wall. I peeked around, scanning the floor beneath the stalls until I saw her simple black flats. "Mom?" I said again.

In a meek voice, she answered, "Yes?"

"Are you okay?"

"I'm fine, Sylvie. Don't worry. A little car sickness snuck up on me. That's all. Give me a minute to breathe, and I'll be good as new."

"But I heard your mother say nobody better touch her," that waitress was telling Rose when I turned around. "Why's that? Is she . . . *haunted*?"

"Not haunted." My sister moved closer to Penny, voice low still. "She just doesn't want us getting her dirty. But your hands are clean. So go ahead. Touch her."

"Rose," I said.

My sister looked at me. "Who's Rose?"

"I mean, Sabrina. I don't think you should—"

"Just ignore her," Rose told the waitress, all but whispering now. "Esmeralda's a worrywart. Your hands are clean. So like I said, go right ahead. Touch her if you want."

I watched as the waitress bent down and put her face up to Penny's. "Hey there, dolly," she said in a voice as quiet as Rose's. She reached out a nail-bitten hand and stroked all the red hair my sister hadn't gotten around to plucking. "When my girl was little she had a doll just like you, but smaller."

Penny stared back, expressionless and indifferent as ever.

"Weird," the waitress said.

"Weird?" Rose repeated.

"I mean, she's just an old Raggedy Ann. A dime a dozen. But this one, well, she feels different somehow. I don't know. Maybe it's those marks."

"Marks?" my sister said.

"Fingerprints. Your doll has them all over her neck. Or where her neck should be anyway. I guess it's just the seam where her head is stitched to her body. Anyway, looks like maybe somebody's been choking her."

I stepped closer. The waitress was right: gray smudges lay all around the seam between Penny's body and head.

"Plus, she's got that dainty gold bracelet twisted tight around her wrist. Looks like somebody—one of you, I guess—has been hating on her and loving her at the same time."

My sister said nothing, and neither did I.

"Well, unless I want to end up with fingerprints on my neck, I better get back to my tables," Shawna told us. "Nice to meet you girls. Hope your mom feels better."

And then we were alone in the restroom. Once more, I asked my mother if she was okay. This time, her voice sounded stronger when she told me to stop worrying, that she just felt queasy from so much driving in a single day. As she spoke, I looked to my sister, but Rose stared down at her hands.

"Is that woman gone?" my mother asked from inside the stall.

"Yes," I called back.

"She didn't touch Penny, did she?"

Rose was still studying her hands, so I gave my mother the answer she wanted and told her the waitress had only looked. With that, my sister walked to the sink farthest from Penny. I watched her crank the hot water and pump the soap dispenser before scrubbing away. When I asked what she was doing, she said her hands were greasy from the popcorn and chocolate at the movies this afternoon. But I knew better.

I walked to the trash can and pulled out the red yarn, which I'd slipped in my pocket before leaving the car, since I didn't want my parents to see. Beneath the humming fluorescent lights, those strands appeared brighter, more alive than they had while driving in the dark. I moved my hand over the trash can and let go of the doll's hair so it landed on top of the waitress's damp paper towel. As I crossed to a sink and washed up too, I couldn't help but stare over at Penny.

"You could do surgery with those mitts," my sister said when I kept pumping the dispenser and worked up a good lather. "Let's go."

"What about Mom?"

"Alive in there?" Rose called out.

"No need to wait," my mother said after a moment. "Go on back to the car. I'll be there shortly. Keep Penny where she is, though."

I worried about leaving her, but there seemed no other option but to listen. Rose and I left the bathroom then weaved among tables, spotting that waitress who looked up while pouring coffee and winked at us. We passed the register, where my sister scooped a handful of pinwheel mints out of a donation box. Outside, our father was waiting in the car, all buckled in and ready to go.

"What happened to your mother?" he asked.

"She's inside," I said.

"Is she okay?"

"So she says," Rose told him.

It took a while for my mother to emerge from the doors with Penny in her arms. As I watched her get closer, I couldn't help thinking again that she seemed not herself. When she got in, my father asked if everything was okay. Her answer was the same: motion sickness brought on by so much travel in a single day. He started the engine, and as the wheels began to turn, I told Rose, "I'm surprised you remembered those names."

"What names?"

"The ones I gave my horses."

"Well, I pay more attention to things than you might think, Sylvie. Sabrina's the white one with blue eyes and a genuine horsehair tail. Esmeralda is black with rippling muscles and glowing green eyes. Am I right?"

I nodded, more surprised than before. "How do you remember that?"

"It's all you used to talk about. I can tell you about the others if you want."

Something told me to let the moment be. And soon Rose closed her eyes again and drifted off. Despite my mother's insistence that she felt fine, as we drove on in the dark, it became apparent she was anything but. In the course of my childhood, I couldn't recall another occasion when she came down with anything more than a case of sniffles. My father was the one who fell prey to the flu and bronchitis and strep, not to mention the troubles with his back. Rose and I carted home the expected stomach bugs and fevers from school. Always, my mother had been the one to deliver ginger ale and soup to our bedsides, to smear VapoRub on our chests and slip a thermometer in our mouths, so it felt strange to see her so ill.

For the remainder of the trip, the radio stayed off. Instead of preachers bellowing about how to avoid an eternity in hell, my mother's soft, suffering moans filled the car. She pressed her cheek to the window, because the glass felt cool against her skin. Thirty or forty minutes a stretch—that's the most we were able to drive before she asked to pull over. Each time, my father clicked on the emergency flashers and stopped on the side of the highway. In a frenzy, my mother unbuckled her seat belt and burst from the door. Cars and trucks roared past, headlights brightening and receding over her as she carried that doll—more loosely than before—into the tall grass. In the silence between passing traffic, we could hear her heaving, until growing quiet and emerging from the shadows to climb into the car once more. Somehow, my sister managed to stay asleep the entire time. But my father and I remained alert, silent except when it came to asking my mother if there was anything we could do.

"Let's just get home." That was her response each time. "I'm fine."

And so, after making countless stops, we turned into our driveway just as the sun began sifting daylight into the sky. More wearily than before, my mother unbuckled her seat belt and climbed out of the car. I woke Rose, and we got out too. My father took my mother's arm and led her to the door, where he found an envelope wedged between the knob and the frame. He squinted at the words before shoving it in his pocket.

Once the door was unlocked, my mother entered first, moving through the dark to the kitchen. I heard her fill a glass of water while my sister shot up the stairs. My father followed, carting our luggage to the second floor. I used the time to move around the living room, snapping on lamps. When I was done, I saw him at the bottom of the stairs again, the letter from the door in his hand. His face looked grim, and I couldn't help asking if something was wrong.

"Huh?"

"I was wondering if something is wrong? You look worried."

"Things are fine, angel."

I might not have asked who had left a letter for him, but I felt tired enough from the long night that the question slipped out.

"*This?*" He held it in the air. His normally neat hair was mussed, and I could see in his eyes that he was worn out from the trip too. "Oh, it's just from that reporter. Sam Heekin. I've been letting him interview me for his book."

The two of us must have sensed her standing there, between the kitchen and living room, because we both turned to see my mother. Now that we were home, I kept waiting for her to put down the doll, but she carried it with her still. "What about Sam Heekin?" My father folded the letter, tucked it back in his pocket. "We can discuss it later when you are feeling better."

"I feel fine," she said, but she went to the sofa where she settled in with Penny on her lap. "I think I'll just rest here awhile, though."

"Wouldn't you be more comfortable in your bed?"

She leaned back, closed her eyes. "I would. But the thought of climbing those stairs. I can't just yet. You go ahead. I'll be there in a minute."

"Are you sure?" I asked.

"Sylvie, sweetheart. Is that you?" She said the words without opening her eyes, and I had the impression she'd gone blind, a woman left to feel her way around the world. "What are you doing up? After the night we had, you should be in bed asleep."

"I'm on my way. But I'm worried about you."

"No need to worry. Now good night to you both."

I looked to my father, who hesitated before adjusting the pillows on the sofa so my mother could lie back. When she was comfortable, he tugged a blanket off the armrest and draped it over her. Over Penny too. He leaned down and kissed my mother's forehead. "It was a long day for all of us, but especially you. So get some rest."

I went around the room snapping off lamps I had only just turned on, pulling the drapes shut. Once the room was dark, I went to her and kissed her forehead too, keeping my distance from Penny. My mother's skin did not feel feverish or sweaty as I expected, but perfectly cool and dry, too. Whispering, I told her, "Good night, Mom."

"Good night, my sweetheart. Thank you for being such a good daughter."

Her words made me think of the lie I'd told earlier about that waitress not touching Penny. I thought suddenly of Dot too, the way I'd helped Rose in order to protect my essay from being destroyed. "I'm not always good."

"Sure you are," she said in a weak voice. "You never disappoint us, Sylvie. Now go on and get up to bed."

My father and I climbed the stairs, giving each other a quick hug before heading to our rooms. I flopped on my mattress and fell immediately asleep. Only an hour or two passed before so much morning sunlight spilled in the window that it nudged me awake. In my drowsy state, I lay staring at the shelf above my desk. I'd been too young to remember my uncle giving Rose and me those horses. But my father said Howie frequented a racetrack near his apartment in Tampa. A big win did not come often, but when it did, he liked to buy a few from the collectors' shop there. Since he didn't trust himself not to pawn them the next time he found himself hurting for cash, he gave the horses to us. My father disapproved of his brother's gambling but loved those horses anyway, and especially when he saw how much I loved them too.

But something was different the morning after our return from Ohio.

I got out of bed, crossed the room, pulled out my desk chair, and stepped up on it.

When I saw what had been done to Sabrina—the spotless white pony with glassy blue eyes and a tail made from genuine horsehair, the one Rose had remembered—my lips parted but no words came. I reached for the black pony with rippling muscles and green eyes. Esmeralda—Rose had remembered that one too. I held them both by their bellies, staring down at their limbs, which had been snapped off. Their legs, carved carefully to showcase their knobby knees and broad hooves, littered the carpet below. I climbed down off the chair. One by one, I began picking up the pieces, growing more angry, more bewildered with each that I found.

My sister was the most obvious culprit. But difficult as Rose could be, it was hard to imagine her sneaking into my room and doing something so unprovoked. Even less likely was my father. Besides, he was sleeping down the hall and had no reason. Listening, I could hear the faint rise and fall of his snores. As for my mother, she must have been downstairs on the sofa still, right where we left her, drained of even the small bit of energy required to climb the stairs. That's when I thought of that doll. Cradled in my mother's arms. Smiling her placid smile. Her blank black eyes soaking in our home, a place she had traveled so far to be, bringing nothing more than the fingerprints around her neck, a dainty bracelet twisted tight around her wrist.

BIRDS

People scattered along the winding path in the woods, hands frozen in the air. Heekin instructed me to whisper while we passed, to walk softly so as not to disturb them. When we reached an open space by a pile of twisted branches, he came to a stop. As he knelt to unzip his duffel, I looked down at the wiry gray strands weeding up among his black hair. His thin fingers were wide and flat at the tips, as though somebody had taken a mallet to them. I watched as he pulled out a small plastic baggie and handed it to me.

"What exactly do I do with this?"

"Same as the others are doing. Pour some in your hands, then hold them out."

I did as he said, dumping seeds into my cupped palms. He poured a little in his hands too, before tucking the baggie back in his duffel. "Remember," he said, looking at me with his rubbery face and narrow eyes. "You've got to keep absolutely still and silent."

He lifted his arms and so did I. Even though I was wearing a sweater and coat I had pulled from my closet the night before last, when he had first called, a chill worked its way down my back. "And my mother did this too?"

"Yes. Just like I told you."

"When did you two come here?"

"A number of times. The first was after the interview she granted me while I was writing the book. I had the idea to bring her here when she spoke about the heartbreak she felt after the loss of her father and the smaller tragedy of those birds, which always haunted her. I'm guessing she shared those details of her life with you?"

Embarrassed as I was to admit it, I told him she had not. "I read that part of your book, though, so I know."

"That part?" Heekin said. "I would have assumed you'd read the whole thing."

I told him I'd held off on the final section out of respect for them. "They didn't want Rose and me to read any of it. They weren't happy with what you had to say."

Something changed in Heekin's eyes then, a kind of clouding over. He let out a breath and said, "I feel bad about that and always will. It's the reason I wrote your mother asking if she'd see me."

"And did she?"

He looked at his hands, the mounds of seeds in each open palm. "No."

We stopped talking after that. Down the path, I could see others standing, arms in the air. I raised mine higher.

Finches. Blackhead Grosbeaks. Those were the birds that would land in our hands if we were patient, Heekin had told me. I glanced over at him in his maroon Members Only jacket, zipped up tight. He had nicked his neck—shaving, I assumed—and a dab of dried blood held a torn tissue in place, making me think of Dereck's gloves. Those flecks on the material, that unexpected story of how he'd come to ruin his fingers, my visit with Father Coffey—all of it had lingered in my mind during the long wait on Saturday. Since a deadline at the paper kept Heekin from meeting sooner, I'd spent the day before at home with Rose. The two of us had not spoken since the incident with the money, so the only sound in our house had been the chiming clock at the top of each hour as time slipped away, bringing me closer to the moment I'd have to face Rummel and Louise. This morning I told Rose I was going to the library—a reckless lie, considering the place was closed, but I knew she'd never check—then I met Heekin at the end of Butter Lane. Now he had driven us to the Bombay Hook Nature Preserve across the state line in Delaware, and with only twenty-two hours remaining, I was beginning to think he'd be no help after all.

"Can I ask how you found that letter?" Heekin said. His speech, I noticed, just as I had on that initial call, was nothing like the long-winded sentences he wrote and nothing like the stuttering, rambling man my father once complained about.

"It was in my sister's room. I was looking for one from my uncle, actually. I wrote him weeks ago, but never heard back."

"So it was nowhere special then? My letter, I mean."

It seemed like such an odd question, I couldn't help but feel a flutter of annoyance. "Sorry, but no. Somehow it ended up under Rose's bed, which was why I thought it had been meant for her."

He sighed. "Well, we should stop talking or they won't come. The quiet and stillness attract them, same as the globules your father used to claim appeared to him."

A breeze moved past, shaking the last stubborn leaves that clung to the bare branches. A chill moved through me again that had less to do with the cold, I suspected, and more to do with the sense of betrayal I felt toward my parents. When no birds came after some time, I broke the silence. "Obviously, you didn't believe him."

"Your father? No. Not in the end. Did you?"

I thought of the light in the basement that had yet to go out, of those pictures he showed during his lectures, of the story he told about his fateful first meeting with my mother. "I did and I didn't. It was hard not to, though, when you listened to him talk."

"I know that feeling. The first time I went to see them, your father did most of the talking up onstage. He had the gift of gab. But your mother, she had a greater gift."

We were quiet again, waiting. Not far away, a small bird with black and white feathers perched in a cedar tree but showed no signs of coming closer.

"Where did you write your uncle?" Heekin asked, ignoring his own instructions to keep quiet and sending that tiny creature away.

"Tampa. His address there."

"Well, that explains why you never heard back. Your uncle moved, Sylvie."

"*Moved?* Where?"

"Not far from here, actually. A couple hours away."

"How do you know?"

"I'm a reporter, remember? Maybe not the best one out there, but I've covered every detail of your parents' story for the paper. A number of times I even tried to talk to your uncle, but he refused. Same as your sister when I reached out to her."

On the ride to the preserve, in his wheezing, beat-up Volkswagen, Heekin had told a story that was fast becoming familiar: Not long after my parents' deaths, he stopped by our house only for Rose to turn him away. She said he'd been nothing but trouble for my mother and father and she didn't want to see him again. But he had not mentioned anything about my uncle. "Why did you want to talk to him?"

Heekin shrugged. "Other than you girls, Howard was one of the few people in your parents' circle I never once interviewed. Not while writing the book. Not after they were gone. I just thought he might know something."

"But he was in Florida that night," I said as the note in Rummel's folder floated into my mind. "What could he possibly tell you?"

"I know that. I've read the police reports with his statement that he was home drinking, having lost his job. It was just an attempt—a desperate one on my part—to get whatever answers I could. It doesn't matter, though. Your uncle was as firm and dismissive as your sister when it came to sending me away."

The bird, or one just like it, landed on a nearby branch. I needed to be quiet if I wanted it to take seeds from my palm. Even so, I couldn't keep from asking why he cared. "I know it's your job. But . . ."

Heekin brought his hands to his sides, balling his fists to keep the seeds from dropping. "It's my own guilt. That's the simple answer, anyway."

"Guilt?"

"For betraying your mother by writing certain things in that book. For whatever part I played in the demise of your family. But it's not just that. Even if the Dunns hadn't come forward to offer Lynch an alibi, I never believed the man was guilty."

Twenty-two hours, I thought again. "Why? That's the story that makes sense. He was angry at my parents about what happened to Abigail. So he had a motive. Plus, he was at the church."

"Even if your sister and uncle refused to speak with me, Albert Lynch was willing. I've visited him a few times in jail for the pieces I wrote. And—"

"How did he seem?" I couldn't help but ask, since I was the one who put him there.

"How did he seem? Like a man who has lost everything. His wife, years before. Then his daughter. And for almost a year now, his freedom."

I looked at another tiny bird moving from branch to branch with a blurry flapping of wings. If I really had been wrong, it was hard not to feel guilty. But when I thought of Abigail, I also couldn't help feeling that I'd protected her somehow.

"He's a troubled man, Sylvie. That's for sure. But a murderer? I don't think so."

"I'd like to see my uncle," I said, changing the subject. "Do you think you can take me to him? Maybe he'll talk with you if I'm there. Maybe—"

"Shhhh . . ."

This time the sound did not come from inside my ear. Heekin motioned toward a cedar branch. A bird perched there, closer than before. Rather than hold up his hands, he went still. I kept mine raised, outstretched, doing my best not to move either. I thought of those statues in the church, the way they stared off into nowhere. For a few moments, we were like them, motionless, until in a sudden flurry, the bird flew to me, landing in my palm. Its delicate body felt no heavier than the seeds in my hand. I watched its movements—quick, herky-jerky—as it picked up a seed, tilted its head back, and swallowed. It repeated the motion with a second seed before spreading its wings and flying up into the branches, singing.

Heekin looked at me and smiled. "How did that feel?"

I lowered my hands, letting the rest of the seeds drop. "Like you promised."

"Magical, right?"

"Magical," I told him, because it was true.

"Well, I'm glad you got to experience it. Your mother—she couldn't get enough of those little birds. And they couldn't get enough of her. We used to stand here for hours, feeding them and talking, then trying not to talk so they'd come."

It took work picturing my mother with Heekin on that path in the woods, to imagine the circumstances that led to their being together in the first place. "What did you two talk about when you came here?"

"Lots of things. You girls. Sometimes, if you want the truth, we talked about your father. The way things were between them. Mainly, we discussed her desire to stop."

"Stop?"

"Their work. She found it tiring. I'm not sure you were aware of that. The way she explained it, those feelings of hers came and went of their own accord, rather than something she could switch on and off. But your father needed her to do exactly that. In many ways, their livelihood depended on it. Her times with me here became an escape from all that. They were an escape for me, too."

"Were you two—" I didn't know how to ask my next question, so I stopped.

This time it was Heekin who changed the subject. "You were saying something a moment ago about your uncle?"

"Will you take me to see him?"

"*Now?* What about your sister. Won't she wonder where you are?"

"Don't worry about her," I said.

Heekin opened his fists, and I watched the seeds fall. "Well, we'd have to call first, to see if he's even there and if he'd agree to it. And there's the matter of my car, which is on its last legs, though I suppose it could manage."

"Okay then. And maybe on the way, you can tell me about you and my parents."

He looked down at the violet journal peeking out of my coat pocket, and almost as an afterthought, said, "I once thought I'd be the person to write the definitive book about your mother and father. But I was too cynical. My story got too tangled with their own to be objective. And let's face it, I'm too much of a hack. Who knows, though? Your mother used to tell me about those essay contests you win. Maybe someday, Sylvie, you'll be the person who puts down their story—the one who tells it the way it should be told."

With that, Heekin turned to walk back up the path. I walked with him and we passed person after person who stood in silence, arms in the air. All around, birds moved through the branches, flapping and singing, as people waited for the magic those creatures could bring them if only they were patient, if they were still, if they listened, saying nothing, not a word at all.

He first saw them at a small event at the old Mason Hall in Bethesda—the Masons at the Mason, my father joked from the podium. That night, the story he told was about the Locke Family Farm in Winchester, New Hampshire. A stagecoach traveling south from Montreal in the winter of 1874 broke down not far from the place, and the farmer and his wife took in the men. "Before we go any further," my father said to the group of only a dozen or so, "I should clarify that this is not going to be one of those farmer's daughter jokes." People laughed, and he went on about the travelers being treated to a fireside dinner of roast pig, sweet potatoes, and pumpkin pie. Their stay turned out to be such a pleasure that the men asked to repeat it on their trip north months later, then again the following year. In this way, the Locke Family Farm slowly transformed into an inn that expanded over time to a hilltop structure with twenty-three guest rooms.

While my father spoke about the night that farmer went mad—butchering his wife, children, and seven guests at the inn, all with the same hatchet—Heekin listened intently, though his gaze kept shifting to my mother. She appeared uncomfortable onstage, rocking back and forth in her chair, staring at the floor except for a lone glance up at her husband as he removed the actual hatchet from a small black case. Holding that weapon in his hands, he went on to speak of the years following the massacre, when the hotel fell into disrepair, until finally closing in 1919. By the time he was done describing the strange apparitions that appeared to so many who entered the inn, even Heekin felt as though the family of ghosts had made their way into the room. He pictured a headless Mrs. Locke moving clumsily around the stage. He pictured Mr. Locke in blood-splattered overalls, that hatchet in his hands instead of my father's. He imagined the children, climbing up out of the well where their bodies had been disposed of, joining hands and resuming the game they had been playing when everything went so horribly wrong.

Ashes, ashes, we all fall down . . .

Afterward, Heekin did his best to shake those illusions, drawing on his usual sensibilities and skepticism. And yet, his curiosity persisted. He had first learned of my parents while writing a mundane story for the *Dundalk Eagle* about proposed renovations to the Mason Hall. On his first visit to the building, he noticed a flyer on the lobby bulletin board promoting the event. On this, his second visit, he lingered by the same board following the lecture, waiting for my parents to exit in hopes of striking up a conversation. When the moment arrived, Heekin introduced himself, shaking my father's warm, strong hand, then my mother's cooler, fragile one. At first, my father did not show much interest, Heekin thought, but when he mentioned his job as a reporter, my father divulged more details about their trip to the Locke Family Farm, which was a fully functioning inn once more. The new owners had found the hatchet in an old storm cellar and turned it over to my parents in hopes that it would rid the place of unwanted spirits. Ever since, he told Heekin, things there had been peaceful.

If the news of Heekin's occupation and his interest in writing a story about them caused my father to open up, it had the opposite effect on my mother. She stepped away from their conversation. Heekin kept glancing over at her, trying to catch her eye, but my mother gazed through a window in the lobby, paying no attention to him.

On the ride home—this was a part Heekin did not know until later—my father asked my mother why she had become so taciturn, sullen even, both up on the stage and in the lobby with Heekin. Once again, she stared out the window, not answering.

"I can only gather that it makes you uncomfortable," my father pushed. "Am I right?"

"Yes, Sylvester. The things we do—well, as you know, I've always thought of it as a private matter. A gift we should use to help people, not to draw attention."

My father sighed and they drove in silence for a while, my mother staring out at the dark woods. At last, my father said, "Name a painter you admire."

"I don't know what that's got to do—"

"Just name one."

"Fine. Norman Rockwell."

"A writer?"

"The Brontë sisters."

"A singer?"

"Please, can you make your point, Sylvester?"

"My point is, if any of those people had kept their gifts to themselves, the world would be a less beautiful place. Do you agree?"

"I do," she answered, however reluctantly.

"Well, it's no different for us. We should be sharing this thing that you—that *we* are able to do. We should let others know how many people we've helped. It's a hopeful message, Rose, and if there's one thing the world needs, it's hope. Do you agree with that too?"

"I do," she said again.

"Good. So let's find a way to make you comfortable up there. The last thing I want is the woman I love, that girl with a toothache I fell for at first sight, to be unhappy."

My mother just stared out the window, saying nothing. Later, she told Heekin she'd been thinking of that story my father shared back at the Mason Hall. Outside, in the dark of those woods, she envisioned the Locke family. Among the shadowy trees, she saw that headless farmer's wife, her husband in bloody overalls gripping that hatchet, their children playing ring-around-the-rosy. My mother did not spook easily, but this vision left her unsettled, filling her with a sense of foreboding.

"Are you okay?" my father asked from the driver's seat.

She turned from the woods, from that family, to look at him. "I'm okay."

"Well, I'm happy to hear it." He reached over, took her hand, and held it tight. "So about that reporter. The man gave me his card. Mentioned something about an interview for the newspaper. Don't worry, if it happens, I can do all the talking."

And so a week after that night, Heekin found himself standing on the stoop of our Tudor, ringing the doorbell. When no one answered, he knocked. Finally, my father opened the door and ushered him inside, explaining, "My oldest daughter broke the bell years ago. She thought the little box that contains its mechanics right here on the inside of the door was a bank and kept dropping coins inside. Put in so many the bell stopped ringing. One of these days I'll unscrew the cover and fix it. Probably find a million dollars in there while I'm at it."

Heekin smiled, looking furtively around the living room while taking a seat in one of the wingback chairs that my father offered. He noted the large cross on the wall, the antique clock nearby, the curio hutch stuffed with books, but what caught his eye more than the rest were the framed pictures of Rose and me on a small table in the corner. They were taken when we were in elementary school, our eyes bright, our hair brushed and shiny.

"I take it those are your daughters," he said as my father sat across from him.

"Those are my angels, all right. Lovely, aren't they?"

"Yes," Heekin told him. "You must be a proud father."

"I am. Now, speaking of my girls, they'll be home from school soon. So, if you don't mind, I'd like to get down to business."

Sixty-Three-Year-Old Woman Wins Annual Pie Eating Contest. . .
School Chancellor to Announce New Spending Program. . .
Librarians Create Quilt to Raise Money for New Annex. . .

Those were the sorts of stories Heekin normally covered. They had little depth and required only a handful of questions before the lede, body, and kicker unfurled in his mind. But this interview was different—so much so that it left him nervous. Fidgeting there in his seat, he worried that his old stutter would return. It was something he thought he'd resolved with the help of a speech therapist years before, but whenever he felt uncomfortable it resurfaced. In an effort to keep that problem at bay, he had brought a tape recorder and a reporter's notebook along, filled with questions not addressed in the lecture at the Mason Hall.

How did the two of you get your start?
How do the two of you handle it when one senses something the other does not?
How do the two of you balance your unusual occupation with the everyday demands of raising a family?

But Heekin had drafted those questions with both my mother and father in mind. They were a unit, after all. Yet there was no sign of my mother. He should just come right out and ask, Heekin told himself. Didn't being a reporter mean raising inconvenient questions? But like so many things in life—his failed stint in the air force, his failed relationship with his first wife—he'd never been very good at that. Besides, my father did so much of the talking, unprompted, there was no need to put forth more than a couple of questions.

"The situations you and y-y-your—" Heekin said at one point, interrupting a story my father had already told at the lecture, "y-y-your *wife*. These situations you and your wife encounter sound terrifying. Do the two of you ever feel frightened?"

"We're human," my father said, with a certain amount of pride in his voice. "So fear is only natural. But when we feel it, that's when we pray."

Even though the tape recorder was running, Heekin scratched the answer in his notebook. In truth, he had only asked the question as a way of finally bringing the conversation around to my mother. Not that it mattered, since my father moved swiftly to another topic. "Would you like to see the basement?"

"The basement?" Despite Heekin's skepticism, fear clumped in his throat.

"It's our work area. The place has become a museum of sorts, chock-full of—well, I guess you could call them artifacts—that we've collected on our travels." Without waiting for Heekin to answer, my father stood. "Shall we?"

"Um, yes, s-s-sure," Heekin said, fighting that tongue-tied verbal tic of his.

As they descended the wooden stairs, he kept his tape recorder on—the air cooler, damper, with every step. The place felt vaster than he might have imagined, the darkness in the far corners bleeding into nowhere. In the center, a worn Oriental rug with a wooden desk and an old rocker defined the space. Against a cinder-block wall: a hulking shelf cluttered with books. Against another: a second shelf cluttered with small statues and figurines and a twisted branch, the knots arranged in such a way that a face appeared to be howling in the wood. That hatchet from the Locke Family

Farm was mounted on a wall the way a fisherman would display a prize catch. Beyond it, past the skeleton frame of a wooden partition, in the endless dark of a far corner, Heekin made out what looked to be a mechanical chair of some sort . . . a *dental* chair, he realized with a peculiar shudder. "What . . ." He swallowed. The clump in his throat had sharp edges now. "What goes on down here?"

"I told you. It's where we do our work."

"And what k-k-kind of . . . I mean, if I might ask, what is that back there . . . that I'm looking at in the corner?"

My father turned and looked, then laughed. "Oh, that's just a leftover from my former life as a dentist. When my wife and I first moved into this house, my plan was to set up a home practice. But zoning laws prohibited it, which in the end was a blessing since my heart was never in that line of work. Don't be nervous, though, Sam. I promise not to pull out my old forceps and extract your molars and bicuspids . . . that is, unless you write an unfavorable story about us."

Heekin forced a chuckle and tried to get out a follow-up question about that abandoned career. My father patted him on the shoulder and told him to relax, that no dentists or spirits would do him harm in our basement. Meanwhile, the tape recorder felt brick-heavy in Heekin's hand. He glanced down to see the wheels turning. If he wanted this story to succeed—which he desperately did—then he needed to begin asking the right sorts of questions. He took a breath and out one came, smoothly as possible: "What's that area about to be s-s-sectioned off?"

"It was originally going to be a waiting room for patients, though lately I've begun working on it again. I hope to create a proper room where the occasional troubled soul can stay. Right now, I just set them up on a cot over there. It's not ideal."

"Troubled s-s-soul?"

"That's my way of saying the unfortunate people who come here in need of help."

"What kind of help?"

"Well, put most simply, people whose souls have been occupied by malevolent spirits, spirits that have no intention of leaving on their own."

Heekin looked at my father's dark eyes behind his smudged glasses. He knew about my parents' trips to haunted places. But neither had mentioned anything like this at the lecture. "Do you m-m-mean . . . exorcisms? Aren't those only performed by priests?"

"Usually. But even priests find themselves at a loss in certain cases. Some have even been known to send people to us."

That tape recorder hummed in Heekin's grasp.

"I know what you're thinking." My father held up a hand as if to halt an idea. "You've watched the same movies as everyone else. But in real life, removing an unwanted sprit from a person is nothing like that. No heads spinning around. No green vomit spewing across the room. That kind of thing would guarantee a more colorful story for your paper, I'm sure. But in this house, it comes down to my wife and me calling upon our faith as we spend days and nights praying over and caring for the suffering person."

His wife. Now that my father had mentioned her again, Heekin realized that unless he brought her up soon, he would lose his last chance to ask about her. But the words he wanted would not come, so he followed my father instead to the bookcase against the wall. One by one, my father picked up the items on the shelves, offering a history of each. The details varied, but the stories were unified by similar circumstances: every statue and figurine and even that twisted branch was said to be taken from a haunted place that became peaceful once the object had been removed. On a lower shelf, Heekin noticed a hodgepodge of jewelry—rings and lockets and brooches that had been left by the people who came to our house, my father informed him. "I believe it's best," he said, "if they reenter the world with none of what they came with when the spirit occupied them."

"I see," Heekin said as his next question took shape in his mind. Doing his best to control each word, he put forth the words: "If you believe these items to hold some ill force, doesn't it make you uncomfortable having them in your own home?"

"No," my father said in a calm voice. "Why would it?"

"Well, it seems obvious." Heekin felt more confident now. "If you believe these items once manifested malevolent spirits, isn't it possible they could do the same here? What's more, taken together, it would seem their collective force could create a mass of dark, festering energy beneath your home. I mean, if that's what you believe."

My father was quiet. He rearranged the items on the shelf in such a way that led Heekin to realize the haphazardness was studied. At last, my father said: "My wife and I are extremely devout. We live a clean and honest life in accordance with God's will. That gives us dominion over anything down here."

"What about your daughters? Are they devout? Or do they risk falling prey to—"

"Of course our daughters are devout. They're my children, after all. I wouldn't tolerate anything less."

"Do you allow them down here?"

"It's their house too, so they're welcome anywhere. My wife does prefer that no one go near her old rocker, which once belonged to her father and has sentimental value. As for me, in the same way an accountant, or even a dentist like I once was, would not want children monkeying around in his office, I prefer my girls spend their time elsewhere. Now, speaking of my daughters, they'll be home soon, and I have calls to return before then. Is there anything more you need for your article?"

Your wife, Heekin thought. *I need to talk to your wife.* But despite the fact that he had managed to ask probing questions on other topics, those words still refused to come. "No," he said at last. "No more questions."

With that, my father led him up the stairs. When he stepped through the front door and out onto the stoop, Heekin felt relieved to be in the daylight again. He turned back and managed, "Please tell her . . . your w-w-wife, I mean . . . tell her h-h-hello from me."

My father nodded, but that was his only response before closing the door.

In the week that followed, Heekin sat at his cluttered desk at the *Dundalk Eagle,* playing the tape from the interview and staring at the few scattered notes he'd taken, doing his best to draft the story. He played and replayed the tape, listening to every word, until something jumped out at him:

"I promise you, in most ways, we are the same as any ordinary family.

My wife goes grocery shopping on Saturday mornings. My daughters—"

Maybe, Heekin thought as he stopped the tape, rewound, and played those words again, *maybe I'm not such a bad reporter after all.*

The next weekend found him roaming the aisles of the Mars Market closest to Butter Lane. As a bachelor, he spent little time in stores like that, most nights just grabbing frozen dinners and ice cream from 7-Eleven. He lingered in the market for nearly an hour, picking things up from the shelves and dropping them into a cart, until he began to get suspicious looks from the clerks, at which point he rolled his carriage down an empty aisle and abandoned it, making a speedy exit from the store.

During the next week, he told himself to forget my mother and just write the story based on his notes and the tape. And yet, when Saturday rolled around, he found himself pushing a cart up and down the Mars Market aisles. This time, as he reached for a Hungry Man dinner, a voice came from behind. "Sam?"

Heekin turned to see, not my mother, but my father. At his side: a twelve-year-old *me* with braids in my hair and bright purple bracelets on my wrists. "H-h-hello," he said, that nervous stutter wasting no time in returning.

"Hello," my father said.

"And hello to you t-t-too," Heekin told me. "You must be Sylvie. I've seen your picture in your living room. What's on your wrists?"

I shook my arm, moving the rubbery bands there. "Friendship bracelets."

"Ah. Well, looks like you've g-g-got two good friends. Am I right?"

"Yes. Gretchen and Elizabeth. We all wear the same bracelets."

"So how are you?" my father asked.

Heekin looked around for some sign of my mother. "G-g-good. And y-y-you?"

"Fine. I've been meaning to call and ask when the story is going to run."

"The story? Y-y-yes. That. Well, it is g-g-going to run. I just need to . . ."

"Need to what?"

"Write it," Heekin blurted. "I need to write the thing."

"Write it?" my father said. "We spoke weeks ago. But I guess these things take longer than I realized."

"In this case, it does. Because I need to t-t-talk to . . . I mean, I h-h-have. . . ."

"Follow-up questions?"

"Yes. Follow-up questions. I need to come by again and ask a few more."

"Certainly. Why not come tomorrow? Same time as before?"

The next day Heekin arrived at our door for the second time. On the drive there, he had promised himself to ask about my mother. She was fifty percent of the story, after all, and it made sense that he inquire about her. He rang the bell, forgetting the detail about my sister breaking it with all those coins. The door opened anyway, and Heekin was prepared to blurt the question the moment he saw my father's face. But after so much waiting, it was my mother who stood before him.

"I thought I heard someone out here," she said in a soft-timbred voice. Heekin. "Is everything okay? You look startled, if you don't mind me saying."

"It's j-j-just. I was, well, on the d-d-d-drive over I was imagining . . . not imagining . . . p-p-planning how this visit would g-g-g-go. And I didn't expect—"

"Didn't expect what?"

"You," he managed to say. "I didn't expect you."

"Well, I didn't expect to see you, either. I prefer my husband talk to you on our behalf. I don't feel comfortable doing interviews. But I'm afraid you'll have to see him another time. I will let him know you came by."

My mother stepped outside, pulled the door shut behind her. She gave Heekin a warm smile and started past him toward the Datsun in the driveway.

"I d-d-don't understand," he called after her. "We have an appointment. Where is he?"

"Upstairs in bed. He's thrown his back out."

"I'm s-s-sorry."

"I'm sorry too."

My mother reached the car, sizing it up as though it were a horse she was wary of mounting. Heekin watched as she went through the keys on her chain, determining which would unlock the door. "You hate to drive," he blurted, getting the words out all at once.

She looked up at him with her glittery green eyes. "How do you know that?"

"Your husband. It's on the tapes. The tapes from the interviews, I mean. I remembered him saying that about you."

"Well, you're right. It makes me nervous, because I've never been very good at it. But I manage fine when the situation calls for it."

"I could drive you. Wherever you're going."

My mother did not answer immediately. She stared at something inside the car, jangling her keys, before looking back at him.

"No interview," he promised. "Just some friendly chitchat."

Her errand turned out to be to the pharmacy for my father's pain pills. My mother explained that on occasion he called in prescriptions under her name, since the one thing he maintained from his former career was his medical license. Other than that, Heekin did the talking, stuttering and rambling despite his best efforts. He told her about his lonely year spent in the air force working as a typist. "Not many p-p-people know this b-b-bit of trivia, but H-H-Hugh Hefner also worked as an air force t-t-t-typist. It's the only thing that guy and I have in c-c-c-common."

It was a joke Heekin had told before, one of the few he could count on to get a laugh, but my mother just said, "Forgive me, but Hugh who?"

"Hefner."

"*Heifer?*"

"No. Hef*ner.*"

"Oh," she said. "And who's that?"

"You know, the head of *Playboy* magazine."

Her hand went to her chest. "I'm sorry, Mr. Heekin—"

"Sam. Call me Sam."

"I'm sorry, Sam. But I'm not familiar with those sorts of publications or the people in them."

Their time together was off to a bad start. Heekin wanted to rewind things, to begin again. Instead, he told her about his life at the paper, the bland stories he normally covered, and his dream of someday finding a subject worthy of writing an actual book about. All the while my mother sat in the passenger seat, smelling of rosewater like her name, her delicate hands stroking her black leather purse as though it were a cat purring on her lap.

Empty soda cans littered the floor, and she nudged them away whenever his Volkswagen made a turn.

When they pulled into the strip mall, she asked if he minded parking around back, since she preferred using that entrance in order to slip in and out more easily. He did as she wanted, and my mother told Heekin she'd just be a moment. True to her word, she emerged in no time, pausing unexpectedly to examine a towering stack of thick, discarded books behind the neighboring hardware store, pulling one off the top and carrying it with her to the car. On the drive back to our house, Heekin made up his mind to allow her to do the talking. Beyond the brief explanation about the book, however—filled with wallpaper swatches, a fortuitous find, she said, since she needed help figuring out what to do about the peeling walls in our kitchen—my mother did not have much to say. Most of the ride was spent in silence, her purse on the floor now, as she turned the pages of that book, looking at all the patterns there, asking now and then his impression of a particular swatch. At last, they turned onto the lane, and Heekin could not help feeling like he'd blown his chance at some connection with her. "Good-bye," he told her, a disproportionate melancholy stirring in his chest.

My mother thanked him, unbuckling her seat belt and getting out of the car. But in the last moment before closing the door, she surprised him by leaning in to say, "You seem like a nice man. And this story sounds important to you. Uncomfortable as it makes me, I'd like to help. Why don't you bring your notebook and recorder in for tea?"

"Really?" he said, hearing the childish excitement in his voice.

"Really," she told him.

Inside, my mother asked Heekin to make himself comfortable while she went to the kitchen. Rather than take a seat, he stood in the hallway, running questions he wanted to ask though his mind. My mother had set the wallpaper book and the small white bag from the pharmacy on a side table by the stairs, and the pharmacy bag was open enough for Heekin to see the jumble of amber containers inside: Tylenol with codeine, Vicodin, others with unfamiliar names. After the whistle screeched on the kettle, my mother moved through the hall with a tray to take up to my father, fetching the white bag on the way.

When she returned, they went to the living room. "So," she began once they were seated. "What can I tell you that my husband has not?"

"Your childhood," he said, fighting his nervousness. "He *ne-ne*-never *to-to*-told me . . . well . . . I mean we *ta-ta*-talked about his childhood. But we *ne-ne*-never touched on yours. Could you *te-te*-tell me . . . you know, about it?"

My mother sat patiently, waiting for him to get out all those words.

When he was done, Heekin managed, "Forgive me. It's an old *ha-ha*-habit I've kicked. But it *ha-ha*-happens sometimes when I'm *ne-ne*-nervous."

In a gentle voice, she asked, "Has it always been this way for you?"

"It *s-s*-started with m-m-my father. He used to b-b-b-bark at me, and so I felt uptight around him. The habit comes *ba-ba*-back whenever I'm uncomfortable."

"I'm sorry," she told him. "If you like, we can pray together about it and see what can be done."

"Thank you. But with all *d-d*-due respect, I'm not really a believer in those things."

"What things?"

"You know, prayer and *d-d*-demons."

My mother was quiet, thinking over his statement. At last, she said, "What is prayer but meditation? What is a demon but a fear that lives inside us, one we cannot easily conquer on our own? If you prefer to use those words, it's all right by me. So I make the same offer. If you like, we can meditate together on this fear you can't control."

Heekin's answer surprised even himself. "Okay."

My mother leaned forward in her chair. She took his warm hands in her cool ones, squeezing more strongly than he would have guessed she'd be able to do. He expected her to say something, but her lips stayed pressed together. She closed her eyes, and he took this as a cue that he should too. The only sound was the ticking of the clock, the birds chirping out in the yard.

At first, Heekin felt tempted to open his eyes and peek at her face, so near his, but then he realized he didn't need to, he could see it there, in the darkness behind his lids. Her pale, papery skin. Her thin lips pursed. The silver crosses glinting in her ears. Just thinking of her so close, feeling her fingers against his, put him at ease. His mind drifted to some warm, unnamable place. He was a child hopping the checkerboard tiles of the floor in the grocery store. He was a child riding his bike outside his father's ranch house in Augustine, Delaware. At last, he felt her hands slip from his. He did not open his eyes right away, but instead, he remained as he was, picturing her pretty face once more as she asked, "And how did that feel?"

"Peaceful," he answered, looking at her finally.

"Good," she told him, smiling. "The next time you sense those old fears about to take hold, I want you to remember the special feeling of peace we created here together. My hope is that it will help you to stay calm and get your words out the way you intend them to sound. Okay?"

"Okay."

"Now," my mother said. "Should we try this interview again?"

"Yes." Heekin felt himself breathing more easily. He felt the words come more smoothly too. "Can you tell me about your childhood?"

"I grew up on a farm in the South. My mother was a quintessential farm wife. She disciplined me with a switch and believed children should be seen and not heard."

"And your father?"

"I loved my father," she said in such a way that implied she had not felt the same about her mother. "He was tough too, but he treated me like I was special. Unusual as it was for a man in rural Tennessee, he knew perfect Latin and taught it to me. Not that I have much use for it these days beyond the occasional Latin spoken at Mass in the gym."

It was then, with some prodding on Heekin's part, that she told him the story of the birdhouses her father had built and what she'd done after he was gone.

"That must have been heartbreaking for you," he said when she finished. "And you mentioned that he passed, but you never said how."

In an instant, my mother's eyes welled. Tears did not spill onto her cheeks, but they suspended on her lower lids, on the verge. Even after so many years, he could see how the question had pricked at something raw inside her, so Heekin told her to never mind. It was something no good reporter would ever say, but he didn't care. "You don't have to tell me, Mrs. Mason."

"Rose," she said, pressing her index fingers to the bottom of each eye as though to shove those tears back inside. "You can call me Rose."

"Rose!" my father called from upstairs.

The timing caused them both to laugh. "Apparently, someone else does," Heekin said, making a joke.

And yet, my father's voice broke whatever spell had been working between them. "I should be going," my mother said, standing from her chair. "I hope the things I've shared help with your story and impress your editor."

"I feel certain that they will," he told her.

At the door, Heekin worked up the courage to mention the nature preserve he first discovered when he'd been stationed at the Dover Air Force base. Despite the roar of military planes overhead that so often startled the birds, the place had been his only escape. "Even if I was too afraid to fly, it was comforting to watch those little creatures do it. And if you're patient and still long enough, they land right in your hand. Anyway, if you like I could—"

"Rose!" my father called. "I need your help getting to the bathroom!"

"You could what?" my mother asked Heekin.

"I could take you there sometime," he said, rushing out the words before my father could distract her any further. "No interview. Just a friendly field trip."

He expected my mother to politely decline his offer. But she didn't hesitate. "I'd like that very much."

Heekin smiled, reached in his pocket, and gave her his card. She took it and thanked him before closing the door. As he walked to his car and climbed inside, glancing back at the house, he replayed their last hour together, in particular the moment she took his hands in hers.

I shouldn't have told you all those things," Heekin said as we pulled off an exit ramp after nearly two hours on the highway north. At the stoplight, his car stalled for what must have been the fifth time. He pumped the gas and worked the ignition until it started again just as the light turned green. "Blame the long ride. Blame the fact that you remind me so much of her."

I stared at my reflection in the glass of the passenger window, trying to see the parts of me that led him and so many others to think of her. Out-side on the derelict sidewalks, I watched a woman carrying shopping bags that looked too heavy for her stringy arms. I watched a hunched man push a grocery store cart heaped with empty bottles. It felt as though we were touching down in some strange place, a tiny bird from the preserve gliding its way into some far-flung country on Rose's globe.

When we turned onto the streets of a barren neighborhood, one last unexpected question slipped out: "Did she ever tell you how her father, my grandfather, died?"

"Only that it was some sort of accident on the farm." He paused, before adding, "Your mother was an honest woman, but I got the feeling that was one of the rare lies she told. If I was a better reporter, I might have found out what really happened."

For all his talk of poor reporting skills, Heekin had done an expert job of tracking down my uncle—or rather, never losing track of him in the first place. Before we got on the road, he had insisted we give him a call from a pay phone. When Howie heard my voice, he sounded surprised, and even more so when I told him I was on my way to see him. He stalled, suggest-ing we put it off until some other time. But I insisted. Even if he didn't exactly agree, that's how I made it sound to Heekin when I hung up. Now, after driving all that way, I felt anxious about the possibility that my uncle might not be there after all.

We moved at a crawl through the streets of a dreary neighborhood, squinting at the boarded windows of houses we passed, the shell of a scorched car, the minefields of shattered glass on the pavement that Heekin carefully navigated around. At last, we came to a stop outside a large build-ing. As I looked at the chipped gray paint, the scramble of crooked letters above the row of glass doors, a strange feeling stirred inside me. It made me realize I'd seen this place before, but where?

"Are you okay, Sylvie?" Heekin asked.

I told him I just felt anxious about seeing my uncle again after so many months. "And, well, I don't understand. After all these years, why—how did he end up here?"

"Those are questions your uncle can answer better than I can. And that's what we came here for, isn't it: so you can get answers?"

With that, Heekin pushed open his door. I did the same. We stepped out onto the sidewalk, desolate except for a bodega a few blocks away. Sirens wailed and faded until the air grew silent, thick with something menacing. I remembered the unexpected shyness I felt upon seeing my uncle that night in Ocala as some version of that feeling swooped down upon me now. There was little time for that, however, since Heekin was moving across the street, and I hurried to keep up. All the while, my gaze kept going to the scramble of crooked letters on the old marquee. We had come to the place I'd seen in one of the photos in my father's desk drawer when Dot splashed about upstairs that long-ago night. This was the theater where he had spent his childhood, collecting tickets, sweeping floors, and seeing ghosts—his very first—amid the darkness inside.

THE WELL

The morning after we returned from Ohio, I expected to walk downstairs and find my mother right where we left her, asleep on the living
room sofa. But she was gone. In the late morning hours, my father explained, she must have managed to make it up the stairs and into their
room, because he opened his eyes to find her in the bed next to his.

"Penny too?" I wanted to ask, but something in me already knew the
answer.

For nearly a week after that, my mother remained sealed away in their
bedroom. She did not appear in the mornings before we left for school.
She did not appear in the evenings when we arrived home. Funny how
that waitress had trouble envisioning "someone like her" being a mother,
because during that time, I think all of us in our family realized how good
a job she'd always done. It wasn't just my father's runny mashed potatoes
or dried-out cube steaks; and it wasn't just our unwashed clothes in an ever-
growing heap by the machines. Those details felt insignificant compared
to the off-kilter mood that permeated our house. I would not have been
surprised to have found murky water sloshing in the basement corners,
because that's what we had become: a ship taking on the dark and icy sea,
about to sink.

Still, my father and I tried. In the evenings, we sat with Rose at the
kitchen table—my mother's chair with her book of wallpaper swatches on

top nothing short of a ghost among us—pretending the meal tasted as good as one she would have made from her recipes. To his credit, my father worked hard at keeping the conversation alive. Most often, that meant asking me about school, since my sister had become difficult to talk to. One night, as she was cutting into her sauceless chicken breast, my father took a stab at it anyway. "Rose?" he said. And when she kept cutting, not answering, he tried again, "Rose?"

My sister looked up. "What can I do for you?"

"What can you—" He put down his fork, rubbed his temples. "You can make an effort at some conversation over dinner—*that's* what you can do. Haven't you got anything to say for yourself?"

Rose slipped a piece of chicken between her lips and chewed. "I do, actually."

"Okay, then. Go ahead."

"Well," she said with her mouth full. "I was just wondering when Mom is going to rise from the dead?"

"Rise from the— Rose, your mother is not dead. She's ill."

"If that's the case, then maybe we should take her to a doctor. Or do we not believe in doctors anymore around here? Are we hoping that Jesus will magically—"

"For your information, we did take her to a doctor."

"When?" I asked.

"The other day. You girls were at school. Dr. Zeller gave her a thorough exam."

"*And?*" Rose and I both said.

"And he wasn't sure what to make of her symptoms. The random waves of nausea. The extreme fatigue. All that and yet no fever whatsoever. Could be any number of things, he told us. But most likely a bacterial infection."

"Now that sounds official," Rose said. "Old Doc Z could be a regular on *St. Elsewhere*."

"Saint *what?*" I asked.

"I've said it before, Sylvie; it might do you good to watch crap TV once in a while. Otherwise, you'll end up not knowing anything about the real world, just like—"

"When do you watch that sort of TV?" my father asked.

"I don't," Rose told him. "I only wish I could. But you never know, *St. Elsewhere* might poison my pure mind and heart, and put me at risk of falling prey to—"

"*Don't*," my father said, raising his voice. "We talked about your behavior and that mouth of yours."

We were all quiet then. I couldn't help but think of the murky water I imagined in the basement. I pictured the house sinking, the kitchen slanting, the table and chairs sliding across the floor, dishes crashing, as that icy water rose up and swallowed us alive.

"So when will Mom be better?" I asked.

"Soon," my father told me. "Very soon."

Rose put down her knife, giving up on dinner. Under her breath, she muttered, "Should have handed the doll over to that waitress."

"Waitress?" my father said.

"Never mind," she told him.

"If you're going to say something, follow through. Now what waitress?"

"She means the one from the truck stop," I offered, in hopes of easing the tension between them. "That place near Harrisburg."

My father squinted, remembering. "But we didn't eat there. So how did you girls come to talk to any waitress?"

"She was in the bathroom. And she recognized you and Mom from TV," I said.

This bit of news caused my father to sit up straighter. "Oh, she did, did she?"

"You'd think the lady had never laid eyes on a doll before," Rose said.

"Or at least not one in a bathroom in the middle of the night," I added. "Not to mention the fingerprints on its neck and the bracelet around its—"

"Did your mother put Penny down?" Our father was sitting up straight still, paying careful attention. "And this waitress—did she notice those details about the doll?"

"Yes and yes," I answered.

"She couldn't get enough of the thing," Rose told him. "That's why we should have given it to her. If you ask me, it's got some weird germs that are making Mom sick. Didn't you tell us it belonged to some kid with a disease who died?"

"I did. But it's not Penny's germs that are infecting your mother."

"Well, what is it then?"

My father pushed back his chair and stood from the table without taking his plate to the sink. It was Rose's turn to clear and wash the dishes. If it had been mine, he would have helped, but he never bothered when it came to her. "All this talk made me realize there's a project I need to work on," he told us, before pulling the basement door open and descending the stairs.

The next afternoon, I stepped off the bus and walked down the lane only to hear Rose and my father shouting inside the house. At first, I figured it was more of their usual bickering. As I got closer, though, I began to make out words, more barbed and menacing than I'd heard them use before.

"I warned you in Florida! I told you that was strike one! Now it's strike two! One more, Rose, and I promise you'll be out!"

"Just like that, huh? You'll send me packing, same as you do those freaks who come here once you're done using them!"

"*Using them?* We *help* them! You keep talking like that, and I'll send you away until you can show some respect for your parents and live in a way we see fit!"

That was the most I heard, because when I opened the door, Rose burst from the kitchen and stormed down the hall. She shoved past me, stomping up the stairs and slamming her door. A moment later, I heard my father clomp down the basement stairs after slamming that door too. In the ringing silence that followed, I stood wondering which of them to go after.

That's when my mother stepped from the kitchen and appeared before me in the hallway, smiling. In the stories my father told in lectures, people woke to find a deceased relative bathed in warm light at the foot of their beds. In those stories, the person's heart filled with overwhelming joy at the sight. That's how it felt to lay eyes on my mother. I ran to her and threw my arms around her. "I'm so happy to see you," I told her, breathing in the milky smell of her skin.

"I'm happy to see you too," she said, laughing. "But, Sylvie, you're carrying on as though I've been away. I've only been upstairs with a bug. You could've come visit."

"Dad told us we should leave you alone."

"He did, huh?" She ran a hand over my hair. "Well, I'm sure he was just worried you girls might catch whatever I had. And trust me, you wouldn't have wanted it."

I hugged her more tightly, turning my face in the other direction, so I could see into the living room. That's when I spotted the doll slumped in my mother's old rocker from the basement, head tilted sharply to one side as though someone had snapped her neck. "What's that doing here?" I asked, pulling away.

"Penny? Oh, I don't need to cart her around anymore. I handed her over to your father. From the looks of things, he found a home for her in the living room."

Footsteps trudged up from the basement just then. We turned to see my father emerge, holding his 35 mm camera. "I know it's your first time out of bed in almost a week," he said to my mother, keeping his eyes on the dials and fiddling. "But we've only got a few exposures left on this roll. I want to get it developed before our next lecture. So we may as well put it to good use and get a picture of you—"

"Oh, Sylvester. I can't get my picture made now."

Getting her picture made—that was a turn of phrase left over from my mother's childhood in Tennessee, something I never heard anyone but her say. "How about taking one of Mom and me?" I asked.

"Actually, Sylvie, I was thinking of taking a photo of your mother and Penny."

"Penny?" my mother said. "What for?"

"You know what for, Rose. We'll file it with the others. Maybe show it in our talks or allow that reporter to use it when he writes another article or that book about us."

"That book," my mother said with a sigh. "Sylvester, I'm not sure I want a photo like that turning up in a newspaper or a book or anywhere at all."

"You didn't let me finish. I was about to say, *only if you feel comfortable*. But those were just ideas I was tossing around. We can discuss them later.

For now, let's just take a photo for our records. Best to do it while there's still daylight, since the flash on this thing doesn't always work so well."

I watched as my mother walked reluctantly to the rocker, picking up the doll and propping it over one shoulder, just like during that car ride. She followed my father outside and stood before our Tudor, which looked more run-down than usual in the fading light. My gaze stayed on her as she cradled Penny the way she must have once cradled Rose, the way she must have once cradled me as well. My father wasted no time before snapping away. Despite his reasoning that there were only a few exposures left, I counted nine before I interrupted to ask if he could please take one of my mother and me.

"Oh, angel," he said, looking at the dials and fiddling again. "I just used the last exposure. You should have said something sooner."

"I *did* say something sooner," I told him before I could stop myself.

My father lifted his head and fixed me with a look. "Sylvie," he said. "Your mother and I are doing this for our work, not for fun and games."

"Don't worry, dear," my mother said, heading back in the house with Penny. "I promise to buy a disposable camera at Mars Market. We'll get a nice photo made of us."

After the doll was returned to the rocker and my father returned his camera to the basement, there was homework to be done, followed by dinner. As we sat at the table, Rose's empty chair became the ghost among us, since she did not come downstairs or respond when I knocked on her door. A roast made in the slow cooker—that's all it was, but the food tasted better than anything we'd eaten in some time, since my mother prepared it. It was my turn to clear and clean the dishes, but both my parents helped, and my mother wrapped the bone in aluminum foil and put it in the freezer for some future day when she might need it to make soup stock. When all that was done, I figured we'd gather in the living room to watch a documentary on PBS, but my father said he had a handful of work things to discuss with my mother. The business of that book by Sam Heekin, I guessed. Whatever it was, I left them to it and went up to my room.

When I'd found the broken horses a week before, I waited till morning to take the pieces into the bathroom where Rose was brushing her teeth. "Did you do this?" I asked.

"*Me?*" Her mouth was full of toothpaste, which she promptly spit out. She plucked a leg from my palm, inspected the knobby knee, the broad hoof. "Of course not."

"Well, who else then?"

"I don't know. But what reason would I have?"

"There are lots of things you do, Rose, that I don't understand your reasons for."

"Careful. You're starting to sound like Dad." She returned the limb to my hand, her toothbrush to the medicine cabinet. "You know, Sylvie, when a horse breaks a leg, it's a lost cause. In real life they'd shoot it. If I were you, I'd just toss it in the trash."

Her surprise, her denial—they had seemed genuine, so I left her and went to my desk to begin the careful surgery of gluing the pieces together. Still, I could not believe that my father or mother—or even that doll— could be responsible.

Now, not so many nights later, I listened to the murmur of my parents' voices discussing their work down in the living room while I looked up at that shelf. Inspecting the horses, counting their legs to be sure they were intact, had become a ritual before sleep. The ritual was interrupted when my gaze reached a spotted pony with glimmering brown eyes. Aurora's wooden tail had been snapped off. It took hunting, but I located that tail behind my desk. I felt the urge to march down the hall, to slam my fist against Rose's door, to scream at her that none of this was funny. But I knew she'd only deny it again, doing an even more convincing job the second time around. The obvious solution was to begin locking my door. I locked it then, and found the small hook-shaped piece of metal to lock it from the outside in the future too, before sitting at my desk once more and gluing yet another horse together.

All the while, I heard my parents below. It was not possible to make out their words, but the clipped rise and fall of their speech gave me the sense that the discussion wasn't pleasant. And then, all at once, they fell silent. I heard them climb the stairs and settle into their beds down the hall. By then Aurora was whole again, and though I needed sleep, I stayed at my desk and let my mind wander. For days, I'd been replaying what Rose had said about me ending up like our parents if I didn't pay attention to the real world. Maybe the details about TV shows she tossed out in conversation were meaningless compared to the information in the documentaries we were allowed to watch, but I didn't like the idea of my sister knowing things I did not. That feeling is what led me to unlock my door and sneak downstairs.

Other than a quick glance, I forced myself not to look at Penny in my mother's rocker. I simply pulled a chair close to the TV, turned it on, and lowered the volume. Flipping channels past late-night news stories about Margaret Thatcher and another about Oliver North, I landed on the sort of rerun my parents forbid but Rose might reference: *Three's Company*. It didn't take long to suss out the players and the plot, which had to do with an overheard conversation wildly misinterpreted. Ridiculous as the story was, I kept watching, easing into the unfamiliar sound of canned laughter. During a commercial, I went to the kitchen, where I made myself a sandwich from the leftover roast and poured a glass of milk before returning to the living room. It wasn't until the credits rolled that I looked over at the rocker again. The watery blue light of the television flickered over that chair, over me too, as I stared at the place where Penny sat when I came downstairs.

But Penny was no longer there.

Had she been there when I walked out of the kitchen moments before? I could not be certain. And as I picked over the possibilities, my mind arrived at the same conclusion it did with those horses: my sister was playing tricks on me. I imagined her padding down the steps to watch TV, realizing what I was doing, and getting the idea to move that doll somewhere just to scare me. I moved quietly around the room, peeking behind the sofa and drapes and any other place where Rose and I used to hide. But there was no sign of Penny anywhere, so I gave up and turned off the TV, sliding my chair back into place before climbing the stairs again.

At the end of the hall upstairs, Rose's door was shut. My parents' was cracked open, however, so I peeked inside. The green glow of their alarm clock gave only enough light to make out each of them, lumps in their beds. I thought of the silence that had fallen over them before bed. I rarely heard them argue, and I wondered if they'd gone to sleep angry at each other, which left me with a sudden sense of sadness toward them.

In the morning, I woke early to find my sister's door still shut, my parents still lumps in their beds. Downstairs, the doll sat in the rocker again as though she had been there all along. I walked closer, staring at the smudges around her neck, the bracelet around her wrist. That face—one a child might draw with a crayon—was nothing more than a pair of eyes, a triangle nose, and a curled slash for a smile. And yet, looking at it brought a feeling of dread. I stood there, soaking in that feeling, wondering if I'd imagined the entire thing the night before, as that waitress's voice echoed in my mind.

She's just an old Raggedy Ann. A dime a dozen. But this one, well, she feels different somehow . . .

"You girls having a nice morning chat?"

The voice startled me, and I whirled around to see Rose, showered and dressed, walking down the stairs. *Say something,* I told myself. *About the doll. About the horses.* But I just stood there, watching her move through the hall to the kitchen. I heard the fridge open and close. Cabinets and drawers too, followed by the sound of cereal being poured into a bowl.

"What's wrong with you?" she asked, coming back into the living room with her breakfast, crunching away.

"Nothing." I turned again from Penny's smiling face to see my sister's more serious one. "Where are you going?"

"Hate to break it to you, Sylvie, but there's this place called high school where I have to be in a bit. Another place called junior high where you have to be soon too. That's something I wouldn't expect an egghead like you to forget."

Above us, floorboards creaked. Our parents were getting ready to start their day too. Rose rolled her eyes. "For once I'm actually looking forward to it," she said. "I mean, anything to get me out of this joint for a while."

In the mornings, Rose left the house first, since the high school bus came before the one I took to junior high. But that day, I asked if I could walk with her to the stop in hopes of finding a moment to confront her about the games she was playing with me. After I hurried to dress and gather my books, we headed out the door together. On the way, Rose stopped to pick up rocks, tossing them into the empty foundations and doing her best to hit those rusted fireplace rods at the bottom, which gave a loud *clank* and elicited a "Yes!" from her whenever she was successful. At the end of the lane, she pulled a cigarette from her sock, just like she'd done in that desolate park on Orchard Circle. As she sucked on one end, blowing a hearty puff into the morning air, I heard the rumble of an engine not far down the road. "I don't think what you're doing is funny," I blurted, worrying that the bus must be approaching.

Rose rolled her eyes and let out a groan. "Oh, please, Sylvie. The last thing I need is a lecture from you about smoking. I get enough lectures from Mom and Dad."

"I'm not talking about smoking. I'm talking about my horses and the—"

"Your horses? You're back on that? I told you, I didn't do it."

"I don't believe you." Instead of the bus, a truck rumbled past. But I pressed on with the conversation anyway. "Why should I?"

"Why should you? I don't know. First, you're the only one in our family treating me decently right now. Second, I know those horses actually mean something to you. I wouldn't mess with them. In fact, you can take mine if you want. They're under my bed. Looking at them only makes me think of Howie, which is something I'd rather not do."

"I thought you liked Uncle Howie?"

"*Liked.* Past tense."

"What changed?"

"What changed is that I called and asked if I could come live with him."

"In Tampa?"

"Last I checked that's where he lives, knucklehead."

Just the thought that Rose might actually find some way to leave home caused an unexpected longing to stir inside, because I was not ready to lose her. "Why would you do that?"

"*Why?* Sylvie, open your eyes. In case you haven't noticed, things aren't exactly working out for me here in Holy Roller Hell. I figured it might be better if I stayed with him. You know, finished up school down there then figured out what to do with my life."

As we spoke, Rose ran a thumb over the dial on her lighter. Once in a while, she did it hard enough that a flame reared up. She took another puff of her cigarette, blew smoke between us. "Well, I wouldn't like that," I said.

"And why not?"

I felt silly saying the words, but I said them anyway: "Because I'd miss you."

My sister looked away from me, back down our street at those old foundations where we used to play, before turning to me again. "Oh. Well, I'd miss you too, kid. But it doesn't matter. Our dear old uncle blew me off. Said he didn't know how long he'd even be in Tampa since he had other plans."

"What plans?"

"Pipe dreams, really. Crap he blames Dad for getting in the way of all these years. Anyway, who cares? The point is, I'm not a fan of Howie. So the horses in my room, they're yours if you want them."

"What about Penny?"

"The doll? Well, you can have that too. But you might want to check with the thing's new parents. Mom and Dad, I mean."

I told her that's not what I was asking, then took a breath and explained what happened the night before. But once I was done with all those details, the most Rose had to say was, *"Three's Company,* huh? Now that's a dopey show. Though I'd like living near the beach in California."

In the distance, I heard the sound of an engine again. This time, I looked to see that it really was the bus rolling in our direction. Before it got closer, I said, "Tell me you came downstairs and hid Penny on me last night."

Rose snuffed her cigarette on the bottom of her sneaker before stashing what was left of it in her sock. She reached in her pocket for a stick of gum, folding it into her mouth. The smell of smoke mingled with mint, same as in the park. "That night at the truck stop, when you woke to find the yarn in your hand, remember that?"

"I do."

"I admit to putting it there. I was just messing with you. Having some fun."

"I knew it. And the same goes for last night?"

The bus bore down upon us, lumbering to a stop just feet away with a loud squeal of brakes and the roar of teenage voices laughing and hollering inside. The driver, a vest-wearing woman with a ratty ponytail, swung a lever and the door sandwiched open.

"Sorry, Sylvie. Can't cop to that one. Ever since I heard Mom hacking her guts out, I steer clear of that thing. I wasn't kidding when I said it might have germs."

"Well, then I don't—"

"Are you coming?" the driver called.

My sister moved toward the door, climbed onto the first step. I stood watching, not wanting her to leave just yet. Before disappearing inside, Rose turned back. "We can talk about it later, Sylvie. I've got my own ideas about things that go on inside that house. If you keep your mouth shut, I might tell you."

With that, the door closed. Through the windows, I saw my sister walk clumsily down the aisle in search of an empty seat as the bus began rolling away. After she was gone, I waited for my bus to arrive. Then I waited all day for school to be done, and for the hours of homework and dinner to pass. A day passed. Two. Three. A week. Another week. Never once did Rose give me so much as a hint of the things we talked about that morning. I could have escorted her to the bus stop again and tried to prod her, but I figured she had made up her mind not to tell me anything after all. Meanwhile, things seemed to return to normal at home, or normal as they could be with that doll smiling from my mother's rocker every time I stepped into the living room.

And then came a day when I walked the packed hallways between classes with Gretchen and Elizabeth. We were discussing an upcoming English exam that had us nervous, since the teacher always threw in a trick question. Last time, it amounted to a simple vocabulary word—*exigency*—that not one of us knew the meaning of. In the middle of our guessing what it would be this time, a voice shouted, "I saw your sister!"

Laughter erupted, and as I was looking around to figure out what was going on, Brian Waldrup stepped in front of me. "I mean you, Wednesday. I saw your sister."

"That's not my name," I told him, thinking of the way my mother hated being the center of attention. This was why, I realized, things could turn on you in an instant.

"It's your name now. And I saw your sister."

"I don't— You saw Rose?"

"No. Penny. That's what you freaks call her, right?"

For just a moment, all the noise and commotion in that hallway seemed to cease. There was Brian with his buzzed hair and ripped jeans. There was Gretchen with her mouth full of braces. There was Elizabeth with her horsey face. I stood, watching as their eyes and so many others fell upon me. "She's not my—I mean, it's not my sister. And I don't know what you're talking about."

"I think you do," Brian said, laughing. "So does anyone who looked at today's paper."

Rather than respond, I started moving again, telling myself I'd go to the library the first chance I got to find the paper he was talking about. Gretchen and Elizabeth followed, though that did not stop Brian from calling after me, saying that name over and over: "Penny! Penny! Penny!" I tried to keep my two friends from hearing any more by talking loud and walking fast. It was some made-up story, I said; he exaggerated things, and it was better to just ignore him. But even as I said those words, I detected something flimsy in my voice. They must have sensed it too, because I glanced over to see a mix of curiosity and confusion on their faces, and I knew then that whatever germs my sister spoke of—real or imagined—had spread, irreversibly, to school now too.

When I arrived home, I found my father in the living room, curio hutch wide open as he inspected the books inside. The phone rang and rang, but he made no move to answer it. I'd long since returned the "history" book, but the sight of him there worried me anyway. *Don't bring up the article,* I told myself, sensing that it would be better to discuss it with my mother. "What are you looking for?" I asked, trying to sound casual.

"Just gathering information for a new lecture. We booked two more today, and I'd like to give them a bit more historical context. People are so obsessed with what they see in movies, and I want them to understand the way malevolent spirits can have a more subtle but devastating influence on their lives if they don't keep them at bay. For example, in the 1600s—"

"I don't want to go on those trips anymore," I heard myself say over the ringing phone.

"Excuse me?" my father said, distracted still by the thick book in his hands.

"I don't like missing school. It's too hard to make up."

"You'll be fine." Without looking at me, he flipped the pages, saying, "We tried leaving you girls here alone before. Remember how that turned out?"

The image of Dot, naked and cowering in the corner of their bathroom, came to life in my mind. "But that was because of Rose." *Or* mostly *because of Rose,* I thought.

"Sylvie, I don't know where this is coming from," he told me, shutting the book and paying attention now. "But we're not leaving you here alone and we're not going back to enlisting a nanny service. Besides, I can't say no. I've already agreed to the lectures. They're paying us three times what we normally get."

The ringing fell quiet. And again, I heard myself say something unplanned: "Why?"

"*Why?*" At last, my father looked up from his book with an exasperated expression.

"I mean, why are they suddenly paying more?"

"Well, if you must know, word is getting out about us," he said with a measure of pride. "People are curious about the things your mother and I do."

My mother. The mention of her caused me to glance over at her rocker. Penny was not there. As if to prove my father's point about how in demand they were, the phone began ringing again. "Where is Mom anyway?"

"In bed."

"Bed? But it's barely four o' clock."

"Yeah, well, she's not feeling her best."

"She's sick again?"

"I'm afraid so, Sylvie."

Before he was even done talking, I turned and started toward the stairs.

My father called after me that I should leave her alone so she could rest, but I ignored him, going directly to my parents' bedroom and peeking in.

Since the shades were drawn, the green glow of the alarm clock was the only light in that room. My mother's body was a lump under the covers once more. I could make out only her pale face, eyes closed, on the pillow. Someone must have turned off the ringer on the phone in their room, because inside I heard only the soft rise and fall of her breathing even as down below the sound started up again. I wanted to bring my mother soup and cool washcloths and ginger ale, to take care of her the way she had always taken care of us, but there seemed to be nothing to do at the moment except let her sleep. I stepped away and went to my room, where I found Rose lying on my bed.

"How did you get in here?" I asked, since I had locked the door when I left.

My sister ignored the question, held out a copy of the *Dundalk Eagle*. "I've been waiting for you. Did you see this?"

I looked down at the photo of our mother cradling Penny. "Someone said something at school," I told her. "So, yeah. I went to the library and found it."

"Why do they have to put this crap in the paper? It makes us look insane."

"Don't blame them both. I was there when Dad took that picture. She said she didn't want it turning up anywhere."

"Well, she's an idiot for posing for it in the first place. What does she expect out of him?"

I fell quiet, turning to look up at the horses, counting their legs, counting their tails. I'd taken Rose up on her offer, and now that shelf held her horses too. Fourteen of them crowded for space—a herd that had come to the edge of a cliff. "Don't call Mom names," I said, quietly. "She's sick again. I'm worried about her. Something's not right."

"Yeah, and I'll tell you when it began: the moment they came down the stairs from that apartment in Ohio lugging that doll."

After so many weeks spent waiting for her to broach the topic, there it was at last. "That morning I walked with you to the bus stop. You said you were going to tell me things about what goes on in this house. But you never mentioned another word. Why?"

"You were the one who had it on your mind, Sylvie. You should have asked me again. Besides, I've been busy focusing on other things."

"What other things?"

"My life. Some of us actually have one. Unlike you."

I went quiet once more, returned to counting the horses. It was easier than talking to her, easier than thinking about our sick mother down the hall and our father in the living room combing through those ancient books full of strange stories, and the sound of that phone ringing and ringing. From behind me, in a softer voice, Rose said, "I'm sorry."

Since there were so many horses now, it took longer to inspect them. I kept counting, imagining I was staring into an actual herd, breath blowing from their nostrils, tails swishing about to keep the flies away.

"Did you hear me, Sylvie? I said I was sorry. I know I've got a mouth on me, as Dad likes to point out. But I shouldn't use it on you all the time."

"It's okay."

"No, it's not. I'll try to be better, though."

I had seen how easily her efforts to control her behavior peeled away, so I didn't put much stock in what she was saying. When I finished counting the last of those horses, finding every last one intact, I turned to look at her on my bed.

"You know, I think about it sometimes," she told me.

"Think about what?"

"Growing up here. I'm hardly the sappy type. But once in a while, I can't help remembering."

"Remembering what?"

"Stuff."

"What *stuff*?"

"Stuff like sleeping in the living room under those makeshift tents or drawing our houses in the foundation across the street. I remember those times, even if I act like I don't."

Her words left me with the same awkward feeling as when I told her I'd miss her if she went to live with Howie. I wanted to ask why we couldn't share a more grown-up version of that closeness now, but worried the question would make her defensive, so I kept quiet.

"I remember when Mom and Dad first brought you home from the hospital too. 'Look at its hands,' I used to say. 'Look at its feet. It's so tiny.' And Mom would say, 'Rose, your sister is not an *it,* but a *she.*'" Rose let out a laugh then and paused, lying there with her sneakers on my mattress, staring at that picture of our mother in the paper. I walked over and looked at it again too, my gaze shifting to a passage from Heekin's article:

> "After we returned to our apartment from the hospital, where we had lost our daughter, I put Penny on top of her bed," said Elaine Entwistle. "For some time, I felt too heartbroken to go back into that room. But when I did, I saw the doll's arms and legs were arranged differently than I'd left them. I asked my husband if he'd been in that room, and he said no. I told myself it was my imagination, that I wasn't thinking clearly. But soon, it happened again. That was just the beginning of a series of very strange occurrences, which led us to contact the Masons."

I stopped reading. I'd already been through it once at the library that day. Clearly, Rose wanted to be done with it too, because she crinkled the paper and tossed it in my wastebasket. "I feel sorry for you, Sylvie."

"Me?"

"I've only got another year left. But you've got all of high school with them. It's not going to be easy after this. And according to Dad, the piece got picked up by other papers. Bigger ones."

"Maybe people will forget," I said, detecting that flimsy sound in my voice once more. "Maybe things will go back to normal."

"Keep telling yourself that. But if I were you, I'd get rid of that doll before she does any more damage."

"I thought you didn't believe the things they said about her."

"I don't. But does it matter what I think if others out there believe? Now that people know she's here in this house, Penny will just keep influencing things. Look at Mom and Dad. They believe, and it's changed them already. It's changed the whole feeling in this house too. It's like the air is harder to breathe. That's what belief does, Sylvie. Whether something is true or not is beside the point."

I sat on the edge of my bed, considering. Finally, I asked, "But get rid of her how? Where?"

"You're the brainiac. Figure it out."

Rose looked past me then. Her expression tightened, and I turned to see our father in the doorway. In one hand, he held an ancient book from the curio hutch, so thick and heavy it might have been a weapon. "I made dinner," he said, his voice deep and low.

"I'll be right down," I told him, even though I didn't feel hungry in the least.

"And what about you, Rose? Should I assume you won't be joining us again?"

"No thanks," she answered, quieter than I was used to. "I ate after track practice."

"Suit yourself. I'll take food to your mother, Sylvie, then see you downstairs."

Once he was gone, Rose stood from my bed and went to the door. I asked why she never ate with us anymore and she told me the more she stayed out of his way, the better. "Like I said, I've only got next school year left. At this point, I'm just trying to get through it."

With that, she turned to go. Despite the fact that Rose had gotten into my room anyway, I locked the door and headed down to the kitchen. My father had not set the table, so I did. When he joined me again, he took the phone off the hook, then pulled out the frozen glass tumbler I only ever saw him use at holidays. From the cabinet above the fridge, he dredged out a bottle of scotch and poured himself a drink, and then we sat at the table, Rose and my mother's chairs two ghosts among us now. *If Penny keeps having an influence,* I thought, *someday soon I'll be the only one left.*

It was unlike my father not to bother with conversation while we ate the dinner he had prepared—a flavorless meatloaf that tasted nothing like the one my mother made with onions and garlic and stewed tomatoes on top. I kept trying to introduce topics into the silence, telling him about my upcoming exam and the trick questions my teacher tossed in, but those things did not hold his interest.

"Is something the matter?" I asked finally.

My father sipped more of his drink. Turpentine mixed with rubbing alcohol—from where I sat that's what it smelled like, a smell that made me think of Christmas, since it was normally the only time he allowed himself a glass. "Just nerves," he answered. "I'm meeting that reporter tonight."

"Oh. Is he still writing his book?"

"He's about done with it actually. But our last interview, well, it didn't go the way I wanted. So I convinced him to meet me one more time. He's always got so many questions. Some of them I'm incapable of answering, because it comes down to faith and the way we interpret the world."

"But you've always been good at explaining those things, Dad."

"Yeah, well, I guess the way our lives have been around here lately has me distracted. I want you to know, Sylvie, that this isn't how I intended things to turn out."

I stayed quiet, pushing chunks of meatloaf around my plate.

"I'm talking about your mother upstairs. Your sister as well. The two of us eating dinner alone. When I left home years ago, I dreamed of having my own family. A happy one."

"We are happy," I said, but there it was again: that flimsy sound in my voice.

My father took a few greedy sips from his glass, his Adam's apple bobbing up and down as he swallowed, letting his meatloaf go untouched. And then a horn honked outside. He stood from the table, giving me a kiss on the forehead.

"You're right, Sylvie," he said, sounding less tense. "We are happy. All families have bumps along the way, so why should ours be any different? Things will go back to normal. Anyway, I've checked in on your mother for the night, so it's best just to let her sleep."

After he grabbed his coat and walked out the door, I was left to clear the table before heading upstairs, where I stopped to peek in at my mother again. She lay in her bed, sound asleep, a half-empty dinner plate on the nightstand. I felt the same urge to go inside and take care of her, the way she always took care of us. But I did what my father asked, leaving her to rest and going to my room instead. I pulled that slim piece of metal from my pocket and slipped it into the knob, opening the door.

The moment I stepped inside, I felt it beneath one of my slippers. When I lifted my foot, I saw another of those broken limbs. And then I looked to see not just one but dozens scattered on the carpet. Dozens more on my desk too. I stared down at the chaos a long moment before gazing up at that shelf, where every last one of them had been toppled.

I closed my door. Knelt on the carpet. Hands shaking, I went to work gathering those pieces. When that was done, I put them in a pile on my desk before stepping into the hallway. Last I looked, the rocker had been empty downstairs, but I knew where I'd find Penny. And whether or not the doll was to blame, I wanted her out of our lives.

I walked to my parents' room and stood outside their door. My mother, I could see, was in her bed still. Quietly, I pushed open the door enough for me to step inside.

Her voice sounded thick and sluggish when she stirred, asking, "Sylvie, is that you?"

"Yes, Mom. It's me."

"Is everything okay?"

"It will be. But I wanted to check in on you. To see if you need anything."

"Actually, a drink of water would be nice. I've just been so thirsty. There's a glass here on my nightstand if you don't mind."

I filled the glass in the bathroom sink and brought it to my mother, who lifted her head from the pillow and drank with a loud gulping sound. Meanwhile, I stared around the room, my eyes adjusting to the green glow of the alarm clock. Their dresser. Their nightstand. My father's empty bed. It was all the same. But then I noticed a smaller lump beneath my mother's covers. I reached over and pulled back the blankets.

"Why?" I asked when that blank face gazed up at me.

My mother set down her glass, returned her head to the pillow. "I can't explain it, Sylvie. I had my doubts about the claims that couple made. But your father—he believed. Either way, those people had been through so much, I thought it best to pray with them and remove the doll from their home, to give them peace of mind if nothing else. But now, well, there have been nights when I wake to find her here. Same as what happened to them."

"Well, I think I should take it back downstairs."

I waited for my mother to correct me, the way Rose said she once did to her, saying Penny was not an *it* but a *she*. But she just kept her head on her pillow as her eyes fell shut. For a moment, I thought of going into the bathroom for a towel to avoid touching the doll. But there seemed no time for that. I moved to the other side of the bed and reached down, moving calmly, intently, slipping my hands beneath its body and lifting. And then Penny was in my arms and I was carrying it out of the room.

Down the hall. Down the stairs. Through the living room, past the empty rocker to the front door. Outside, a misty rain had begun to fall, making a faint skittering sound, like mice running up and down the gutters. I stood on the stoop, staring out at the tangle of twisted branches surrounding our house, at my parents' Datsun in the driveway, at those signs my father had painted and nailed to the trees, the words screaming: NO TRESPASSING! Carry the thing into the woods, I thought, bury it there like my father had done with Mr. Knothead years before when the rabbit had been found dead one morning—no more *tic-tic-tic* of its heart. But I had only my bare hands to dig with, and the idea of venturing out there in the dark frightened me.

And then, all at once, I knew.

My feet moved down the stairs and across our mossy lawn until I reached the well we had no use for anymore. Without taking time to consider it, I shoved off the plywood and stared at the shimmering black surface of the water below. I held Penny over the side, took a breath, let go. A faint splash, but nothing more. No scream. No struggle. Of course not. The doll was powerless, after all, except for the power we gave it. If that's what you believed. In that moment, I did. In that moment, I didn't too. In the rainy silence that followed, I reached for the plywood, slid it back over the mouth of the well. I rooted around for rocks to put on top, but the ones at the base of Rose's old rabbit cage were too heavy to lift. The plywood would be enough, I decided, before turning back to the house.

Inside, I went to my room, thinking of my father out there with that reporter, wondering about the things he was telling him for that book. I slipped into my pajamas, looking over at the pile of limbs on my desk.

Tomorrow, I told myself as I climbed beneath the sheets, I'd glue them together one last time. Even if they'd never be quite the same, I could lie in bed at night and stare up at them on the shelf. Despite what happened, those horses would appear whole again. Like my family, I thought, drifting off to sleep, they would be together, happy, unbroken once more.

POSSESSIONS

An upright soldier of an *H*. A slouching *E*. A slouching *R*. The word *BAD*, then a space, then another word, this one missing a letter like a gapped-tooth smile: *DE_IRE*. I stared up at that drooping marquee as Heekin and I drew closer to the theater, putting together the puzzle of those letters. With effort, I managed to conjure an image of the place it had once been: the ticket window clean and shiny, the marquee upright, proudly announcing films like *Casablanca* or *Breakfast at Tiffany's*. But the image vanished when we reached the glass doors plastered over with newspapers and work permits.

"Did your uncle say," Heekin asked as he walked along the row, tugging on the tarnished handles and finding every door locked, "where exactly we should meet him?"

I shook my head, glancing up at those letters on the marquee again as if they might rearrange themselves and offer an answer.

"He *did* want you to come, didn't he?"

Confused, not angry—that's how Heekin seemed, though I wondered how long until that changed. If he had not just shared those stories about his time with my mother, reminding me of her good and honest nature, perhaps I'd have been able to keep the lie going. But considering the larger untruth I'd been nurturing for so many months, there seemed no room for more.

I turned away. Looked down the block at a bodega, a jumble of faded flags over the door, a redbrick church just beyond. "He didn't want me to come. Not exactly anyway." If I turned around, I knew what I'd see behind me: that look on my father's face in the arcade, that look on Detective Rummel's face in the interview room when I confessed my uncertainty. It was the look of a person realizing you were not who they thought you were—or more specifically, not who they *needed* you to be. It seemed to me I had a lifetime of those looks ahead; the world felt that full of endless opportunities to let people down, to break their hearts in little ways, in big ways too, each and every day.

"But you said—" Heekin began.

"I know what I said. And I'm sorry. But he wanted to wait. *Down the road*—that's the phrase he kept using. We should see each other *down the road*."

"But I don't understand. Why did you make me drive us all the way here if you weren't c-c-certain?"

Other than that brief encounter in the grocery store years before—a meeting I did not recall until he spoke of it in the car—it was the first I'd heard him stutter. Standing on that sidewalk before the lifeless theater, something about his faltering voice made me feel all the more guilty for leading us there. Turning back to him at last, I explained that I'd told my uncle we were going to leave the second I hung up the phone. "Since he knew we were on the way, my hope was that he'd feel obligated to be here when we arrived. But I should've known better. My father used to warn me about him. My sister too. Anyway, sorry for wasting your time."

"It wasn't a waste, Sylvie," Heekin told me, that stutter vanishing once more. "We got to spend time together at least. I think your mother might have liked that."

I wasn't certain that was true, but it made me feel a little better to know he wasn't upset with me. Heekin suggested we give it one last try and took to knocking on the row of glass doors. I did the same. For a long while, we stood waiting for someone to answer, though nobody did. At last he suggested that we may as well get back on the road to Dundalk before Rose began to worry.

"We can go," I told him. "She isn't going to worry, though."

"Sylvie, she's your sister. I can only imagine she would."

"Well, Howie is my uncle and look what difference that made."

Heekin paused, considering, until finally saying, "You're right. Just be-cause people are related doesn't always make the difference it should. In your case, however, Rose also happens to be your legal guardian. If she's not taking that role seriously, you need to say something. There must be a social services office monitoring your situation."

I thought of Cora with her dolphin or shark tattoo. I thought of Norman who had failed his real-estate exam, but planned on taking it again come spring. I thought of poor Boshoff with his poems and questions and ailing wife beside him in bed at night. "Rose does okay. I just mean she won't worry, since she thinks I'm at the library studying."

If he believed me, I couldn't be sure. Either way, Heekin let the conver-sation go. Before heading back to his car, he suggested I take a good look at the place, since it might be the last time I'd get to see it. "The city has wanted the building demolished for some time. But who knows? Now that I see those work permits on the door, maybe there's another plan."

I looked at the building—its peeling gray exterior, the alley that snaked off into the shadows on one side—doing my best to form a description to put in my journal later so as not to forget. When I was done, we walked across the street. Inside his car, he started the engine, but rather than it stalling, this time he twisted the key and turned it off.

"What's wrong?" I asked into the quiet.

Heekin pressed his palms against that rubbery face of his. The way he shoved his skin around, he seemed capable of shifting entire features into new positions, his nose nudging toward his left cheek, his left cheek scrunching into his left eye, that eye vanishing altogether. But the moment he stopped rubbing, things fell back into place. "A good reporter wouldn't give up so easily. Not after coming all this way. And like I told you, that's something I've always wanted to be. More than that, after letting your mother down, it would mean a lot to me if I could help you, Sylvie. Let's at least stick around awhile in case he returns. If your sister isn't going to worry, an extra hour won't hurt."

His suggestion seemed worth a try, and yet, I was beginning to think that if my uncle made that much of an effort not to see me, it might be smarter—safer even—simply to stay away. My parents never trusted the man. In the end, neither did Rose. Why should I?

"Tell you what, Sylvie. If you stay here and keep an eye out, I'll walk down to that bodega and see if I can get us some sandwiches and sodas. Would you like that?"

I hadn't eaten anything since leaving the house that morning, so I told him lunch sounded like a good idea. Before getting out, Heekin instructed me to stay put and keep the doors locked. I watched him grow smaller in the reflection of the side-view mirror until he disappeared into the bodega.

Alone, I did my best not to think of the last time I'd been instructed to wait in a car by myself. I stared down at the floor of Heekin's car, thinking of my mother sitting in that very same seat, nudging soda cans away from her feet while turning the pages of that swatch book plucked from the pile behind the hardware store. If she really was as tired of their work as Heekin said, it made sense that something as ordinary as a book of wallpaper samples would excite her. I remembered her showing that book to me, making no mention of her excursion with Heekin, simply turning the pages, gazing at the bursts of colors and designs with a kind of wonder in her eyes.

"Each has a mood, the way each person has a personality," I remembered her saying. "Which would you be, Sylvie?"

"You mean, which would I want for our kitchen?"

"No. Which would best match who you are?"

The sharp and sudden sound of knuckles banging against the car window startled me. I looked up to see a man with a withered face and long yellow teeth that made me think of old piano keys. He made a rolling motion with his fist, wanting me to lower the window. Instead, I made sure my door was locked then glanced back for some sign of Heekin. The most I saw were the faded flags above the door of that bodega.

I figured the man outside the car wanted money, and I nervously waved him away. He stayed put, though. On the other side of the glass, I heard his muffled voice say, "Sylvie?"

My name passing those wrinkled lips should have allowed me to relax, but it only left me more nervous. "Yes?" I offered in a tentative voice.

His mouth began moving again, but the *shhhh* made it difficult to piece together all that he was saying. At some point, he must have read the confusion on my face, because he stopped talking and made that winding motion with his fist again. At last, I cranked the window down a couple inches. "That's better," he told me. "A little anyway. You *are* Sylvie, right?"

"How do you know my name?"

"That's what I was trying to explain. I know your uncle. Knew your father too when he was young, before he went off and got famous. Before— Well, I wasn't exactly the nicest to him back when he was a kid. He probably never mentioned me."

As he spoke, the stories in Heekin's book came back to me. "Are you . . . *Lloyd?*"

He let out a breath, smiling with those piano key teeth. "You got it. I wouldn't have known it was you out here, except I saw that reporter and remembered him from when he came poking around months back. I was with Howie when you called earlier. Put two and two together. Anyway, *bingo*. Hello there, Sylvie."

"Hello," I said, warmer, though not lowering my window any farther.

"Guess I'll get to the point. Howie wouldn't appreciate me doing this, but if you want to see him, I suggest you come with me."

"Come with you where?"

"Easier if I just show you."

In the side-view mirror, there were only those flags above the bodega door. I imagined Heekin inside, watching a clerk smear mustard on our sandwiches or roaming the narrow aisles in an effort to excavate something edible among the cigarettes and magazines. "If you don't mind, I'll wait until that reporter gets back so he can come too."

Lloyd looked down the block, making a tapping sound with his tongue against his teeth. "Try seeing your uncle with that guy in tow, and things aren't going to go so great. Tell you that right now. Howie doesn't want to talk to reporters. Especially that one."

"Why doesn't he want to talk to him?" I asked, even though what I most wanted to know was why he didn't want to talk to *me*.

"Better off letting him do the explaining. If that's what you want, come with me."

I studied Lloyd outside the car—his thick fingernails, chipped and worn and yellow as his teeth. Hadn't he been one of the people to laugh at my father? "Why are you here?" I couldn't help but ask.

Lloyd shifted his feet, kicking one of his work boots against the curb. Having this conversation through the narrow opening of the window frustrated him, I could tell. But he didn't say anything about it, leaning forward instead, putting a hand on the roof of the Beetle. "Back when your grandparents were alive, I was the maintenance person around this building. I hung on to the job even when it became a different sort of place. Now that Howie's back, I'm still here. So like I said, I'm making you the offer before your reporter friend shows up again. You want me to take you to your uncle or not?"

Some instinct warned me not to trust him, to roll up that window and wave him away as if he really were a vagrant begging for money. Even as those thoughts filled my mind, however, my hand reached for the door handle and pushed it open.

Outside the car, I saw that Lloyd was smaller than I realized, not much taller than me, in fact, with a loose belly and long, monkeyish arms that dangled at his sides. Rather than say anything more, he simply motioned with one of those arms. We walked back across the street, and I thought he might pull a key from his paint-splattered jeans for one of the doors out front. Instead, he went to the alley around the side. Before stepping into the shadows, I glanced down the block to see if I might catch a glimpse of Heekin exiting the bodega, our lunch in his hands. No sight of him, though. Considering that I'd dragged us there on what amounted to a lie, and he'd already been kind enough to forgive me, I knew it was wrong to wander off. But it seemed too late to turn back.

Inside that alley, void of garbage cans or graffiti or anything more than a single enormous Dumpster with a motorcycle parked behind it, we came to a stop at a flight of iron stairs. The stairs looked no different than a fire escape, I thought, and after a moment I realized it *was* a fire escape.

"See that door?" Lloyd pointed one story up. "It's unlocked. Just go on up and head down the hall. Third door on the right."

I stood there, not moving.

"Don't wait for me, Sylvie. If I take you to him myself, he's going to be pissed. So do me a favor: just act like you figured it out on your own. I'll consider this one small way of making something up to your father." With that, Lloyd turned and walked out of the alley. Gone as quickly as he came.

If I allowed myself to hesitate, I knew Heekin might return and find me there. I put my foot on the first of those steps and began climbing. At the top, the metal door swung open easily, and I found myself in the dimmest of hallways. What little light there was inside flickered as I walked along. *Singin' in the Rain, Some Like It Hot, Ben-Hur, All About Eve*—posters for those films lined the walls. Whenever the lights blinked brighter, I glimpsed old movie stars smiling at me, like ghosts behind glass frames. "Third door on the right," I whispered again and again, in an attempt to drown out the *shhhh* in my ear and the *tic-tic-tic* of my rabbit heart.

When I reached that door, it was open enough for me to see inside a room not much bigger than my bedroom back on Butter Lane. A wooden desk, littered with papers, filled the small space. A reading lamp on top flickered in the same sporadic rhythm as the other lights in the theater. Behind that desk was a narrow cot, the sort my father used to request in our hotel rooms on lecture trips. I looked past the rumpled blankets on top of the cot at the back wall, where milk crates were stacked floor to ceiling—makeshift shelving, I gathered from the clutter they contained.

I stepped into that office or bedroom or whatever it was and waited. From somewhere in the dark of that building, I heard sounds: a clanging pipe maybe, footsteps maybe too. It was difficult to decipher on account of my ear, which distorted things more than usual. I did my best to study the room without touching anything. On the desk lay more work permits like those on the doors downstairs and a calendar with red X's slashing the days that had passed, blank spaces in the ones yet to come. Inside those milk crates, I saw boxes of cassettes. The handwritten labels made me think of the tapes from my father's lectures, only these were marked with names and phone numbers. I went over to the cot, where an ashtray filled with cigarette butts sat atop the pillow. On the floor nearby lay a chaos of newspaper clippings:

INFAMOUS MARYLAND COUPLE MURDERED

DEMONOLOGISTS SLAIN BEFORE ALTAR

DEACON AND WIFE VICTIMS OF BIZARRE CHURCH KILLING

"What are you doing here?"

Startled, I turned to see him in the doorway: *Howie.* When the lights flickered, he appeared to light up for a moment, same as those movie star ghosts in the hallway. He looked thinner than when I'd last seen him, hair clipped close to his scalp, beard gone, his face less ruddy.

"I told you we were on our way," I said, in a nervous, wavering voice. "When the front doors were locked, I found the entrance at the top of the—"

"I know what you told me, Sylvie. I asked you not to come. I said we'd see each other down the road."

Maybe it was the empty promise of that phrase tossed out again: *down the road.* Maybe it was his resemblance to my father—those wrinkles in his brow, those dark eyes. Maybe it was that the last time I had seen him had been after the court hearing where Rose was appointed my legal guardian. Whatever the reason, tears welled in my eyes.

"Hey," Howie said, coming closer. "Hey. Hey. Hey." He wrapped his heavy arms around my body.

"You never came back," I heard myself saying into the sudden warmth of his sweatshirt. "You told us you were going to Florida. All that talk about tidying up your affairs. All those phone calls. Then nothing."

"But I did what I said. It took longer than planned, but here I am. This place—"

His words caused my head to whip up. I pulled away, wiping my eyes. "You never once came to see us! Or bothered to write me back! And now I come here and I find—" I didn't know how to say the things I was thinking, so my gaze just fell to the floor, where all those headlines screamed some version of the same truth: DAUGHTER IS KEY WITNESS IN MURDER OF FAMOUS PARENTS . . . SUSPECT NAMED IN CHURCH KILLINGS . . . DRIFTER ACCUSED OF DOUBLE HOMICIDE AWAITS TRIAL IN MD MURDER CASE. I kicked them away, the words scattering across the floor, that image of my mother and Penny, which appeared in almost every article, multiplying before our eyes like a magic trick.

"I can explain, Sylvie. Please. Just give me a second."

I waited, saying nothing. A foggy silence billowed into the room, those odd noises from somewhere in the vast belly of the building fading away.

Howie pulled a chair over from the desk. I sat on the edge of that bed and he sat across from me, pushing up the sleeves of his sweatshirt. In the tattoos on his forearms, I saw dice and dollar signs and playing cards, an entire casino bursting to life on his hairy skin. "The first thing I want to say—" he began, then stopped. "I mean, the thing I might have said, *should* have said, on the phone if you hadn't caught me off guard, is that I *did* come back to see you girls, just like I promised."

"You came," I said, staring at Penny's face repeating all over the floor, my mother's face too, and remembering my father's promise that the photo would be just for their records. "But Rose sent you away."

"She told you that?"

"No. It's just, she's done it to other people."

"Well, my story might be a bit different from the others."

"Different how?"

Howie paused a moment. It was an odd feeling, being so close in that small room, speaking with such a sense of *exigency*—a word I recalled from that English exam years before. In most ways, we were strangers.

"When I got back to Tampa," Howie began, "I sent cards with cash to you girls any time I managed to hold on to a few bucks. Wasn't much, but it was my way of doing something to show you were both on my mind. But there was never any word back. I called, left messages. No word then, either."

I thought of the way Rose was always so possessive of the mail, and the way she used to roll her eyes whenever we got Howie's messages on the answering machine.

"Eventually, I figured the calls and cards and cash—all of it was useless. I came to the conclusion that before he died, your father poisoned your minds against me. Same as he did your mother's years before."

"Judging from that night in Ocala, you gave my mother plenty of reasons not to like you."

Howie stared down at those casino arms of his. Ace of spades. Queen of diamonds. Snake-eyed dice in a permanent tumble. I watched the muscles beneath his tattoos tighten as he balled his fists before lifting his head again. "I regret so many of my actions, Sylvie. You have no idea. That night is one among many. I didn't believe the things they did, not one bit, but it wasn't right to ruin their lecture like that."

His voice, his expression, every part of him seemed genuinely sorry. "When you didn't hear back from Rose and me, you gave up . . . just like that?"

"At first. And after the shock of everything that happened, I started drinking more. Doing things I'm not proud to admit. Things got so bad, there were only two ways to go: keep falling down the dark hole until it was over or crawl back out of it. It wasn't easy. It's still not. But I started going to meetings. I got sober. Stopped doing a lot of things I never should have in the first place. And now, here I am."

We both looked around the small, dim room, and I couldn't help but wonder how this was any better than where he'd been. "My father never even talked about this place," I said. "I figured it was closed or torn down a long time ago."

Howie let out a short, exasperated laugh. "That would have been too easy. After your grandfather died, this theater was left to your dad and me. We couldn't sell it. Nobody wanted it, considering what the neighborhood had become. So the place sat vacant for years, until an offer came to rent it—as a movie theater, of all things, only not the kind that showed the sort of films that used to play here."

"My father—he never would have gone for that," I said.

"What choice did he have? We needed to cover the taxes that drained us every spring, taxes your father usually ended up paying. And then I had this idea of taking back the place. Doing something *better* than renting it out."

"You mean, making it a regular movie theater again?"

"Afraid not, Sylvie. The days of people getting dressed up to come to this neighborhood and see a film are long gone. I had another idea. Making it a venue for bands. Something I'll tell you more about. But your father wouldn't allow it. Despite his grandiose morals, he preferred to let it stay what it had become, rather than give his own brother a chance. When he passed, since there was no will, the property went through probate. In the end, his half went to you and your sister."

"Rose and me?"

"Yes. This place, crumbling as it is, belongs to the two of you as well. You might not be aware of it, since Rose was made your legal guardian and she has the say for both of you. When I told her what I wanted to do with it, she agreed so long as I send half of whatever money I make. And so long as—" Howie stopped, considering his words.

"So long as what?"

"So long as I stayed out of your lives."

I thought of that morning at the bus stop when Rose scoffed at Howie's "pipe dreams" and told me about his refusal to let her come live with him. I wanted to find some way to ask about all that when a noise came from out in the hall—footsteps, I was certain this time. Howie must have heard them too, because we both turned just as Sam Heekin stepped into the doorway.

I had been so caught up in seeing my uncle again that I'd momentarily forgotten about Heekin, and his abrupt appearance surprised me. Howie stood, shoving his sleeves farther up his arms, displaying more tattoos. In a voice so gruff it seemed to come from a wholly different person than the one who had just been speaking to me with such tenderness, he shouted, "What the hell are you doing here?"

"He's—" I began, but Heekin was already talking, though not doing a very good job of it.

"I d-d-drove here with—"

Howie cut him off. "I made it clear I didn't want to see you around here again."

"Hold on," I said, standing too. "He brought me here. He's a friend of our family."

"*Friend?*" My uncle all but spat the word. "I read his book. Read every one of his articles, too. A lot of what this guy has to say hardly seems like something a friend would write."

Heekin shut his eyes and took a deep breath. When he opened them and began speaking again, his voice was calm, his words clear. "I don't deny my mistakes, and all the things I've done that might have seemed unfair to this family. But I'd rather not do any more harm when it comes to Sylvie. That's why I found my way inside here. I wanted to make sure she was all right."

Howie kicked the articles, sending my mother and Penny and Albert Lynch, who I glimpsed among the photos too, spinning around the floor. "Of course she's all right! She's with her uncle!"

I could only imagine how skeptical Heekin felt about that comment, since I felt the same. Neither of us let on, though. Instead, Heekin gazed around the room, making a quick study of the place. "I'm okay," I told him at last. "We'll just be a little longer."

"Okay, then. If you need me, I'll be waiting outside."

I expected Howie to make another jab, but he just watched Heekin step back into the hall. When we heard the metal door opening and closing, Howie told me he was sorry. "Can't stand filthy reporters and scumbag detectives poking around my business. And that guy does *not* give up. There's something about him I don't like."

"My mother was the best judge of character I knew, and she liked him. In the beginning anyway."

"Yeah, well, your mother was human too. Like the rest of us, she could have been wrong. And I'm telling you, she was wrong about that guy."

I sat on the cot again, doing my best not to look at those pictures on the floor. Even if what Howie said might have been true, I didn't like him talking about my mother that way. I stared blankly at those milk crates as he walked to the desk and fished an envelope out of a drawer. "I want to show you something, Sylvie," Howie said, sitting beside me on the cot, the thin mattress sinking in a way that brought our bodies closer. I felt his arm graze mine as he opened that envelope.

From inside, he pulled a few black-and-white photos, like those in my father's desk, only with none of the blurry shafts of light or mysterious figures. The first picture was of the theater—not the ramshackle place it was now, but back when the building looked majestic, when that marquee stood upright just as I'd imagined. In the crowd out front, I saw women with dark lipstick, spidery eyelashes, and dresses so glittering they seemed to be made of hundreds of tiny flashbulbs. The men at their sides sported dapper suits and bowler hats. Howie let the picture speak for itself before handing me another of a man and woman dressed more simply. The man twisted the crank on a taffy machine; she held the finished product in the air, stretching it thumb to thumb, laughing. Something about them seemed familiar, and I felt a stirring in my chest.

"Are they—"

"Your grandparents, Sylvie. In the candy shop that was once part of the theater."

We looked at them for a long moment. I studied their faces, hunting for glimpses of Rose in my grandfather's strong chin, of myself in my grandmother's wide eyes. In each, I saw my father, Howie too.

"I must be getting old," my uncle told me, speaking more calmly, "because I've never been the nostalgic type until lately. But I'm finding it's a strange thing to be the last one left in a family. You spend a lot of time thinking about the past, wondering why things turned out the way they did."

His words led me to glance away from the photos and down at that messy carpet of newspaper clippings. My mother and Penny and all those headlines.

"You must be wondering why I kept those," he said.

I nodded, then said, "Yes. I am."

My uncle tucked the first two photos back into the envelope, holding on to the third facedown so I couldn't see it just yet. "If there's one place drunks love, Sylvie, it's a public library. Nice and quiet when you're nursing a hangover. You can sleep the day away without anyone bothering you except maybe some nag of a librarian. The Seventy-Eighth Street Community Branch in Tampa—that was my favorite whenever a rent check bounced and the landlady padlocked my door. In my more sober moments, I used to dig around there for stories about my brother. Even if I didn't believe the things he claimed, I felt proud he'd made something of himself. Jealous, too, since he was keeping me from the dreams I had for the theater. Later, after what happened, collecting those papers became a kind of obsession—one I've kept up since I got here. Guess I'm still trying to make sense of it all. Thing is, all those articles list the same facts. I know how hard it must be, Sylvie, but you were there that night. Can you tell me what happened inside that church?"

Shhhh. . .

As he drew closer to that question, the sound in my ear grew steadily louder. Useless, I knew by now, but I pressed a finger to my ear anyway. The thought of Rummel and Louise filled my head. "I tried," I said, offering an answer I did not plan, but one I might well have given them, because it was true, "always to be their good daughter, the one they could count on and be proud of. But when it mattered most, that night in the church, I failed. Not only couldn't I save them, I can't even identify their killer with any real certainty now that they're gone."

"But the papers—"

"I know what they say. But I'm telling you otherwise."

When he spoke next, I heard something different in Howie's voice, a kind of hunger. "Are you saying you don't know who you saw?"

I shook my head, staring at the final picture in his hands and waiting for him to flip it over. "What is that last photo?"

He let out a weighted breath and handed me the picture: two shirtless boys cannonballing off a rocky cliff into a pool of water. It was taken, he explained, at an old Indian well a few miles from the theater. "Our dad used to drive us there on hot days when the AC broke in this place. Lucky he got that shot, because it was one of the few times your father actually jumped with me. He was always so nervous and preferred to walk the path down to the water. I swear he was more at home with the things he thought he saw in the theater than out in the real world."

"That night in Florida," I began, bringing up something I'd always wondered about, "when you and my sister drove off in your truck, she told me later you said things that made her stop believing our parents. What did you tell her?"

My uncle took back the photo and returned it to the envelope, then thought better of it. "Here, Sylvie. Why don't you keep these? They're the few pieces of our family history I have to offer. And who knows? Maybe they'll give you some small comfort if ever you need it."

I thanked him and took the photos, slipping them into my coat pocket next to my journal.

"I have an idea," Howie said, standing from the cot. "Come with me."

We headed out into the hallway and on deeper into the building, passing more movie star ghosts as we went. On each side of the hallway, open doors led into other shadowy rooms like the one where Howie had been working and living. So black and boxy, those rooms would put anyone in mind of a prison cell, and in every single one, I imagined Albert Lynch, pacing or sitting, gazing out at me with a desperate, penetrating glower.

When it became too much, I looked away, just as Howie took my hand, guiding us through a minefield of missing floorboards. All the while he spoke with an excitement in his voice I'd not heard before about his long-time dream for the building—the dream my father kept him from in life, but no longer could in death.

"The Philly Chamber of Commerce started an initiative to revitalize the neighborhood," he told me. "They've even helped me secure a loan. Nothing short of a miracle considering my credit. It's barely enough to make some basic changes, bring the place up to code. That's okay. I'm banking on the look of the old place to give it a certain coolness."

We arrived at a set of double doors. Howie released my hand and pushed them open, leading us out onto a balcony inside the theater. In the flickering light, I could see hundreds of seats filling the orchestra below, hundreds more on the mezzanine above. Despite the peeling paint and web of cracks in the ceiling, the ornate chandelier and the stage with velvet curtains flanking a blank movie screen offered hints of former glory. "Used to be an old vaudeville house before your grandparents owned it. Your dad and me, we spent our childhood between these walls. Scouring the floor after people left in search of dropped change. With this many seats, you'd be amazed at how much we made. If we got lucky, we'd come across jewelry or a wallet—*that* was hitting the jackpot."

"Did my father make you return it?"

Howie laughed. "Difficult as it might be to imagine, even your dad was a kid once. A pretty devious one when he wanted to be. The jewelry got pawned with Floyd's help. We gave him a cut, of course. Wallets, we agreed to keep secret and split whatever cash was inside. Well, that was supposed to be the way things worked."

"Supposed to be?"

"Yeah, until E-19." Howie aimed a finger at the orchestra seats, ticking his way up from the stage until he was pointing to one chair in particular. "That seat right there. Doesn't look any different from the others. But it's where your dad used to stash most of what he found in a tear on the side of the cushion, so he didn't have to share it with me. I used to think the reason I turned up so much more loot than him was because I was older and faster and had a better eye. Then I caught on to what he was doing."

The lights in the theater blinked—*off* and *on*, then just *off*—causing my uncle to fall silent. Things remained dark long enough that I wondered if they'd come back on at all. Waiting out on that balcony, Howie's figure became nothing more than a hulking silhouette beside me, one that put me in mind of those statues by the altar. I listened to the sound of him breathing, smelled the smoke on his breath from his last cigarette. "Is everything all right?" I asked into the blackness, feeling a tightening in my throat as his heavy shoes shifted on the floor beneath us.

"Should be. The wiring inside this monster is just so damn ancient. That's one of the things I'm spending the loan money on: updating the electrical. Anyway, give it a minute and the lights will—" Just then, the theater blinked to life, allowing us to see again and allowing Howie to finish his sentence with relief, *"come back on."*

I gazed out at all the empty seats, imagining the boys from the photo scrambling among them, imagining my father standing down near that one seat in particular, hiding whatever he found from his brother. "And this is where my father first saw . . . *things?*"

My uncle nodded. "Let's go see the view from downstairs." Back in the hall, he led the way to a set of threadbare drapes, the fringe as gray as mop strings. We were about to step through to the staircase just beyond when Howie stopped. "You know what, Sylvie? Why don't you go on ahead while I grab the blueprints from the office?"

I stared past the drapes at that empty staircase, feeling that tightening in my throat again when I looked back at him. "Why?"

"Because I want to show you the exact plans. So just go on down to the orchestra level. I'll catch up in a minute."

Missing floorboards, faltering lights, the things my father used to speak of seeing among the seats—all of it left me wary. "I think," I told Howie, "I should probably go."

"*Go?*"

That odd tightening in my throat grew tighter still. When I spoke next, my words came out in awkward clumps. "There's an appointment I have. In Maryland. At the police station. The detective there—he wants to talk to me. I need to figure out what I'm going to tell him."

"Tell him about what?"

"I don't know. But, well, Sam Heekin is waiting for me. I shouldn't—"

"Don't worry about that guy, Sylvie. Like I said, you own this place too. Now that you're here, I want to show it to you. Who knows when Rose will let us see each other again. Now get down there."

Get in the truck . . .

Unlike that night in Ocala, when I managed to avoid giving into his order, this time I couldn't see a way out. I turned and stepped through the threadbare drapes, the drab fringe brushing my shoulders like limp fingers when I passed. Had there been a banister at some point during the building's history, it was long gone; I was left to trail my hand along the wall while descending the steps. When I reached the first floor, I walked through another set of drapes and kept going out among the orchestra seats until I stood in the center aisle.

How many people had filled that place when it was a legitimate movie theater? How many more when it was a vaudeville house before that? I tried to imagine them, holding hands, laughing or crying about the world come to life before their eyes on the screen or stage. Somehow, though, the great yawning maw of that open room felt stronger than the past, making it difficult to envision. Instead of those people, I ended up thinking of their possessions—coins and bills and bracelets and necklaces and wallets—all dropped to the floor, unknowingly, over the years. The thought led me to move in the direction of the stage, where the movie screen was plagued with cracks. At last, I stopped at one aisle in particular.

After so many years, it would seem someone would have repaired the tear in seat E-19, but reaching down, I felt the slit on one side of that cushion. How could I resist slipping my hand inside? How could I not wonder if I might pull out some long-forgotten treasure? But only a few stray puffs of loose foam filled my hand.

I let it fall to the floor, straightening up and waiting for Howie, who had plenty of time to get what he needed by then. When he didn't show, it occurred to me that I'd not seen any blueprints on his desk or among those makeshift shelves. No sooner did that thought come than I began to wonder why there were no signs of renovations in the place. No tools or extension cords. No sawhorses or paint cans.

"Hello!" I called into the belly of that theater.

The word was tinged with a pleading sound. It was met with only silence before the lights flickered then snapped out, drowning me in darkness once more. As I stood with one hand on the back of my father's torn seat, at the very place where he must have first seen those otherworldly visions, my own demons came seeping from the shadows:

Dot calling, *Hello? Yoo-hoo? Girls?* My mother saying, *When you feel afraid, I want you to pray.* And then there were the strange rumblings from our basement in those early months after our parents were gone—the breaking, the rustling, the shifting about—that led me to plead with Rose in a quivering voice, *You're crazy if you don't hear those things. They're pissed off. They're sad. They want them back. I can tell. . . .*

"Howie?" I called in an effort to keep those voices, that darkness, and my own rising panic at bay. "Lloyd? Hello?"

Still no answer. I couldn't wait any longer. I knew I was at E-19, so I told myself to track my way out to the center row then back toward the exit. I began doing just that when something brushed past the periphery of my vision, leaving me with the same chill I felt when the limp fingers of that fringe brushed my shoulders.

Howie—that was my first thought—he had come to find me in the dark. Then I saw it again: not my uncle after all, but a blur of motion among the seats nearest the stage. The movement stopped, and I watched it, a pulsating shadow that contained no light yet had a presence all its own. I should have realized right away what I was seeing, but like those people who stood on our doorstep wondering why no one answered when they rang the bell, it took a moment to puzzle things out. Once I arrived at the truth, I did not want to be near it any longer.

E-18. E-17. E-16. E-15 . . .

Fast as I could, I moved toward the center aisle, where my hand found the next row of seats. I began tracking the alphabet toward the rear of that theater. *F . . . G . . . H . . . I . . . J . . .* When I reached *K,* I came to a stop. That lightless mass was in front of me now, a few rows away. The way its shapeless figure rose and fell, rose and fell, it appeared to be breathing, before skittering off into the darkness again.

K . . . L . . . M . . . N . . . O . . .

At last, I let go of the seats and ran full speed toward a slip of light beneath a door not far away. I burst through the door, stumbling into a lobby filled with sawhorses and lumber and spools of cable, all lit by the muted sunlight filtering through the newspapers and permits on the glass doors. I fumbled along the doors, slamming my hands against the handles. None opened until I reached the very last, which I lurched through into the daylight. As the sun washed over me, making it impossible to see, I kept moving until I slammed into something—or *someone*, I realized as I felt hands take hold of me, gripping my body tight.

"Easy there, young lady. You okay?"

I stepped back, almost falling to the sidewalk. My eyes adjusted, and I made out Lloyd's withered face before mine. "Where's Sam Heekin?"

"That reporter?" Lloyd twisted around, pointed to the Volkswagen parked on the far side of the avenue. "Right there."

I looked to see Heekin in the driver's seat of the VW bug, a newspaper spread over the steering wheel, reading and popping potato chips into his mouth.

Footsteps sounded behind me then. The same door of the theater opened, and my uncle stepped outside, no blueprints in his hands. My voice wobbled more than I liked when I shouted, "Why would you do that . . . not just to me but to *him*?"

"So you understand then?" Howie said.

"Yes. And you could have just told me."

"I'm sorry, Sylvie. But when you asked what I said to Rose that made her stop believing, I thought the best way was to show you. And now you know."

I stood there, crossing my arms, waiting for the confusion and fear of the last few moments to leave me. "But why?" I asked again. "And how?"

"It began as something of a joke. Well, not quite a joke, since I was trying to teach your dad a lesson. I first got the idea when Lloyd"—he stopped and nodded to Lloyd, who must have realized then what we were talking about—"was sampling some light filters in the projection room one day when I was here after school. I snagged some lenses, slipped a black one over a flashlight, and shined it up at the chandelier to create the effect."

"But my father was smart. He would have figured it out."

"How old was Sylvester at the time?" my uncle asked Lloyd. "Nine? Maybe ten?"

Lloyd made that tapping sound with his tongue against his teeth, nodding. "About that, I'd say."

"Young enough that he was more susceptible to the possibilities of what he was seeing," my uncle told me. "That first time, I expected him to scream and go running out of the place. Figured it would teach him not to sneak back at night and get what he'd hidden in that seat. Instead, your father stood stock-still, watching those shapes move around him. I swear, it looked like he was communicating with them somehow."

"So you were both in on it?" I asked. "And you kept it up?"

"Not really," Lloyd said. "When I caught Howie with the filters and realized what he was doing, I had a little fun at your father's expense too. But after a few weeks, I told him enough was enough."

"In the end, Sylvie, it was just a prank that got pulled a handful of times before it was over. At least I *thought* it was over. Months later, I came home to find my mom and dad laughing around the kitchen table, my brother looking serious and upset. I asked what was so funny, and they told me I should ask Sylvester to describe what he saw in the theater."

"And that's when he told you he saw—"

"*Globules*," Howie said, resurrecting that word from Heekin's book. "But even stranger than that name he'd concocted for them: I asked when he last encountered those things and he told me he'd been seeing them every day for months."

"Are you saying my father made it up?" I asked, wondering how much of what he said I should believe.

Howie didn't respond right away. He and Lloyd just looked at each other, and I had the feeling neither wanted to answer the question. "I don't know, Sylvie," my uncle said at last. "Sometimes I wonder if he lied to us. Other times, I wonder if he lied to himself. Maybe his belief gave that light a power all its own."

His words made me think of Penny, the things my sister once said about the doll's power over our family, power that only seemed to grow stronger instead of weaker after I dumped it down the well. "So he never knew what you'd done to him?"

"Years later, when your dad was in dental school in Baltimore, I drove down on my motorcycle on a whim to see him. Should've known better, but I got this idea in my head that the two of us might have a brotherly visit. Shoot pool. Throw darts. Your father actually seemed happy to see me and was a good sport when I dragged him to a bar. A miracle considering what a Bible thumper he had become. He even drank two beers. Me, I drank too many. At some point during the night, he started talking about the things he saw in the student housing building where he lived. Even a little bit of booze always loosened your father's lips, and he went on about how they had followed him from the theater. He had quit calling them that strange name by then, saying they were ghosts, plain and simple. Anyway, that's when I realized I never should have let it go on so long. So I told him."

"What did he say?"

"Nothing, actually. He just finished his beer and said he wanted to walk back to his apartment, since it wasn't far. We weren't ever big on hugging, so he shook my hand. I remember standing outside in the parking lot, watching him go. I didn't see or hear from him again for almost ten years, when Rose was born. I showed up to see her in the hospital, bringing the first of those horses from the track as a peace offering. But it was never the same between your dad and me. The truth was, it hadn't been since we were kids."

I glanced across the avenue. If Heekin had noticed us, he gave no sign. We had come all that way, but none of what I'd learned put me any closer to the answer I needed most. "That night last winter," I said to Howie, "I mean, the night they died, where were you?"

He looked to Lloyd, who stood quietly beside us on the sidewalk still, before turning back to me. "I've told you before, Sylvie. I was home in my apartment in Tampa. I'd lost another job and was drowning my sorrows in booze the way I used to do. I didn't come out of it for a few days."

As he spoke, I thought of my mother teaching me how to sense what was inside a person. And though I didn't really believe I had any of her gift, I did believe that Howie was telling the truth.

"Sylvie!" Heekin had noticed us at last and rolled down his window. I called back that I'd just be another minute. And then I told my uncle I really did need to go.

This time, Howie didn't try to keep me there any longer. Instead, he told me he was glad, after all, that I'd come to Philly. He also said he never planned to go along with Rose's request for long. "That's why I kept telling you we'd see each other down the road. Once I got the place up and running, and started making money, I planned to revisit—well, let's call it the terms of my agreement with your sister. Even if she's resistant to the idea, I want to help you. I want to be a part of your lives."

I stared down at his arms, noticing a tiny horseshoe among the playing cards. My uncle reached out and pulled me close, tighter than before, in a final hug. He spoke into my ear, choosing the good one by chance, and telling me to call anytime, that Rose wouldn't have to know. When he let go, I said good-bye to him and to Lloyd too, before crossing the avenue.

I expected Heekin to begin grilling me the moment I climbed into his cramped car. The thought of explaining all I'd learned before thinking it through myself felt daunting, and so I was grateful when the most he said was that I must be hungry, and to help myself to the sandwich and chips he had bought for me. I did just that, fishing lunch from the bag while the car's engine sputtered to life. As we chugged away from the curb and moved down the street I watched Howie and Lloyd grow smaller and smaller in the side-view mirror, standing beneath the drooping marquee with its crooked letters until they were gone.

It wasn't until we were on the highway south, sandwich and chips demolished, that Heekin spoke. He told me that even though it was just three o'clock, I probably felt tired after the long day. He said we could talk about whatever went on inside the theater when I was ready, same went for the unfinished stories he had begun telling on the drive up about his involvement in my parents' lives. I did feel tired—drained by it all, in fact—so my only answer was to nod and lean my head against the window. It felt as though only a short while passed before we were rolling down the off-ramp of the highway then winding our way through the narrow streets of Dundalk. That's when Heekin broke the silence at last, saying, "While I was waiting for you outside the theater, I thought of something."

I looked away from the window at him. Those weedy gray strands of his hair caught the fading sunlight, the unusual hills and valleys of his face. "What's that?"

"Earlier, you mentioned you never wanted to forget certain things.

It made me remember the tapes from my interviews with your parents. Their voices are on them. The police made me turn over the cassettes, but you should ask the detective for them, so you can have those pieces of your parents at least."

By then, we had reached Butter Lane. Heekin stopped in the exact spot where I'd met him that morning. I told him I would inquire about the tapes, and then he gave me his business card with his home number written on the back in case I needed to reach him. I thanked him and pushed open the door. The question I'd started to ask him back at the preserve had been niggling at my mind ever since, and it made me stop. "Were you and my mother—" I paused, finding it hard still, to say the rest of what I wanted to know.

"In love?" Heekin said, doing the job for me.

I nodded.

"No, Sylvie. I would have wanted something more between us. But she was loyal to your father and to you girls too. I'd be lying if her rejection didn't fuel some part of my motivation in refusing to change certain details in my book." He stopped and let out a sigh that seemed weighted with regret. "Anyway, speaking of my book, whatever more you need to know can be answered in the pages you've been avoiding. Maybe it's best if you discover it there. It might not be tomorrow or next week or next year. But I'm guessing at some point, you'll be ready."

Even as he said those things, I knew the time had come. When I was alone in the house again, I needed to dig that book out of the police bag in Rose's closet and finish it at last. There seemed no point in telling Heekin that, however, so I just thanked him again and got out of the car. Daylight had begun to slip away, so he flicked on his headlights to help me see as I headed down the lane. When I reached the house, I listened as his VW bug stalled out before he started the engine again and sped off down the main road.

Standing at the edge of the property, not far from the NO TRESPASSING! signs that had never done much good, I looked at Rose's truck in the driveway, the light in the basement window, which still glowed. Once I walked through the front door, I knew I wouldn't walk out again until it was time to go to the station in the morning. Fifteen, maybe fourteen hours left, I guessed. The thought, coupled with the idea of facing my sister, made me want to put off going inside a little longer.

As night fell, I wandered to the empty foundation across the street. For a long while, I stood on the edge, not far from the twisted roots of the fallen tree. Same as Rose used to do, I reached down for a handful of rocks, tossing them at the metal rods that snaked up out of the cement in one corner. And then my memory of Rose was replaced by a memory of Abigail, sketching a map on the wall with a stone in the moments before blood pooled on her palms.

Now do you get it, Sylvie? Now do you understand how much I need your help?

When I grew tired of thinking about Abigail, tired of tossing rocks too, I sat on the ledge, legs dangling over the side the way a person sits by a swimming pool. Enough time passed that the last of the sun disappeared and the moon began to loom over the edge of the woods. And then, amid the never-ending *shhhh,* came the sound of an engine, like an animal rumbling down the street. I looked to see the glow of headlights against the bare tree branches. They came to a stop halfway down the lane, not far from the spot where I witnessed those two witches kissing on Halloween night.

Slowly, I stood. I saw a figure step out of the car and walk in the direction of our house, carrying an object of some sort. Another teenager with a doll to throw on our lawn—that was my first thought, since the person was difficult to make out with the car's headlights so bright behind. But when the figure came closer, I realized it was the woman with the grim, head-on-a-totem-pole face, wearing the same sort of frill-less dress.

Just as I'd done while waiting for birds to land in my hands, I did not move. The woman reached the edge of our property and paused. I waited for the moment when she stepped into our yard—and *that's* when I began moving, hurrying along the far side of the road in the direction of her idling station wagon. She had left her door ajar, and I slipped inside, leaning across the seat and reaching for the glove compartment, which popped right open. First thing I pulled out was a bible, thin pages highlighted and dog-eared same as my mother's. I dropped it on the floor and fumbled for an envelope, pulling out a yellow slip of paper. In the dim glow of the dashboard, I looked to see:

Nicholas Sanino, 104 Tidewater Road . . .

Nearby, I heard footsteps and what sounded, oddly, like my mother's humming. Lifting my head to look back, I saw that the woman had already left our property and was on her way to the car, close enough that she'd see me if I stepped onto the road. That's what I should have done, of course: gotten out and confronted her. But panic compelled me to shove everything back in the glove compartment then throw myself over both sets of seats, until I landed with a *thud* in the very back of the station wagon. I reached around and found a blanket, gritty with sand, which I tugged over my body.

A moment later, I heard her arrive at the car. That song she hummed was too full of false cheer, too easily recognizable, to be anything like my mother's, I realized. And where my mother's tune had a way of slowly fading from her lips, the woman's stopped abruptly. In the silence, I braced myself for the wide back door of the station wagon to swing open, for the blanket to be yanked off and for her to discover me. But there was only the sound of a door closing up front in a quiet click, the sound of a buckling seat belt, the sound of the car shifting into gear, and then the feeling of motion as the woman turned the station wagon around.

When we reached the end of the lane, the *tic-tic-tic* of my heart felt more frantic, more explosive, than Rose's rabbit's ever had beneath its soft fur. The *shhhh* grew louder too. I slipped my hand into my coat pocket to feel those pictures of my grandparents and my father and my uncle—even if I could not see them, I hoped they might bring some small comfort the way Howie said. But as the station wagon pulled onto the main road and picked up speed, moving faster and faster, I fished around that pocket, then another, before realizing the pictures must have fallen out somewhere. Same as all those people's possessions in the theater years before, they were lost. But that wasn't all. My violet diary, the pages filled with so many secrets of my parents' lives, so many secrets of my life as well, it was gone now too.

GONE

In those thick old novels my mother used to force upon me, characters were forever having foreboding dreams. Jane Eyre dreamed of infants, sometimes wailing, other times hushed in her arms. Pip suffered through feverish nightmares in which he found himself no longer human, but rather a brick cemented into a wall, unable to move.

The night I dumped Penny down the well, then slipped beneath the sheets of my bed while those horse limbs lay piled on my desk, it only made sense that I should be haunted by turbulent dreams too. My subconscious could have churned up any number of images: Penny climbing out of that watery grave, my mother waking to find her soaked body oozing dank well water on the mattress beside her. Worse, I might have dreamed that it was me trapped down there beneath the earth, crying out for help. Instead, I slept more peacefully than I had in the months since that doll came to our house. Not a single disturbance until the sound of angry voices in real life began weaving their way into my tranquil subconscious.

"I've done everything you've asked! *Everything!*"

"I don't believe you! I'm sorry, but I don't! You've used up all your currency! Spent! Done! Gone!"

"Please. The two of you calm down. Now tell us what you did to her."

"*Her?* You mean *it!* And I told you, nothing!"

"How about telling the truth for a change? Now spit it out!"

"You want the truth? Okay, the fact is this: there is not a single thing wrong with me, but there is something very wrong with the two of you! Who else would put—"

"Don't start that up again! I warned you! Now stick to the subject!"

"I *am* sticking to the subject! Because it all comes back to the way we live our lives around here! It's not normal!"

I opened my eyes. Sun streamed through the window. Quickly, I got out of bed and threw on some clothes, making my way down the hall and the stairs. When I stepped into the living room, my mother was seated in her rocker, wearing her bathrobe and slippers, while my father paced back and forth by the curio hutch.

"There's Sylvie," Rose said. "Ask her. Go ahead. She'll tell you."

"Tell them what?" I asked.

"Tell them that I didn't touch their fucking spooky old rag doll!"

"Rose!" my mother said at the same time as my father yelled, "Watch your mouth, young lady! We don't talk like that in this house!"

"Oh, that's right, because it's so holy around here!"

"It's true," I said when they stopped speaking long enough for me to find a way in. "Rose didn't touch it."

My words brought a blanket of silence over the room. Something made me think of those horses again. The first time I glued a broken one back together, I'd taken another down from the shelf to compare. I remembered tugging at the legs of the unbroken horse and realizing how difficult it would be for a person to snap them. A hammer, a saw, or at the very least, a good hard whack against the desk—that's what it would take.

"Sunshine," my father said in a softer voice, "it's very noble what you are trying to do, but I don't want you lying to cover for your sister. That doll is our property and an important part of the work your mother and I are doing."

"I'm not covering for her." My voice remained calm, though I felt a churning inside. I took a breath and told him, "Rose didn't drop that doll down the well. I did."

My parents looked at me, stunned, which was no surprise. My sister, however, looked stunned too, making me wonder if she hadn't really expected me to go through with it, if perhaps she'd just been shooting off her mouth the night before.

"Sylvie," my mother said, speaking up first. "Why would you do such a thing?"

Before I could answer my father held up his hand. "Stop right there. I still don't believe Rose had nothing to do with it. I know you, Sylvie, and this is not something you'd ever do. Not on your own anyway."

"So here she is *confessing* and you're still calling me a liar?" my sister said. "There is something wrong with you, Dad. You see the world the way you want to see it. Even when all evidence points to the contrary."

I assumed talking to him that way would bring about more shouting, but instead my father turned all his attention to me, coming closer, pulling off his glasses. "Look me in the face, angel, and tell me truthfully that your sister had nothing whatsoever to do with it."

That churning started up again. I stood there, feeling trapped. For as long as I could remember, I had wanted to be their good daughter, the one who lived up to expectations, the one who won essay contests and brought home perfect grades, the one who gave honest answers. But in that moment, I wanted to protect Rose too.

"The truth," my father said quietly.

"The truth," my mother said from her rocker.

"Okay," I said. It was just one word—*truth*—but with it they cast a spell on me. "Let me back up and tell you why we did it."

"*We?*" Rose shrieked.

"I knew it," my father said. "I just knew it."

"Not *we, me*. I did it," I said. But then I turned to my sister. "Rose, I just want to explain why we thought the doll had to go. That way they understand the truth."

"Sylvie, *don't*," she said, panic rising in her voice. "Not now. You don't understand."

"All you have to do," my father said to me, "is tell us what happened."

His face was before mine still, and I could see small pouches beneath his eyes. It made me wonder how things had gone the night before after he downed that icy tumbler of scotch and headed out the door for his final meeting with Sam Heekin. I watched Rose throw herself on the sofa, crossing her arms and kicking her feet on the carpet in frustration.

"Go ahead, Sylvie," my father said.

After a breath, I began. First, I told them what happened in the truck stop bathroom: how we allowed the waitress to touch the doll, how I worried for my mother inside the stall and later on the drive home when she became ill. I told them that after we returned home with Penny, nothing felt the same, from the broken horses in my room to the all-consuming tension that filled the house. And then I confessed to sneaking downstairs one night, only to duck into the kitchen and find Penny gone from her rocker when I returned. I told them how I let Rose in on what I discovered and how my mother confirmed that something similar was happening when I pulled back the covers and saw Penny in her bed the night before. I spoke faster as I neared the end, telling them about stepping into my room and noticing all the horse limbs scattered on the floor. And so, I said, Rose and I had started talking about the need to get rid of that doll, because of the power it had, or the power we were giving it. But even though the two of us discussed the idea, I made it clear that *I* was the one who carried out the act.

"Before things got any worse around here," I told them, looking at my father's weary face then at my mother in her chair. "I made up my mind to protect us. I'm sorry. Maybe it wasn't right. But that's exactly what happened. I know it's part of your work, but I felt afraid. Not just for myself. But for all of us."

For a long moment after that, no one spoke. My sister had stopped kicking the rug a while before, so the only sound in the room was the ticking of the clock. At last, my father said, "Rose, go upstairs and pack your things."

"Pack?" I said. "What for?"

Rose stood from the sofa. "I told you, Sylvie," she said on her way toward the stairs. "You should have kept your big mouth shut. You think you're the smartest in this family, but you're really the stupidest of all."

"Enough of that," my father told her. He was no longer yelling, though, nobody was. "Go to your room. We'll leave in a half hour."

"Leave?" I said to my parents as I saw my sister slip out of the living room and walk away up the stairs. "Leave where? I told you I was the one who did it."

"From what I just heard," my father said, "it was Rose who kept urging you to sneak downstairs and watch TV. Am I right?"

I was quiet, because the truth was being used against us both now.

"And it was Rose who told you the smart thing to do was get rid of Penny. Am I right there too?"

Again, I did not respond.

"So it's apparent that Penny is not the one having a bad influence around here. It's your sister controlling things. Putting ideas in your head too. And I'm tired of it."

My mother kept her eyes on the floor. "But Sylvester, can't we try one more time? What about her senior year?"

"We talked about this. Enough trying. It's not just about what happened last night. It's about getting Rose's head right."

I opened my mouth to try and convince him not to take Rose wherever they were going, but I knew it was useless. Instead, I turned and ran upstairs and down the hall to my sister's room. When I stepped inside, the cinnamon-colored suitcase we shared was wide open on the floor, a heap of clothes tossed inside along with her black sneakers. I wondered if she might yell at me about what I'd done, but Rose stayed quiet, grabbing things at random: a stash of heavy metal records, a few half-melted candles, a carton of cigarettes hidden in the back of her closet, even her old globe. I watched her, saying nothing until she reached under her bed and pulled out a forgotten horse. Pure white with shimmering blue eyes and a mane made of miniature white feathers like an Indian headdress. Same as me, Rose tugged at a leg to see if it might snap off. When that didn't work, she pulled two limbs in opposite directions, wishbone style, but that wouldn't break them either.

"Here, Sylvie." She handed the horse to me. "You might as well keep the last unbroken one. Write and let me know how long it survives after I'm gone."

"Where are you going?"

"Jail. Or something close to it."

"I'm serious, Rose."

"Some school. Saint Julia's, I think it's called. Ask Mom or Dad about it."

"Let's talk to them again. Convince them not to—"

"It's too late, Sylvie. Especially since you're the one who did the convincing in the first place. Besides, this isn't as sudden as it seems. Dad's been cooking up this scheme for a while now. He had the place ready and waiting for me, as soon as I made a wrong move. Only it turned out I didn't need to. You did it for me. I should probably thank you, though, since anywhere will be better than here."

In another part of the house, the phone rang, sounding shrill. Someone must have answered it quickly, because after the second ring things fell quiet.

"I don't want you to go," I told my sister.

Rose did her best to force the suitcase closed, but it was too full. She jettisoned the globe, placing it back on her dresser, then yanked out some clothes, leaving them in a pile on the floor. After that, I helped her by sitting on top of the suitcase. "Yeah, you do, Sylvie," she said, the buckles releasing a solid *thwack* each time one snapped into place. "You just don't know it yet. Life will be more peaceful here without me."

"But when am I going to see you again?"

"That's a question for Mom and Dad too. I bet they'll tell you it'll be as long as it takes to get my head right. Isn't that the line of crap they like to say about me? Either way, let me give you some advice: You know how they always tell us about their rule that we can share anything with them?"

I nodded.

"Don't believe it."

The final buckle snapped shut, sealing the suitcase tight and putting an end to the topic. My sister stood and went to the door. She must have wanted at least a few minutes to herself, but I stayed put a moment longer, looking around the small space, which felt somehow void of her presence already.

"You know something, squirt? I always knew you were bright. But you're pretty brave, too. Dumping that doll down the well."

Sitting on that overstuffed suitcase, I didn't feel so brave. What I felt was foolish. But what point was there in telling my sister that? When I stood and stepped past her into the hallway, I felt the urge to give Rose a hug. It had been years since the two of us had done that, however, and it made me nervous to think of how she might react. Instead, I said simply, "I'm sorry for ruining things."

Rose looked away, fixing her gaze on that suitcase we shared on all those trips with our parents. "Don't worry about it, squirt. It's not all your fault. Now leave me alone so I can finish up in here."

I didn't want to, but I turned and retreated to my room. Inside, I sat on the edge of my bed, absently petting the soft feathers of that last unbroken horse. All the while, my mind could not help but fixate on Penny down in the well. Despite my wishes, despite any rational thought, I kept wondering if the doll was still having an influence from where she lay in that cold, murky water.

Thump, thump, thump—I listened to the sound of my sister dragging our suitcase down the stairs. One last time, I told myself that I should do something to keep her from leaving. But when I went to the window and saw the car idling in the driveway, trunk popped open, I knew there was no undoing things now. Our father and mother stood by the road examining our mailbox, which had been knocked off its post. The trash cans were down, too, though they ignored those for the time being. I watched our father pick up the mailbox, inspecting the buckled sides and the bent red flag that spun round and round like some whirligig carnival game. He attempted to balance the thing on the post again, but it wobbled before toppling to the ground. My father kicked it away in frustration.

And then the front door opened and Rose stepped outside. She lugged our suitcase down the stoop to the car. Despite his back trouble, my father went to her and heaved it into the trunk. As he walked to the driver's side, our mother pulled an envelope from her jacket and pushed it into Rose's hand. My sister refused it, but my mother insisted, shoving it in Rose's pocket. And then our mother did what I had felt too nervous to do, putting her arms around Rose, pulling her close. My sister did not return the hug, standing there stiff as that headless mailbox post.

From that moment on, things moved quickly: Rose got in the car and buckled her seat belt. My father did too, shifting into Reverse. As they backed out of the driveway, I waved to my sister, willing her to look up and wave too. But it never happened, even though I kept on waving until the Datsun pulled onto the lane and rolled away.

For a long while after they were gone, I looked out at the empty drive-way and my mother lingering on the front lawn, gazing down the road as though she hoped for them to return. With the exception of a few occasions when she mentioned her father's passing, I'd rarely seen my mother cry. As I stood at my window, however, I watched her hands move to her cheeks, wiping away tears. When I couldn't bear to watch any longer, I turned to my desk and began sorting those horse limbs, lining them up until they were side by side, ready for the odd surgery I'd grown accustomed to performing.

Hours—that's how long it took for me to carefully glue them together. All the while, so many questions about Rose and when exactly she'd be back knocked around my mind. When all the horses were returned to my shelf once more, it occurred to me that, ringing phone and chiming clock aside, there had been no sounds inside our house for some time. I stepped out of my room, locking the door behind me, listening for my mother. When I still did not hear anything, I made my way to the first floor. At last, I opened the front door and found her sitting on the stoop, wearing her robe and slippers still, a thick stack of white paper in her lap and more tears in her eyes.

I stepped outside and sat beside her. Above us, birds chirped in the misty air, and squirrels scrambled along the branches of the birch trees. I looked over at my mother's crumpled face. The tears that rolled down her pale cheeks seemed capable of washing away the hints of blue from the veins beneath her skin.

"Can I ask," I said, finally, "where Saint Julia's is?"

Her hair had fallen out of its pins and looked wild as hay. She brushed it from her eyes, telling me, "Your father gave me the name of the town. But my mind—well, it's been so muddled lately. This fatigue. I just haven't felt myself. Anyway, it's a nice place in upstate New York where they help people like her. Troubled girls, I mean. Your father found out about it. Made all the arrangements. If I felt better, I might have been able to keep stalling him the way I have for months now."

"When will she back?"

"I don't know, Sylvie. In some ways, that's up to her." My mother looked out at the empty driveway, hands resting on the thick stack of paper in her lap. When I asked what those pages were, the question brought more tears. I reached over, rubbed my hand on her back, feeling the knobby bumps of her spine. At last, my mother took a breath and told me that when she woke that morning, she made up her mind to fight her weariness and get out of bed to cook us breakfast. After being cooped up in that bedroom, however, she first wanted a glimpse of the sun. That's when she opened the front door and caught sight of the vandalized mailbox and toppled trash cans. "I made my way to the street and picked up some of that trash, then lifted the mailbox off the ground only to discover this manuscript stuffed in there. It's from that reporter your father welcomed into our lives."

Inside the house, the phone rang. It had begun to sound like small screams to me. "Do you need to get that?"

My mother shook her head, waved it away. She looked down at the title on the top page. I did too: *Help for the Haunted: The Unusual Work of Sylvester and Rose Mason* by Samuel Heekin. "Your father," she said, when the ringing stopped, "thought he was going to persuade the man to omit certain details he apparently told him one night when they were out having a drink after an official interview. But Sam—*Mr. Heekin*, I mean—had already finished the book and has no plans of changing even a single word. It will be published in another few months. September, actually. Heekin intended to give it to your father last night, but chickened out—that's the only way to say it. Instead, he slipped it in our box after he dropped him off. Before whoever came by and knocked it off the post."

"How do you know all this?" I asked.

I glimpsed an odd expression on my mother's face then: a wide-eyed flicker that left me with the feeling she'd said more than she intended. Her mouth opened to answer, but just then the phone burst into another series of shrill screams. I asked once more if she needed to get it, and she told me, "Eventually, I should. But he'll call back."

"*He?* Who is calling?"

"Well, I don't mean *he*. Not exactly anyway. After all, there are plenty of people calling. More reporters who want to interview us. And these people who call themselves *lecture agents,* who want to book your father and me all over the country for more talks. And so many strangers have been calling too, more than ever before, seeking our help. But there's one person who has been more persistent than the rest. *Relentless,* in fact.

"But enough about that," she added, looking at me with her glittery eyes. "What's most important, Sylvie, is that I need you to promise you'll *never ever* read these pages, even when the book is published. This reporter no longer has a good opinion of your father. And whoever's fault that is— your dad's, mine—I don't want you going forward in life with disillusioned feelings about your own father, who loves you very much and would do anything for you."

"I promise," I told her, meaning it. "I won't read any of it. Not a single word."

"That's my good girl." She brushed back more hair, wiping her eyes too. "I knew I could count on you. And now, Sylvie, I need to ask your help with something else. Between what's happened with Rose and now this book, your father is going to be pretty upset when he gets home. I'd like there to be one less thing that frustrates him."

We sat for a long moment, side by side, silent except for the sound of our breathing, the sounds of birds and squirrels all around. My mother did not need to say anything more; I knew what she was asking. Even though a sizable part of me wanted to refuse, another part—the part that wanted to please her, the part that felt so dogged about using my smarts to solve any problem—had already begun dissecting the matter. It took little time before arriving at the most obvious method. I stood and told my mother I'd be right back, before making my way into the house and down the basement stairs.

When I tugged the string that dangled from the ceiling, the bare bulb came to life, illuminating the hatchet on the wall, the hulking bookshelf blocking the crawl space, my father's desk in the center, and the empty area where my mother's rocker had been before they lugged it upstairs for Penny. I went to the desk and pulled open a drawer. Those tarnished instruments lay inside, bound by a rubber band, same as they'd been so many years before. I removed the dental scaler and orthodontic pliers then used the pliers to bend the tip of the scaler until its shape resembled a hook. Next, I went to my mother's knitting basket, grabbed a spool of yarn.

When I got back outside, my mother was still on the steps, alternately turning more pages of Sam Heekin's manuscript and looking up to observe what I was doing. Pushing off the plywood, staring into that dark well, I located Penny, facedown and floating in the water. I slipped my makeshift fishing line over the edge, lowering the scaler and moving it in a figure-eight motion. A hand, a sleeve, a strand of that strange red hair—I hoped to hook any such part of that doll. Twice I managed, but no sooner did I begin lifting than the weight of its waterlogged body became too much and Penny slipped free. Before the line broke or the hook came loose, I brought it up again—tripling the yarn, doubling the knots, testing to be sure things were secure. Dropping it down and circling once more, eventually I felt the *gotcha* feeling a fisherman must when something is on the hook. Carefully, I lifted. The closer the doll got to the surface, the louder the rainstorm sound of water gushing from its body. I kept tightening the line, winding it between my hand and elbow, until at last I was able to reach down and grab Penny.

My mother had put aside Heekin's manuscript by then and joined me at the well. She watched as I dropped the doll on the ground. Water pooled from its body, trailing in small rivulets around my mother's slippers and my sneakers.

"There," I said, brushing my wet clothes. "That's what you wanted."

She stared down at Penny—a few dead leaves in the doll's hair, but otherwise no worse for wear. "Thank you, Sylvie. And I'm sorry too."

"Sorry?" I said.

"Your sister was right. Your father and I—we used to keep you girls separate from our work, as much as possible. As time's gone on, I've realized we failed at that."

The mention of Rose and the things she said before leaving only stirred the sadness and guilt I felt about her being gone. In an effort to change the subject I said, "Last night, you told me you didn't believe them at first."

"Believe who?"

"That couple in Ohio. The Entwistles. When I came to your room, you said you didn't believe the things they claimed about the doll. What do you believe now?"

My mother let out a heavy sigh, watching as still more water drained from Penny; it seemed the doll had soaked up a never-ending supply. "I felt badly for them," she said. "That much was certain. But from the letters they sent, I had the sense they were simply a couple mourning the loss of their daughter, hoping for something to be true that was not. And I told your father as much."

"Then why did we go there?"

"At first, they wrote to say that in its own strange way the doll had brought hope back into their lives. But over time, they reported that her presence seemed to be responsible for disruptive occurrences."

"What sort of occurrences?" I asked, thinking only of the ones in our lives.

Again, my mother sighed. She never liked talking about this sort of topic as much as my father, and I worried she might cut it short. But she continued, "Broken dishes. A shattered mirror. A fire in the store below their apartment. More than any of those things, however, they described a pervasive, off-kilter feeling that plagued their home. Eventually, your father convinced me that we should visit and help them if we could. But from the very moment we watched you girls drive off to the movies, I had the same impression as when reading the Entwistles' letters: this was a couple struggling with overwhelming grief. At first, that opinion was based solely on those feelings I get. But the details of their lives confirmed it. Their daughter had been dead nearly three years, and yet, when the Entwistles showed us the girl's bedroom, it was just as she left it, right down to her barrettes on the nightstand and her dirty play clothes in the hamper. Most nights, Mrs. Entwistle informed us, she slept right there in the twin bed with her daughter's doll cradled in her arms, rather than in her own bed with her husband."

"So were they lying to you and Dad about the things they claimed Penny did?"

"Not lying exactly. What they were doing, I believe, was sharing with us a kind of truth they had created for themselves. In some ways, it's not so different from what many people do in this world. Their truth was a story that they had woven together in the years after their heartbreaking loss—one they kept adding to, seizing any scrap of evidence to support their belief. You'll see as you get older, Sylvie, even if the examples aren't so extreme, there are times when it is easier to fool yourself than swallow some jagged piece of reality. Does that make sense?"

I nodded. "What about—" I paused, wanting to finish with: *the snapped limbs on my horses, the doll missing from the rocker that night, the way it had of turning up in your bed.* But I held off, asking instead, "What about the broken dishes and the shattered mirror? What about the fire?"

My mother could not explain those things with any certainty, she said, except to tell me that it was not so unusual for objects to break. As for the fire downstairs, Drackett's Used Goods looked more than a little cluttered when she glanced in the window. "All those ancient things crammed inside probably made for a fire hazard."

At last, the water letting from the doll's body had slowed. My mind was full of more questions, but I brought up one in particular. "When we knocked on the door, Dad had a scratch on his hand that was bleeding. What happened?"

"That's probably the least mysterious thing of all. Mr. Entwistle was showing your father pieces of the broken mirror that he kept in a plastic bag. Your dad cut himself. Simple as that."

"I see," I told her.

"I know what you're thinking, Sylvie."

"You do?"

"Yes. I bet you're wondering why, if I did not believe the things they said about Penny, did I go along with your father and remove her from their home?"

She was right, that had been on my mind.

"Whether or not I believed them was beside the point. Getting the doll out of their home was what they wanted, and it seemed like the most sensible—the most *kind*—thing to do in order to help them move on. Besides, your father believed what they said. That's happened many times, in fact. He sees things a certain way that I do not. When we prayed with them, he felt strongly that a door had been opened inside that apartment. For that reason, he asked me to keep the doll away from anyone else until we got home. He especially didn't want either of you near her—" My mother stopped. "Near *it*, as your sister pointed out. I suppose I should break that habit at least."

This time, the mention of Rose led me to try and picture her at that moment, in the passenger seat for a change, while my father sat at the wheel. I imagined the thick silence between them as they sped north toward the New York border and that school beyond. Maybe she was right, I thought. Maybe any place would be better for her than our house, considering how strange things had become.

Keeping my eyes on the doll, while digesting the things my mother had said about how harmless it was, I couldn't help but tell her, "I still don't like the idea of having Penny around. I don't like seeing it in your rocker. And however it happens, I don't like it ending up in your bed. Plus, I don't like that its picture was in the paper. Kids in school, people in town, they all know what's going on here, Mom. And knocking down our mailbox and trash cans is their way of showing us they don't like it."

My mother fell quiet before telling me, "At the moment, there's nothing we can do about what people out there think. But we can do something about Penny. And whatever the truth about the doll, at the very least we can put it someplace where you won't have to see it. Someplace where, no matter what anyone believes, it will seem incapable of doing harm." She got up and walked toward Rose's old rabbit cage, where Mr. Knothead once lived, twitching his wet nose, devouring the endless carrots my sister fed him, dropping his stinky pellet turds through the metal bars to the lawn beneath. It was not so terribly big, that cage. Not so terribly heavy, either. That's something I learned when my mother detached and slid it out from the wooden stand, then asked me to give her a hand. Together, we wedged our fingers between the bars and carried it across the lawn, up the stoop, inside the house, and down to the basement. The most out of the way spot, we decided after some discussion, was atop that hulking bookshelf by the crawl space. We steadied the cage up there, and then my mother disappeared up the stairs, returning with Penny in her arms. After placing the doll's wet body inside, she closed the door and fastened the latch, letting out a breath.

"Tell me, Sylvie. Does that make you feel better?"

The sight of Penny shut away behind those metal bars should have done something to alter my feelings. But looking at the thing on the other side—leaves gone from its hair, bracelet twisted tight around its wrist, candy-cane legs crossed daintily over each other, smiling just the same—the truth was, I felt no different. Still, I knew what my mother wanted to hear, so I opened my mouth to give her the right answer.

Just as the phone had interrupted my mother earlier, it released a shrill ring from upstairs at that moment, interrupting me as well. The sound startled us both. And this time, it kept ringing well past the point when the machine should have picked up. My mother sighed. "The tape must be full. I should probably get the phone, in case your father is trying to reach us from the road."

She walked to the string dangling from the lightbulb. She was about to give it a tug when she stopped. "I was just thinking," she said, "about when I was a girl. During long nights on the farm, I used to sometimes feel scared sleeping in my room. When that happened, my father used to leave the light on for me. He said it would be harder to imagine bad things happening when there was light to see by. I think the same applies here. Let's leave this one on. How does that sound?"

As that phone rang and rang above our heads, I looked up at the rafters and felt an odd sense of alarm. But I told my mother her suggestion sounded like a good idea, and with that, she let go of the string, leaving the light burning in the basement as the two of us headed up the stairs.

Back in the kitchen, with the door shut behind us, I plopped down at the table and began flipping through that swatch book while my mother picked up the phone. The Paisley Party. The Bloomsbury House. The Littlest Stars. Each of the patterns had a clever name, and the day my mother brought the book home she asked which design best matched the person I was. I'd been unable to choose then, and all these months later, still none seemed right.

"I'm sorry," I heard her say into the phone. "But I'll have to ask you to call back when my husband is home. He handles that sort of thing. Thank you." When she hung up, my mother looked to see what I was doing at the table, asking if I'd found anything close.

"Not yet," I said, just as the phone rang once more. The sound caused us both to groan, and our groans caused us both to laugh.

"I understand now the way a receptionist must feel," my mother sighed, before answering again. There was a long pause, and then, in a voice that sounded cooler, less polite than on the previous call, she asked, "At a pay phone where? Mars Market? I see. You're quite close actually."

The Purple Parade. The Stars and Stripes. The Milky Way. I kept flipping, searching for the perfect pattern.

"Well, I suppose it would be okay. I can't promise I'll be of much help, though. It doesn't work that way. Besides, my husband is not here and normally he—" She paused, then continued, "If you take a left out of the lot onto Holabird Avenue, you'll come to an intersection. There, you take a right. Well, no, actually. Not a right. You know something? It's funny, I don't often drive the route myself, so I'm not the best source of directions. Tell you what, ask someone there. Since our street is easy to miss, I will walk to the end of the lane and meet you. Okay then, Mr. Lynch."

The name caused me to look up. I shut the book and waited as she said good-bye. The moment she put down the phone, I repeated: *"Mr. Lynch?"*

"That's right. I'm not sure you remember, but we met him and his daughter a few years back in Ocala."

Even after so much time, the memory of that night lived vividly in my mind. I heard the apprehension in my voice when I asked, "What does he want?"

"Well, *he's* been the persistent one I was referring to earlier. Calling for days on end, in fact. Now, apparently, he's turned up right here in town. Says his daughter is having troubles again, worse than before, actually."

I could still see him calling into the bushes. I could still hear her snarling. I remembered the girl's strange silence as her mouth moved up and down like a marionette's beneath the lights of that parking lot. "Maybe you should have told him no."

"Sylvie, that doesn't sound very Christian of you."

She was right. But I kept going anyway. "Just because he decides to show up in Dundalk does not mean you're obligated to drop everything and walk to the end of the street to pray over her."

By then, my mother was about to exit the kitchen. She stopped in the doorway, took a breath, and said, "A prayer does not cost a person anything, Sylvie. Remember that. Now I cannot guarantee I'll be of any help this time, but taking a few moments out of my day to at least *try*, well, it's no great burden. So I'm going to change my clothes and meet them."

In the middle of that book there was an entire section of white swatches that I'd flipped through before. While I listened to the creak of floorboards upstairs as my mother got ready, I turned to them again. The Whitest Clouds. The Whitest Seashells. The Whitest Cotton. I studied each until my mother returned downstairs. Her hair had been swept up into pins once more. Silver crosses dotted her ears; another cross hung around her neck. She wore one of her many gray dresses.

"Did you always dress that way?" I couldn't help but ask.

My mother tilted her head, fidgeting with the back of one of those crucifix earrings. "No. Some years ago, your father suggested it. He thought it best that we present a consistent version of ourselves to the world when we're working."

Not quite beneath my breath, a word slipped out: "Costumes."

"Pardon?"

The way she said it gave me the sense that she genuinely had not heard. I looked up at her and tried explaining, "Those dresses. That jewelry. Dad's brown suits and yellow shirts. They're like costumes."

"Well, I suppose that's one way to look at it, Sylvie. For me, it's simply easier not having to wonder what to put on. There's no time wasted shopping or standing in front of my closet debating—neither of which I care to do. Anyway, I hope to be back home in a bit. After that, let's try to salvage what's left of the day and do something fun."

Once she said good-bye, I went back to flipping through those swatches, listening to her move down the hall, the front door opening and closing. All those patterns did nothing to take my mind off where she was going. When I couldn't stand my curiosity a second longer, I shoved the book aside and stood from the table.

Outside, I caught up with my mother just as she started down the lane. When we arrived at the corner, a van was already parked there, emergency flashers blinking away.

The Forgotten Followers: A Ministry—those words were painted on the side, under a thick coat of grime. Someone had doodled on the muck too. I made out a stick-figure animal, headless, with an endlessly twirling tail, and random letters and numbers in a helter-skelter pattern: *M, A, Z, 6, 13.*

As we drew near, Albert Lynch gave a hesitant wave from the driver's seat. Something about the sight of him sent a peculiar shudder through my body. My mother didn't give even a hint of uneasiness, however, so I just followed along. The man's smooth, babyish skin—a detail I remembered from that night in the parking lot—looked the same. But he sported a pair of bug-eyed glasses now, and a wispy mustache had sprouted above his lip. That night in Florida, Lynch had been wearing a baseball hat. Without it, I could see his bald head, so shiny it seemed polished.

Rather than open his door, Lynch disappeared between the seats into the back and slid the side door open. From what I could tell, whatever seats had once been in the back were all ripped out. Abigail lay on a thin mattress inside, looking as limp as Penny.

Slowly, the girl turned her head to see us, blinking and gazing out with a dazed expression. Her stillness lasted only a moment, however, because the second she noticed my mother, Abigail shook off the blankets wrapped mummy tight around her legs. She sat up, then pushed her body to the edge of that van, hopped out, and walked toward us with a slight but no-ticeable limp.

"Well, hello again," my mother said as the girl took her hand.

A rustling came from the van. My mother and I looked to see what was going on, but the sound caused Abigail to slip behind her, hiding. Since the girl was paying no attention to me, I took the opportunity to study her. Fifteen, I guessed. Maybe sixteen. Somewhere between Rose's age and my own. She was not a child as she had been that night in Ocala; she was taller and had breasts now, the start of them anyway—enough to give a hint of shapeliness beneath her ratty tee. That blond hair of hers, messy as ever, fell to her waist. Her feet were bare, a few toes on her left, black and blue.

"Mr. Lynch?" my mother called into the van.

I stepped closer to peer inside. Sleeping bags and pillows and books were strewn inside. A cloth painting of the cross with the sun setting behind it covered what I could see of the far wall. In front of that painting stood a cardboard box flipped upside down and littered with half-melted candles and more books. A makeshift desk, I thought, or quite possibly an altar.

After rustling around in the back of the van a bit longer, Albert emerged, arms full of rumpled clothes. He looked down at the blankets Abigail had shaken off, then looked up to say, "Did she—"

"Did she what?" my mother asked.

"Did she walk out there on her own? Just like that?"

"Just like that," she told him as Abigail stayed tucked away behind her, dragging those bruised toes against the pavement with enough force that it looked painful.

Lynch must have had plenty of practice getting in and out of that van, yet when he set those clothes aside and stepped out, he did so without accounting for the steep drop, and stumbled, nearly falling, before steadying himself. Once his feet were planted on the pavement, he came closer, bringing a cloud of stale cologne or maybe the air-freshener smell from that van along with him. "Thank you," he said to my mother in the astonished voice I remembered. "Thank you. Thank you."

"Please, there's no need to thank me. I haven't done anything yet."

"You agreed to meet me on such short notice. And you don't realize it, but I haven't been able to get my daughter up and out of that van in nearly a week."

Abigail's foot stopped grazing the pavement a moment as she peeked out from behind my mother. When her father noticed her wide blue eyes looking at him, he gave the same hesitant wave he'd given us, but the girl just flinched and ducked behind my mother again, pancaking her face so hard into my mother's back I worried it hurt them both.

The exchange, or lack thereof, caused Albert to heave a sigh. "I suppose the best thing for me to do now is leave you to it. How long until I should come back and get her?"

"Leave me to it?" my mother said.

"Trust me. If I'm around, it will only distract while you are working on her."

"I'm sorry, Mr. Lynch. But you must be mistaken. I don't *work on* people. I'm not some auto repair shop or child psychologist at a hospital where you can—"

"Good. Because I've tried the psychologist route already. It failed."

When he saw the displeased expression on my mother's face, Lynch grew quiet. He glanced down at his heavy black shoes—the sort Father Coffey wore, the sort my father wore too. Looking up again, he told my mother, "Forgive me, ma'am. Those were the wrong words to describe what you do. The last thing I want is to insult you. I love my daughter. No father has gone to the lengths I have to keep his child close. To keep her safe. But as much as it pains me, there's no other way to say it: Abigail has something, well, she has something *in her*. She needs help. *Your* help."

"I—"

"I saw you Mrs. Mason," Lynch said, cutting her off. "You helped her find peace once before. Over the years, I considered seeking you out again, but I was foolish, thinking I might find some better, more permanent solution. I wasted so much time. I mentioned the shrinks. But there were healers. And preachers. Plus, so many people who claimed to be modern-day soothsayers. One con artist after another put on a big show, and in the end, they did nothing but fleece me."

In her most gentle voice, my mother told him, "I'm sorry."

"Me too. But then, the other day, I had an appointment I'd been waiting months for. That's the way it works with these people. They keep you waiting so you get the impression they're in demand and it's going to be worth it. In this case, it was three old women who call themselves the Sisters. I drove Abigail to their house at the end of a windy road on a mountain in Rangley, Maine. Nobody around for miles except me and my daughter, maybe some moose out in the woods, and those rickety old women hunched and shriveled the way you'd imagine in a fairy tale. Holy as those ladies were supposed to be, they demanded their money up front. I peeled endless twenties from the wad in my pocket and forked them over. And then they had the nerve to act bothered when I told them they needed to come to the van and see Abigail, since she would not come inside."

"And did they?"

Lynch nodded, peeking around my mother to glimpse his daughter. The girl's face was hidden away still, and she had resumed that dragging motion with her foot.

"What did those women do?" my mother said.

"Nothing. After the same sort of spectacle I've grown accustomed to—chanting and shaking their arms in the air and tossing herbs and rubbing oils on my daughter—not a single thing changed. I stood outside that van, looking off into the mountains. I might have cried if the tears hadn't dried up inside me a long time ago. Meanwhile, the Sisters packed up their props and exited back toward their house, telling me that sometimes it takes months for their work to be effective. I've heard that line before, so I smiled and said nothing while watching them walk to their house. But then, as I stood there, willing myself to get back in the van and drive down the mountain, their front door opened, and I looked to see one of the Sisters coming back to me. I'd say she was the youngest, but it was hard to tell, since they were all so old; either way, there was something different about this one. I guess it was that she had more light, more compassion in her eyes. She whispered to me about—well, I'll give you one guess who she told me about."

My mother kept quiet, looking down at the ground. The only sound was Abigail doing that thing on the pavement with her bruised toes.

"*You*, Mrs. Mason. She told me about you and your husband. Only she didn't say your names right away, so I didn't realize. She said she had read of a certain couple and the things they'd been able to do. She suggested that this couple might be able to help my Abigail too. That's when she pulled out a clipping from the newspaper, and I looked down to see a photo—*your photo*—and I read about all the things you've done since I last saw you."

"I see," my mother told him. "Listen, Mr. Lynch, I don't want to be one more person who adds to your disappointment, so I need to be up front. As I told you on the phone, I cannot guarantee I'll be of any help. My husband and I don't claim to have any sort of magic powers. When it comes down to it, our only method is prayer in its most simple and basic form. It's all I have to offer. And that said, your daughter is a minor. I can't have you leaving her here and disappearing on us."

"I'm not disappearing. I'll be back. *Of course*, I'll be back. But you and your husband are good people. At the very least, I know my Abigail will be safe here with you. And I can use a day, two days, three—however long it takes, to get myself together and calm my nerves before I do something I—"

When he stopped abruptly, I expected my mother to prod, but she allowed the silence to do the job. She waited—we both did—watching him look down at those heavy shoes once more. When he lifted his head and spoke next, his voice crept close to tears. "It's been so hard. This life. You have no idea. Or maybe you do. But there are times when I'm afraid I'll lose my patience. Afraid that, despite my good intentions and faith in our good Lord Jesus Christ and the love in my heart for my daughter, I might snap and do something I'll regret."

In the distance, we heard a car motoring along the main road. All of us, except Abigail, looked to see a red convertible with flashy hubcaps moving closer. At the sight of Lynch's grimy van pulled to the side, emergency flashers blinking away, the driver slowed to get a glimpse of us there before speeding off.

When the convertible was gone, I made up my mind to put an end to this situation before things went any further. "Sorry for your troubles, sir," I began. "We really are. But you will have to come up with another plan. You can't leave your daughter here."

Considering how unusual that sort of bluntness was coming from me, it sounded pretty convincing—that's what I thought anyway, before Lynch fixed his gaze on me with such intensity, it was as though he was realizing for the first time that my mother had family who might interfere with his needs. A smile—so slight, so awkward, I was not quite certain that's even what it was at first—formed on his thin lips. I had the feeling he might start laughing at the things I'd said.

"Sylvie," my mother said. "It's okay."

"But—"

She reached over, put a hand on my arm, and squeezed, while keeping her gaze on Albert Lynch. "I can try to help your girl," she told him. "But I must inform you that I've not been feeling my best the last month. And these things—well, they take focus. They take energy from me. Still, I can try."

That not-quite-a-smile turned into something more full-fledged when Lynch heard what my mother was saying. After another rush of *thank you*'s, he turned toward the van and wasted no time gathering up rumpled clothes, a toothbrush, a hairbrush, sneakers, books. I stood watching, having a hard time imagining his daughter brushing her teeth or hair or wearing sneakers, never mind reading.

When Lynch turned to carry the pile toward us, something that had been swept up inside dropped out of the bottom. My mother and I watched it fall to the pavement and skid toward the front tire. In his excitement,

Lynch must not have noticed, otherwise he wouldn't have asked me to hold out a garbage bag so he could stuff his daughter's things inside.

"She likes this book," he said, showing us a copy of something called *Legends of Faith*. "Or she used to like it. When she was younger, I read it to her. Sometimes, I still do, in hopes that it will bring back memories of happier times."

"Mr. Lynch?" my mother said.

"And now that she's up and out, I should warn you that it might appear as though things are relatively fine with her. That's how it goes. For weeks at a stretch things seem almost normal. But just when you get comfortable, that's when—"

"Mr. Lynch?" my mother repeated.

This time, he stopped talking and looked at her. "Yes, ma'am?"

My mother did not answer. She didn't have to; his gaze trailed hers, mine too, to where a small black pistol with a blunt silver nose lay not far from the front tire. I watched Lynch's hands begin to tremble as he shoved the last of his daughter's things in the bag, then he walked quickly to the van and scooped up the gun.

"*Please,*" he said, once it was stashed inside beneath the driver's seat. "Don't get the wrong idea. I'm a good Christian. A man of faith. But for a lot of complicated reasons, my daughter and me—we live our lives on the road. That means sleeping in campgrounds. Rest stops. People out there, they're not always as nice as you. I learned that the hard way. I've never used this gun. Never plan to. It's just to scare people when the situation calls for it."

"Well, you're scaring me plenty right now," my mother told him. "No matter what your reasons, you shouldn't be so careless about where you store that pistol."

In the tone of a scolded child, he told her, "I'm sorry, ma'am. And you're right. I won't be so careless anymore."

"Well, okay then. Now that that's out of the way, why don't we agree that you will call in a few days and we can see how things are with your daughter. How does that sound?"

"Sounds good to me. And thank you one more time. I may not look like it, but I do have access to a little money when I need it. So I can pay something in return. Or if there's something else I can do, let me know, and I'll find a way to give it to you."

In response to that offer, my mother said nothing. It was not like her to discuss a fee for the things they did, that much I knew. So she just waited; I did too, watching Albert Lynch climb back into his van. He flicked off the emergency flashers, rolled down the window, and called out, "Abigail, I know you can hear me. I'm going to leave you for a bit, but I'll be back. My hope, my prayer, is that your time here will help you get better."

If the girl heard him, she gave no sign. She stood behind my mother's back still, though turned around now, looking down our street riddled with those gaping foundations like a mouth full of cavities. Albert gave up waiting for any response, or maybe he never expected one. Either way, he offered us a last wave, less hesitant than any previous, before pulling away from the curb. As he vanished in the same direction as that red convertible, my mother took the bag of Abigail's belongings from me. Without a word, we began the walk home. The slow, careful way she moved made me realize that my mother must have felt fatigue washing over her again.

In those early moments inside our house, Abigail did not seem so much a person with "something in her" as she did a houseguest, albeit an awkward one. She moved slowly around the living room, peering too closely at the clock, the cross, and the books imprisoned behind the glass of the curio hutch. She leaned in to study the grade-school portraits of Rose and me for so long, it felt as though she was touching them in some way, putting her fingerprints all over the frames.

"What exactly is wrong with her?" I asked my mother, since she seemed different from the only other haunted person I'd encountered in our house, that man at the kitchen table in the middle of the night years before.

I had followed her to the washroom, where she emptied the bag of Abigail's belongings and inspected the broken zippers, torn hems, and tattered material. In a tired voice, she told me, "You don't have to be a part of this, Sylvie. Once I get her cleaned up and fed, I'll get her settled in the partitioned area that your father finally just about finished. In the meantime, you can go to your room and read or even go to the living room and watch TV for a change."

She seemed so weary that I couldn't help but want to be of some use to her. "Here, Mom. Let me get this laundry going while you help her settle in."

My mother debated the idea, then put down Abigail's clothes and went to a cabinet by the dryer. She pulled out a gift box with a torn scrap of Nativity wrapping paper taped to one side. Since my sister wore sweats to bed and walked around the house barefoot until the soles of her feet turned gray, I was never sure why my parents bothered getting her certain gifts. Now, my mother took out an unworn nightgown and slippers they'd given Rose the previous Christmas. She held up the gown, and it unfurled like a pale spirit before her. She carried that spirit, those slippers, from the room.

A Grand Canyon T-shirt. A Mount Rushmore T-Shirt. A Jesus Loves Me T-Shirt. From where I stood feeding all those frayed shirts into the machine, I could hear my mother and Abigail in the kitchen. My mother offered her food but got no response. My mother offered her a shower but got no response to that, either. At last, she must have managed to convince the girl to wash her hands and face, because I heard water running in the sink for some time. I poured a double dose of detergent into the machine as I heard my mother say, "There we go, Abigail. That's better—for the time being anyway. Now, I imagine you must be tired. Am I right?" The girl must have nodded, because after a pause my mother said, "I thought so. And you know what? I'm tired too. So let's get you settled downstairs. We can say some prayers, read a bit of scripture, then I think I'll head to bed early myself."

I cranked the knobs on the washer, realizing my mother and I would not be having any of the fun she promised earlier. Considering the way things had been lately, I should not have been disappointed, but I was. I didn't have time to really get upset, though; no sooner had I lowered the lid and the machine started thrashing away than a crash came from the kitchen, followed by the sounds of a shrill yelp, furniture toppling, and dishes smashing. I hurried to the kitchen to find my mother holding open the basement door, the light we'd left on glowing below. The table had been shoved into the center of the room. The chairs where my parents normally sat had been knocked over. A fat strip of peeling blue wallpaper stripped from the wall.

"What happened?" I asked my mother.

She shut the basement door, looked down at that wallpaper book on the floor. It had fallen open to a pattern I recognized by now—The Tiniest Hearts. "I wanted to take her downstairs but she shook her head. I told her it would be fine and held out my hand. But as soon as we reached the top step, she pulled back so suddenly and with such force that our hands came apart and she fell into those chairs. She grabbed for something and caught that wallpaper, which peeled right along with her as she fell to the floor."

"Where is she now?"

"I don't know."

Once more, my mother told me I didn't need to be a part of what was happening. But I ignored her. She picked up Rose's nightgown and slippers, and we roamed the house. I expected to come upon Abigail tucked in the back of a closet or behind a hamper or beneath a desk, burrowed away like an animal in hiding. Instead, when my mother and I reached Rose's doorway, we spotted her inside, slipped beneath the covers, eyes closed, as though she had been asleep for hours.

More to herself than me, my mother said, "I can't have this."

"What should we do?" I asked.

She did not answer right away. Instead, we lingered in the doorway, watching Abigail. I thought of the story her father had told about the Sisters, those hunched old women who took his money but did nothing to help beyond pointing him to my mother and father. After so much false promise, no wonder the girl did not trust anyone to lead her into an unfamiliar basement.

My mother must have been thinking the same thing, because as I watched, she entered the room, reached out, and made a sign of the cross on the girl's forehead again and again. It went on long enough that I looked away, staring at my sister's globe and giving it a spin the way she used to do, planting my finger down on random locations: Hong Kong. Ontario. Bombay. I wondered if Rose had arrived at Saint Julia's by then. Maybe she'd even checked into her room and begun making friends with other girls there, realizing already that it was the best place for her after all.

"I don't like the idea," my mother said to me in a hushed voice when she was done making crosses. "But we could leave her here for just tonight. Do you feel comfortable with that, Sylvie?"

I lifted my gaze from the globe and looked at Abigail asleep in Rose's bed. "For now, I guess it would be okay."

"When your father gets home, he can help us make other arrangements." She stood, leaving that white gown Rose had never bothered with at the foot of the bed, those slippers on the floor. My mother joined me in the hallway and was about to close the door when we heard something from inside the room: a voice, worn as those tattered clothes in the washer, saying, "Thank you."

My mother and I looked at each other to be sure we had actually heard it. And then, through the small crack in the door, my mother spoke gently, telling her, "You are welcome, Abigail Lynch."

CANDLES

In the dark beneath that scratchy wool blanket, the station wagon's wheels turning beneath me, it became difficult to keep track of time. Had an hour passed? Or only twenty minutes? The woman turned on the radio, and an announcer's voice filled the chilly air inside the car. His was a syrupy, southern drawl I recognized as one my father sometimes tuned into when we were driving. The preacher spoke of things I'd heard him say before: that the end was near, that the listeners better hurry up and get right with God. Normally, there was a menacing edge to the sermons but tonight even he sounded tired of it, rattling off the scripture as if it was old news, which in every possible way, it was.

The woman at the wheel must have grown bored too, because she turned off the radio without warning. I wondered if we were getting close to our destination, but then the car picked up speed and I felt us climbing upward, heard the whir of cars and trucks passing. We were merging onto a highway, and I realized I'd slipped into the backseat without considering that Delaware license plate on her car.

When I couldn't bear the darkness a second longer, I peeked from beneath the blanket. Above me, headlights from passing vehicles shape-shifted on the ceiling. I lifted my head just enough to make out the driver's hair yanked into a tight bun. I wanted a better look, but didn't dare risk her catching sight of me. Instead, I did my best to read the dozens of road signs we moved beneath, though it was impossible to see more than a blur. Beside me lay a few Tupperware containers, like so many she brought to our house, only these were empty.

After what felt like ages, the station wagon finally slowed. I heard the *clicking* of the turn signal, and we moved off the highway, stopping a few seconds before picking up again at a slower speed. Once more, the woman began to hum that same hackneyed tune as we made a series of rights and lefts. I tried to memorize the order in case I needed to follow the path in reverse when finding my way back home, but after too many, I lost track. And then we made one final turn before the car came to a stop—her humming stopped too.

In the silence that followed, I worried she might hear me breathing. I slipped back beneath the blanket, pressing my face to the floor and feeling the sand and grit there against my cheeks. When I heard the woman gather her purse from the front seat, I realized she might also want the containers next to me. She opened the door and got out while I bit down on my lip, bracing myself again to be discovered. But then came only the sound of her footsteps clicking away.

A moment later, I poked my head out and was considering sliding back over the seats when a car rolled up and parked directly behind the station wagon. A police car, I saw when I turned. I ducked and listened as the officer got out and slammed the door, his footsteps heavier than hers.

"Where were you?" a male voice asked.

"Errands." The woman's voice, like her humming, sounded full of false cheer.

"More *errands*?"

"Yes. You know, post office, grocery store."

"Where are the bags?"

"Bags?"

"The grocery bags."

"Oh. Well, I just stopped to see if they had more of those potpies you like. The turkey ones. I had a coupon. But they were all out. I swear the stores do that just to get you in the door, figuring you'll buy something at full price instead. Not me. I turned around and walked right out of there."

Things were quiet, and I considered lifting my head to look around again, but waited to be certain they'd gone.

"What's the matter?" the woman asked at last.

"Why do you think something is the matter?"

"The way you're staring at me right now. Like you're angry, Nick. Either that or I've got food in my teeth." She laughed, but if he did, I couldn't hear it over the *shhhh*.

"I'm just hungry is all. Bad day. Very bad day."

"Sergeant again?"

He mumbled something I couldn't make out before saying, "Let's just eat. Then I'm going back down there and talking some sense into that jackass."

A door opened and banged shut, and the voices disappeared. Still, I lingered beneath the blanket in case they returned. When I lifted my head finally, the world came into view in pieces. There was that police car with the gumball lights on top. There was the front lawn, or not a lawn really, but a strip of crushed shells with a small plastic windmill spinning away in the center. There was the house, tall and narrow, white with black shutters, the roof full of peaks and dips—the sort of place I remembered from nights trick-or-treating in my parents' old neighborhood. Except this must have been near the ocean: I could smell salt in the air, hear the faint sound of waves crashing.

Slowly, I slipped over the seat, making as little noise as possible when I stepped from the station wagon. Outside, I looked at the side of the police car: Rehoboth Township. The sight should have made me feel safer, but somehow it worried me more.

I gazed up at the house again. Lights glowed in the windows on the first and second floors. Nervous as it made me, I followed the path of crushed shells to one side of the property, where a row of garbage cans and a chain-link fence divided the backyard from front. In the moonlight, I could see a cement patio, a picnic table, and a kettle grill. In the yard stood a statue of the Virgin Mary, vines winding up her open arms and obscuring her face. In the corner was a wooden shed, newly built with two sturdy locks on the door.

"I cooked it earlier today."

The woman's muffled voice from inside the house startled me. I looked up to see that I was beneath a small window. Now that I was paying attention, I heard water running, the clatter of dishes and silverware. The sounds faded as I moved into the yard, keeping near the fence, until I reached the shed. I couldn't hear anything from this vantage point, but I saw them through a picture window, seated at a table. The man was bald and wore a white T-shirt that hugged the bulky muscles of his arms and shoulders. I watched as they bowed their heads and closed their eyes, then the man made a quick sign of the cross before shoveling food in his mouth without so much as looking up. The woman didn't eat more than a few bites and simply stared across the table at him, until finally standing to clear the dishes.

As they moved from the window, I returned to the side of the house where I'd be able to hear what was going on inside. At first there was only more of her humming while the water ran. From somewhere deeper in the house came the sound of footsteps moving about. A toilet flushed. A door closed. All the while that woman kept humming until the footsteps moved into the kitchen, and I heard his deep voice telling her, "Not that song."

"Sorry. All day long, I find myself halfway through before I realize. I try not—"

"Well, try harder."

She fell quiet, before asking, "Don't you ever wonder?"

"No. Not anymore. I've let it all go, and you need to do the same."

I stood there waiting for something more when without warning a porch light snapped on in the backyard, flooding the cement patio with light. I froze there in the shadows a moment as the back door swung open and the man stepped from the house, carrying an overstuffed garbage bag. He moved directly to where I stood by those trash cans, so I turned and slipped quickly through the gate. Out on the street, I paused along the sidewalk, looking back to see him drop the bag into a can and press down the lid, then start dragging the can toward the road.

The narrow front lawns in the neighborhood and so few trees left no easy places to duck out of sight. If I stepped behind a car in a neighboring driveway, I worried someone might see from a window and snap on their light too. So instead I simply walked down the street as though I belonged there. Before I got too far, I crossed to the far side and turned back in order to get a better look at him. He was no longer dressed in just a T-shirt but wore a police uniform, the buttons of his shirt still undone.

While dragging the second can to the curb, the man glanced up and caught sight of me across the street. He lifted his hand to his forehead, visor style, and asked in the same gruff voice he used to speak to that woman, "What are you doing out here?"

I couldn't tell if he recognized me, though I certainly didn't recognize him. "I'm just . . . here," I said.

"Are you on your way home? And do your folks know where you are?"

"Yes and yes," I said.

"Well, get there safe."

He turned away from me and finished up his business with those cans before retreating to the house and snapping off the light out back. So I was a stranger to him after all, I thought, walking to the corner and wondering what to do now. A few minutes later, the roar of an engine filled the quiet air, and I glanced back to see the police car come to life and roll out of the driveway. Windows down, I heard the static squawk of the police radio inside. When he passed me, the officer looked my way and waved.

The moment his taillights disappeared around the corner, I turned back again, feeling braver now that it was just the woman alone. *Knock on the door,* I told myself. *Ask her point-blank who she is and why she has been coming to Dundalk.* I was about to work up the nerve when I saw the garbage cans. I knew from the times when vandals tipped over our trash that all sorts of personal information could be revealed that way.

I looked up at the house. A glow came from the windows still, but the curtains were drawn. Quickly, I lifted the lid of the nearest can and tore into the plastic, then held my breath and reached in among the crumpled papers and dirty napkins and balled foil.

It didn't take long before I pulled out an envelope that offered more information: *Nicholas and Emily Sanino, 104 Tidewater Road, Rehoboth, DE.* I tried to recall if I'd ever heard those names before.

"Can I help you, young lady?"

The sudden voice led me to drop the trash can lid. If it had been the old metal kind, there would have been a loud clatter. Instead, the plastic made a dull thud at my feet. I looked at her and searched for the right words. None came so I just held up the stained envelope. "Are you Emily Sanino?"

The woman stepped nearer, swooping down for the garbage can lid, placing it back on the can. Her face, I saw, looked softer up close. In the streetlight, I could see a web of faint lines around her eyes and mouth. She snatched the envelope from my hand. "Who are you? And what are you doing out here in the dark digging through our garbage?"

"I'm Sylvie," I told her. "Sylvie Mason."

The woman was pressing down on the lid to be sure it was secured, but the moment I spoke my name, she stopped. A hand went to her mouth. "Rose's sister?"

I nodded.

"How did you—" Her voice faltered. "What are you doing here?"

"Trying to find out who you are."

Emily Sanino stared at me, considering what I'd said, before asking how exactly I had found her. When I explained, she let out a long breath. "Does your sister, or anyone else, know you're here?"

I shook my head.

"Okay, then. Why don't you come inside? But you can't stay long. My husband will be back soon."

I followed her around the side of the house to the back door. The wood-paneled kitchen smelled of garlic and stewed tomatoes, whatever it was she had cooked for dinner. The smell caused my stomach to grumble, since the last thing I'd eaten was that sandwich Heekin bought me from the deli in Philly.

I ignored my hunger and looked at the speckled white countertops scrubbed clean, a bright blue mixing bowl on top, a bag of flour, an egg-beater, and her simple black purse with a lone gold buckle. "I was going to bake something," she explained. "It calms my nerves. But I realized I didn't have any eggs. I went out to the car to go to the store. That's when I saw you."

"Were you baking for us?"

"Us?"

"You know, more of the things you leave at our house?"

She shook her head. "Not tonight. I left a cake at your house earlier."

I wondered if Rose had found the cake on our stoop on her way to Dial U.S.A. and tossed it in the trash just like all the rest.

Emily Sanino returned the mixing bowl to a cabinet, the flour and milk to the fridge. I peeked down the hall to the living room. I saw a rocker, like my mother's. Just beyond, I noticed a row of framed pictures on a side table, a cluster of trophies with little gold figures on top.

"You know," I told her as she moved about the kitchen, "I'm sorry to say but nobody eats the things you leave for us."

She had swung open the door to the refrigerator but turned back to look at me, visibly perplexed. "And why not?"

"My sister and I have no idea who's leaving it."

Emily Sanino considered that a moment. I had the sense that she was debating something in her mind, before closing the fridge and saying simply, "I see."

"Why do you leave it? I mean, if you don't know us."

"You're right. I don't know you." She stood by the table now, staring straight at me and speaking in a stiff voice, as though choosing her words carefully. "I only met your sister a handful of times. Still, I have enormous sympathy for you girls, considering what you've both been through."

"Did you know my mother and father? Were you someone who came to them in need of their help?"

She ran her hands over her plain dress. "You know what? Let's go into the living room. That way I can listen for my husband's patrol car. We have to make sure he doesn't find you here when he gets back."

I considered telling her that I'd spoken to him outside, but I kept it to myself; the last thing I wanted was to distract her when we had so little time together. In the living room, I went to that side table and looked at the trophies, five in all. On top of each, the miniature gold figure—running, jumping, swinging—was a girl. The framed photos showed a dark-haired toddler wearing a soft pink dress, the same girl a few years older at the beach in a bright bathing suit, hair long and wet, sand stuck to her elbows. In the next frame she was a lanky adolescent, mouth full of braces, wearing a T-shirt that said GOD'S LOVE SUMMER CAMP. Finally, I saw the girl had grown into her teens. She had wide shoulders and womanly breasts, her hair looked darker and shorter.

"That's my daughter," Emily volunteered when she saw me looking.

I glanced at the staircase on the far side of the room, remembering the lights I'd seen on the second floor when I stood out front earlier. She took a seat on a recliner. I went to the rocker and sat too. "Is she here?"

"No. I'm afraid not."

I saw something pass over her face. Sadness, but something more that left me with a hunch about where this was going. Like the Entwistles, the Saninos must have reached out to my parents for help. There seemed so much to say, but neither of us spoke for a long moment, and then without any prompting from me, she simply began.

"We wanted more children, an entire brood, but my husband and I, well, we started late. So we were just grateful for the blessing of her. She got all the attention. She had better clothes than we did. She got sent away to summer camp. There were endless sleepovers and birthday parties."

"It seems like a good way to grow up," I told her.

"It was. But raising a child holds no guarantees. You can follow all the right steps, do all the right things, and still something can go wrong— Actually, *no*. That's a word my husband would use. I won't say wrong anymore, I'll say differently than planned. That's what happened to my daughter when she reached her teens."

I remembered Albert Lynch, standing at the end of our lane, warning us that Abigail could seem perfectly normal until suddenly everything changed. I remembered the girls I'd read about in that "history" book years before too.

"As a mother, you think you know your child. You brought her into the world, after all. You changed her diapers and picked her up when she cried. You read her stories each night before bed and slipped coins under her pillow so she believed in the Tooth Fairy. But then, despite all that love and effort, years go by and one day she turns sullen. She keeps secrets. She doesn't want to be near you. I used to ask her what was wrong, but she always told me the same thing: I wouldn't understand.

"Then her grades dropped. She began skipping school. She didn't want

to be with her old friends anymore. Despite all that, she managed to graduate. We sent her off to a good Christian college in Massachusetts. We
thought the freedom of being away from home would help. But after a
month, we received a call from the dean informing us that she had stopped
attending classes. Worse still, her behavior had become erratic. She was
caught breaking into someone's dorm. When the R.A. reported her, she
threatened the girl with a knife." Emily stopped and looked toward the
window, listening. When there was no sound, she smoothed her hands
over her dress and told me, "I don't think she would have done the things
she did if my husband had not been so hard on her."

"Is that when you turned to my mother and father?" I asked.

Mrs. Sanino tilted her head, her mouth dropping open into an oval
shape that made me think of a Christmas caroler. "Your parents?" she said
after a moment. "We never took her to them. Although I read all about your
mother and father, and saw them interviewed on TV, we did not meet."

"But if you didn't seek them out, then how—"

"My daughter came to know your sister when we sent her away to
Saint Julia's."

This was not the story I'd been expecting after all. I needed a moment
to adjust things in my mind, but Emily Sanino didn't allow for that.

"As you no doubt have learned about me," she pushed on, "I'm not
afraid to take a road trip while my husband is away from the house. Nick is
an officer three towns over, so he doesn't get home certain days when he's
doing a double on patrol duty. I'd tell him I was going to see my sister over
in Dover. Really, I snuck away to visit our daughter. During those trips,
that's when I met Rose. Did you ever go to see her there, Sylvie?"

"No. My father promised that we would, but he kept putting it off. He
told us the staff prohibited visits, because it created setbacks in the behavior
of the girls there."

Emily scoffed. "Well, he wasn't lying. That was their policy. No visitors. For the first thirty days anyway."

"Ninety," I said, remembering how endless that summer seemed without her.

"No," she told me. "I'd remember if it was *that* long. But either way,
they didn't welcome the influence of the outside world at that place. Still,

I didn't care. I never wanted to send her there in the first place. Even if I couldn't bring her home for good, I found a way to sneak her out for the day. And those times, well, they were the first in a great while that my daughter actually seemed happy to see me. Rose usually managed to sneak out too and join us."

"Where did you go?"

"No place special. Hiking. Walking in the park. But it *felt* special. Those girls were like prisoners set free. Every little thing made them laugh. We'd stop for ice cream before heading back to Saint Julia's, and it was as though I was giving them the treat of their lives. They were that grateful, that happy."

I tried to place my sister in the scenario she described, laughing, eating ice cream. Instead, what I conjured was the memory of trips to the ice cream parlor with my parents during the months Rose was gone, the strange guilty peace I felt during that time. Those memories led me to say, "My sister didn't last there more than that summer."

"Neither did my daughter."

"What happened?"

"I don't know exactly. She had agreed to stay there originally for a full six months. But then one morning, the psychiatrist from Saint Julia's called to tell us they found her room empty. She left just like that. And, really, she was free to go all along since she was of age."

"Did she come home?"

"She knew better, I'm sure. Her father would have sent her right back. So instead, she just . . . disappeared."

"Disappeared?"

Emily Sanino stood and went to that side table and pulled back the curtain to look outside. I wanted to tell her that we'd hear the patrol car well before seeing it, but instead I simply repeated the word, *"Disappeared?"*

"We've not heard from her since," she said in a stiff voice, letting go of the curtain and pressing her fingertips to the sides of her eyes, as though forcing back tears. After a moment, she took a breath and turned to me. "Now that you know everything you came to find out, we need to get you out of here. How will you get home if you—"

"Wait," I said. "I still don't understand why you've been coming to our house."

That question gave her a long pause. She stared at me, blinking, before saying, "When I read about what happened to your mother and father, Sylvie, I thought of how special those days with Rose had been. The idea of that poor girl on her own raising you, well, it broke my heart. I remembered how she used to devour the food I brought on those trips, so I decided the least I could offer was more of that nourishment. It's what the Bible teaches, after all: charity of the heart."

"Well, thank you for remembering us. I only wish you'd left notes, so we knew who it was from. Didn't you ever think to do that?"

"Yes. But I didn't want to open old wounds. I'm sure Rose doesn't exactly want reminders of her time at Saint Julia's. My guess is she never speaks of it. Am I right?"

I nodded. My brain felt fuzzy with the events of the day. I tried to think of what more I could ask, but just then, Emily Sanino's back stiffened. A moment later, I heard a car motoring down the street. "I need you to leave," she said, peeking through the curtains as the flash of lights washed over her. "How will you get back to Dundalk?"

"I don't know," I told her, standing. We walked to the kitchen, and she pressed a hand on my back to get me there faster.

"What do you mean, you don't know?"

"I didn't plan things. I just came here without—"

Outside in the driveway, a door slammed. Emily grabbed her purse from the table and told me to hold out my hands. When I did she shook the contents of her wallet—coins, bills, stray coupons, shopping lists—into my palms. A few stray pennies fell to the floor and scattered at my feet, but I didn't bother to pick them up. "I'm sorry," she told me, her voice an urgent whisper. "But I can't let my husband know about any of this. There's a pay phone in front of the firehouse on West Shore Drive. You can call a taxi from there. You should have more than enough money to get home."

"West Shore?" I said as she opened the back door and all but pushed me outside. Emily Sanino glanced in the direction of the living room, where her husband's feet pounded up the porch steps. "Left out of the driveway.

Right at Bay Breeze, then follow it to West Shore. The firehouse will be in front of you. Across from the ocean."

"Should I give Rose any message?"

"*Message?*" she said, eyes wide. "Absolutely not. Don't say a word to her about this visit. Trust me. It'll be better that way."

With that, she closed the door and snapped off the light. I was left standing on the cement patio with only the moon to see by. A moment later, I heard her voice inside as she greeted her husband with all that false cheer lacing her voice once more.

I turned and walked through the alley to the street, her rushed directions blurring in my mind, along with everything else she told me. For nearly an hour, I moved through the sleepy streets of that oceanside neighborhood, making too many wrong turns before backtracking and looking up at last to see the fire department, with a pay phone out front. After dialing 411, I got the number of a taxi company. The man on the other end told me it would cost sixty dollars to get back to Dundalk. While he waited, I counted what I had, but it only totaled up to thirty-four. I asked if he could do it for half price, and the man said, "Yeah, if my driver only takes you halfway. How's that sound?" I told him not very good then hung up. That's when another idea occurred to me. Squinting at the buttons, I punched in a combination I hadn't thought of in some time. After dumping in enough coins, the phone rang and a sleepy voice came on the line.

"Cora?" I said.

"Yes?"

"It's Sylvie."

"Sylvie? How did— Oh, *RIBSPIN*. That's right. I forgot about that."

You forgot a lot of things, I wanted to say, *including* me. "You told me I could call this number anytime I needed something."

Last I'd seen Cora, she'd had on all that goopy green witch makeup, and even though it didn't make sense, that's how I pictured her now: lying in bed at the apartment she shared with her mother, noodly fingers brushing aside her mottled wig and gripping the receiver as her black lips formed the words, "I did say that, didn't I?"

"Yes. And this is one of those times."

"Sylvie, are you okay?' she asked with genuine concern in her voice.

"I will be if you could come get me. I need a ride home."

She fumbled with the phone. "I'm sorry. But I lent my car to Dan. You know, the Hulk's owner. We have a bit of a free trade situation. His dog. My car. Not sure who gets the better end of the deal. Except my mom, she likes having the dog around. Says the Hulk makes her feel loved. As if I don't give her enough love . . ."

I'd forgotten Cora's habit of rambling, and I cut her off to say something I couldn't keep in any longer, "I saw the two of you. Kissing, I mean."

Silence. While I listened to the faint electric hum on the line, I stared at the fire department. Through the glass windows, I glimpsed the tops of the red trucks inside, the jumble of lights and ladders. The air felt so impossibly damp it was hard to imagine anything catching fire for miles around.

At last, Cora let out a breath. Something about the sound washed away the image of her in that witch makeup. Instead, I saw her the way I did when we first met: holding her clipboard, dressed in her carefully pressed clothing, with her ankle bracelet and that shark or dolphin tattoo, not to mention her intentions to make me dress warmer and see a doctor again about my ear. "I am not going to lie to you, Sylvie. That's wrong, and I've already done plenty of wrong by you. The truth is, I never thought I'd get caught up in the sort of thing that happened with your sister. But I don't have to tell you the way Rose can make things happen. Do you know what I mean?"

"I do," I said, thinking of Dot, thinking of the night in Ocala when we snuck into my parents' lecture, and thinking most of all of her call that lured us to the church that snowy night last winter.

"Well, she also has this way of making you feel like the most special person in the world when she wants to. That is, until something changes and she doesn't make you feel that way anymore. That feeling—it was too much to take. I asked the department to switch me to a new case. I'm sorry."

There was more hurt in my voice than expected when I told her, "You could have said good-bye."

"I know. Again, I'm sorry. It's just, well, I'm not always as good at things as I set out to be. But I'd like to help find a way to get you home. Tell me where you are."

"Rehoboth, Delaware."

"Rehoboth? Why?"

"I came to find out who has been leaving all that food on our steps."

"I really don't think you should be there, Sylvie. It doesn't seem like a good idea. I'd leave whoever it is alone. Now let's focus on getting you out of there. Maybe you should just call Rose."

It was clear Cora would be of no help, so I told her I would then said a rushed good-bye and got off the phone. Since no part of me intended to reach out to my sister, I did what I should have in the first place and tried the number on the card Heekin had given me. His answering machine picked up. I rambled into it about where I was and what I'd learned about Emily Sanino and Saint Julia's. In the middle of it, I realized how desperate I must have sounded, so I stopped short and hung up on that call too.

After that, there was only the crashing of the ocean waves, the light of the moon, with me beneath it, lingering by the pay phone for a long while. I looked at Emily Sanino's shopping lists—flour, unsalted butter, and all the rest made me think of Boshoff and his cookbooks and poems and his sick wife beside him in bed. And then I had a thought and picked up the phone again.

Four-one-one connected me right through and Dereck answered on the first ring, as though he had been waiting for me all along. "Of course I'll come get you," he said when I explained where I was and that I needed a ride. "But you'll have to sit tight. It'll take me a bit to get there."

I was so relieved that I didn't mind waiting. After we hung up, I sat down on the curb. If I'd had my journal I would have used the time to put down the events of the day, beginning with the visit to the nature preserve with Heekin and ending with the moment in Emily Sanino's living room. I would have read over what I'd already written about Abigail and the things that happened that summer too. Instead, I tried to think of all the places I might have dropped it: in the dark of my uncle's theater, in Heekin's VW bug, down in the foundation across the street from our house.

At last, I looked up to see Dereck's jeep pull into the lot. I climbed inside, feeling relief but also an unexpected awkwardness. Now that he and my sister were over, what connection was left between us?

We pulled onto the street, and it was as though he knew the way by heart, making rights and lefts without checking the map on the floor between the seats. "Do you mind if I ask what you were doing here?" he said after a while, keeping his eyes on the road.

"Trying to figure some things out," I told him, which was the simplest explanation.

"And did you?" was all he asked.

"Yes and no. Really, I ended up with more questions."

"About your parents?"

"Them, and my sister, too."

Dereck didn't respond. We reached the highway and picked up speed. The haphazard rise and fall of lights all around, and the constant shudder of the canvas top, made it difficult to talk. We tried anyway, but it was awkward small talk—details about those turkeys mostly—and it made me think again how quickly any connection was dissipating between us. At last, we passed a WELCOME TO MARYLAND sign, and Dereck took his ruined hand off the steering wheel and pointed to the floor between the seats. "By the way, I brought something to show you."

"A map?" I said and laughed a little, despite myself.

"No. Look underneath."

I peeled the map away and found a chestnut brown yearbook from Dundalk High School, the year 1988 in raised gold numbers across the top.

"It's from my senior year. I grabbed it out of my junk drawer when you called. I want to prove something to you. Page sixty-four."

With that same hand, Dereck clicked on the interior light. I opened the book, and a newspaper clipping slipped out onto my lap. I left it there and turned the pages until arriving at the one he specified. "A picture of the exchange student from Peru?"

He smiled, showing those wolfish teeth. "Not *that* photo, Sylvie. The one beneath it."

"A group shot of the Honors Society?"

"Recond row, rour reople rover rom ra reft."

I traced my finger up to the second row, four people over from the left until landing on Dereck, grinning big and wide.

"Ree, R-I'm rot a rope, rafter rall."

"I never thought you were a dope. Even though you make it hard to believe considering how much time you spend talking like a cartoon dog."

Dereck laughed, and the moment made me feel close to him again. "Well, thanks for your faith in me."

Before closing the book, I stared a little longer at the photo. "You look happy."

"And I don't now?"

"You do. It's just, I don't know, a *different* look on your face back then."

"Well, that's when I had all my fingers. That's also before I realized high school would end, and I'd actually need to make a plan for my life."

"Couldn't you still make a plan?"

"Maybe. First, I have to get through the last of the season with the turkeys. Thanksgiving is only three more days away as of tomorrow."

I thought of those mornings when I paused on the path to stare at the birds in the field, how empty it would feel without them, how empty it would feel without Dereck there too. We pulled off the highway and navigated the dark roads of Dundalk until turning onto Butter Lane at last. I told him to go slow, shining his high beams on the pavement as I looked out for my journal. He even pulled off so I could look around by the foundation too. But my little violet book wasn't there, either.

It had only been twelve hours, more or less, yet it felt like ages since that morning when I first left the house and met Heekin at the end of the lane. Rose's truck was still in the driveway, her bedroom light on. Otherwise the house was dark, except, of course, for the light in the basement, which filled me with the same nervous fear as it had for weeks.

"Thanks for coming to get me," I told Dereck. "I have a little money for gas if you—"

He held up that hand with the missing fingers. "This one's on me. I'm happy you called, Sylvie. Feel free to do it again if you ever need my help."

I told him I would then reached for the door handle, remembering how he hugged me last time, how his stubble brushed against me as he pressed his lips to my cheek and the warm, earthy smell of him enveloped me. I wondered if he might do it again, but the moment did not present itself. Probably those four years between us, I thought, all the differences they made. And so I opened the door and got out, that newspaper clipping from inside his yearbook slipping off my lap and falling to the ground as I did. I reached down, picked it up. "What's this?"

"Oh. That's the other thing I meant to show you. The article that came out after the freak accident I told you about. The one that cost me my fingers."

I glanced at the headline, some part of me expecting to see the name Albert Lynch, since those were the only stories I paid attention to anymore. Instead, the headline read simply: DECK COLLAPSES, DOZENS OF TEENS INJURED.

"You can hang on to it," Dereck told me. "Personally, I'd rather forget that drunken afternoon. But like I told you, it was big news around here."

I stuck the clipping in my pocket and thanked him again for the ride. Dereck flicked on his high beams and waited for me to get inside before backing out of the driveway. He beeped his horn a few times, and I flashed the porch light to say good-bye.

After he was gone, I went upstairs and changed and washed up before making my way back down to the kitchen. Rose had replenished the supply of Popsicles, but I was tired of them. Apparently, she had tossed whatever Emily Sanino had baked, since it wasn't on the steps or the counter.

I skipped any sort of dinner and stood beside the kitchen table, reading the article Dereck had given me. The story confirmed everything he had told me about that accident and how he lost his fingers. Two photos accompanied the article. One showed the splintered deck in pieces on the ground, the toppled grill and kegs and broken chairs all around. The other was of the lawn scattered with teenagers, some lying on the grass as paramedics attended to them, others standing in the background, unharmed.

I was about to put down the clipping when I remembered Dereck saying that my sister had been at the party. Just as I'd done with his yearbook photo, I traced my thumb over the crowd until, sure enough, I spotted Rose standing blank faced in the crowd. I stared at her fuzzy black-and-white image a moment before noticing the person beside her too.

I must have stared at that image for a solid ten minutes until I put the clipping aside at last and went to the cabinet beneath the sink. When I swung it open, the garbage can was empty, a fresh bag placed inside. I shut the cabinet and looked at that clipping again, tracing my finger over the people in the crowd until stopping in the same spot. This time, I put the paper down and walked to the front door, stepping out into the moonlight and heading for the trash cans my sister must have dragged to the street earlier.

Back in Rehoboth, I'd lifted the lid and used my finger to puncture the bag. I did the same here. Once more, foul odors rose up as I dug inside, churning through the entire bag until my hands grew sticky from handling Popsicle wrappers and crumpled paper towels and squashed soda cans. When I finished with that bag, I reached for the one below. The work wasn't strenuous, but something had me breathing heavily anyway.

And then I felt the first of what I was searching for: slim, like a firecracker between my fingers with the same sort of wick at the tip, blunt and brittle from use. And not long after I had found one, others began to appear. Like some rabid raccoon, I tipped over the can and knelt on the ground picking among all the papers and wrappers and trash smeared with frosting. And when I located them all—twenty-five slim pink candles—I held them up in the dark. Even though they'd long since been blown out, it didn't matter. It was as though they lit the entire sky above. It was as though they lit my way when I stepped into the church that snowy night the winter before, because at long last, I knew who it was I had seen. At long last, I knew.

EMERGENCY EXITS

May I please have seconds? I don't want to be in the way . . . Sylvie? I have the same dream almost every night . . . When I say it is both good and bad, what I mean is that it starts out good—my mother is showing me the emergency exit rows, explaining about the lighted path in the aisles, the oxygen masks that drop from the ceiling—but peaceful as it begins, the dream always turns bad. It is that way with most things in life, my life anyway. Probably, it is the way things will go during my time here with you and your family—even though that is not what I want . . . My wish is that things stay good. My wish is that we stay friends, Sylvie, always and forever . . .

Even the greatest blizzards begin with one or two seemingly innocent snowflakes drifting down from the sky. That's how it was with those simple words of gratitude—*thank you*—spoken by Abigail after she tucked herself into Rose's bed and squeezed her eyes shut: they were the innocuous beginnings of all that was to come.

But I should not be talking about snowstorms, not yet. It was summer still, the sunniest and hottest I'd experienced in my life. Odd as it may sound, considering my sister had been plucked from our family and Abigail deposited in her place, it also came to be the happiest summer I recalled in a long time, that last summer my parents were alive.

When my father returned the following morning, he carried the empty suitcase Rose and I shared. She had no need for it there, I heard him tell my mother when she met him at the door, and seeing it would only keep thoughts of leaving the place thriving in her mind. Those weren't his ideas, but protocol at Saint Julia's, he explained. According to him, that same protocol prohibited family contact for the first ninety days to allow students time to detach from their former lives and acclimate to a new environment, one with rigid structure, firm values, and a strictly enforced disciplinary code. That was the most I heard him say about my sister, since my mother began telling him about all that had transpired in his absence— most important, how Albert Lynch and his daughter had shown up the day before, how she was with us still.

"*With us?*" my father said. "Downstairs?"

"No," my mother told him. "Why don't you come with me, Sylvester? I'll show you."

Since my mother had shut Rose's bedroom door the day before, Abigail had not been outside the room and no one had been inside—as far as I knew, anyway. I assumed my father would make immediate adjustments to the sleeping arrangements, and since he left the suitcase by the stairs, I carried it to the second floor to see how things would play out. When I reached the top, though, my parents were already stepping out of Rose's room and closing the door behind them. My father came to me, took the suitcase, and gave me a hug hello, before asking, "How would you feel, sunshine, if our guest stayed in your sister's room a little longer?"

"Guest?" I couldn't help repeating.

"Yes, Sylvie. You wouldn't mind if Abigail stayed in your sister's room while she's here, would you?"

"What about that partitioned area in the basement? I thought—"

"You thought it was done. I know. So did your mother. But after all these years, that little project of mine has a ways to go still. There's no electricity, for one. Not the best furniture either except for that cot and old dresser. So even though no one exactly invited our guest into Rose's room, now that she's there, it seems kinder to let her stay put. For a few nights anyway."

The basement was good enough for all the other haunted people who had come here before, I wanted to say. But I held back because I knew the response he wanted—didn't I always? And even though it left me feeling all the more guilty toward my sister, I gave it to him anyway.

In the days that followed, it hardly mattered. Whenever I was on the second floor, I stayed in my room with the door closed. Not a single time did I so much as glimpse Abigail. If she used the bathroom, if she descended the stairs to the kitchen, I never saw.

And yet, things remained quiet inside our house. My parents slipped in and out of Rose's room so discreetly it was as though they were coming and going from a confessional. Early mornings, I heard my mother's gentle voice praying on the other side of the wall. Evenings, I heard her reading scripture. Most often, it was the same passage from deep in the Book of Philippians, one I came to know by heart; if Abigail was paying attention, she must have come to know it too:

> *Do not be anxious about anything. But in everything, by prayer and petition, with thanksgiving, present your requests to God. And the peace of God, which transcends all understanding, will guard your heart and your mind in our Lord Jesus Christ.*

Those words were not intended for me, but I tried my best to heed them anyway. Fighting off any anxious feelings, however, became just that: *a fight.* It did not help that the phone kept shrieking at all hours, until at long last my parents turned off the ringer and let calls go to the answering machine. It also didn't help that I woke some nights to the sound of a car motoring down our street, bass thumping, as people shouted from the windows about Penny and Satan and things they believed were happening in our home. And it did not help that, despite my father's reports to the police and his careful work of regularly resurrecting the mailbox, we discovered it knocked over, along with our garbage cans, again and again.

The initial arrangement my mother made with Albert Lynch—that he should call in a few days and see about getting his daughter—was not mentioned. Instead, a few days turned to four, four turned to five, five to eight, and on it went. One afternoon, I glimpsed my mother slipping into Rose's room, carrying a tray of food like some do-good nurse in a ward for the infirm, when it occurred to me that Abigail had been with us a total of two and a half weeks. *Seventeen days,* I thought, working out the math in my head.

By then, it was early July. The official holiday had come and gone, but backyard fireworks could still be heard, popping off now and then like distant gunshots in the night. Temperatures had spiked to such a sweltering degree that my mother took to preparing cold dinners—beet soup, tuna sandwiches, tomato and cucumber salads—meals she normally reserved for the thick of August. Window fans worked overtime, whirring all over the house, blowing hot air around.

On this particular evening, my mother must have felt tired of those *nonsupper* suppers, so she baked a vegetable lasagna from a recipe clipped out of the newspaper. The idea sounded good, but after the oven had been on for over an hour, it created a sweltering, junglelike atmosphere in our house. Nevertheless, we took our same old seats at the kitchen table.

"I remember," I said, swatting a mosquito that had made its way inside, "when Rose and I were little, and it got this hot, you used to take us swimming at that pond over in Colbert Township." It was a memory none of us had talked about in years, but I could still see my sister and me in our bright bathing suits, splashing in the water, burying each other's feet in the rocky dirt on the shore. I waited to see if my parents remembered too.

My mother kept eating, or not eating exactly, but dissecting the dish she had prepared, segregating peppers from onions from tomatoes on her plate. During the previous seventeen days—since Penny had been put in the cage, since the light had been left on below, since Abigail had arrived and my father returned home without Rose—my mother had not uttered a word about feeling unwell. And yet, I couldn't help but sense that something about her, something unnameable, was no longer the same and, if I was truthful with myself, had not been since our trip to Ohio.

The way my father's gaze lingered on my mother in certain moments, as it did then, made me wonder if he noticed the change in her too. He waited to see if she might respond to what I'd said; when she didn't, he told me he remembered those swims, adding that when he was little, his father took Howie and him to an Indian Well outside of Philly to cool off some summer afternoons. Then he asked my mother, "Didn't you used to swim in a pond on the farm in Tennessee?"

My mother quit segregating her food and looked up. "Yes. But someone once drowned in that pond, so I was always afraid of swimming there. Plus, it was such stagnant water it made for a buggy place. I only went when I felt desperate for—"

She stopped abruptly, and my father and I waited for her to finish. Window fans whirred. Moths beat against the screens in a haphazard rhythm. More mosquitoes hummed in the air. All the while, my mother just stared at the entryway of the kitchen. And then we turned to see her in the white nightgown intended for my sister.

She looked different than she had that first afternoon. There was the fact of that gown—cleaner, more simple, than the tattered clothes she arrived in. There was the fact of her hair, brushed so all the curls had gone straight. There was also the fact of those bruises and scrapes on her feet, healed now, I discovered with a quick glance down. But there was something more to it than those physical details. I couldn't help but sense a deep and noticeable calm about the girl, a calm that had not been there before.

"Well, hello, Abigail," my mother said.

"Yes, hello," my father said too.

"Would you like to join us?" my mother asked. Rather than wait for a response, she stood and quickly set an extra place at the table.

Abigail lingered in the entryway long enough that I thought she might turn and retreat upstairs. Finally, she walked to the table and slipped into Rose's chair. None of us said a word as she placed her napkin on her lap, picked up her knife and fork, and took the first hesitant bites of dinner. She kept eating, quickly and simply, until her plate had been cleaned. Then she looked up and said in a smooth and serene sort of voice, "May I please have seconds?"

My mother nodded, and she helped herself to another portion. That's when I made an effort to bring back the previous moment, asking my mother to finish what she was saying about the pond on the farm. She didn't elaborate on the topic, though, telling us it was just a pond and not a very nice one at that.

At last, Abigail wiped her mouth and said, "Lake Ewauna. Or Lake Ewaumo."

"Pardon?" my father said.

"When we used to live in one place. Out west. There were so many lakes near the ministry, one in particular we loved. I could never say the name, but it was something like that. We used to go swimming there. Only at night, under the moon, when no one was around."

"That sounds lovely," my father told Abigail.

She gave a shy smile and went back to eating.

"Maybe we could go to that pond in Colbert and swim some night," I said, trying again to yank back the conversation. Pushing my luck, I added, *"Just us."*

Those words should have had some effect, but Abigail kept her head down and went on eating. My mother told me she was not even sure the pond was still accessible to the public. "It was owned by some farmer, I believe. Ever since they opened the town pool, I never hear of people going there anymore."

"You know what?" my father said. "All this talk of late-night swims has given me an idea. How about we go out for ice cream? It'll help us cool off."

All my life, we had never been a family that went out for ice cream. Back when we were younger, Rose and I used to get the idea in our heads and take to begging only to hear the same lecture from my father about how absurd it was to shell out money just so some kid could fill our cones. Instead, my mother kept a tub of sherbet in the freezer, or Popsicles when she wanted to give us an extra treat.

That night, my mother pointed out that she had both sherbet and Popsicles in the freezer, so there was no need to make a trip across town to the ice cream shop. Unlike my father as it was, he told her to forget that. "It'll be good to get out of the house. Before we pass out from the heat or these mosquitoes eat us alive."

"What about . . ." My mother allowed her voice to trail off, but he understood.

"Abigail," he said, turning to the girl. "How do you feel about this idea?"

Her plate was empty again. I wondered if she might ask for thirds. Instead, she just stared at it the way she had those photos of Rose and me, as though seeing something there no one else did. "I'll be okay here by myself."

That was all I needed to hear. I pushed back my chair and stood to rinse my plate in the sink with the intention of going up to be sure my bedroom door was locked before leaving. Nothing had happened to my horses since Penny had been put in the cage and Rose had been sent away, but I wasn't taking chances. Then I heard my father say, "You're misunderstanding me. I'm asking how would you feel about coming *with* us?"

"Sylvester," my mother said. "I think perhaps—"

My father held up a hand, keeping his eyes on Abigail, so that my mother fell silent.

"Oh," she said. "That's very nice, Mr. Mason. But I don't want to be in the way."

"Don't be silly. We're happy to see you up and about."

Maybe my mother did not tell him about that warning from her father, how the girl could seem normal—or *almost* normal—but that's when she changed. Or maybe my mother did tell him, and he thought he knew better. Either way, even if no one else was thinking about Albert Lynch's words, they whirred in my mind like those frantically spinning window fans. On the few occasions I'd been in Abigail's presence, never once had she looked at me—not directly anyway. It was something I hadn't realized until, there in our kitchen, she did for the first time. The effect was that of seeing some strange, poisonous flower bloom before my eyes, opening its petals and turning its face toward me. I watched as she lifted her gaze from her empty plate, fixing those wild blue eyes upon me, while speaking to my father in that serene voice. "Sylvie doesn't want me to go."

"Nonsense," my father told her.

"It's okay," Abigail said. "If I were Sylvie, I wouldn't want me to go either. It sounds like a family thing. And I get the feeling it's important to her."

That tub of sherbet, those Popsicles—my mother chimed in about both again, but those things had become consolation prizes nobody wanted, least of all me. My mother must have sensed it, because her next offer was to stay home with Abigail while my father and I went and brought back ice cream for everyone. But my father seemed determined we go together.

"Sylvie, tell her it's not true. We didn't raise the kind of daughter who leaves out a guest in our own home."

They were all watching me, but it was Abigail's gaze I felt most. I looked into her wild blue eyes and my mind filled with the memory of the afternoon her father slid open the van door to reveal her lying on the thin mattress inside. I thought of how calm she seemed now, so different from the girl with snarled hair and bruised feet who hid behind my mother, who toppled the very chairs where my parents sat, who shredded our wallpaper. But despite that newfound serenity and my mother's days and nights of prayer and scripture, I did not feel comfortable having her around.

Even so, I looked back at Abigail while speaking to my father, same as she had done to me. "I'm not sure where Abigail got the idea I don't want her to come. But I don't mind. If that's what she wants."

It was, of course, exactly what Abigail wanted.

After changing into a T-shirt with a faded Saint Louis arch decal and shorts my mother had repaired days before with a needle and thread, she got into the Datsun along with us. On a night that hot, any ice cream shop would have been mobbed; the one in Dundalk was no exception. The parking lot teemed with so many vehicles, my father settled on leaving ours a block away.

The moment we got out of the car, my mother noticed what none of us had before: Abigail was in bare feet. Too late to do anything about it, though, so we walked right past the NO SHIRT, NO SHOES, NO SERVICE sign on the door. As soon as we joined the line snaking through the place, a lull rippled through conversations all around. When it came to driving by our house at night, shouting from car windows, batting down our mailbox and trash cans, and speeding away in the dark, people had plenty of courage. But beneath the fluorescent lights of that ice cream shop, they stuck to whispers. They stuck to nudges and stares.

My parents paid no attention, of course. If Abigail noticed, I couldn't tell, since she stayed busy studying all the ice cream behind the counter. I kept expecting someone to kick us out, but the line just inched along until I found myself waiting by a freezer with smudged glass doors. Inside, cakes filled the shelves. All those blue ice cream flowers, and blank surfaces, like snow-covered ponds waiting for happy messages to be squiggled on top, made me think of the *Rosie* cake, which had a way of hollowing me out right there on the spot.

"What flavor are you going to get?"

I was so caught up in thinking about Rose and how much our lives had changed that it took a moment to realize the person asking was Abigail—and she was asking *me*. I turned away from those cakes and looked at the decal on her shirt, plagued with so many delicate cracks it was like gazing at an old painting. I tried to guess which flavor my sister would have ordered if she had been with us, then made up my mind to do it for her. "Chocolate," I told Abigail.

"Oh," she said, smiling. "That's what I'll get too. I mean, if you don't mind."

The line lurched ahead. I stepped away from that freezer, away from Abigail as well. "Of course I don't mind. Get whatever you want."

At last, when our cones were in hand, the four of us headed outside to a row of picnic tables where customers congregated. In the dusky sky over Colgate Park, someone was shooting fireworks. I was glad for the distraction, since people were too busy gazing up at the bursts of Roman candles sputtering over the treetops to care about the Mason family and their guest. Even we became hypnotized, while ice cream trickled down our wrists, melting faster than any of us could keep up. When the show was done—cones eaten, napkins balled in our sticky palms—my father looked down and spoke in an oddly remorseful voice. "Maybe I was wrong," he said, "all these years about it being a waste of money to go out for a night like this. It's important for a family to share certain moments. When Rose gets back, let's be sure we do this again."

After so many days of no one saying a word about my sister, the mention of her, particularly the notion that she would return and that we would do something as a family, lifted my spirits more than ice cream or fireworks ever could. As we walked back to the Datsun, my happy feelings even led me to wonder if I should be nicer to Abigail. After all, strange as she was, the girl had nothing to do with Rose being gone, and like my father said, she wouldn't be with us much longer.

While we drove the dark streets, I stole glances at her. The windows were down and, same as my sister, she did not tuck back her hair. It whipped

all around, random strands reaching out and snapping at my cheeks, sting-
ing my skin. I held my hand out the window, cupping my palm and letting
it ride the wind, up and down, down and up. Had I not been paying so
much attention to Abigail and to my palm, I might have noticed my father
take a detour.

"Sylvester," my mother said, eventually. "Where are we going?"

"You'll see."

Two words—that's all they were, but enough to seize our attention.
I quit hand-surfing. Abigail gathered up her hair. We leaned forward between the seats, looking out the front window until we made a series of
turns and the headlights shone down a narrow dirt road with a strip of wild
grass in the middle. We were in Colbert Township, I realized, heading to
the old pond. Judging from the way the trees pressed in on both sides and
the lack of any official signs, it appeared my mother was right about no one
going there anymore.

"Sylvester," she said again. "What are we doing?"

"Just checking things out."

"Why?"

"Why not? I don't know about you, but I'm in no rush to go back to
that hot house."

"I don't think this is a good idea. We have no clue if this place has
become private property. What if someone contacts the police?"

My father shrugged. "If the Colbert cops are anything like the dolts in
Dundalk, who sound half asleep when I call about the vandals having fun
with our mailbox and trash cans, I doubt they'll care. And if they do, well,
then I just might give them a piece of my mind."

My mother gave up protesting, but I could tell by the way she folded
her hands on her lap that she did not like this impromptu excursion one
bit. It didn't take long before the trees opened up to a clearing and our
headlights fell upon the glassy surface of the pond. Not far from the water's
edge, my father stopped the car, then turned off the engine and the lights.
We were four shadows, no sound but the crickets and cicadas and night
creatures all around.

I thought my father might instruct us what to do, but my mother spoke instead, saying she wanted to have a private talk with my father for a few minutes. "You and Abigail can go on outside for a little bit."

"But we didn't bring our bathing suits," I told her.

"That's because we are not swimming," she said in a stern voice. "But you can have a look at the old place if you like. Don't wander too far, though."

My father's gaze found mine in the rearview mirror. "Sorry, tadpole. Consider this a reconnaissance mission. If things look good, we can come back tomorr—"

"*Sylvester,*" my mother interrupted. Then to us, "Go ahead, girls. But like I said, no wandering off."

Abigail's hand had been on the door handle for some time, but she kept watching me for a signal that it was okay to get out. When I opened my door, she did the same. She followed me to the pond and bent to rinse her sticky hands in the water, just like I did. Just as I'd imagined, moonlight shimmered on the surface of the pond so that it glowed like some living, breathing force. Too many stars to count twinkled in the inky sky overhead. Across the water, in a marshy area thick with reeds, I made out what looked to be a half-sunken dock.

"Is everything okay?"

Not just on account of her oddly serene voice, but because she had been quiet for so long, it was still something of a shock to hear Abigail speak. In some way, it felt not much different than if Penny's mouth were to open and words were to come tumbling out. I quit rinsing my hands and stood to look at her. "What do you mean?"

"Are they fighting?"

The moment we shut the back doors of the car, my mother had launched into the conversation she wanted to have with my father. Muffled as their voices were, I caught their opening gambits before stepping away.

"First the trip out for ice cream, now this detour. What are you trying to do?"

"Show us a good time for a change. After everything that's happened, I thought you'd like that. I thought the girls would too."

So the answer to Abigail's question was yes. But I didn't think it was any of her concern, and that's exactly what I told her before turning away. While I was busy looking into the water, she stepped into the pond. I heard her before I saw her: *plunk, plunk.*

When I glanced over, Abigail was submerged up to her ankles. My parents said we wouldn't be swimming, but they didn't mention anything about wading, so I decided to slip off my flip-flops and step into the cool water too, my feet sinking into the mud, shifting away from stones that pricked my soles like sharp teeth.

"I bet this isn't like that lake in Oregon," I said, making a stab at conversation.

Abigail swirled a foot around, mixing the mud and rocks into something soupy. "No, it's not."

"Can I ask why don't you live there anymore?"

"We still live there."

"That's not what you told us earlier. You said when you were little you used—"

"To live in one place. That's what I said. Now we live lots of places. Oregon is just one. But we're usually there for a few weeks in the winter when it's too cold to swim."

Behind us, the doors of the Datsun opened. Immediately, Abigail retreated back to the shore. I didn't move fast enough, though, and my mother arrived at the water's edge to find me ankle-deep. She glanced at Abigail's feet, slick with water, then looked at her slim watch and said, "Now that we're here, your father and I agreed you might as well take a dip. It'll help you sleep tonight at least. So go in with your clothes on if you like. You've got ten minutes. And let's hope we don't get arrested or find out this place has become a toxic waste site."

If Rose had been with us she would have let out a loud *Wooohooo!* Abigail simply waded in again, deeper this time. When the water reached the hem of her shorts, she turned to my mother, my father too, who had just arrived at the water's edge, looking shaken. Neither protested, so she sucked in a breath and slipped under.

In the silence that followed, the three of us stood waiting and waiting for her to emerge. Abigail seemed strange enough that she might have been capable of sprouting gills and fins, capable of swimming down to some watery underworld, or out into the shadows of those trees and the starry sky beyond. At last, however, her head emerged, small and turtlelike, far out in the pond. Since we didn't have much time, I waded up to my shorts too, trying not to think of creatures beneath the surface as I slipped under as well. When I came up again—sooner than Abigail, closer to the shore—I saw that she had swum the entire way to the reedy area with the half-sunken dock. Rather than follow, I floated on my back and studied the stars dotting the sky.

If I kept my splashing to a minimum, it was possible to hear my parents. My mother took a seat on a slanted bench not far from the water's edge and my father stood next to her. "We've received requests for lectures that pay more than ever," he was saying. "Not to mention all the places people want us to investigate. There's an old estate in New Zealand that a widow refused to leave after her husband died. Now she's deceased as well, and people there are reporting some pretty bizarre occurrences."

To all of this, my mother said only, "New Zealand."

"That's right. They'll fly us there. All expenses paid."

"What about the girls?"

"They'll fly Sylvie too. And Abigail if that's what we want. *We* hold the cards now, my dear. How's *that* for a change? No more sharing the stage with that phony Dragomir Albescu and his fingers full of fake jewelry. No more humiliating myself at Fright Fest just to make a—"

"Abigail is not our daughter, Sylvester."

"Excuse me?"

"When I asked about the girls, I was talking about our daughters. You remember who they are, don't you?"

"Of course I do," my father said, clearly exasperated and offended too.

"Well, you didn't mention Rose coming on this trip of yours."

"First of all, it's not *my* trip, it's *our* trip. And who do you think worked so hard at finding a way to help Rose? *Me*. But since we'd have to go to New Zealand soon, I assumed she wouldn't be able to join us."

"Then I won't be either, because I don't feel comfortable traveling so far from home with her at that . . . that place. Never mind taking a trip with someone else's daughter. So we'll just have to decline or put it off until things are back to normal."

"Okay, then," my father said. "Okay. Okay." I watched him walk to the edge of the bench. He seemed to be looking for some way to sit beside her, but it was too crooked for that. At last, he gave up and remained standing, telling her, "I understand what you're saying. Besides, we've got other offers closer to home. And come fall, Sam's book will be out. By then, we'll be even more in demand. That night I saw him a few weeks back, he told me his publisher has already been getting quite a bit of interest from the media."

I looked to my mother on that bench—bouncing her legs, biting her lip—responding only with, "Ninety days."

"Pardon?"

"That rule at Saint Julia's. It just seems like an awfully long time."

"Oh, yes. That. Well, it'll go by in a blink. You'll see."

"Maybe so. But I'd at least like a phone call to—"

"To what? Fight the same old fights with her?"

"To hear her voice. To know she's okay."

"She's fine. She's better than fine, she's improving. We're going to get her back good as new."

After that, they grew quiet. I must have drifted, because I found myself in a particularly cold patch of water. It seemed to move through me the way my father said spirits do, with an unmistakable chill. I swam away, making a show of splashing about so they did not suspect me of eavesdropping. Across the pond, Abigail perched on that half-sunken dock, a mermaid at the bow of a doomed ship, pale arms and face bathed in the moonlight, hair curly once more from the water. She stared back at me, back at my parents too. From that distance, I doubted she could possibly hear them. Still, the way she looked so intently left me wondering if their voices carried across the water.

"Eventually, the summer will end," my mother was saying as I went still in the water once more. "School will start up. Sylvie will be in eighth grade. We could get Rose enrolled in a few classes at a local college. Come fall, what I'd like most is for all our lives to be back on track. Which means . . ."

Like a radio losing reception, I lost their words a moment. Hoping they wouldn't notice, I allowed myself to drift closer again.

"Saint Julia's is far from cheap," my father was saying when their conversation came clear once more. "The extra money—frankly, we need it. Especially if you're telling me you want to hold off on the lectures now too."

"No matter how badly we need the money, it's only reasonable to expect more than that one call in all this time. I can't help feeling that we should . . ."

"We should what?"

"*Do* something."

"Like what?"

"Like—" As though working to stay afloat same as me, my mother paused, measuring each breath, before saying, "I don't know. Report the situation to some agency. Tell them her father has not returned for her."

"And how would that look for us? Besides, I don't see what harm it's doing. The man is sending checks, so it's not as though she's been abandoned. And look at tonight, it's been a perfectly lovely evening."

"I'm aware of that, Sylvester. If only you made this much effort to have *perfectly lovely evenings* when our other daughter was at home."

After all my father's uncharacteristic efforts that night—the ice cream, the detour to the pond—at long last her words pricked at something inside him. I sensed him deflating there on the shore. He looked out over the water, and I dipped under and swam through a tangle of vines. When I came up, I heard him calling my name, calling Abigail's name too.

"Here!" she called back.

"Here!" I called back too, as though answering some sort of roll call.

"We should get going," he said, his voice echoing around us, sounding weaker than usual. "Consider this your three-minute warning."

After that, there were no words for some time. I looked to see Abigail in the distance, still watching them just the same. I turned to see my father walking back to where my mother sat on that crooked bench. Something about the way he stepped toward her reminded me of that story about their meeting. The girl on her suitcase. The girl with a toothache. The girl in a snowstorm. Now, instead of lifting an icicle from her cheek, he leaned down and kissed her. "I'm sorry," he said.

"I'm sorry too," she told him.

"Let's make a deal. We enjoy the summer. No work other than the few lectures I've already booked. In the fall, we'll be sure Abigail is back with her father. And if Rose is ready, we'll be sure she is home with us again. How does that sound?"

My mother lifted her hand and touched her fingers to her lips, then her cheek, as though touching the kiss he had planted there, the place that icicle had been so many years before. I heard a splash on the far side of the pond and looked to see Abigail had leaped off the dock and was swimming back. I began swimming back too, thinking the things my father suggested made for a perfect plan, except for one detail: my mother had yet to tell him what she knew about Heekin's manuscript and the damage it would do to their reputations when it was published come fall. But even as I thought about that, I arrived at the shore and stood again, feeling the sharp rocks and mud sinking beneath my feet, while my mother stared up at my father, telling him, "That sounds good to me."

Sylvie?"

I woke in my bed. My room was empty, except for those horses on their shelf, fighting for space. For a long moment, I lay there, counting limbs and tails as best I could, wondering if I'd dreamed the sound of someone calling my name. But then came the knocking. I kept still, listening to the faint *tapping* until the voice that first woke me said again, "Sylvie?" It was coming from the other side of the wall, from Rose's bedroom.

"Yes?" I said.

"Are you awake?"

"I am."

"Sorry to bother you."

My sister and I had never spoken through the wall, since her bed was on the other side of her room. I wondered if Abigail had taken it upon herself to rearrange the furniture in all the time she'd been living there. Seventeen days had turned to twenty then twenty-four, and now, somehow we were tiptoeing into August. If there were signs of things returning to normal—of Rose coming home soon, of Abigail leaving—I had not noticed. Instead, the four of us went about our lives, discarding old traditions and creating new ones. At church on Sundays, people stared and whispered

about the new addition to our family and the conspicuous absence of my
sister, until one day, my father announced we would not be going to church
at all, that it was better for us to simply pray at home. In the evenings, it
became a custom to go for ice cream after dinner, followed by a swim at
the pond. My mother insisted my father track down the owner to ask for
permission. The old man told him he used to love people swimming there
and was all too happy to know people would be enjoying it again.

How could any girl my age not be happy—or at least placated by nightly
trips to the ice cream shop and swims in a pond beneath a blanket of stars
before bed? Guilty as it made me feel, I enjoyed those times. I sensed Abigail did as well. The two of us had begun occasional conversations, though
until the night she knocked on the wall, the topics were limited to our
choice of ice cream flavors and our favorite spots in the pond.

"It's okay," I told her now. "But it's late. Is something wrong?"

"I have the same dream almost every night. About my mother."

"Is it a bad dream?"

She was quiet. Perhaps, I thought, she had drifted back to sleep, and
that would be the end of it. Then she said, "It's a good dream and a bad
dream. When we used to live all year long at the ministry in Oregon,
my mother and I had a ritual before bed. Did you ever have that with
your mom? Something that made you feel safe before she turned out the
light?"

I thought of the prayers my mother used to say with me, a song she
used to sing when I was younger, back before that other song took its place,
the way she sometimes stroked my hair and kissed my forehead before
leaving the room. "Yes," I answered, feeling an unexpected nostalgia for
those rituals. "We did."

"Well, did you know my mother was once a flight attendant?"

"No," I said, surprised. "She was?"

"That's how she met him. He was on a flight to South Africa with other
missionaries. That's where my mother is from. Capetown. They fell in love
and he convinced her to join the ministry too."

By "him", I assumed she meant her father but did not ask. Maybe it
was the tense conversation between my parents at the pond our first night

there, the secret my mother was keeping about Heekin's manuscript, but something made me ask, "Did they stay in love?"

"He did. But she didn't. It wasn't just him she fell out of love with, though. She started to hate life at the ministry too."

I tried to imagine what that life would be like but came up blank. "Why?"

"A million reasons. She used to say it was like living in a bubble. One day, she finally left that bubble and took me with her. We got as far as the Portland airport before he found us and kept me from going with her."

"Your mother went anyway? Without you?"

"Yes."

"But how could—"

"She said she had to. And that she'd figure out some way to come back for me. She gave me her word."

"And did she come back?"

"Maybe. That was a long time ago, though. Even if she did, he made it so she would have a very hard time finding us. Who knows? By now, she's probably given up and gone back to her country."

"Is that why you wander?" I asked. "In case she's still looking for you, I mean."

"Yes. Most of the year, we are on the road. Except for a few weeks every winter when we go back to the ministry in Oregon. At that place, even the coloring books are about Jesus. Since there was never anything new to read to me, my mother used to do her old preflight routine before bed. You know, 'Ladies and gentlemen, the captain has turned on the Fasten Seat Belt sign. Please stow your carry-on luggage beneath the seat in front of you or in an overhead bin. Make sure your seat back and folding trays are in an upright and locked position. If you are seated next to an emergency exit, please read the instruction card located in your seat pocket. . . .'

"She used to look so pretty, my mother, with her long blond hair and blue eyes, standing at the foot of my bed, pointing up and down the imaginary aisles. It made me feel like we were about to take off, that our dreams were these great adventures. But then, the day we were supposed to take a real flight together . . ."

Abigail allowed her voice to trail off. It didn't matter, since now I understood.

We were quiet for some time, until at last she said, "When I tell you the dreams are both good and bad, what I mean is that they start out good—my mother is showing me the emergency exit rows, explaining about the lighted path in the aisles, the oxygen masks that drop from the ceiling—but peaceful as they begin, the dreams always turn bad. It is that way with most things in life, *my* life anyway. Probably, it is the way things will go during my time here with you and your family—even though that is not what I want."

I wasn't sure what to say so we went back to being quiet after that. I tried to picture Abigail on the other side of that wall. Had she moved the bed the way I imagined? Or was she simply kneeling there in that white nightgown originally intended for my sister? I never did find out, because soon I drifted off to sleep and Abigail must have too.

The next night brought another trip to the ice cream shop, another swim in the pond where I kept watch on my parents sitting calmly side by side on that crooked bench back on shore. Afterward, on our bumpy ride back down the dirt road toward home, I stuck my hand out the window and surfed the air once again. Abigail did as well, though she told me I was doing it wrong. It never occurred to me that there was a *right* way to hand-surf, but she said, "I can tell you're in your head too much, Sylvie. You need to give yourself over to the air and motion. Stay in the moment."

"What makes you such an expert?" I asked.

Abigail fixed me with a look, and I thought of that van she had first arrived in, all the years she and her father had spent wandering. "The secret is to not think so much," was all she said. "Just feel the air. Just let go."

After that, I pulled my hand inside and simply watched her, since I felt suddenly self-conscious about the whole thing. And as we drove the dark streets, I couldn't help but notice how comfortable she seemed beside me, living Rose's old life. Thinking that caused some suspicion to awaken inside me, one that kept nagging at me the rest of the ride home.

And then, hours later, I woke in my bed. No one had called my name, but I sensed her presence lingering on the other side of that wall. This time, I knocked.

"Yes, Sylvie?" Her response was almost immediate.

"They aren't real, are they?"

It was, finally, the words that had festered in my mind ever since watching her in the car earlier, though they seemed to have been there long before that, I realized. In some way, it seemed I had always known.

The question brought about a pause, longer than any during our conversation the previous evening. I wondered briefly if Abigail knew what I meant. But at last she said, "The answer isn't a simple yes or no, Sylvie. It's harder to explain than that."

"Then try."

"Okay, then. But do you promise not to tell anyone? Because my wish is that things stay good. My wish is that we stay friends, Sylvie, always and forever."

Is that what we had become? I was not so sure, but I was hungry for whatever she was about to tell me, so I said what she wanted to hear, "I promise."

Abigail sighed loud enough that I could hear it through the wall. "Other than those few weeks in the winter when we're in Oregon, we live in campgrounds and rest stops. We hardly ever see anyone at all. The only thing we do is go to whatever religious services he finds. One day, years ago, we slipped into a healing service in some auditorium in some town. I don't even remember where since they are all pretty much the same after a while. People singing the identical songs, raising their hands in the air, falling to the floor when they think the Holy Spirit has overtaken them. But at this one service, the preacher announced that his inner circle was going to pray over a boy whose soul had been occupied by an unwanted spirit. They brought out the boy and laid hands on him. In big, booming voices, as he snarled and scratched at them, they ordered the devil to be gone. Looking at it all, I thought *I* could be that boy."

I didn't understand what she meant at first. "Why would you—"

"My father never listened to what I wanted—until I behaved that way. Then he paid attention. It put me in control instead of him. At first, that power meant nothing but making sure he was as miserable as me. But in the end, it led us here, to me living with your family instead of him."

"I see. He'll come back for you, though. Eventually."

"I worried about that at first too. But it's been so long now I'm pretty sure he's given up. Before we came here, I made it so I was impossible to live with. He's afraid of me now. *Terrified,* in fact. I did some pretty awful things to him. So if he's smart, which he is in his own way, he'll keep staying away. Because I want to live here for good, Sylvie. I want to go to school here in this town like a normal person, to have a normal family and a normal life."

Abigail Lynch might have been the first person ever to look upon our family as normal, but I didn't tell her that. Instead, I simply kept listening.

"Your father mentioned a lecture date he's got coming up. He asked if I'd be willing to go onstage, the way your sister never would, to talk about how he and your mother helped me."

I tried to recall an occasion when my father had ever asked my sister to join them onstage, though no such memory came. "What did you tell him?"

"That I'd do it. Happily."

"But you'd be lying. And my father wouldn't—"

"Please, Sylvie. It doesn't matter as long as I do a good job for him. Besides, it's not all a lie. There is something inside me, just like my father told you and your mother that first day. Some people might call it a demon. All I know is it's something that made me live my life this way. It's made me do terrible things too."

Given the things she was saying, I felt grateful for that wall between us then, since I did not want to look at her. All summer, I'd been thinking about the deal my parents made, the one where things would return to normal come fall. I'd even been ticking off the days until early September arrived and we would make the trip to see Rose and maybe even bring her home. All along, I'd envisioned Abigail being gone by then, returning to that life she lived with her father. Now, I was not sure what would happen, but I didn't say another word about it and neither did she.

In the days that followed, we lived two lives: the one where Abigail and I were those disembodied voices, communicating through the wall in the dark of our rooms. In that life, we stayed away from any difficult conversations. Instead, she taught me her mother's preflight routine, and I repeated it back to her each evening, a kind of prayer that comforted her before sleep. And then there was our second life, the one we lived during the day. No longer afraid to go to the basement, Abigail spent hours down there, practicing her part in the talk with my father. He told her that all she had to do was get up onstage and tell her story, but she wanted every word, every gesture to be approved by him beforehand.

And then, just as my mother predicted, summer ended and school began. The publication of Heekin's book was just weeks away, and though my father called him to request a copy, he never heard back. Meanwhile, my parents' lecture came and went with Abigail joining them onstage to great success according to my father. I waited in the greenroom, like I used to with Rose, taking that old copy of *Jane Eyre* along, studying the words I underlined years before, and wondering what I'd seen in certain passages.

Eighth grade should have been something I looked forward to, considering it was my last year of junior high. But from the very first day I stepped through the doors to see the same old teachers and Gretchen and Elizabeth, who had never been quite the same toward me since that article appeared in the paper, I couldn't help but feel that the year ahead was simply something to be gotten through.

What I looked forward to most was our visit to see Rose, since the ninety days would soon be up. My mother informed me that we would be going to Saint Julia's the weekend after school began. No one mentioned enrolling Abigail as she'd hoped. Instead, she walked me to the bus stop each morning in her bare feet and met me there each afternoon.

Only a few days into the first week, I stepped off the bus to find her waiting for me the same as always. Even before I saw the fresh scratches and bruises on her toes, I sensed something different in her expression, which appeared glazed and distant. As the bus lumbered away, Abigail said in a voice less serene than the one I'd finally grown accustomed to: "Let's not go home for a little while, okay?"

"Okay. But why not?"

"Your parents. There's someone in the house with them."

"Your father?" I said. There was a certain inevitability and relief in my voice. "Did he finally come back?"

"No," she told me. "Not yet anyway. But that's what I need to talk to you about. Your mom told me that he'll be coming to get me any day now."

She had begun walking, and I trailed along. Soon, she led us to the foundation directly across from our house, where Rose and I used to create our imaginary homes. The crumbling cement steps, the twisted iron rods in one corner, the fallen tree resting in a puddle—I looked over the edge at all those things, trying to imagine us playing there now.

Despite her bare feet, Abigail started down the steps. I worried she might cut herself, but she so rarely bothered with socks or shoes that she seemed unfazed. When she reached the bottom, Abigail picked up a stone and used it to write on the wall the way Rose and I once did with our pastel chalks. An X and a Y—that's what she drew, placing them at a distance from each other. The sight of those letters put me in mind of that helter-skelter pattern on the van the day she arrived, the doodle of that headless animal with its endlessly swirling tail.

"If you're in the mood to do algebra," I said, trying a joke as I looked down at her inside the foundation, "I have plenty of homework in my bag. It's all yours."

"That's not what this is," she said in a serious voice.

"So what is it then?" I asked, glancing across the lane at my house, feeling impatient.

"It's more like a geography lesson. One you are going to teach me." She paused and looked up at me, and I couldn't help glancing away again across the lane, until she called out. "If I'm at X, which is right here in Dundalk, but I want to be at Y, which is the Baltimore Train Station, what's the best way to get there?"

It felt odd to have such a serious conversation in the daylight, rather than through the bedroom wall. "Ask my parents. They'll—"

"They'll tell me to forget it, Sylvie. They'll make sure I stay put until my father comes to take me back. And I can't do that again. Not anymore."

I stopped and looked at her down in that foundation, the X and Y on the gray wall. "Where are you planning to go?" I asked at last.

"My mother used to have a friend—a nice lady who left the ministry before we did. The two of them wrote letters all the time. I remember that friend's name and where she moved to."

"Where?"

"I'm not telling you, Sylvie. Because once I'm gone you'll feel obligated to tell your parents, to give them the answer they want."

She was right, of course, but I couldn't help feeling surprised she'd figured that out about me. I would always give them the answers they wanted. "Well, even if you get to this friend of your mom's, then what?"

"Then she will help me contact my mother."

The two of us stood there a moment, staring at that X and Y.

"It's not the best plan, but it's the only one I've got," Abigail said finally. "So *please*. Help me."

At last, I put down my books and descended those crumbling stairs into the old foundation, where I took the stone from her hand. The last time I had drawn on that wall, it was to create a pretend window, one with pink curtains that looked out onto a yard with lime-green grass and lavender flowers. Now, I drew a map of the path through the woods, past the poultry farm to the spot where you could hear the highway in the distance. "This would be your quickest way," I told her. "The path opens up right behind this foundation. Just follow it to the highway. Then follow that into Baltimore. There must be signs for the train station, I'm sure."

"Thanks," Abigail said, sounding genuinely grateful. "But there's one more thing. I need money, Sylvie. Enough for a train ticket at least."

At some point during our late-night talks, I'd let slip a mention of those essay contests and how proud I was of winning them, how I'd been saving the money for something special, though I didn't know what that was just yet. "Let's go back to the house and have dinner," I said, stalling before she mentioned the obvious. "Maybe go get ice cream and swim. It's still warm enough."

"No," she told me. "It might still be warm enough for that. But it's almost fall now, then winter will come. And he'll be here to get me long before that. I have to do something. And I have to do it now."

"I'm sorry," I said, giving the answer I know my parents would have expected of me. "But I can't help you."

I turned again toward the stairs, put my foot on the first step as a few chunks of the cement crumbled away. From behind me, there came a shuffling sound. A moment later, when I reached the top of the steps, I heard the smallest of moans before Abigail shouted, "Sylvie! Look at me!"

Something in me did not want to turn back, but her voice grew louder as she called out again. And when I looked at last, I saw that she was standing by those twisted iron rods, the ones Rose speculated had once been the start of a fireplace. Blood pooled on one of her open palms. The sight caused me to gasp.

"Now do you see?" she said. "I do have something inside of me? It may not be the demons other people talk about, but it's something that makes me capable of hurting myself if I need to. Hurting other people too unless I get what I want. So please. What I want is your help."

It seemed I should have made some sudden move, scrambled back down the stairs to help her by trying to stop the bleeding. Or run quickly as I could away from her before she tried to harm me too. But, no. I just stood at the top of those stairs, staring at her a long moment, watching blood drool down her fingers and drip onto the cement of the foundation. Neither of us said a word. And then came the sounds of another voice, calling "Sylvie! Abigail!"

It was my father.

"I have to go," I said. "We both do. You've got to clean that wound and bandage it up."

Abigail still did not speak, but she reached over and dragged her other hand across one of those rods, releasing another moan, louder this time as her face contorted in pain. When she was done, she held her blood-smeared hands out to me and said simply, "The money. I know you have it. I can't ever promise to pay you back, but please."

"Okay," I told her at last, since it seemed the only way to make her stop. Still, I couldn't help stalling if only to give me time to figure out the best way to handle the situation. "I'll give it to you tomorrow."

"I can't wait until tomorrow. I need that money tonight. When I'm asleep down in the basement, bring it to me."

"The basement?" I said, surprised. "Why would you be sleeping down there?"

"Because, Sylvie, that's the other thing I have to tell you. Your parents are putting me downstairs on the cot tonight. That person I mentioned, the one who's at your house right now with them, well, it's your sister. You won't be going to see her this weekend, because Rose has come home at last."

HELP FOR THE HAUNTED

Most people, they are afraid to believe in ghosts. Me, I'm afraid not to believe. Because, well, what then? If there really is nothing else—nowhere to go after this, no way to linger on this plane to finish unsettled business if we must, then that means each moment, each breath, each passing second, is as ethereal as the wind. It means all we do here on earth—the going and coming, the loving and hating—it is all for naught. So, no. Ghosts don't scare me. But no ghosts—that terrifies me.

Enough about that, though. Back to what I was saying previously, Mr. Heekin. Forgive me, I mean, Sam. What I have always wanted, more than anything, is to build a good life for my daughters and my wife. To have a family of my own with proper values. Growing up, my father drank too much. He was not abusive, but his remote nature was in its own way a form of abuse. My mother and I had our tender moments but shared such different interests that we were never close. And my brother, well, he did things I can never forgive. For all those reasons, I ended up creating my own world.

What's that? Excuse me?

No, no. That is not what I am saying. Those things I
saw—still see—are every bit real. What I mean is that I created my own life apart from the family I was born into. I
moved away. I found the Bible. I came to believe that a life
lived in the light, free of sin and reproach, protects us as we
move through this world. It keeps the darkness at bay.

The tape came to an end, and the cassette player in Detective Rummel's car automatically ejected it. He asked if I wanted to listen to the other
side. "Depends," I said, my father's voice echoing in my mind still. "How
close are we?"

Rummel lifted a hand from the steering wheel, pointing to an impossibly high metal fence in the distance. I looked to see barbed wire curlicuing
across the top, a compound of low-slung brick buildings on the other side.
"We've got a little time still, Sylvie. But why don't we wait until after to
hear more, so you can clear your head?"

Days. Weeks. Months. It might have taken that long to arrange a meeting with an inmate on the other side of that fence. But the morning after
I found those candles in the trash, I drove in silence with my sister to the
police station. The two of us had barely spoken since that fight in her truck
over the money from Dial U.S.A., and our silence had become so palpable
it felt as though we were both holding our breath, daring the other to let it
out first. Once they separated us—Rose on that bench in the hall, me inside
that achingly familiar interview room—Rummel and Louise asked if I was
prepared to either recant or uphold my account of the evening last winter.

And that's when I told them I wanted to see Albert Lynch. I refused to
say anything more or even see my sister again until they made arrangements. Louise stepped out into the hallway to speak to Rose about the
need for her permission, since I was a minor after all, and she was my legal
guardian. While waiting, I asked Rummel about those interview tapes
Heekin had told me about. For all the trouble I had given him, the detective maintained his kindness toward me. In an almost tender voice, he said
that if I thought the tapes might help somehow, I was welcome to give
them a listen. He brought a cassette player into the room, and my father's
interviews with the reporter filled the air around me. At different points on

the recordings, Heekin's faltering voice could not be heard, so it was just my father speaking between the occasional pause.

By midafternoon, Rummel poked his head into the room to inform me that the prison had okayed the visit and that Rose had begrudgingly acquiesced and granted permission too. The only thing we were waiting for was to find out if Lynch himself would agree to see me.

A short while later, word came that he did.

Nearly five hours after I entered the station, I walked out, carrying the one cassette I had yet to play. In the hallway, Rummel and I passed my sister on that bench, flipping through the same old safety brochures. It startled me to see her, since I assumed she had given up and gone home by then.

"Sylvie," she said when she laid eyes on me.

Head down, I kept walking. Some part of me felt the urge to take the detective's hand for comfort. Instead, I squeezed the cassette harder, bracing myself for this moment with Rose, bracing myself for the trip to the prison that lay ahead.

"Sylvie!" She tossed those brochures on the floor and stood. "I'm talking to you!"

"I'm just going to see him," I told her over the rising *shhhh*.

"Why?"

Absolute certainty—that was why. I wanted to be sure this time that what I believed was the truth. I wanted to be right for Detective Rummel and Louise. I wanted to be right for my mother and father. I wanted to be right for me too.

But I did not explain that to Rose. Instead, I just kept walking as she stood there in the hall calling after me.

SUSSEX COUNTY CORRECTIONAL INSTITUTION—I stared at the sign as we drove through a series of gates at the prison. That very first night I opened my eyes to see Rummel at my bedside in the hospital, the man had seemed strong and impenetrable, a statue come to life. But as he spoke to the guards at the gates, the guards at the front doors, and still more guards in the maze inside that rambling brick compound, the detective seemed impossibly human. Something in his heavy footsteps, his quick breaths and occasional sighs, left me with the feeling that Rummel was nervous about this visit too.

Beforehand, we had agreed that he would stay with me the entire time, so when yet another guard led us to a room full of tables and told me to take a seat, the detective lingered nearby. That long, rectangular table where I sat waiting for Lynch was not unlike the ones in the school cafeteria. Thinking of school led me to think of Boshoff and the diary he had given me. I hadn't been able to find it the night before, and now my only hope was that it was lost somewhere in the bowels of Howie's theater, like so many dropped possessions of the people who came before me, only never to be found.

I kept thinking about the diary, and all I had written inside, until a door opened across the room, different from the one Rummel and I had come through. I looked up to see Albert Lynch being escorted in by another guard. Slowly, they walked to the table, Lynch in an orange jumpsuit, his gaze on the floor instead of me. The guard pulled back the chair, legs scraping the floor, and Lynch flopped into the seat. "Thirty," the guard said, pointing to the large clock on the wall.

The half-hour limit was yet another detail that had been agreed upon beforehand. I knew we didn't have much time, and yet for an extended moment, neither of us said anything. Lynch sat there, staring at me. Without his odd bug-eyed glasses, I was not sure how well he could see, but I wondered what I must have looked like to him. I felt much older than that girl who had witnessed him calling into the bushes outside the convention center in Ocala, more world-weary and wise than that girl who had walked to the end of Butter Lane with her mother to find him and his daughter waiting for us in their van.

Lynch had never been a heavy man, but he had lost a considerable amount of weight since those days. The hollows under his eyes and his sunken cheeks gave the impression of a tent collapsing from the inside. That smooth, babyish skin of his had gone crepey around the mouth. At last, he opened his thin lips and said quietly, "All these months in this god-forsaken place, the only visitors I've had have been lawyers and detectives like your friend here. When they told me I had a visitation request this morning, you were the last person I expected."

I stared down at my hands on the table. "No one has come to see you?"

"Who would, Sylvie? No one knows where my daughter is. She was my only family. My only life, in fact."

I closed my eyes, for just a second or two, but long enough to conjure the memory of that conversation in the foundation with Abigail and the way I had turned from her, racing across the lane toward home the moment she informed me that my sister had returned. When I opened my eyes again, I told myself to put that memory away, to stay in the here and now. "I came," I said, forcing my gaze upon his, "because I want to talk about that night in the church. The conversation you had with my parents, before—"

"You don't need me to tell you, Sylvie," he said, making no effort to hide his contempt. "I've given my account to the lawyers and detectives, including the one you brought with you. Just ask him for the transcript."

I heard Rummel's heavy shoes shift on the floor behind me, heard him let out another of those faint sighs. In the moments after I had made the request to see Lynch, the detective had offered the same option: that I could just look at the transcripts. But that's not what I wanted. What brought me to the prison was that long-ago conversation with my mother in the bed of our hotel room, the one where she told me I could sense the truth inside a person if only I allowed myself. "I want to hear what happened from you," I told Lynch.

He did not respond immediately, or at least not directly. Instead, Lynch told me, "I've had a lot of time to read in here, Sylvie. Guess which book I spent the most time on?"

"The Bible," I said, since the answer seemed obvious.

"Wrong. That's for other people in here. I've decided at long last that I've had enough of that book. Enough for a lifetime actually. So, no. The one that's been keeping me company is the book about your mom and dad. The reporter who wrote it had a few interesting things to say about your old man, Sylvie. Have you ever read it?"

"Yes," I told him.

The night before, after I'd found those candles in the trash, I'd cleaned up the mess, then returned to the house. Since Rose was up in her room, I couldn't get the book from her closet. Instead, I scoured the house for a second copy, finding one crammed inside the curio hutch with all those other old books of my father's. That fall when it was published, my father sat quietly in his chair reading the book. The clock ticked. My mother made tea. She kept busy flipping through those wallpaper patterns until he was done. That's when my father told us we were never to speak of the book or Heekin again. All that and yet, there were those few extra editions in the hutch anyway. For so long, I had told myself that what kept me from reading the final pages had been the promise I made to my mother that morning on our steps when she held the manuscript in her hands and wept. But it was something more, I realized. I was afraid to read that final section—"Should You *Really* Believe the Masons?"—because I did not want to face what it might say.

"So," Lynch was saying now. "You know the things your father told that reporter."

Be direct and clear, I thought, repeating those survey rules in my mind. "That's not what I want to talk to you about. I want to hear what happened in the moments before I entered that church."

Lynch looked behind him at the guard, no more than ten feet away, then at the clock on the wall. Twenty-one minutes—that's all we had left. He turned to me again, but said nothing.

Rummel came closer, put his hand on my shoulder, and squeezed. "We can go, if you like."

"No," I told him. "Not yet."

I waited for him to step away again, and when he did and the clock showed only nineteen minutes remaining, this is what I offered Lynch: "If you want, I can tell you what happened that summer you left your daughter with us. I can tell you what I know of her last night in our home. The things that went wrong."

That got his attention. Lynch raised his head and said, "If you're planning on feeding me the same lines about those demons who drove her from your house, then save it, Sylvie. I already heard that crap from your old man before he died."

I swallowed, noticed that my hands were shaking. I moved them beneath the table and took a breath, trying to calm the rabbit beat of my heart. "I'm not going to tell you the same story as my father. I'm going to tell you the truth of what I know. So long as you do the same for me."

"Okay, then," he said. "You first."

How much easier might this conversation have been if I had never lost my journal, if I could simply open to the pages where I'd written all about that summer, all about that last night in particular, then slide the book across the table for Lynch to read?

I remember that when I ran across the street and burst through the front door, the first thing I wanted to do was hug my sister, since I had not hugged her the day she left home. But the sight of Rose made me stop abruptly in the entrance to the living room.

"What are you gawking at?" Rose said. "You look like you've seen a ghost."

"Your head," I told her. "What did you . . ."

She reached a hand up and ran it over her scalp, still nicked and bloody from the razor. "Funny, I had a full head of hair when I got here this morning. But when I found someone else sleeping in my room, wearing my clothes, living my life, I thought I better do something to set myself apart from her."

"Rose," my mother said. "Your father and I explained why you found things the way you did. You never should have—"

The front door opened and my mother grew quiet. A moment later, Abigail padded up the hall in bare feet until she was standing beside me. Why had I failed to notice earlier that the shirt she wore was not one of those tattered things she had arrived with, but rather a simple black tank that belonged to my sister? How many other days and nights had she taken to wearing her clothes without my noticing?

"Abigail," my father said, his voice rising with alarm. "What happened?"

I watched as she held out her palms, blood still drooling and dripping from each, as her mouth moved open and closed but made no sound. First my father, then my mother, rushed toward her. In a moment, they had whisked her off to the kitchen, where I could hear water running and my mother praying too.

Meanwhile, Rose and I had been left alone in the living room. There was a little blood on her hand as well from when she ran it over her scalp. But nothing she couldn't wipe away on her jeans, which she did just then. "Well, squirt," she said. "I can see things have really normalized while I've been gone."

How could I tell her that in their own strange way, things had seemed normal—happy even—all those months? There was the ice cream. There were those late-night trips to the pond. There were the conversations Abigail and I had through the bedroom wall.

Instead, I said, "I'm glad you're back. Are they going to let you stay?"

"They're not happy about it, but I'm not giving them a choice. No way am I heading back to that place. And I'm not going back to school again either. I'm going to stay here through the fall and winter, save my money then get an apartment of my own."

I thought of that globe up in her room, the way she used to spin it, plunking her finger down on random locations. Warsaw. Buenos Aires. Sydney. "Get a place where?"

"Don't know. Haven't figured that out yet. But it won't be Dundalk or even Baltimore. It'll be someplace a safe distance from this madhouse."

I stood there, saying nothing. All summer long, I had wanted the same things as my mother: for Rose to come home, for Abigail to be gone, for things to return to normal. But I realized then that things would never go back to the way they had been. When Rose left that morning months before, she may as well have left for good.

"Sylvie," my mother called from the kitchen. "Can you run to our bathroom upstairs and get some bandages and peroxide?"

I turned away from my sister and did what our mother asked. When I stepped into the kitchen moments later, Abigail held her hands above her head to slow the bleeding. "Does she need stitches?" I asked.

"I don't think so," my father answered, then looked to Abigail and asked her, "How did this happen?"

Her mouth moved up and down again, but no words came. You're good at this, I thought. If I didn't know better, I'd have been fooled too.

"You were with her, Sylvie," my mother said at last. "Tell us."

Abigail's eyes caught mine then. I thought of that morning when I

*spoke the truth for Rose and how badly that had turned out despite my
intentions. Let them believe what they want, I decided before answering
only with, "I don't know what happened to her."*

*Abigail's eyes were on mine still as my parents walked her to the
basement door. Her mouth was no longer moving, though I could
imagine words slipping out anyway, saying: "The money. Tonight, after
I'm down there asleep, don't forget to bring me the money."*

"And then what?" Lynch said. He was not exactly leaning forward at
the table, but he was sitting up at last, his spindly fingers pressed to the
surface. "You went down there and gave her the money?"

"Your turn," I told him. "Tell me about the deal you made with my
sister."

He balled his hands into tight fists and seemed about to drum them on
the table, but shook them in the air a moment instead. "Fine," he told me.
"It's nothing I haven't said before. All that fall and all that winter, I kept
searching for Abigail. I had ideas about where she might have gone. Back to
the ministry in Oregon. Or off to find a friend of my ex-wife's. Or to a town
in the south where we once stayed for a few months, since she seemed to
like the other children at the church there more than other places. But she
never turned up anywhere. All the while, I kept calling your house, but
your parents just let that stupid machine answer. I couldn't go to the police,
because of the way we had been living. Besides, I didn't know if my ex had
some sort of report filed against me. I found out from one of the lawyers
after I was in here that she never did stop looking.

"I started coming to your house again. That fall. That winter too.
Eventually, your parents didn't even bother to open the door. By then, I had
read that book by Sam Heekin, which meant I knew about the Mustang
Bar where he took your father after he apparently popped a few of those
pills he liked to take when his back was hurting. The day of the storm, I
went through the same routine: hammering away on your front door to
no avail until I gave up and found myself sitting at the Mustang Bar too. It
had been ages since I'd had so much as a drop of alcohol, never mind the
few shots of whiskey I tossed back that night. As I sat at that bar, drowning
my sorrows, some girl kept coming in and ordering drinks. Eventually, I

realized she was sneaking them outside to the car. When I stood from the stool and made my way outside, who do I see but your sister? She looked different from that night I saw her in the parking lot in Florida, but I remembered her face."

"And that's when you made the deal?" I asked.

"Yes. Fifty bucks to call your parents and get them to talk to me. I told her that's all I wanted to do and she believed it."

"Then what?"

"She made the call from a pay phone right outside the bar. Meeting at the church was a detail she came up with all on her own. I was expecting to go by your house, but Rose told me that if your parents thought they were going to meet her, that if she was willing to pray with them to get things right in her head, they would venture out into the storm to see her."

"Only it was you they would be seeing."

"Exactly."

"So then you went to the church?"

Lynch glanced behind him at the clock again. I did too. Thirteen minutes. "Uh-uh," he said. "Your turn."

I took a breath, thought of those pages in my journal, and began:

> Abigail never came back up from that basement—not that I was aware
> of, anyway. My mother, however—she emerged a few hours later to
> throw together a quick dinner for Rose and me. While my father took a
> tray down for Abigail, my mother said she was sorry that we could not
> eat together as a family, but that any day now, perhaps even the very
> next, Abigail's father would return for her at last. A shame, my mother
> said, that after a perfectly fine summer, this is how he would find the
> girl. She said she had tried her best, but there were some haunted people
> she could not help after all.
>
> Once our mother made us two turkey sandwiches then returned to
> the basement, Rose told me that most nights at Saint Julia's, she snuck
> her dinner back up to her room. That's what she wanted to do then too.
> It had been so long since I'd seen my sister, I agreed to whatever she
> wanted. Inside her room, I watched as she shoved the bed back to where
> it used to be against the far wall, then stripped the sheets Abigail had

been sleeping in and piled them, along with all the girl's clothes, into the cinnamon-colored suitcase we once shared.

"She can have the old thing," Rose said. "It just brings back bad memories."

After I hunted down fresh sheets and helped make the room hers again, the two of us lay on her bed and picked at our sandwiches. It was then that I asked Rose more about Saint Julia's, but she told me she preferred not to talk about it, except to say that she had left on her own and was never going back. The worst experience of her life, that's what she said, but also the best because it taught her once and for all who she was. There in that bed, lying side by side the way we used to in those makeshift tents in the living room, we fell asleep.

At some point, I was woken by the sound of footsteps padding down the hall, and I looked to see my father, then my mother, slipping into their bedroom and closing the door. For a long moment, I lay there gazing over at Rose who, with her shaved head, looked nothing like herself. In some ways, it was like sleeping next to a stranger. And I couldn't help but feel that's what she was becoming to me. I lay there, wondering about her plan to stay in our house without returning to school and how many more feuds that would cause with our parents. Finally, I decided to stop worrying and instead do my part in making things better.

I got up. I went to my room, where I stood on my desk chair and reached for that shelf full of horses. There was one in particular, a horse I'd named Aurora, that came with a small compartment inside its hollowed belly. I used a dime to pry it open and pulled out the wad of money I'd stashed inside over the years. Six hundred dollars—that's what all my work on those essays had totaled up to.

Despite Abigail's presence in the basement, my mother had left that bare lightbulb on just as we'd agreed. When I made my way down the stairs, I saw Penny smiling inside Mr. Knothead's old cage. I looked away and walked to that partitioned area where the light did not fall and where I found Abigail fast asleep on a cot with one of my mother's knit blankets draped over her body. Some part of me thought to turn back and head upstairs, to forget about giving her the money. But as I stood there, staring at the moonlight shining on those bandages around her hands, I could not help but wonder what worse things she might be capable of doing to herself—or to my family—if she did not get her way.

"Abigail," I whispered.

Her eyes opened. She sat right up. When she spoke, it made me think of earlier in the summer when it was still a surprise to hear her voice. "I've been waiting for you, Sylvie. Did you bring what I need?"

"Yes. But I still don't like the idea." As much as I wanted her gone, I couldn't keep from saying, "How will I know if you'll be safe?"

"It's not your problem," she told me. "I'll be fine, though. Don't worry, Sylvie."

There seemed nothing more to do but give her the money. All of it, because she'd need more than cash for a train ticket. Abigail might have been among the few haunted people my mother could not help, but in my own way, I could. With one of her bandaged hands, she took the wad of bills from me, not bothering to count any of it. "Thank you," she said.

"You're welcome," I told her, noticing a foggy sort of expression move over her face as she lay back on the pillow. "Are you okay?"

"Yes. Well, no. Not really. I feel wiped out, I guess."

Who knew if this was just part of her act? I couldn't be certain, but I put my hand on her forehead anyway. Like that time I had kissed my mother's and found it cool, I was surprised to find hers felt the same. "Do you need food? Maybe something to drink?"

"No. Your father brought dinner down to me a while ago. And there's a glass of water right there on the floor by my cot."

We were quiet a moment, the two of us breathing in the shadows of that basement. At last, I asked, "When will you leave?"

"Sometime tomorrow. But instead of following the path through the woods, I have a better plan. Since it's Saturday, your mother will want to go grocery shopping. Let's go with her, and I'll sneak off when she's busy at the register."

It seemed as good a plan as any, so I agreed to it. And then, although I meant to say good night, a different word slipped out, "Good-bye."

Abigail let out a weak laugh. "Sylvie, I just told you I'll see you tomorrow, so it's not time for good-bye just yet. But before you go back upstairs, can you do one last thing for me?"

"What?" I said, but then I understood. "Oh. Yes. Sure." I looked down at her head on that pillow, hair fanned all around as moonlight shone through the sliding glass door, making her face appear ghostly but beautiful. In that moment, she seemed like the spirits my father so often spoke of, an energy trapped between this world and the next. "Ladies and gentlemen," I whispered, "The captain has turned on the Fasten Seat Belt sign. . . ."

Abigail listened. She smiled. She closed her eyes.

"Then what?" Lynch asked.

"I was about to ask you the same thing. After you made the deal with my sister and drove to church, what happened next?"

Lynch rubbed his face, glancing up at the clock. Eight minutes before our visit would come to an end.

"Stop wasting time," I told him.

"I'm not wasting time!" he burst out. "You come here! You demand this story I've told a thousand times. You tease me with this information about my daughter! So I need a minute to clear my head!"

Rummel's heavy steps moved toward the table, but I held up a hand and they stopped, then retreated. "Okay, then," I said to Lynch. "I understand. Take a minute. But we haven't got long."

The man blew out a breath and rubbed his hands over his bald scalp. "I parked on the street behind the church. Your parents knew my van by then, so I figured if they caught sight of it, they would turn right around and leave. Your sister told me the key was kept in the window boxes at the church, a detail she recalled from your father's days as a deacon. Sure enough, there it was. I let myself in."

"And you brought your gun along—the one I saw the day you showed up at the end of our street?"

"Yes. But it was just to scare them. I promise you that was my only plan. I wanted the truth from your father and mother, instead of the silent treatment I'd been getting and the lies before that. My intention was to turn on the lights inside the church, but I couldn't find the switch. All the better, I decided in the end, since the darkness might give me an advantage. I waited up front in one of the pews near the altar until I saw the headlights of your car pull into the snowy parking lot outside."

He stopped a moment, and although some part of me wanted to prod him to keep going, I knew better. Besides, my mind flashed on the three of us turning into the parking lot of that church, of my father getting out and walking through the snow toward the red doors before disappearing inside, of me asking my mother, "Do you ever feel afraid?"

"I waited there," Lynch said at last, "bracing myself until the door opened and I heard your father call into the darkness, 'Rose?'

"'No,' I told him. 'It's me.'

"'Who?' he asked in a confused voice. And then he took a few steps closer into the darkness and said, '*Albert?* I don't understand. What are you doing here?'

"'I came to get answers about my daughter,' I told him. 'Once and for all.'

"Your father turned to go then, but I raced after him, tugging on his coat and pulling that pistol from my pocket, making sure he saw the flash of silver in the dim lights of your car through the stained-glass windows. 'You're not going anywhere,' I told him."

Lynch leaned back from the table. "There," he said. "Your turn."

This time, I didn't even look up at the clock. "I finished Abigail's nighttime ritual, then headed up to my bedroom and fell asleep. In the morning, I walked into the kitchen and heard my parents' voices in the basement, so I went down the stairs again. That's when they told me she was gone. Only the basement looked nothing like it had the night before."

"What do you mean?"

"Everything was strewn about. The things from my parents' work—a doll we kept in a cage was on the floor. A hatchet too. So many rings and trinkets and leftovers from their trips were scattered everywhere. It looked like—" I stopped, feeling an ache in my chest as I remembered the strained look on my father's face when he knelt on the floor to pick it all up. Then later as he wrote out that sign—DO NOT OPEN UNDER ANY CIRCUMSTANCES!— and attached it to the front of the doll's cage.

"Like what?" Lynch prodded.

"Like someone had done battle with a demon down there. At least that's what my father suggested."

"Uh-uh, Sylvie. You told me you weren't going to make the same claims as your father."

"That's not what I'm telling you," I said, thinking now of Heekin's book and the tapes from the interviews and the things Howie told me too. "I think my father wanted it to seem that way."

"Why?" Lynch said.

"It was one more story to tell. One more way to make people believe him."

"And what do you believe, Sylvie?"

"For a long time," I began, but stopped, thinking of all those words I'd put down in the pages of that journal, all the conversations I'd had over the last few days, the way certain details about my parents began to sift from the mess of our lives so that I began to see them differently than before. Again, I said, "For a long time, I wouldn't let myself think so many things. But now, well, I have come to believe that, for one, Abigail did plan to leave that night. That she only told me about her idea to slip out of the grocery store to put me off for a while. Who knows? Maybe she worried I'd change my mind during the night. Anyway, I think that after I left she opened that sliding glass door and stepped out into the night. And then, the next morning, as we all stood in the basement looking around at the chaos, we heard the knocking coming from upstairs."

"Knocking?" Lynch said.

"Yes," I told him. "It was you. You had come for your daughter."

"But what—"

"The church," I said, cutting him off.

Just then, the guard announced, "Time's up." From somewhere in the prison came a loud buzzing sound. I could hear the rumble of footsteps outside the walls of that room where we sat.

"The church!" I said. "Finish telling me about the church!"

The guard came up behind Lynch and put his hand on the man's arm, all but lifting him from the chair. When he was standing, Albert leaned forward and told me, "Your father gave me the same excuse he did that day I showed up knocking on your door. Demons had driven her away. He apologized. Oh, believe me, he apologized. I told him I didn't buy it. I had wanted to come earlier in the summer, but every time I called, he insisted that he and your mother wanted—*needed*—to keep Abigail longer in order to help her. And I just let him fleece me, sending money and apparently giving him one more story to tell in his lectures."

"The church," I said again. "Stick to the church."

"He said all the same things that night, but I still didn't believe him. And then your mother came inside. Your mother—she was different, Sylvie. You should know that much by now. Maybe she and your father were a team, but they were not the same. Somehow, and I'll never know exactly how, she managed to calm me down. She sat with me in a pew. She prayed with me while your father lingered in the shadows by the altar. And then I saw the person I had become: a man wielding a gun, making idle threats, looking for his daughter who had never wanted to be with him in the first place."

"So what did you do?"

"I tossed down my gun and fled the church through the front doors. I got in my van and drove toward the highway, faster than I should have in the snow. And then I stopped at that Texaco, where I saw that old man in the restroom and helped rescue his wife's dogs out in the parking lot. That's the truth, Sylvie. So help me, that's the truth."

As the guard pulled him back toward that door where he had entered, toward the sound of all those footsteps, I sat watching, thinking of that song my mother used to hum and trying my best to sense the truth inside him the way she believed I could. The moment the door clanged shut, Rummel and I were left in a vacuum of quiet. He approached and put his hand on my shoulder again. I stared down at his heavy black shoes a moment before getting up. The two of us were led by another guard back the way we came, through the series of doors and gates, until we were outside in the car.

As we drove away, I stared at all the barbed wire and thought of Dereck telling me to keep my fingers off the fence that first day we met in the field. For all I knew, he was slaughtering turkeys at that very moment, since Thanksgiving was only a few days away now.

"Are you okay?" the detective asked.

"Yes," I told him.

"You know, Sylvie, when you work long enough doing what I do, you begin to develop a sixth sense about people and whether or not they are guilty. But I've learned that no matter my feelings, I have to put them aside and look at the evidence and listen to the testimony. So that conversation in there, you shouldn't let it sway you too much one way or another. The facts are the facts."

"I understand," I said. And then at last I told him, "But I didn't see Mr. Lynch that night in the church."

The car wheels spinning on the pavement. The wind whistling through Rummel's partially opened window. The crackling static of his police radio. Those were the only sounds for some time. "Are you sure?" the detective asked finally.

"I'm sure," I said. "So what now?"

"We need to talk to Louise Hock. Like I told you, Lynch will be released. Since it's gotten so late in the day, all that's going to have to happen tomorrow. If you like, I can pick you up myself first thing in the morning."

That was the plan we made. And when he dropped me off at home, my gaze went to the empty front step. Emily Sanino was likely all done with those gifts, for a while anyway. Rose's truck was gone, and that yellow glow from the basement window shone even in the daylight.

Inside, I went to my parents' room where the red light on the answering machine was blinking away. I ignored it for the time being and went about finding my father's old cassette player tucked in his nightstand with an empty prescription container, and oddly, a wrench wrapped in a towel. I put that aside and, from my pocket, pulled the cassette tape that had been in Rummel's car. Since it was evidence, I figured he wouldn't let me keep it overnight. That's why I'd slipped it from the recorder when he let me back in the car at the prison and went around to the other side. Now, I popped in the tape and pressed Play. For a moment, there was nothing but static, and I thought perhaps this side of the tape had become warped after so long. But just as I was about to hit Fast Forward, a voice came alive in the room. Not my father's, but Heekin's. I turned the volume as loud as it could go.

HEEKIN:	As I've been writing the book, I've grown increasingly frustrated with some discrepancies in your narrative.
MY FATHER:	(woozy-voiced) You are beginning to sound like my brother and some of our other critics. I thought you had become a friend, Sam.
HEEKIN:	I am a friend. But I am also trying to do a job here. My job is to report the truth.
MY FATHER:	The truth is that a lot of the people who come to us are lost causes.
HEEKIN:	Lost causes?
MY FATHER:	Yes. I guess you could even say they're not all there. Crazy even. You know how I first started? By placing an ad in the back of a newspaper. "Help for the Haunted" it read then offered our services. Tell me, what sort of sane person answers an ad like that?
HEEKIN:	So what are you saying?
MY FATHER:	I'm saying write the book, make it appropriately scary and you'll have done your job. That's what people want, isn't it?

Heekin cleared his throat, and I had the sense this conversation had gone in a direction that left him flustered. He rambled and sputtered the way he did when he was nervous until there was a loud click and the tape went silent. And then, a moment later:

HEEKIN:	Can I ask about your children?
MY FATHER:	Sure.
MY MOTHER:	I'd rather you not.
MY FATHER:	My wife likes to keep our work and home life separate.
HEEKIN:	And you don't?
MY FATHER:	These things have a way of melding. Besides, I said you could ask, I did not say we would answer.
HEEKIN:	Well, then. Allow me to try. What do your daughters make of what you two do?
MY FATHER:	We don't talk too much about it.

His voice sounded clear, not at all woozy, and I realized the tape had cut to another conversation from some other time when my mother was present.

HEEKIN:	And do you find, Mrs. Mason, that either of your daughters shares your gift?
MY MOTHER:	I do, but let's leave it at that.
HEEKIN:	So they are accepting?
MY FATHER:	As much as any children are accepting of their parents. (Laugh) I guess what I am trying to say is that we are like any other parents. We are trying to raise our daughters with good Christian values in a world that is increasingly secular. It is not easy with all the immorality out there. Take our daughter, Rose—
MY MOTHER:	That's enough, Sylvester. We don't need to go into that.
MY FATHER:	(after a pause) My wife is right. See how much I need her to keep me in line? I guess I'll just say we've had more than our share of trouble with Rose. My wife and I have done a lot of praying that she will come around to our values again.
HEEKIN:	Values?
MY MOTHER:	I think we've gone as far as I feel comfortable on this topic. If you don't mind I'd like to conclude the interview for the day. Thank you very much.

This time when the tape went silent it stayed that way. A dull, empty hum filled my parents' bedroom. I sat there watching the wheels of the recorder spin round and round until I heard the sound of an engine and screechy music moving closer down the lane and coming to a stop in our driveway.

Instead of looking out the window, I went to the answering machine and pressed Play. "Sylvie, it's Sam Heekin. After you left that message last night, I did some digging. I uncovered some things you should know about. Call me right away." While that played, I pulled the newspaper article Dereck had given me from my pocket and stared at that picture again, my father's words about values ringing in my mind.

Rose had yet to walk through the front door, so I slipped down the hall to her room. Quickly, I slid open her nightstand and dug out that laminated prayer card she had saved. Clutching it, I went down the hall to our parents' room again and picked up the phone on their nightstand.

"Saint Julia's Home for Girls," a man's voice answered after I dialed the number on the back of that card.

It felt like ages since I'd made those survey calls, but I summoned that grown-up voice I used to interview all those people. "Hello," I told the man on the other end. "I'm looking for a school for my daughter."

I waited for a moment to see if he would ask how old I was. But he did not. "Well, this isn't exactly a school. You know that, don't you?'

"Yes. My daughter, um, she needs a place to go to"—I paused, remembering my father's long-ago words—"to get her head right. I assume that's the sort of situation you treat there."

"Yes. We treat young women who have developed a sexual confusion. One that goes against the teachings of the Bible," he told me. "But you should know we have rules. Once you sign your daughter into our care, you entrust her well-being with us. Our treatment is quite serious and not to be taken lightly. One of the first things we require is that no one from the outside have contact for the first thirty days of admission—"

The door opened and closed downstairs, and I slammed down the phone. Rose's feet came pounding up the steps. She rounded the corner and stopped when she saw me there, sitting on the edge of our mother's bed. "What the hell are you doing?" she asked.

I lifted that torn newspaper article, showing it to her the way I had been tempted to do for days. "Who is this in the picture with you?"

"What picture?"

I stood, walked closer to her out in the hallway. "This picture. It was taken after you came home from being sent away. After the accident where Dereck lost his fingers. Who is that with you?"

Rose made a show of squinting at the photo, but I had the sense she wasn't really looking. "I don't know. I have too much on my mind for your egghead crap today, Sylvie. I've signed up for GED classes and I have homework to do. You, more than anyone, should be able to sympathize with that."

"Franky?" I said.

"Who?" my sister asked, but I could hear a knowing quality in her voice.

"Frances? Frances Sanino, the daughter of Emily and Nick Sanino?"

Rose's face took on a stunned look, as though she'd been slapped, a look she quickly tried to conceal, pinching her lips together and sucking in a breath. "I don't know what you're talking about—"

"Yes, you do. Because her mother has been the one leaving food here on the steps. And I know why you didn't want us to eat it. It wasn't because you thought it was poisoned. It was because you were saving it for someone else. Franky."

"Shut up," Rose said. "Shut the hell up, Sylvie. You think it's easy for me? Do you? All I wanted was to be free of this place, and now I'm stuck here taking care of you. And what do I get in return? Nothing but a bunch of ungrateful back talk. I'm sick of it. So I'm going to my room. If I were you, I'd steer clear of me for the night, because now you've put me in a mood."

"I know!" I screamed at her. "I figured it all out!"

"You didn't figure anything out," Rose said. "You are crazy. You told the police and the reporters and everyone else that you saw Albert Lynch that night. And it turned out you were wrong, because that old couple came forward. Now you are waving some newspaper article around and getting ready to make God knows what new accusation. You think you are so smart, Sylvie, but you are dumb. Really, really dumb."

"You can say that all you want," I told her, stepping past her and starting down the stairs. "But I'm about to prove you wrong."

"Where are you going?"

I did not answer as I made my way to the first floor, then cut through the living room toward the door that led to the basement. The entire time Rose was right behind me. When I pulled open that door and stared down into the shadowy darkness below, lit only by that yellow glow, she stepped in front of me and said just one word: "No."

"Yes," I told her. "Now move."

Rose lifted her hands and shoved me. I stumbled back, losing my balance and falling. The newspaper article slipped from my hands, landing in the space between us. I stared at my sister's sneakers on her small feet, thinking of that day in the truck when I crawled around, scraping for the money I'd earned only to end up with loose change.

All our lives together, Rose won every fight with her words and with her might. Never once did I stand a chance. But now as my hands began to shake, as my heart banged in my chest, I stood and reached up and, with everything I had in me, I shoved her back. In an instant, she lost her footing and stumbled toward those stairs. For a moment, it seemed like we could stop what came next. She reached her hand out, and I grabbed for it, because I hadn't meant for this to happen. But our hands didn't catch one another in time, and so she tumbled backward down the stairs.

After Rose hit the cement floor with a great crash, a thick silence followed. I thought of that cassette tape when my parents' voices had stopped, those tiny wheels spinning round and round as their words echoed in my mind: *I guess what I am trying to say is that we are like any other parents. We are trying to raise our daughters with good Christian values in a world that is increasingly secular.* A feeling of shame, a feeling of pure horror, filled me up at the realization of what I'd done. Useless as it sounded, I spoke to her down in the basement. "I'm sorry, Rose. I'm so so sorry."

My sister did not respond, and the dread that this could be more grave an accident than I first understood took hold. I pounded down the steps to where she lay, her right leg bent in the most unnatural position. "Are you okay?" I asked. "Please tell me you are okay."

"It's my leg," she said, and I heard in her voice that she was crying, releasing the kind of exhausted sobs I'd never heard from Rose before. "You did something to my leg."

Those flyers on the bulletin board at the police station—in my panic, they came back to me. Hadn't one advised never to move a person in the event of an accident? Get help—that was always the advice. I was about to go back upstairs to the phone and do just that when Rose spoke through her tears, "Remember that rule they always used to say?"

"Who?" I asked.

"Mom and Dad. The rule that we could always tell them whatever we were thinking or feeling, and they would do their best to understand. Do you remember that, Sylvie?"

"Yes," I told her. "But let's not—"

"It wasn't true," Rose said. "It wasn't true."

I didn't want to talk about any of that now, but even so, I heard myself asking, "What do you mean?"

"When I was fourteen, I first told them. They encouraged it, after all, always repeating that dumb rule. But when I said I felt different from other girls, you know what they did? They acted like it was some sort of fucking *possession*. They prayed over me like one of those supposedly haunted people who came here in need of their help. And they told me to keep my feelings a secret. The more it didn't change, though, the more they prayed. I tried to give them the daughter they wanted. I tried to be more like you. I brought all those boys home. But it didn't work. So they sent me away to that home where I was supposed to get better. And you know what? I did get better. I met Franky.

"Even though Franky's parents had sent her there too, she already knew the place was a joke. She made me realize there was nothing wrong with the way I felt." Rose's words sputtered out as her crying grew stronger. "'Her coming was my hope each day,'" she said in a broken voice, "'her parting was my pain; the chance that did her steps delay. Was ice in every vein.'"

"Rose, I don't know what you're talking about. But we've got to get—"

"Those are the words from that book you used to underline. *Jane Eyre*. I remember it, because it's how I felt about Franky. And anyway, we planned to get out of there and save money and find some way to live a normal life together in time. But when I got home, I'd already been replaced by Abigail. So I gave up trying. And the fights with Mom and Dad—Dad, in particular—got worse. And so one night I'm out. And who do I run into but Albert Lynch?"

"I know," I told her. "You don't have to say. We need to get you help. And I told you, I figured it all out."

"No, you didn't!" she screamed. "Because I bet you didn't figure out the way I felt in all of this, did you?"

The rage, the sadness—those things in her voice frightened me into silence.

"Did you?" she screamed.

I shook my head.

"Fifty bucks to talk to Mom and Dad. That's what he offered me. And happily, I arranged it. But Franky knew what I was up to. She was the one with me at the bar, after all. Since I wasn't of age, she kept sneaking in and getting us drinks then bringing them out to the car. After I made the call to Mom and Dad, she gave me some bullshit excuse that she wanted to go back to a friend's house where she'd been staying ever since we left Saint Julia's. So I let her go. Only Franky didn't go to her friend's. She went to see them at the church too."

Rose stopped. For a moment, I caught us both looking around that basement, the strange world my parents had created down there. That hatchet on the wall. The old branch with what looked like a howling face in the bark. The dozens of trinkets and objects hanging from the ceiling and filling the shelves. Those dusty old books about demons. And, of course, Penny in the old rabbit cage, smiling that placid smile.

DO NOT OPEN UNDER ANY CIRCUMSTANCES!

The sign was still there just the same.

"You know what can make a person possessed, Sylvie? It's not Satan or Lucifer or any of that nonsense. Do you know what it is?"

"What?" I asked her, desperate to let her finish so I could get help.

"Love and hate. Greed. Revenge. Pride. Those things turned Dad into his own demon. He knew the things he was doing were dishonest. Mom's gift wasn't powerful or controllable enough for him. He needed something greater to get the attention he craved. He needed all of us to support his stories, so he set out to make us believers too."

Famous? I remembered the way my father shimmied against that nozzle, rain sopping his hair, dripping from his lashes as he said, *Well, now that you mention it, I suppose it would be nice to show them.*

"And so, when those people stayed here in the basement, he messed with them. Putting all kinds of pills he had access to in their food. They weren't in their right minds to begin with, but after he messed with them, who knows what sort of delusions they experienced? It was the same with Mom. He did it to her. Abigail too—"

"How do you know that?"

"You think you're the only one to figure things out? I watched him. Made a study out of it. And I caught him one day in the kitchen crushing a pill and mixing it into some food. When I asked, he told me it was just some medicine. But I knew better. I'd read those labels on the prescription containers in his desk drawer. And the fact that I knew he was a fraud only made him resent me more."

I pressed my face into my hands, remembering my mother being so ill and unlike herself after that trip to Ohio. Had he done that to her because she wanted to stop their work the way Heekin told me? Or was it so that she would have no choice but to believe in the power of Penny and so many other claims he made? Is that why Abigail did not feel well that last night? There was so much to understand but I found myself asking, "What did you mean about love and hate? Were you talking about Dad?"

"Yes. But I mean me and Franky too," she said. "Those things made us demons as well. First her. And then me."

I waited for her to tell me more, but she was crying again.

"Rose," I said, deciding once and for all that this conversation had to wait. "I am going to call an ambulance. We need to get you help."

I stood, went up the stairs. In the kitchen, I walked to the phone on the wall, only when I picked it up, there was no dial tone. I clicked the receiver a few times, but the line was dead.

Hands shaking still, I went to the freezer and pulled out an ice tray to get ice for Rose's leg. But the tray was empty. Instead, I grabbed a bunch of Popsicles, wrapped them in a dishtowel, and rushed back down the stairs.

In the brief time I had been upstairs, the air in the basement had changed. Outside the window, the light was just the same. That bare, yellowy bulb still glowed on the ceiling as well. The dank, loamy smell still hung in the air. And yet, I had the sense that something had shifted. "Rose," I said, pressing that cool towel to her leg. "The phone isn't working."

"Sylvie, you better go."

"What? Go where?"

"Anywhere. Just not here."

"I'm not leaving you."

I heard a sound in the corner of the basement then, from behind that partition. I stood, remembering the reason I had been so determined to come down here in the first place. I thought of Emily Sanino humming "Happy Birthday." I thought of that cake she left. I thought of all those can-

dles too. And then I walked over and stepped to the other side of that pan-
eled wall. There was only the empty cot covered with rumpled sheets. On
the small dresser by the sliding door that led out onto the backyard, I saw
a stack of empty Tupperware containers that had been left on our stoop.

I stepped back to the other side and looked at my sister, who had
propped herself up into a slumped position against the stairs and was nursing her leg. "So those noises I heard, they were her?"

Rose nodded. "She was here for a few weeks after the murders. But
then we agreed she had to go. Any plans we had made could no longer be.
At least not until you were grown and gone and nobody suspected anything. But then—"

Again, I heard a noise somewhere behind me in the basement. I turned
and looked into the shadows, where my father's old dental chair remained
untouched still. Just beyond, I could see the fuse box and a tangle of wires
on the wall. It was then that I realized the phone cord had been cut. I was
not sure what to do so I turned back to Rose. "But then what?"

"But then Franky didn't stay away. She couldn't. And the truth was, I
didn't want her to. So without telling me beforehand, she came back. On
Halloween night, while I was out and you were here alone, she slipped in
through the sliding door and waited for me. That's when you first saw the
light on again. I told her it was better to just leave it on, because I knew it
would keep you from coming down here, since you thought it had to do
with Mom and Dad and the things they did when they were alive. I knew
you still believed."

I stood for a moment, staring at my sister, wondering how she was
capable of keeping so much hidden for so long. "Did you . . ."

"Did I what?"

"Did you kill them?"

She shook her head.

"Say it!" I shouted. "I want to hear you tell me that you didn't!"

"No," she said, crying and shaking her head more. "No. No. No. It was
Franky. She did it, Sylvie."

I felt cold all over. Pinpricks up my arms and down my legs and across
my stomach. My entire body was shivering now and I could do nothing to

stop it. Voice trembling, I asked, "How could you cover for her, Rose? How could you let me go on thinking I had seen someone I did not?"

"Because I loved her. And she did it because she loved me."

No noise came from behind me, but I saw Rose's gaze shift over my shoulder. I felt a presence there, and so I turned around.

For an instant, all those pictures in the living room of Emily Sanino flashed in my mind. I saw the young woman before me as a dark-haired toddler in a pink dress, a few years older at the beach in a bright one-piece bathing suit, as a lanky adolescent with a mouth full of braces and a T-shirt that said GOD'S LOVE SUMMER CAMP. I remembered the trophies with the little golden girl on top. Track awards. And now that track star Rose had dated was standing before me, head shaved to the scalp just as it must have been that night at the church, one of the few details that had led me to believe it was Albert Lynch who knocked me down on his way out the door. In one ear, she sported a small silver cross, the sort my mother used to wear, but the effect was menacing instead of peaceful. When she spoke, her voice was more composed than I would have imagined. She asked, "What did you do to Rose?"

Voice still trembling, I told her, "She fell."

"She fell? Or you pushed her?"

My sister spoke before I could. "Franky, leave Sylvie alone."

"Why?" Franky said. "She's the same as your parents. No good for you."

"I don't care," Rose said. "Leave her alone. Let me handle this."

"You've been handling this for months and where has it gotten us?" Franky shouted. "Look at the mess she's made of you."

She stepped out of the shadows then, coming closer. I thought of that night last winter, the sound of the gun so close to my ear before I fell to the floor and crawled beneath that pew. Like some sort of alarm the *shhhh* seemed to grow louder in that instant, so loud I almost did not hear Rose shouting, "Sylvie! Run! Get out of here!"

I turned toward the stairs and stepped over my sister's leg, bent the wrong way still, like those turkeys in the field on the other side of the woods. But I only made it up a few steps before I felt a hand snatch the back of my old T-shirt. I grabbed the banister and hung on as Franky pulled and pulled, until finally, I felt the fabric start to give and then suddenly the shirt came completely free. The dank air against my bare skin sent a shiver snaking through me as the sudden shift of pressure caused me to stumble forward. My hand slipped through the space between the slatted wooden steps, and Franky came around and grabbed it from beneath. I wrenched my hand free, pulling away from her with such force that I stumbled back down the stairs again, barely missing my sister.

"Stop it!" Rose screamed as I scrambled to my feet. "Please stop!"

"I'm not stopping," Franky told her, "because if she gets out of here, she's going to tell the police and everyone what she's learned. And then you and me, Rose, we are going to be sent away for a long time. And where they put us is going to make Saint Julia's look like a funhouse. I'm not letting that happen to us."

I looked at my sister's contorted face and could see tears rolling down her cheeks, shimmering in the yellow light. "I'm sorry, Sylvie," she said. "I'm so, so sorry. I never wanted it to be this way. I know you won't believe that, but I didn't want any of this."

What would I have told her if I had the chance? That I forgave her? That I understood? That I would make sure things would turn out okay? But none of those things was true in the moment. The most I knew was that I felt trapped there in the basement, since Franky had made her way around from the back of the stairs and was now holding the hatchet from the massacre at that old New Hampshire farm turned inn. I thought of the Locke family my father talked about in his lectures, the bloody end the mother and children all met, the way their souls were said to haunt that old hotel for years afterward.

As if to warn me that she intended the same fate for me, Franky reached up and whacked the hatchet into the stairs. The blade sunk into the wood and she yanked it back out. It caused Rose to let out a shriek.

And then Franky reached up and used the hatchet to smash the lightbulb. In an instant, the basement grew dark and full of more shadows, lit only by the stray shafts of sunlight that made its way through the casement window. I turned and ran toward the partition. Tangled in the blankets, I saw something I had not noticed before. When I pulled back the covers, there it was: my journal, wide open and facedown. There was no time to reach for it, so I went to the sliding glass door just beyond. When I tried to pull it open, nothing moved. I looked down and saw a broomstick wedged at the base to keep the door from opening. I pulled and pulled on the broomstick, but she must have nailed it there, because it would not budge.

When I turned, Franky was watching me calmly since she knew I could not get out that way. The only thing I could think to do was to reach for those Tupperware containers. I picked them up and hurled them at her, then stumbled toward the dental chair, where I reached into a nearby drawer, grabbed a handful of old dental tools, and hurled them at her too. None of it did anything to keep her from coming closer still, moving steadily, as though nothing would ever stop her from attacking me with that hatchet.

I ran to the hulking bookshelf, thinking I could pull it down to get into the crawl space. Penny and the cage wobbled on top as I reached around the back and began pulling. The bookshelf rocked a bit, but was too heavy. One by one, I began throwing those old tomes about demons and possessed girls my age from so long ago at Franky. She just swatted them away with the hatchet while I exhausted myself. When I cleared the shelves of most of the contents, at last I pulled again and this time knocked the entire piece of furniture over. That shelf and the remaining books and the old rabbit cage and Penny went toppling down in a loud clatter. I wasted no time pulling my body up into the gaping hole in the cinder-block wall that led to the crawl space. Only once did I glance back to see that Penny had come free from her cage and landed, lifeless and still, on the cement floor while Franky stood there looking momentarily stunned by it all.

I kept moving, crawling into the darkness, the only light a small rectangle in the distance created by an air vent on the other side of the house. My hands were grimy with dirt by the time I reached that light. I put my fingers on the metal grate and pulled. Who knew how many years it had been there. Long enough that it wiggled the slightest bit but refused to come loose.

Behind me, I could hear grunting as Franky lifted herself into the crawl space too. It made me tug on the grate even more frantically. Over the sound of the *shhhh,* I heard her drawing closer with every second. *Soon, she will be upon me,* I told myself, *and it will all come to an end there in the darkness beneath our house.*

With every last bit of strength I could muster, I pulled on that vent until it came loose. Fast as I could, I slid my body out into the daylight. As my feet were about to slip free, I felt Franky grab at them. But I kicked and wriggled loose before she could get hold. And when I was standing, I turned to see her hands reaching out from the vent. It would not stop her, I knew, but I stomped my foot on her fingers. The force caused her to release a loud howl, and another when I stomped again.

As Franky withdrew her hands into the crawl space, I looked around and wondered where to go. That's when I thought of Dereck on the other side of those woods, slaughtering turkeys in time for Thanksgiving. I began running across the street, toward the path beyond the first of those empty foundations.

But Franky had made her way out of the crawl space by then and started running too. Just as I got to the edge of the foundation, she caught up and shoved me so hard from behind that I found myself falling over the edge. I landed in a murky puddle at the bottom and looked up to see Franky standing up above. My mind felt so dizzy that her image shifted and reshaped itself.

My back, my arms, my legs—*all of me*—felt in too much agony to move. And yet, I needed to since she was making her way to the crumbling cement stairs. As I lay there, so many memories and thoughts flashed in my mind: There was Abigail drawing a map on the walls around me the night before she left. There was my sister and me creating the details for our imaginary home over and over again: a window, a painting, a doorway. There were my parents, who had come to this neighborhood and bought the lot across the street, starting their lives out like any other new couple. How could they have known they'd be the only people ever to live here? How could they have known how horribly wrong things would go for them . . . and for all of us?

I tried to get up. The most I managed was to roll over onto my stomach as the murky water splashed around me, soaking my jeans and sneakers. Franky ambled down the stairs, slipping on the rocks but not falling, hurrying to reach me. When she did, she grabbed a hank of my hair and pushed my face into that dirty puddle, holding me there so that I was unable to breathe.

The *shhhh* in my ear grew louder still, the sound warping itself into something higher pitched and hysterical. And then it became an altogether different sound—it became a kind of tune instead, one I recognized. For the first time, I heard the words as my mother's lilting voice sang that song she used to hum:

> We gather together to ask the Lord's blessing;
> He chastens and hastens His will to make known.
> The wicked oppressing now cease from distressing.
> Sing praises to His Name; He forgets not His own.

Franky lifted my head by the hair and yanked me out of that water. For a few fleeting seconds, I saw the cracked gray walls of the foundation. I saw the fading daylight. I saw the fallen leaves around us. And then she shoved my head down, smashing my face against the cement. In the white light and blistering pain that followed, that *shhhh* warped itself into the sound of my mother's voice once more. I heard her there, so close now, singing that old choir song to me:

> Beside us to guide us, our God with us joining,
> Ordaining, maintaining His kingdom divine;
> So from the beginning the fight we were winning;
> Thou, Lord, were at our side, all glory be Thine!

Again, Franky lifted my head, and again she brought it down. The force was so great that this time it felt as though the world had stopped. I tried to open my eyes but could not. I heard no sounds, not even my mother's singing.

And then, after what felt like a long stretch of time, my eyes blinked open into the gloom of that water, and I had a vision of her: my mother, standing on the other side of some great abyss, that dirty water an ocean between us. She wore the beige trench coat from the video I played that day in the basement so long ago while Rose messed with the fuse box and Dot bathed in the tub upstairs reading her silly book. For a moment, the image flickered and blurred just as it had done that day on the TV screen.

I'm losing her, I thought. *Once again, I will have to let her go.* But then her image sharpened. And when her lips moved, she spoke in a serious voice.

"This is what I will tell you, Sylvie," my mother said. "Each of us is born into this life with a light inside us. Some, like yours, burn brighter than others. As you grow older you will come to understand why. But what's most important is to never ever let that light go out. Do you understand what I am trying to say?"

"Yes," I opened my mouth to tell her, only to take in more dirty water, swallowing it, filling my lungs.

"That's a good girl," she said. "It won't be easy, but you have to believe. And you have to fight. Okay?"

This time, I knew better than to open my mouth to answer. Besides, it no longer mattered, because that ghost, that globule, that memory of her—whatever it was—had vanished into that murky green water. At the same time, Franky made her greatest effort yet. She lifted my head by the hair. And when I was delivered back into that world of air and fallen leaves and the gray autumn sky growing dim above, my free hand scrambled along the cement floor until I found what I needed. Before she could send me down a final time, I squirmed around until I was on my back, pinned beneath her. And then I used my free hand to bring a rock against the side of her head.

Once. Twice. A third and fourth time, until I saw blood. After that, her body went slack and she fell to one side of me.

For a moment, after I let the rock drop, I lay there catching my breath. As soon as I could manage, I forced myself out from under her. I stood, wet and bloodied, and looked down at Franky. Her back rose and fell with each breath, but otherwise she was motionless.

I walked away from her and began the climb up those crumbling stairs. At the top, I stared back at my house. All those NO TRESPASSING! signs my father had nailed to the birch trees, which had done nothing to keep danger away. My sister was still inside, and though I thought to go and help her, I chose the path instead. Dripping and muddy and shirtless, I stumbled along the twisted trail to the field, where I stood so many mornings and afternoons. Over that barbed fence I climbed, careful not to do any more damage to myself. I walked across the trampled grass, where those turkeys had been for so long, most of them gone now. I kept going until I reached the doors of the barn.

"Dereck!" I called, knocking and knocking. "Dereck!"

When no answer came, I slid the doors open. A man who was not Dereck stood on the other side, wearing headphones and chopping meat on a wooden block. He had gray hair and a kind face. He looked the way I imagined my mother's father to have looked. When he saw me, he yanked the headphones from his ears and came to me. "What happened to you, young lady?"

"I'm here for Dereck," I told him.

The man removed his white smock and draped it over my shoulders. He led me through a maze of shelves and bins and small cages to a back room, where the air was chilled. He told me to wait a few seconds. And it really did seem like just a few seconds before Dereck appeared, covered in blood too.

He took one look at me, then went to a locker across the room and pulled out his battered barn jacket. Like that day I had jumped from my sister's truck, he offered it to me, this time slipping it over my arms and zipping up the front. As he did, I began to cry, the tears warm against my skin. Dereck put his arms around me. "What happened?" he asked and asked again, though I could not force the answer from my mouth. Not right away. Not for some time to come. And still he kept repeating that question, "What happened? What happened? What happened?"

But the words would not come. All I could do was take his ruined hand in mine and lead him away from the farm, back across that trampled field, back over the barbed-wire fence, along that twisted path in the woods toward home.

FARAWAY PLACES

I did not take much from the house when I moved out. My journal, of course. That lone white horse Rose had given me, the only one that had never been broken. A bag full of clothes. My mother's silver cross necklace, which I have not taken off, even seven months later, along with her slim gold watch I use to tell time. With the exception of a few other odds and ends, I left the rest behind. It would be boxed up, I was told, put into storage or sold off. My father's old competition, Dragamir Albescu, surfaced and offered good money for the haunted artifacts in our basement. Rather than let the man pick and choose like some sort of rummage sale, my uncle offered him an all-or-nothing deal. In the end, every last relic from their unusual career—including the hatchet from the Locke Family Farm, Penny in Mr. Knothead's cage, even my father's old dental chair and my mother's rocker—all of it was loaded onto a moving truck headed for Marfa, Texas, where Mr. Albescu maintains the Marfa Museum of the Paranormal.

Before he and the movers drove away, Albescu told my uncle that a special room would be dedicated just to my parents and their contribution to the field. When Howie made some mention of Heekin's book and asked if the things he had written might keep people away, Albescu waved one of his jeweled hands in the air and scoffed, "Not at all. In fact, these things in our line of work are like a shuttlecock in the game of badminton. They need to be swatted back and forth in order to keep people paying attention." Then he told us that we were welcome to visit the museum anytime, free of charge.

I can't imagine a day will ever come when I'll want to do that.

My life is different now. And the way things are looking, it is going to get more different as time moves forward, though I don't think I'll ever forget the life we lived in that house on Butter Lane as Rose once predicted. At the moment, I am staying a few towns over in Howard County, at the home of a couple named Kevin and Beverly. They take in foster children, which for the time being anyway, I am.

When I arrived on their doorstep, escorted by a brand-new caseworker, and carting along my journal, that horse, a bag of clothes, and only a few other possessions, they told me their names were easy to remember, because they rhyme. My mind was in such a daze still that I could not understand how that made any sense. But then Beverly—who wears a never-ending supply of oversized sweatshirts in bright pastels and keeps her hair tugged back in a never-ending supply of scrunchies—let out a bubbling, infectious laugh and said, "You know, *Kev* and *Bev*. It'll be hard for you to forget us, Sylvie. Trust me. Now come on in."

They showed me to my room, which is clean and simply furnished. There is a single bed with an oak headboard, a matching dresser and night-stand with a simple white lamp on top. The window beside the bed looks out over their fenced yard. The view is not unlike the one I used to draw outside the imaginary windows on the walls of the old foundation across the street. It is late spring now, so I see tufts of grass out there and all sorts of colorful flowers. Most days, there is a bright sun shining in the sky. Sometimes, I sit quietly in that room on the edge of the bed and spin my sister's globe, which was another thing I took from our house. When I plunk my finger on a random location—Tokyo, San Francisco, Mexico City—I think of the way she used to do the same.

Places like that—faraway places, I mean—they're where I want to go someday . . .

I hear her voice saying those words and, inevitably, I think of that final afternoon when I took Dereck's hand and walked back through the woods. I should have noticed that Rose's truck was gone from the driveway. But we were too preoccupied by the sight at the bottom of the foundation.

When I'd fled not long before, I remembered glancing behind to see her back rising and falling. Now, though, the body had gone motionless. Whatever I'd done in the commotion with that rock had brought an end to a life down there. The sight made me shudder, and Dereck pulled me away across the lane.

"Rose!" he called, pushing open the door to our house.

The antique clock ticked. The oversized cross hung on the wall. The curio hutch showcased my father's haphazard stacks or books behind the glass. Considering all that had occurred, it seemed even those things should offer an indication of being altered somehow. And yet, it all remained the same, indifferent as ever.

"Hello!" Dereck called when we did not hear an answer.

Words refused to come to me still, but with my hand in his, I guided us to the kitchen and that door to the basement. For a long moment, we stood at the top of the wooden stairs that so many of those haunted people had clomped down in hopes of leaving their demons behind. We stared into the shadowy space, where I had last seen my sister. There was my torn T-shirt. There was the dishtowel with Popsicle juice dripping in all sorts of bright colors from the steps to the cement below. But there was no Rose.

It must have been the man who first opened the door back at the farm who thought to call the police, because soon sirens wailed in the distance and drew closer. Before long, car doors slammed outside, footsteps pounded up the front steps and around back of the house. At least a half-dozen officers arrived on the scene, maybe more. Many of them I recognized from the hallways at the station, or perhaps in my vague, flickering memories of that winter night when I was pulled from beneath the pew at the church. The last to arrive was Detective Rummel, since he had already gone home for the day. By then, Dereck and I were sitting on the steps outside. Yellow police tape had already been set up around the foundation across the street. Officers were unspooling even more around our yard too, stringing it among the birch and cedar trees. I wore Dereck's barn jacket still and rocked and back and forth, since my body carried a chill I could not shake.

Same as he did that first day at the hospital, Rummel took my hand in his. He spoke gently, saying, "Tell me what happened, Sylvie."

And so, at last, I found the words to tell him all that I'd come to know and exactly how I'd come to know it. The story took time as I explained about my visits with Father Coffey and Sam Heekin and my uncle and, of course, Emily Sanino. It took longer still to tell him about Abigail and my parents and the things I'd learned about my father. After a long while, though, I came to the end of that story. When I finished speaking, the detective gazed at me with his bright blue eyes and asked the very question I'd been wondering since returning to the house: "Where is your sister?"

Seattle. Montreal. Madrid.

Sometimes, I sit on the bed in my room at Kev and Bev's house and spin that globe, imagining I know the answer. I try to picture her life in any one of those places. I try to imagine her happy too, which I hope is so. The most I know for certain, the most the police know as well, is that her truck was found the next day in a rest stop off the highway in Pikesville, Maryland. Whatever money she had, Rose took from the house, right down to the coins inside the old doorbell box, which she had put there as a child, not knowing that someday she would rip it off the wall and retrieve every cent before leaving home forever.

These days, Howie comes to visit me quite a bit. Often, he is full of updates, since he's been working with the courts again in an effort to be appointed my legal guardian. His plan—*our* plan, I can safely say as the days pass and we spend more time in each other's company—is that I will go to live with him in a new apartment he is renting in Philadelphia. The place is situated on a quiet street, near a good school, and has a second bedroom that he says I can decorate any way I want in the few years I have left before college. The theater is up and running again, and even though there's only a smattering of bands booked to play the stage in the summer ahead, Howie tells me it's a sign that someday there will be more. When I mention those details to Kev and Bev and the caseworker who comes by regularly to check on me, they all say the same thing: a good home and a successful business will work wonders in helping my uncle to get custody this time around.

Howie sold off his motorcycle and bought a Jeep like Dereck's. On the days when he visits, we take rides together, usually going by the old house just to look at the place with a For Sale sign out front. Even though I avoid the newspapers still, my uncle told me there was a recent story in the *Dundalk Eagle* by Sam Heekin about a new developer who plans to buy up all the properties on the lane, finish building houses atop those forgotten foundations at last, then sell them off. So far, things there look the same, but I can already picture what it will become, since I'd been imagining real houses there for years.

Just today, when my uncle came to get me, the weather was warm enough that the top was off the Jeep. He asked if I wanted to take our usual route by the house, but I told him there was another errand I needed to run first. Rather than pull my hair back as we drove, I let it whip around me the way Rose used to do, the way Abigail used to do too. My hand surfed the wind, and I did my best to stay out of my head as I'd been taught that summer on our way to and from the ice cream shop and the pond.

By the time we pulled in front of the school, it was nearly the end of the day. Since I'd opted to finish the academic year with a home tutor, I had not been inside the building for months. It was the last day before summer vacation, and when I walked past the smoking area beneath the overhang with its ratty furniture, on through the front door, the air hummed with a palpable excitement. I moved through the halls until arriving at the windowless office Boshoff shared. Inside, I found him peeling his Just Say No posters off the wall, rolling them up, one by one. I stood in the doorway, watching him a moment before he saw me.

"Sylvie," he said, smiling. "What a nice surprise. Please, come in. Sit."

I stepped into the space but did not sit. "I can't stay long. My uncle is waiting."

Boshoff put down the posters, and we stood gazing around at the walls covered with bits of stray tape. Everything else was gone. "Each June," he said, "the maintenance crew tells me and the other faculty to leave the place bare, so they can paint over the break. The thing is, they say that every year and no one ever does a thing."

We both laughed, and that's when I handed him the package I'd brought, wrapped up with a bow.

"Sylvie, you didn't need to get me a gift."

"I wanted to," I told him.

Boshoff tried his best to neatly undo the paper before giving up and simply tearing it open. Inside, he found a cookbook—not one I'd bought, but rather, one I'd made by gluing a wallpaper swatch over two pieces of cardboard then sandwiching a dozen or so empty pages inside. With duct tape from Kev's toolbox, I bound it into a book, which looked less home-made than I imagined. Even if I never managed to find wallpaper that perfectly matched my personality, I found one that suited Boshoff's book just fine. The Keep Calm—that's what it was called. The pattern was the deep blue of a nighttime sky with a dusting of dim yellow stars placed here and there. It seemed the sort of thing that might calm anybody who had trouble sleeping at night.

I watched as Boshoff opened the book to see that I'd filled the pages with recipes. Beef barley soup. Pork piccata. Lady Baltimore Cake. Those and the others were the meals my mother used to make during my child-hood. Before leaving home, I'd found them written in her careful cursive on index cards she kept tucked in a kitchen drawer. It seemed important that she be remembered for something besides the strange artifacts on display in that room in Marfa, Texas. What I wanted was for some people—even if it was just the two of us—to remember her as a mother first, because that was the more important role she played during her time in this world. For that reason, I also filled the last of those pages with passages I once under-lined in the books she made me read, like:

> If all the world hated you and believed you wicked, while your own conscience approved of you and absolved you from guilt, you would not be without friends.

That was just one, but there were others. I thought those lines were like poetry in their own way too, because you had to stop and think about them in order to understand their connection to things around you.

Boshoff turned the pages, clacking a cough drop against his teeth, but not saying a word. After some time, I worried he did not understand what it was meant to be, so I explained, then finished by saying, "It's just a little something to read at night when you can't sleep. That's all. Anyway, how is your wife?"

When he looked up, I could see his eyes were rimmed with red at the lids. He blinked a few times, and I thought he was about to deliver sad news when he told me, "You are a very thoughtful young lady, Sylvie. Thank you for this book. It will remain special to me, always. And thank you for remembering my wife too. You'll be glad to know that she's doing well actually. In remission for a few months now, which is the biggest blessing we could ask for." He closed the book and said he wanted to save it to read at night the way I intended. "Now, tell me about you. How is your ear?"

"My uncle took me to a doctor," I said. "Turns out the *shhhh* I heard all this time is caused by tinnitus brought on by the gunshot that night in the church. The doctor said it will come and go for a long time, since there's no cure."

"I'm sorry."

"Don't be. It seems to be getting quieter every day actually. I get the feeling that, pretty soon, I won't hear it at all."

"That's happy news. And your sister? Have you heard anything?"

"No word," I told him, thinking of that globe spinning and spinning, all those faraway places. "But someday, a long time from now, I bet I'll hear from her."

"Well, it is important to stay hopeful," Boshoff told me.

With that, the bell rang. The sound broke some spell between us as the halls filled with the roar of students eager to leave this part of their lives behind and start the next. I supposed I was one of those students now too. "I should go," I said. "While I can still escape the stampede."

"Okay, Sylvie. Thank you again for thinking of me."

"Thank you," I told him.

When I stepped into the hallway, I turned in the direction of the crowd, which did not part the way it used to do, but rather, carried me along until I was moving out the front doors into the daylight once more. When I climbed into the Jeep, my uncle was waiting for me. He had rolled down his sleeves so I could see only a hint of his tattoos, not that I minded them. "All set?" he asked.

"All set."

We managed to beat the buses and pull onto the main road ahead of the traffic. Howie asked if I wanted to go by the old house or maybe go visit Dereck at the garage, which was something we sometimes did. But I told him that maybe we could skip those things for today. Instead, we turned up the radio and just drove for a while, as I leaned back and felt the sun on my face. Sometimes, when we were together, I glanced over and glimpsed my father in his resemblance. Whenever that happened, my mind flashed on the morning I went down to the basement to find Abigail gone and my father cleaning up the chaos with a strained look on his face. Why had she decided to go against our plan and leave during the night, stopping at Father Coffey's house on the way? And when my father discovered her gone, did he decide right then and there to make it look as though she had left on account of those things in our basement, arranging the scene just so in order to support that story? And did that wrench wrapped in a towel in his nightstand have something to do with those horses and the way they were broken? Some answers, I still did not know and supposed I never would. Mostly, I found myself wondering if he really did send Rose away because of his beliefs or if it was simply convenient once she caught on to what he was doing.

When all that becomes too much to think about, I turn to my journal still. There was only a handful of empty pages left when I arrived at Kev and Bev's, and I've since filled them with those things I wonder about, hoping the answers might be made clear. Just last night, in fact, I realized I had come to the final page. Instead of putting down any more questions, I decided to write about something else instead. This is what I wrote:

> Sometimes at night, when it is dark inside my room, I get down on my knees to pray. First, I pray for my sister. And then I pray for my parents' souls. Whenever I do that, I feel something change in the air around me. It is more than their memory returning; it feels like their spirits. Despite all the things that haunted my mother and father during their time in this world, despite the mistakes they made too, the feeling of having them close brings me comfort somehow.
>
> When I am finished praying and get into bed and close my eyes, I picture my father. Only not the person I knew. Instead, I conjure him as a young boy standing in the dark of that theater, watching shadows dance around him, having no idea about the truth of what they were and how they would change the course of his life.

*And then I think of my mother beside me, hair fanned all around
on the pillow the way it had been that night in our motel room so long
ago. If I keep my eyes closed, I feel her there again. I hear her breath,
hear her voice telling me, "Each of us is born into this life with a light
inside of us . . . What's most important is to never let that light go out,
because when you do, it means you've lost yourself to the darkness.
It means you've lost your hope. And hope is what makes this world a
beautiful place. Do you understand what I am trying to say?"*

I think about those words a lot, and I think about their spirits too.

If you believe in those sorts of things.

I do and I don't believe.

But mostly—mostly, mostly—I do.

Acknowledgments

I'd like to thank three amazing women in my life who make everything happen: My talented, insightful, and patient editor, Kate Nintzel, read endless drafts and helped to shape this story and keep it moving. My incredible literary agent, Joanna Pulcini, offered inspiration and devoted countless hours discussing these characters and figuring out their world. And Sharyn Rosenblum, my friend and book publicist, brings boundless energy and so much fun to our work together.

Also at HarperCollins, I am enormously grateful to Liate Stehlik, Michael Morrison, Lynn Grady, Virginia Stanley, Kayleigh George, Annie Mazes, Tavia Kowalchuk, Carla Parker, Beth Silfin, Andrea Molitor, Laurie McGee, Kim Chocolaad, Caitlin McCaskey, Erin Simpson, Jennifer Civiletto, and Margaux Weisman.

I am indebted to the Corporation of Yaddo, where I began writing this story in earnest while living in an old Tudor in the woods not unlike Sylvie's old Tudor in the woods. In particular, Elaina Richardson, Candace Wait, and Jonathan Santlofer helped immensely with my two generous residencies there.

Also tremendously helpful were homicide detective Dennis Harris of the Boston Police Department and Cory Flashner, the assistant district attorney of Suffolk County, Massachusetts, who sat with me in an interview room at the station and answered my endless "what if?" questions.

Plus, Ed McCarthy answered all my questions about how certain things might happen in an old theater.

The careful responses and encouragement from my early readers were invaluable: Stacy Sheehan, Elizabeth Barnes, Carolyn Marino, Jennifer Pooley, Ken Salikoff, Katherine Hennes, and Jessica Knoll.

On the film and foreign fronts, I am indebted to Matthew Snyder and Whitney Lee for all they do on behalf of my books. At *Cosmo*, I'm thankful to current Editor-in-Chief Joanna Coles. I also had the great fortune to work side by side with *Cosmo*'s previous longtime Editor-in-Chief, the one and only Kate White, and I owe her a huge thanks.

And then there's the people I'm just lucky to have in my life: Susan Segrest, Amy Chiaro, Betty Kelly, Michele Promaulayko, Abigail Greene, Isabel Burton, Amy Salit, Colleen Curtis, Cheryl (Cherry) Tan and Nicholas (Butter) Boggs, Ross Katz, Fred Berger, Kate Billman, Carol Story, Wade Lucas, Jamie Brickhouse, Esther Crain, Blake Ellison, Glenn Callahan, Boo Wittnebert, Brenda Tucker, Lucy (Lulu) Puls, Jeremy Coleman, Oscar (Oscy Pants) Gonzalez, Danielle Atkin, Adriana Trigiani, Hilary Black, Matthew Carrigan, Dean and Denise Shoukas, Bob Sertner, Alan Poul, Zoe Ruderman, Andrea Lavinthal, Ashley Womble, Christie Griffin, Dan Radovich, Diane Les Becquets, Jan Bronson, Ruth Calia Stives, Michael Taeckens, Kristin Matthews, Bethane Patrick, and David (Doo Doo) Vendette.

Finally, I'm always grateful to my family: Mom, Dad, Keri, Ray, Tony, Joyce, Mario, Birute, Paul, Beth, Christian, Yanna, and most especially, Thomas Caruso.